S0-BJI-418

A NOVEL

# *A TALE OF THREE WARS*

BY

EDWARD B. ATKESON

ARMY WAR COLLEGE
FOUNDATION PRESS
CARLISLE, PA.

Army War College Foundation Press



ISBN 1-889927-00-7

Library of Congress Catalog Card Number 96-061618

Manufactured in the United States of America

Army War College Foundation Press
122 Forbes Avenue, Carlisle, Pennsylvania 17013

# FOREWORD

If you are lucky enough to join the ranks of successful authors, some amazing things start to happen in your life. Suddenly you are bombarded with requests to write editorials, magazine articles, testaments, book reviews, book forewords, and book endorsements, particularly endorsements to be used on book jackets. Even more amazingly, you are offered cold cash for your contributions and the less the subject matter has to do with any recognized expertise you might have, the more money you are offered. If you are someone who struggled as hard as I did to make it through the English Department's "theme-a-week" requirements during Plebe Year at West Point, you begin to think that such requests are motivated by something more than a desire to tap your literary genius. In short order, you become a skeptic and decline all such offers. It was therefore a most pleasant surprise to be asked to write the foreword for this book. First, the story is something I know about because I lived it. Second, no one offered me anything to write the foreword. But most of all, it is a story about soldiers and a war like none we had ever fought before but one we may be compelled to fight again.

A Tale of Three Wars introduces three protagonists; I have met all three, or their twins. Ted Atkeson presents an infinite number of multinational villains and I have known most of them as well. My friends Captain Hop, Major Hao, and Sergeant Hung are well represented here by the valiant and dedicated Vietnamese officers and NCOs who move this fast-paced story toward its unexpected but inevitable climax. The Americans, most of them brave, selfless, dedicated, competent professionals, and some who were their opposite, self-serving, ticket punching, careerists, cowards, were also assigned to the 1/6 and the 23rd Infantry. I knew them well; the reader will better understand the current Army when he meets them between the covers of this book and out of harms way. I will resist the temptation to identify the villainous Vietnamese or

Americans. General Atkeson has changed their names and no useful purpose would be served by unmasking them.

The charm and danger of the countryside and of small Vietnamese villages, the love of home and home place displayed by ARVN junior officers, together with the fear and confusion of the Vietnamese farmer, splash across South Vietnam from I Corps in the north to the IV Corps in the south, and across the pages of this book. There may be a strategic lesson to be learned here, but there is little of the sights, the smells, or the sounds of ground combat. The point is that these three wars are viewed from the standpoint of middle management -- a bug's-eye view of the "wars." This perspective is vital if not indispensable, to understanding the vivid emptiness, loud silence, and odorless stench of insurgency and counterinsurgency. Here, soldiers struggle as hard to understand as they do to survive and to succeed. This is the story of the storm tossed, not the storm. As this tale teaches, the former has little impact on the latter.

This is also a tale of what counts. It is a story of how to measure success and failure in an environment where the line establishing the traditional dichotomy between things political and things military melted and evaporated in the heat of conflict. General Creighton Abrams established a positive tactical correlation between the direction of testicles and the bearing of hearts and minds. This book begins the search for an operational counterpart.

The need to contrast this tale with Robert Strange McNamara's memoir, *In Retrospect*, is apparent. They seem to have their genre mixed. Secretary McNamara would have us believe that he and the whole military establishment were shamefully ignorant of the "guerrilla movement." Well, Major Nguyen Van Do and LTC Paul McCandless, two of the more important tellers of this tale, knew and understood only too well. Secretary McNamara would still have us believe that if it can not be measured it can't count. Do, McCandless, and almost any soldier who was there, knew that if you could count it, it counted for very little: nothing profoundly new, just a reaffirmation of Napoleon's oft repeated but seldom listened to maxim, "The moral is to the material as three is to one." They did not teach Napoleon at the Harvard "B" school, but they did in Vietnam.

From these "Three Wars" one can gather or "regather" three essential facets of war:

- War is hell any way you view it -- worm, bug, sparrow or eagle.
- Leadership is an art not a science; it is of the heart not of the mind.
- Fiction is a better teacher than history -- it is less personal, less painful, more likely to be true, and less likely to be put in loose leaf folders for ease in revision.

A Tale of Three Wars is a comfortable and pleasant read but a lot more. Professionals, amateurs, and the just curious will enjoy it and be informed of it. What more could you want?

H. Norman Schwarzkopf
General, USA Retired

# PREFACE

# A TALE OF THREE WARS

For a quarter of a century many Americans have looked upon the Vietnam War as a form of high folly in foreign affairs. For a variety of reasons citizens have cited the conflict as a prime example of national policy gone awry and gross misuse of the power of the state. Some critics have focused upon decisions at the highest levels of government -- among the "best and the brightest" of the American political elite. Others have turned their scorn on military leaders for lending their skills to the endeavor or for instances of (largely accidental) bombing and shooting of civilians. Still others (including screen writers and directors) have suggested the existence of a conspiracy of rogue elements within the government, especially within the Pentagon and the CIA.

The following narrative makes no attempt to explore any of these matters in detail, but seeks to bring the reader both a thrilling story and the texture of the struggle as seen through the eyes of three men: one an American intelligence officer, another his Vietnamese counterpart, and third a Viet Cong battalion commander. Many of the incidents described actually happened, but not necessarily to persons with whom they are associated in the story. A number of Viet Cong figures are identified by their *noms-de-guerre* where they are known. Most of the situations depicted on the enemy side have been taken from captured documents and the interrogation of prisoners of war and *hoi chanh* (defectors and returnees).

A key purpose of this book is to illustrate how participants on all sides were obliged to fight battles, not just with armed enemies, but within their own organizations. In spite of some remarkable successes in the field, each of the principal characters, Major (later

Lieutenant Colonel) John Paulding ("Paul") McCandless, his Vietnamese friend and staff college classmate, Major Nguyen Van Do, and their common nemesis, Patriot (Comrade) Van Ba, found himself operating under heavy organizational pressures which he believed to be a barrier to the accomplishment of his principal mission. Neither high military professionalism nor elan could save them from their common fate.

Some readers may find certain parallels between situations encountered by the warriors in Vietnam and some involved in subsequent struggles in Africa and Europe, where the United States has had occasion to deploy troops for other, but still fundamentally altruistic purposes. Whatever the faults critics may find in American intervention in Southeast Asia, one must recognize that our motives never included imperialism or selfish economic gain. On the contrary, in the 1990's, as in the 1960's, participants in American military expeditions overseas are moved most strongly by a sense of obligation to protect the powerless and to bring the hope of health and security to others less fortunate than ourselves. The lessons one may find by analogy in this book (for those looking for more than a good read) relate primarily to the dangers of misapplication of good intentions.

A word about VC dialog is necessary here. Readers will notice a degree of rather stilted formalism about much of it. This is largely due to the rigid communist orthodoxy prevalent throughout the Movement during the war years. It is preserved here to give the reader a feeling for the doctrinaire atmosphere in which the members were obliged to live and operate.

Westerners often have difficulty with Vietnamese names. It is important to note that in Vietnam the family name appears first of usually three. The last is the one normally used for address by acquaintances. Thus, Major Nguyen Van Do, may be referred to as "Major Do" or simply "Do" in most conversations. The Viet Cong assigned cover names to most of their soldiers and officials, sometimes using only two words, such as Van Ba in this book. The

VC leader is known as "Ba," just as he would be if it were his real name.

This book is published by the Army War College Foundation Press as its initial effort to make available works of special value which might not otherwise find a place on the list of mass market publishers. The publication should not be construed as an endorsement of the work by either the Department of Defense or the U.S. Army War College. The Foundation is a separate, private institution which supports the goals and activities of the Army War College. A major portion of the proceeds received from the distribution of this book will be used to further the eduction of the next generation of military leaders. In learning from the past and present, may they become the consummate strategic leaders of the future for which this book cries.

William F. Burns
Major General, USA, Retired
President, Army War College Foundation

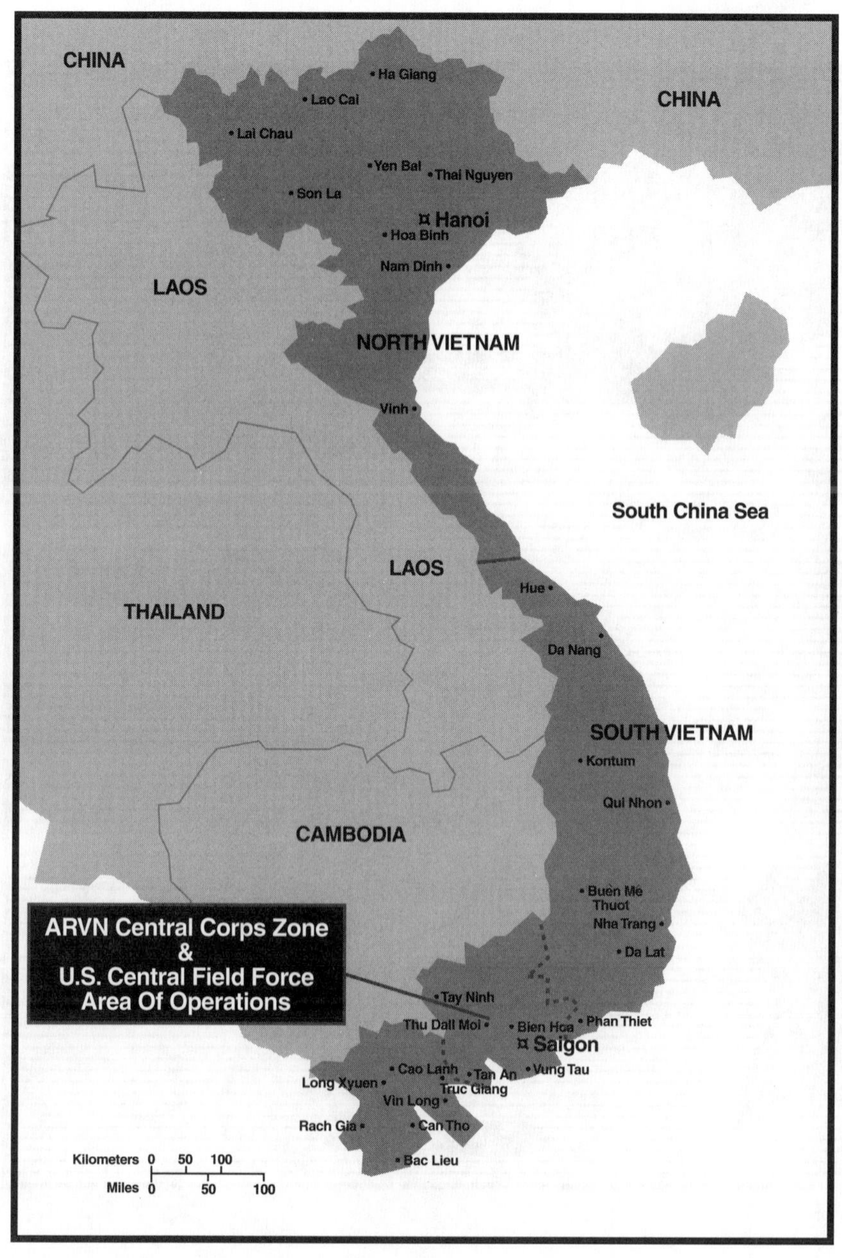
CHINA
Ha Giang
Lao Cai
CHINA
Lai Chau
Yen Bai
Thai Nguyen
Son La
Hanoi
Hoa Binh
Nam Dinh
LAOS
NORTH VIETNAM
Vinh
South China Sea
LAOS
Hue
THAILAND
Da Nang
SOUTH VIETNAM
Kontum
Qui Nhon
CAMBODIA
Buèn Mé
Thuot
Nha Trang
Da Lat
ARVN Central Corps Zone
&
U.S. Central Field Force
Area Of Operations
Tay Ninh
Thu Dau Moi
Bien Hoa
Phan Thiet
Saigon
Cao Lanh
Tan An
Vung Tau
Long Xyuen
Truc Giang
Vin Long
Rach Gia
Can Tho
Bac Lieu
Kilometers 0 50 100
Miles 0 50 100

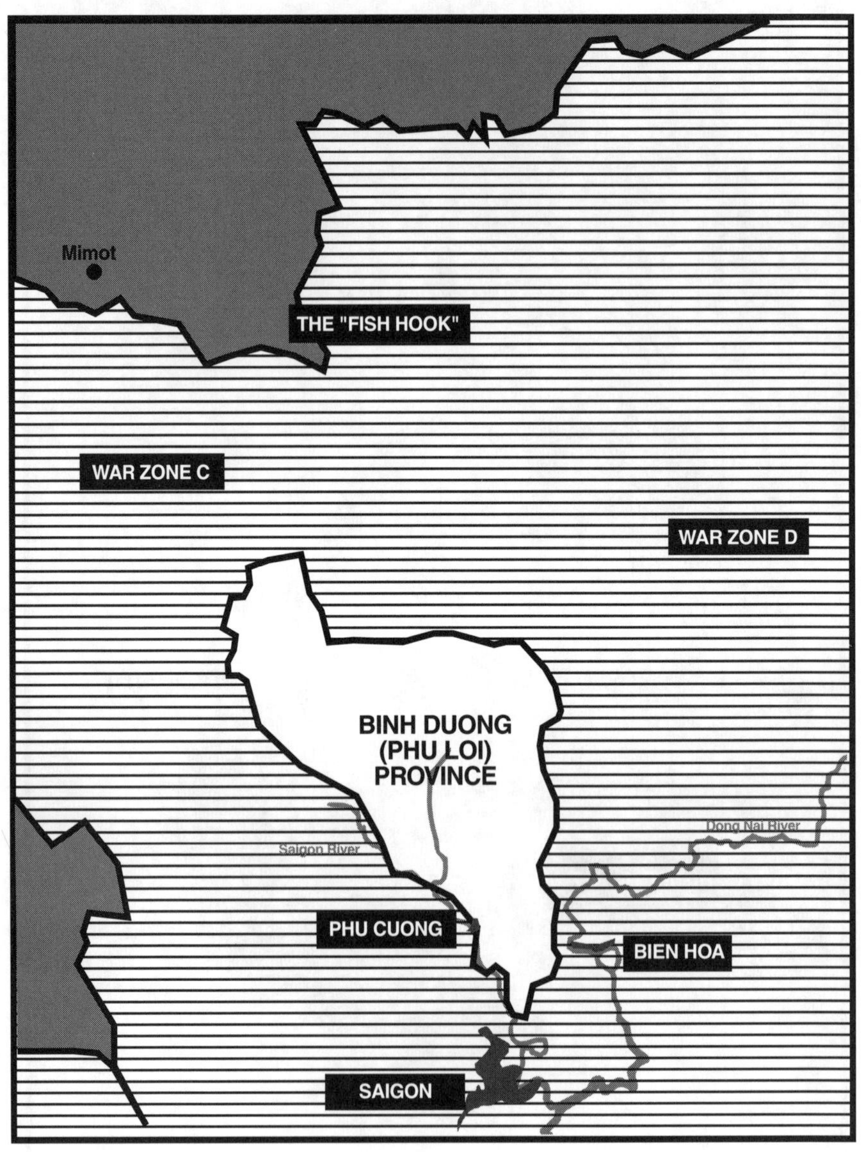
Mimot
THE "FISH HOOK"
WAR ZONE C
WAR ZONE D
BINH DUONG
(PHU LOI)
PROVINCE
Saigon River
Dong Nai River
PHU CUONG
BIEN HOA
SAIGON

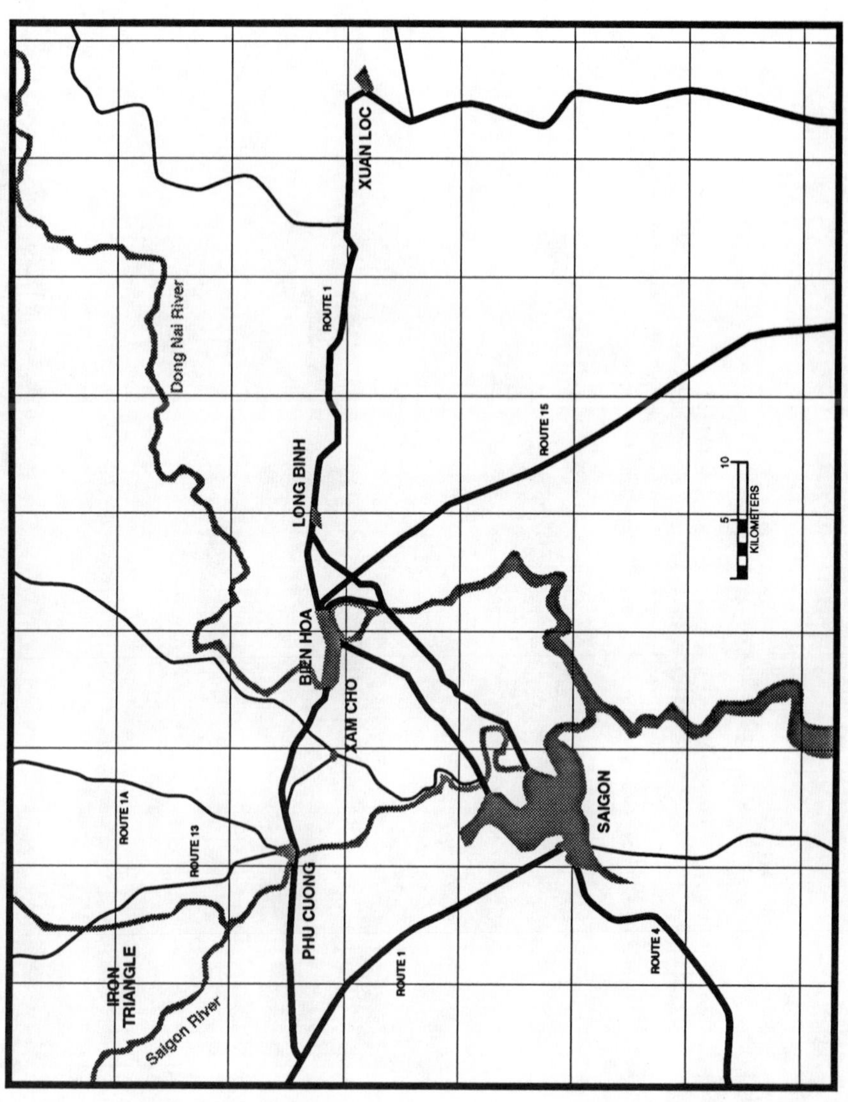
XUAN LOC
ROUTE 1
Dong Nai River
LONG BINH
ROUTE 15
5
10
KILOMETERS
BIEN HOA
XAM CHO
SAIGON
ROUTE 1A
ROUTE 13
PHU CUONG
IRON TRIANGLE
Saigon River
ROUTE 1
ROUTE 4

# *PROLOGUE*

## *PHU CUONG BARRACKS, SOUTH VIETNAM, 1966*

The boom and roll of distant thunder quickened as the storm drew nearer — standard fare for the summer months. Captain Dinh Tan, motor officer for the 5th Armored Cavalry Regiment of the Army of the Republic of Vietnam (ARVN), had experienced a fretful day. Begrudgingly he dragged himself awake to the growing noise. It took a painful effort to get up and close the French casement. What time is it? 2:45. Shit.

It had been raining cheerlessly most of the evening; now the wind was rising and the size and intensity of the raindrops increasing. Tan knew that the splatter would soon become a deluge; but by morning it would be gone. That was the way in

Vietnam's rainy season. The lapses between flashes and thunder diminished steadily. No longer booming and rolling, it was as though a movie sound track had been switched to "jarring crashes."

Stumbling back to bed, Tan was content — it felt good to be lying down again, whatever was happening outside. But he soon found he couldn't ignore it. The wind began to beat water against the panes like the clawing of a wild animal. Crash! The room lit up as though a searchlight had picked it out among the many in the dingy officers' quarters. The lizards on the ceiling scurried for cover behind a lifeless florescent light fixture. The next crash was so close it cracked one of the panes.

Tan sat up. It's a bad one, he thought. Crash! The building shook. My god. That last bolt could have struck the roof. There was a bright after-glow coming from below. We've been struck, and something's on fire. Tan reached to the wall for his trousers.

Another crash shattered the window and sent a spray of glass across the room. The captain was on the floor groping for his boots. Wet shards stuck to his hands and feet, forcing him back onto the bed to pull himself together. Maybe he was cut. This is more than a summer storm. Coming under VC attack in the Delta two years before had taught him to stay out of line with the window. He had taken a 7.62 mm round trough his left shoulder that time, later joking that he might be a slow learner, but he had grasped the essentials of that lesson in a split second. Now, the unmistakable hammering of a machine gun and the growing intensity of an oil-fed fire in the courtyard confirmed the core of his jumbled fears.

Tan snatched up his webbing, already loaded with extra clips and hand grenades. He grabbed his M-16, slapped the camouflage-netting-covered helmet on his head and wrenched open the door.

Dashing along the corridor, he paused to bang his fist on the next door. No response. Damn! His assistant was out. He scurried to the next one. Is there nobody here? Where the hell is everyone — shacked up in town? The sole of his boot, soaked when the window caved in, slipped on the fourth step, hurling him backwards onto the heel of his left hand and a hip. His hand hurt like hell. It had never been quite right since he took that bullet in his shoulder. He might even have fractured it in the fall. No time for that now. A grenade flipped loose from his webbing and bounced down the stairs. Damn!

Stunned by his own stupidity, but frozen in fascination by the tumbling bomblet, he waited for the explosion. The object of his probable doom rattled to a stop at the foot of the stairwell. Stale air rushed from his lungs. He scrambled down to scoop up the grenade. He jammed the lever into his belt, and thrust open the front door.

Outside, the deep wet blackness of the sky was torn where it met the walls of the compound in a spray of colors. White searchlight beams and bluish white phosphorous flares contrasted with yellow sheets of flame from burning gasoline stores. Reddish-orange rocket exhausts trailed as projectiles shrieked through the smoke and rain, exploding in fireballs somewhere off to Tan's right. Less spectacular muzzle flashes spat hate here and there. The captain couldn't tell whether they came from enemy weapons or the defenders'. He knew from previous firefights that much of the shooting was a simple matter of survival. A cowering enemy is a lot less likely to do you in than one up and bounding right at you, he had drilled himself.

Tan's eyes darted around as he tried to make sense of the bedlam. The rain darkened backs of a half dozen soldiers hunched behind a concrete grease rack and firing haphazardly showed where at least some of the friendlies were. The rest could all be VC as far as he could tell. No, there's intense fire at the front gate. Some of the others must be friendlies, too. Who the hell is directing the defense? Where's the post commandant? How about the staff? Where are they?

Without time to even guess at the answers, Tan dashed up behind the grease rack group, squeezing in between two of the soldiers. "How're you doing here?" he puffed at those closest to him.

"We're all right — sir," came the noncommittal reply from a sergeant he recognized but couldn't quite match with a name. "You're the first officer we've seen."

Tan swallowed the veiled rebuke. "What are you firing at? Where's the enemy?"

"We're just shooting and trying to stay alive, Captain. Nobody's here to tell us what to do." The sergeant raised his rifle over the top of the rack and loosed a spray of bullets without sighting.

Tan bobbed his head up to see if the act had any effect. The darkness, rain and smoke made it impossible to see anything at all until another gas drum exploded, momentarily bathing the area in light but revealing little more than dark buildings, now pockmarked with bullet holes.

Ducking back into the relative safety of their refuge, Tan sized-up the situation. The real fight around the front gate seemed to be progressing without much concern for the grease rack group. These men are just killing time, he thought.

His mental train was interrupted by a huge explosion. Ears ringing, Tan glanced over the rack just in time to make out a dozen or more dark figures racing through a cloud of smoke and cement dust. The whole damned wall's gone! We'll be swamped! Instinct told him to jump to his feet and bolt. God! I'd be shot for that. I'm an officer — maybe only the motor officer, but these men are looking to me to lead them. I'll do my best until we can find the rest of their company.

He looked around. His eyes focused on the squat cinder block mass to his left — his motor maintenance office, oddly untouched in the flow of passion and mayhem around it. It offered shelter for the group. If the phone was working he might be able to make contact with whoever was directing the defense — if anyone was. Or perhaps he could reach someone on the outside who would send help. It was worth a try.

"All of you, follow me," he shouted as he turned and splashed his way through the mud surrounding his objective. He mentally thanked the Americans for supplying the stout blocks that went into the humble structure. The keys! I left them on the table in my room. Damn! No time now. A quick burst from his M-16 destroyed the lock, the knob, the whole caboodle. He kicked the door open. Inside, he held it back for the men.

Not wasting a second, even as his foot braced the door open, he checked his weapon and used its butt-end to knock out a louver slat, clearing the window for fire. "Sergeant, put one of your men here to cover the breach in the wall — with someone to back him up. Put two more on the other side to support him."

The sergeant nodded and hand-signaled his men.

Turning to the others, Tan asked, "You all all right?" Three grunted replies. The others just nodded. Tan picked up the phone and cranked the ringer. No answer. He tried again. A scratchy voice came on: "Central."

"Connect me to the commandant's office, quick."

"I'll try, but no one's answered there tonight."

"Never mind that. Try again. It's important."

Tan waited.

A soldier at the window opened fire, then unleashed a second burst. He seemed about to pull back to check his clip when he was hurled backward onto the floor. Tan looked down to see the soldier's face, now a tangle of louver splinters and blood. The soldier's back-up man bent over him, and then looked up at the sergeant, his face drained. "He's —he's dead."

"Take his place," the sergeant snapped back with a nod. Then he added, "Knock out the rest of those slats, and don't stick your head out so much."

The sergeant turned to Tan. "They know we're here now, Captain. Next thing they'll have an RPG 7 on us."

The warning brought up an image of the reddish-orange rocket trajectories. Tan wondered momentarily what they must look like when they headed right at you.

"I know that, Sergeant, but we have to find out who's directing the defense. We can't just squat behind the grease rack." Now it was the sergeant's turn to ignore a rebuke.

A distant-sounding voice on the line diverted his attention. Tan shouted his reply, "Captain Dinh Tan here. Is the Commandant there? Who's this? Well, if he's not there, who's in charge? How about the Deputy Commandant? Are any of the staff there? Where are they? Look Corporal, you find somebody and tell them that Captain Dinh Tan is in the motor maintenance shed with five men holding our ground. We're under intense fire and already have one K.I.A. Got that?"

The men at both windows were firing now. If there was a reply, Tan couldn't hear it. The phone line was silent. Just as he was about to crank it again, there was a terrific explosion just outside, sending gravel and mud smashing through the windows. One man dropped his rifle and caved in, cupping his eyes. Tan could see his mouth open. He may have been screaming, but the blast had deafened everyone.

The sergeant was indeed right. The enemy was getting the range with a rocket launcher — the next round could come right through the window, or even the wall.

Tan hurled down the phone receiver, grabbed the sergeant and pointed to the door. The sergeant hesitated a few seconds, then grasping the meaning, slapped the first soldier he could reach and motioned him out, then another, and another. Slinging his rifle over his shoulder he lifted the blinded man and led him to the door.

Tan followed the last man out, pulling the door as far closed as he could without a handle to grasp — that way it might help attenuate the expected blast. He crouched against the building; the sergeant motioned everyone to squat down against the wall. All waited for the next shot; some held their ears.

Long seconds stretched into a minute, then another. After a few more moments, Tan sensed his hearing returning. But either the firing was slackening off or the RPG had done real damage to his ears. He stretched his jaw to open them up. No, occasional shots and bursts of fire were distinct enough. But there was another sound. Engines were starting up!

Tan gave a silent *Huan Ho!* — Hottcha! He knew the sound of an M-41 Walker "Bulldog" roaring to life as well as he knew his own name. He was the motor officer and had tinkered with most of the machines in the lot. We'll cream them now!

Tan pushed a soldier aside and bobbed his head around the corner. It was true! The bulk of the first tank was just breaking through the smoke. His spirits soared. He couldn't make out the driver's face, but he waved to the squat, sturdy vehicle and gave the thumbs up gesture. A second tank followed the first. It was glorious.

The lumbering beasts headed for the front gate. Tan could see the silhouettes of other figures waving. It was a clear rout. But the tanks weren't firing. They must realize that the enemy holds the gate. Maybe the VC fled at the sight of the tanks. It must be a complete victory. We've driven them all off! He stepped out from behind the building to join the celebration.

* * *

Drifting into groggy half-awareness, Tan wondered where he was and why. Everything seemed to be white, even his arms and hands. He wasn't aware of pain until he tried to move. Then it overwhelmed him, like a thousand daggers in his neck and chest. The sergeant, whose name he still couldn't remember, seemed to be asleep in a chair at the foot of the bed where Tan suddenly realized he now lay. He tried to speak, but couldn't form the words.

The sergeant stirred, looked up at him and gave half a smile. "Good morning, Captain, how do you feel?"

No matter the effort, Tan found he couldn't reply. He barely moved his head.

"The corpsman says you took two rounds in your rib cage and one in the arm. I would've sworn it was more than that. It seemed that every VC in the place was shooting at you. We couldn't get to you for five or ten minutes. Every time one of us tried they would open up with a hail of bullets. They never did fire another RPG, but they sure let us have it with small arms. We wondered what made you step into the open the way you did. Maybe when you can talk you'll tell us about it."

Over the next few painful days Tan began to understand that he had been badly wounded. His whole body hurt like hell. He also began to suspect that something was amiss. No one seemed inclined to talk about it, and he couldn't get out the words to ask. At the end of the week he was moved to a hospital in Saigon — to a private room. He wouldn't have believed that a captain would be treated so well. But before long another suspicion began to creep up on him: few junior officers were treated the way he was. He was somehow special, but he couldn't imagine why.

Tan would have liked for his family to visit him, but only his deputy showed up. The lieutenant seemed pained, and clearly was choosing his words carefully. Of course there was a victory. The enemy was driven off "with heavy losses." That had already been announced in the press. But it would be sometime before the captain would have other visitors. In the meanwhile, his deputy said, there would be no discussion of the matter until the investigation was complete. What matter? What investigation? What the hell happened?

# *ONE*

## *LONG BINH PLANTATION — A FEW WEEKS EARLIER*

Paul couldn't have imagined that it would be quite like this. The rain was again pelting the tent without affording any discernible relief from the oppressive heat inside. Everything was bloated with the humidity, and the ground around his cot was a quagmire. Thank the Lord for cots.

They had pitched the tent in the blackness of the sodden night, and it would have been difficult to have found a worse spot. After an eleven-thousand-mile flight, jackknifed in a bucket seat, followed by a two-hour truck ride through monsoon rains from Tan-Son-Nuht airbase to God- knows-where, no one had been very particular as to where the tent should be erected. The peak bar was missing, so the filthy canvas sagged and fluttered and leaked in the middle. The conditions had seemed so hopelessly miserable by three a.m. when the shelter was finally up that Paul had felt himself carried uncontrollably along with the others in a fit of self-pitying laughter. It washed cathartic tears down his face and wrung out his spirit. It was a paradoxical mixture of wretchedness and shared experience that he could not have appreciated at the moment as the essence of military esprit.

He glanced outside through the flap and got a vague picture of surrounding scrub and a gaggle of other tents, each one seeming to fade into the others. The rain raced diagonally from the black sky, dancing and bubbling on the tents before pouring to the ground. The water was running in little rivulets under his feet, and he had to shift his weight to prevent his boots from sinking too deeply into the mud. There didn't seem to be any resemblance at all between this sodden terrain and the ground he had studied so carefully months before on crisp map sheets back at Fort Meade.

For Christ's sake, he said almost aloud, maybe they brought us to the wrong place. Who would know with no lights, in the middle of the night, and the whole damned South China Sea falling on our heads every twenty minutes?

A couple of hundred yards away he could see the boxy bulk of an armored personnel carrier pitching and yawing its way through the tangled brush up to the crest of the rise ahead.

I wonder if those damned things leak too, he thought to himself. But the sight of the APC was reassuring. It meant that the encampment had not been defenseless during the night, and if they had encamped in the wrong place, the infantry was screwed up, too. Maybe they made compensating errors. Maybe that was what war was really like, anyway — a whole series of compensating errors.

Paul had studied war most of his adult life, but he had never before had personal exposure — never "heard a shot fired in anger." He had been too young for World War II, and during the Korean fracas he had been sent to Europe with an armored artillery outfit. Years of subtle references by his West Point classmates to his having missed the action had grated on him and developed into a barely conscious infection in his mind.

To hell with it, he had often told himself. You're not a run-of-the-mill professional soldier, anyway. Fixing bayonets and charging up San Juan Hill isn't your style. Neither is painting the stones white at Ft. Bragg. There is more to it than that. At least he hoped there was. He couldn't be sure whether he really believed it or whether he was still trying to convince himself.

Now he was an intelligence officer — whatever that was. Some years before he had been assigned to the American Embassy in Helsinki as an assistant army attache, and that had begun his estrangement from the mainstream of the profession.

He had taken the warnings of old friends in stride. They were sure it would "ruin his career." But it had sounded interesting in the late fifties, and God knows there wasn't much else going on. Besides, Cicely had liked the idea. It meant the modest prestige of the diplomatic list, and, although she had no particular gift for languages, she wasn't afraid to try. She instinctively liked people and took a relaxed attitude toward the dozen odd Finnish declensions. In three years she had become superficially fluent in the language, and no one had the poor taste to correct her grammar. Only Paul had joked that she could small-talk her way through a two-hour cocktail party and never conjugate a verb.

This was his first intelligence command, an MI detachment with the Tenth Armored Cavalry Regiment. It wasn't much of a command — about the size of a couple of platoons — but then most people said it wasn't much of a war either. Not many West Pointers had gone into intelligence; maybe that was why he had had so little difficulty in picking his assignment. Perhaps there was a faint glimmer of romance in it. Sort of like chasing Pancho Villa over the border.

The words of the regimental commander at the departure ceremony at Fort Meade stuck in his mind. This was to be the greatest experience and adventure that most of the men would ever know. Only here in this drenched jungle did Paul add his own sequitur, ...and maybe the last for some. But that wasn't the issue now.

Stan was gone. What in hell had he gone out in this weather for? The question was answered as quickly as he formulated it. The squish of boots and the grudging retreat of the flap at the other end of the tent announced the entry of Sergeant Stanislaw Garowski, a hulk of a man from what had once been eastern Poland.

Garowski had grown up with little idea of what peace could be. His village had been seized by the Russians when he was eleven, by the Germans when he was thirteen, and again by the Russians before his sixteenth birthday. But by then he was gone. He had been a messenger with the Resistance during the Nazi occupation and had been captured and deported to a slave labor camp in Germany the year before. Only his tender age had saved him from an SS firing squad.

Garowski had a gift for languages. Besides his native Polish, he spoke Russian and German fluently. When liberated by the Americans he rapidly added a GI version of English. His French came along when he hired on as an interpreter for a displaced persons ("DP") camp in Baumholder. His linguistic skills and his instinct for survival eventually combined to win him an enlistment in the U.S. Army, and ultimately citizenship. He served for four or five years with an MI detachment at Kassel, running agents — some of them old friends — across the border into the Eastern Zone, and occasionally beyond into Poland. He was pretty good at it for a while.

The nineteen sixties were upsetting for Garowski. *The Stars and Stripes* carried articles about the new administration in Washington pumping new life into the Army, long starved for money and in somewhat of a crisis of identity in a world that seemed to make anything but atomic bombs obsolete. President Kennedy talked about Green Berets and "low intensity" struggles in other parts of the world. Garowski had wondered where the hell this Vietnam place was that everyone seemed to be talking about.

When his old contacts dried up and tighter Russian control on the borders reduced his batting average of successful penetrations in East Europe, he gave in to the personnel clerks and accepted reassignment to Ft. Bragg to learn the business of Special Forces. That seemed to be where the action was going to be.

Parachute jumping and skinning snakes were something new to him, but the operation of clandestine radio nets, the handling of foreign weapons, and techniques of silent mayhem were little more than academic icing on a cake he had baked years ago in the ovens of practical experience. Even on his first tour in Vietnam, when he took a half-dozen mortar fragments in his back, they only added to the scars he had collected in his teens. Stripped to the waist, his body looked like an old golf ball.

"Coffee, Major?" he grinned, proffering a mug of brew diluted with rainwater gathered on the way back from the mess tent. Paul returned the grin. The major felt an inner gratitude to the man who, in an instant, had given him something to be grateful for — not the coffee, which was foul, but the human act of thoughtfulness. The rain had turned the contents tepid, but his heart felt a warmth that in other circumstances, and even with a better cup of coffee, he might only have sensed in his stomach.

Paul instinctively liked Garowski. He respected his education in the School of Hard Knocks, but he admired the man even more. He liked the way he handled the other men. He was authoritative and demanding, but patient with them and tireless in his instruction on interrogation techniques and on aerial photograph interpretation. Paul had selected him to be a member of the advance party for the detachment in its move to Vietnam because he had developed a smattering of the language, and because the major knew he would be a damned fool if he didn't.

The rain ended abruptly. Gradually the slanting rays of the sun found the peaks of the tents, confirming their dirty brown hue. For all the exhaustion of the previous night, the camp was stirring in all of its dimensions, and a line was forming at the mess tent. Those who were early enough had already taken their fried eggs and ham to a spot where the water was beginning to steam off, for a moment of physical and psychological rehabilitation. The food was hot and plentiful and went a long way toward convincing the soldiers that they were still on the earth to which they had been born — the majority of them less than a score of years before.

Paul joined the officers of the regimental staff at a makeshift picnic bench. He was senior to most of them, but rank counted for little in the circumstances. And he really wasn't one of them. They recognized him, but they were never quite sure just what he did — something mysterious about intelligence. Anyhow, that wasn't important now. What counted was getting a hot meal inside the ribs and sorting out the havoc of the night before.

There was little talk among them, just the bare essentials: arrangements for shifting the guard and tracking down missing baggage. There wouldn't be any mail for a week or two. Most of the chores seemed to fall to Captain George Robertson, the assistant adjutant.

Robertson was a slender Negro in his late twenties. The blackness of his skin seemed to make his fingernails glow in contrast. He wrote everything down in a notebook, even points Paul knew were only suppositions by the other officers. Paul felt sorry for the captain. The regimental executive officer, Lieutenant Colonel Gordon Dreier, who was now in charge of the advance party, was a coarse man who tended to bully the staff, and George Robertson seemed to catch more than his share of the flak. It would be a month or six weeks before the main body of the regiment would arrive in country, taking the long rail route across the United States to San Francisco and shipping out from there. Paul wondered whether the captain would survive the verbal abuse of the exec for that time. Paul had seen another young officer go to pieces under the bitter barrage of expletives that had become the norm at staff meetings. The poor fellow had become completely ineffective and had to be transferred out. Paul wondered what had become of him.

He wondered, too, what the regimental commander thought of his exec. Colonel Gates was aloof, almost serene. The contrast between the two was razor sharp. The colonel must have been aware of Dreier's rudeness, but he never showed it. He was a father image in whose name the exec lashed and berated the staff. Now Colonel Gates was on the other side of the world, and Dreier was the unrestricted law in the camp. Paul plunged his fork into his eggs and grimaced at the thought of it. This first month in the war zone could be the longest — with a lunatic in charge. Bring on the VC!

The acting sergeant major stepped up to the officers' table and announced that there would be a staff conference in the exec's tent at zero eight-thirty.

Conference, my ass! Paul thought. It will be a bloody forty-five minute harangue with sweat in every crotch and armpit.

The news came as no surprise, but it didn't improve the palatability of the food. Not a word was said. "Disloyalty" was a monstrous word in the Army. Paul thanked the sergeant major, noting that the others kept their eyes down on their mess kits. One by one they finished their meals and excused themselves. A single night in the bush could not destroy the facade of courtesy customary in the mess. Paul thought back to a story he had read some place about how General Custer called his officers together repeatedly to lecture them the night before the Battle of Big Horn. Was there a parallel?

Colonel Dreier had exhausted his repertoire of four- letter words in the first ten minutes of the meeting and had run back through them for a second and third time. The upshot of the matter seemed to be that the camp was a disgrace to the Army and that in his opinion most of the staff officers were incompetent, lazy, or both. Things were going to be ship-shape by sixteen hundred hours or the flag pole that was to be erected by fifteen-thirty would sport the asses of every last son-of-a-bitch on the staff.

The session was a monologue, punctuated only by "yes sirs" and finally by a flutter of salutes. The growing heat of the tent was inconsequential to the heat of the exec's remarks, so the fresher air outside made escape doubly welcome. The most dexterous of the officers were out of the doorway first. Paul noticed that the assistant adjutant was not the last to leave.

The rough flag pole was in place twenty minutes early. Even before that, the tents had been collapsed and re-erected in orderly rows — parade ground fashion. Small groups of men were at work in the area filling sandbags that materialized from somewhere in a heap on the roadside. A sagging tent peak was a cause for some alarm among the staff lest it trigger the colonel's blue-flamed tongue.

Two brief but drenching rain squalls slowed the work, but by sundown the area looked like a caricature of a military encampment in the nineteenth century. A sentry with a makeshift arm band guarded the "gate," and the few vehicles were drawn up in a precise row on the western edge. The infantry, still deployed in a rough circle around the camp, snickered at the spectacle and occasionally whistled and cat-called to the perspiring toilers. In no time at all the advance party had earned a reputation for the regiment as a "chicken-shit states-side outfit that couldn't punch its way out of a fuckin' paper bag."

Armored cavalry — bullshit! This crap went out of style with the Indian Wars! This was Vietnam, 1966. Charlie would eat these toy soldiers for breakfast.

"Just look at those homemade three-holers at the end of each row! The Cong will use the center hole as an aiming point for mortars tonight. There will be shit spread wider than the mortar fragments. Goddam! What a sight!"

Whether the opinions of the infantrymen ever fell upon the exec's ears or not was not apparent. Each day became a routine of back-breaking work during alternating periods of scorching sun and torrential rains under the steady drone of mosquito attacks and Colonel Dreier's unrelenting drive. The advance party had the principal mission of hacking a base camp out of the jungle for a regiment of four thousand men and almost a thousand tanks, APCs, wheeled vehicles and helicopters which were on their way from the States. Food, water, ammunition, gasoline and oil, jungle uniforms, malaria pills and toilet paper had to be assembled in huge quantities for the moment the main body would arrive.

Paul was continuously surprised at the quality of his relations with the colonel. Paul was not a member of the staff; the fact seemed to spare him most of the foul language and possibly contrived anger of the chief. Only occasionally, as when Sergeant Garowski was returning from one of his notorious "foraging expeditions," did the MI detachment seem to catch Dreier's eye at all.

"Goddam! What the hell is that supposed to be?" it began. At the first break in the torrent of questions and comment, Garowski glanced furtively around and replied in a conspiratorial tone, hinting that the large aluminum object under the tarpaulin in the back of the truck was something of special significance in the occult world of intelligence. The less said about it the better — particularly within earshot of the men. Dreier was no fool, but neither did he wish to risk some unknown trouble in an area in which he was not sure of himself. The armed soldiers "riding shotgun" in the back of the truck lent credibility to the driver's suggestions. Dreier chose to wave the vehicle on through, shouting to the guard to keep his "goddam trap shut" about what he had just seen. That night, under cover of darkness, Garowski filled the salvaged casket with fresh water and had his first full-fledged tub bath since leaving the States.

Garowski was a master scrounger. Somehow wooden freight loading pallets were found to form floors for the tents the detachment would occupy. One afternoon Paul returned to his tent to find that an ancient French barracks locker had been installed, with a dim electric light in the bottom to counter the gray-green rot that went to work on anything left in a closed container. Garowski had worked something out with the first sergeant of an engineer company which allowed him to tap into one of their generators. And within three days he had contacted the head men of the surrounding villages and begun the recruitment of a small army of peasants to speed the work of filling sandbags and digging bunkers.

"Major McCandless, let me introduce Father Nguyen Ca Baptiste, director of the orphanage at Ho Nai. Father Baptiste and his flock were refugees from the North in '54."

Good Lord, thought Paul, now he's scrounged up a chaplain! But he replied, "Thank you, Sergeant Garowski." And, "Very pleased to meet you, Father." The major extended his hand.

The priest gave a silly little giggle and a fragile handshake. He spoke no English, so Garowski translated, switching to French when his Vietnamese failed him.

The contact was a fair one. Father Baptiste endorsed the work which the people seemed eager to do anyway for a pitifully small wage, and provided basic information about the lay of the land and its inhabitants. But Paul detected a tendency in the old man to fail to understand questions that related to the enemy.

"Oh, no. No VC here. Everybody Vietnamese. Everybody work hard. So glad to have Americans here."

Paul tried two or three times to bring the conversation around to the war, but by either skill or stupidity the holy father kept throwing it off track.

"So glad to have Americans here. Our people very poor. Need money to buy food. Someday I like to go to America," and on and on.

Paul became impatient, but he could tell by the look in Garowski's eye that he had arrived at the same judgment — they had nudged the old man about as far as he would go right now. There was bound to be a good deal of valuable information behind that wizened old face, but it was increasingly apparent that it wasn't going to come out just now; better to wait a while and look for opportunities to deepen the relationship.

A heck of a note, Paul thought as the old man left. He knows perfectly well that we are here to fight the very people who drove him and his people from their homes a dozen years ago. The field telephone sounded with a metallic rattle.

"Major McCandless," he answered mechanically. "Who did you say you were? Calm down, soldier. You've got what? Well, I'll be damned. Right. I'm coming right now. Hang on!" The major threw the handset on the camp table and raced out the door, stumbling over a tent rope, barely catching himself from pitching headlong into the slime outside.

"Come on," he shouted to John Farthing, his surprised warrant officer, who couldn't remember ever having seen his commander in such a hurry. Somewhat bewildered, Farthing dropped the half-full carton of size 9 jungle boots he had managed to winnow from an officious supply clerk at the depot down the highway and plunged cross-country after the major.

"What are we after?" he tried to call out, but the exertion was rapidly sapping his wind. "And what the hell will we do when we get there?" he ended up panting to himself. The stitch developing in his side was discouraging, but the sudden realization that he was unarmed was almost panicking. They might be up against something serious! The major was too far ahead to hear Farthing's breathless queries, and too intent upon his objective on the east side of the slope to notice.

A curious infantryman poked his head out of his poncho "hooch," pitched beside an APC and watched the men scrambling by. He couldn't get an intelligible answer out of the second guy when he called to him, so he shrugged and plopped back onto his sleeping bag. Only the sound of more men crashing through the underbrush stirred his curiosity enough to prompt him to pull on his boots and to stand up outside.

A hundred yards away men were converging on an overturned jeep and pulling on what seemed to be a telephone pole wedged in the axle. But the "pole" was alive and fighting like mad. The soldiers had a hold on a twenty-foot python which still gripped the jeep, and neither party seemed inclined to let go.

There was not much else Paul could do when he arrived than to grab an unoccupied foot or two of the snake and haul with the rest. Farthing was exhausted from his effort and collapsed in the grass, delighted that there didn't seem to be a space left to grasp. The serpent soon found itself outnumbered fifteen-to-one and released its connection with the jeep. Paul led a chorus, "One, two, three, heave!" The snake arched through the air, crashed down through the brush and disappeared from view.

"Now, just what the devil happened here? Who was driving?" the major wanted to know. A pimply-faced kid with a torn jacket held up his hand.

"Major, me and Rodgers were just returning from the garbage run when that goddam thing dropped out of the tree onto the hood of the jeep. It looked like it was going to eat us up! Goddam! It was something! Rodgers ran off the trail and the whole fuckin' thing turned over. I'll tell you, sir, it was something! This is a hell of a place! I'll be damned if I'm going on that fuckin' garbage detail again! I've had it! Not me! Sergeant Kranz can find himself somebody else for that shit. Goddam!"

The diminutive private identified as "Rodgers" seemed badly shaken. Paul guessed that he had a broken shoulder and ordered him to lie down. The major strode over to the guard post and pulled out the same field phone that the terrified soldier had used to call him. In a few minutes he had an ambulance on the way up the trail.

What a hell of a place this is, he echoed to himself. He could imagine the tales that were already being hatched for transmission in a hundred letters to girls, wives, mothers and friends that night about this woebegone corner of the world. He was wondering how he would describe it to Cicely, himself.

# TWO

## *SOMEWHERE IN BINH DUONG (PHU LOI) PROVINCE, SOUTH VIETNAM, 1966*

Van Ba was not his real name. He didn't even really like it, but it had become increasingly dangerous to use one's given label. For ever larger numbers of young men and women shadowy second — and even third — lives were becoming more the real identity, and old connections were being forgotten or allowed to wither. Ba had been assigned his *nom-de-guerre* for reasons which had not been explained, and he had accepted it the way he had come to accept ambivalence in so many things.

He had done well in internal medicine at the Sorbonne, hiring out in the early morning hours, unloading produce at the city market to supplement his scholarship. His family in Saigon was comfortably situated so he had not been pressed to send money home. His father, a partner in a small ceramics plant, had been enormously proud of his aspiring physician son. When Ba had returned to Saigon to take up residency in the Pasteur Institute, his father had held a very expensive party for him. Ba had been delighted to see his grandparents, uncles, aunts and cousins, but he had inwardly cringed at the extravagance. It had been like Tet with firecrackers and gongs, and his sisters in their very best *ao-dais*. His father had toasted him with rice wine, "To my son, a physician!"

The recollection moved Ba. How far away that all seemed now. And how little time he had any more for recollections of how things had been. He hadn't seen his father now for over four years.

"Comrade Ba." The voice brought him back. "The comrades are assembled as you ordered."

Earlier the stiff formality of the report would have been unsettling to him, but that was the way it had become now. They really were comrades in the Movement, so the term seemed appropriate enough.

"Very good, Truc. I won't keep them waiting." He got up from his field desk and strapped on his pistol belt. The story was that the desk had belonged to a Japanese commandant during the World War. There were markings inside that meant nothing to Ba, but he felt good about putting the box to a better purpose than the expansion of Tokyo's "Greater East Asia Co-Prosperity sphere." He patted his sun helmet in its place on the bamboo pole that served as his coat-tree while he considered whether to wear it for the short walk up the trail to the main bunker. Deciding to leave it, he ran his fingers through his short black hair and nodded to Truc to lead the way.

He knew Truc had a real name, too, and that it was filed in the young man's self-evaluation form along with much more than anyone other than the political officer might want to know about his former life. Ba recalled that Truc had been drafted into the government army some years back, and had deserted; but the details were lost to him among the thousands of similar details he had read about others in the Movement. It wasn't important now. He followed the younger man up the trail.

The main bunker was almost invisible from twenty meters away. On one occasion, before the trail had become so worn, he had missed it entirely in broad daylight and had spent twenty minutes searching for it. A sentry had challenged him from an unseen position in the trees above and had called back to the bunker for an escort. It had been embarrassing for him. Only days before, he had been elected commander of the D group, and it seemed an inauspicious beginning.

The two men bent double and began to descend the ramp into the bunker. The corridor made an abrupt U-turn to the left, then revetted steps led steeply downward. The guard's niche on the right was so dark that Ba couldn't tell whether it was occupied or not, but he heard a scraping noise from the recess as he passed. Truc went ahead with the lantern, extinguishing it as they entered the main compartment. Ba had heard that it had taken some fifty young men and women the better part of four months to dig the principal network of tunnels and the four large compartments of the complex. There were three entrances, plus two others intentionally left incomplete which could be dug out in an emergency.

The main compartment was illuminated more brightly than usual. Truc had ordered extra lanterns placed on the central map table for the conference. The six figures in the room bowed slightly as Truc stepped aside and the D group commander entered. Madam Tran Hua, the political officer, raised her arm in a clenched fist salute. The others imitated her a little less fulsomely.

"Comrade Ba," she began, "we eagerly await your orders to smash the evil lackeys of the hated criminal regime that presently sits in the Palace in Saigon!"

Oh, for heaven's sake, Ba thought, but he replied, "And that we will do, Comrade Hua. But we must plan carefully, and we must await the right moment to execute our plans."

As he said this he thought: that woman is a pain. She's so full of that silly propaganda that she can't tell a grenade from a horseapple. But Ba knew that tolerance for Hua and her interminable lectures to the patriots was a price he had to pay for the precious support he received from COSVN, the Central Office for South Vietnam. COSVN could supply good Chinese- and Russian-made machine guns, mines and ammunition. Ba knew that his D group would become increasingly disadvantaged if it had to rely entirely on captured materiel. A lot of the weapons in the hands of his men were old French and American stuff, better suited for a museum than for the sharp, mean little engagements that were becoming the norm. And spare parts were impossible. Many of the fighters had to fashion their own parts for their weapons. One boy had blown out his right eye when he fired his rifle — he had relied on a faulty locking lug that he had welded onto his rifle bolt when the original one became worn. For all the National Liberation Front's propaganda about self-reliant guerrillas, Ba knew how much he depended on supplies from the outside.

He turned to the oldest of the group in the room. "Patriot Suc, what do you have to report this morning?"

Duan Suc had been the D group's supply officer for but a short time, but Ba had great confidence in him. Ba listened closely as the man began reciting from neatly penned columns in his notebook. "We have received six RPD machine guns, four 60 mm mortars, twenty directional mines, eight torpedoes, ten field telephones, and five kilometers of class three wire that can be used either with the telephones or to detonate the mines and torpedoes. Also, we have purchased five more bicycles for the reconnaissance B unit. All of the equipment, except the bicycles, is cached at Location Tiger, here," he said, stabbing at the map.

"Tomorrow we will issue one mortar to each C unit to expand training. Very few of the patriots have any experience with mortars, and we can anticipate that ammunition will be precious. The crews must be well trained."

"Where are the bicycles?" Ba asked.

"They are temporarily hidden at Patriot Phe's family house in Ben Suc," the logistician replied. "They are fairly safe there, and we can get them when we want them. They are old, but Patriot Phe has inspected them and assures me that they are in serviceable condition."

Le Phe beamed at the reference to his report. At eighteen he was the youngest on the group staff. He had two years' experience fighting with an A unit, and had been recommended for a citation. Ba had asked him to join the D group because he had a good record and because his family, which had already suffered the loss of one son to government fire, lived in Ben Suc. Phe served as a useful go-between for supplies and messages with the village. The village chief was an unknown quantity — he could go either way; but as long as visits were restricted to members of families who lived there, the risks were minimal. Mme. Hua had questioned the selection of Phe at first, but ultimately gave her consent.

Ba had heard about other D group commanders who had ordered the liquidation of any village chief who seemed untrustworthy. Certainly it was a legitimate measure to insure the security of a unit or its patriots, but he resisted suggestions that he do the same. Hua had argued with him, pointing out the potential threat which these chiefs posed, but Ba demurred. He didn't see a real benefit to be gained. He would much rather that the people support the Movement from sincere desire than from fear. Also, he didn't want to provoke government reaction in the province over a secondary issue. Anyway, more and more village chiefs were coming to look the other way — if not actively supporting patriot operations — when it counted. In time they would all turn to the Movement. And if they didn't? Well, there was plenty of time to deal with them later if something serious had to be done.

Ba had found that where politics weren't persuasive with petty government officials, a few *dong* on the side would often bring them around. Of course they preferred the government currency to revolutionary paper, but it was not too hard to get the good stuff. One of the patriots had a cousin in the government treasury office who could usually skim off enough bills to meet their needs, and the risk of getting caught was not too great, as long as the higher ups got paid, too. Occasionally the D group would set up road blocks on the principal highways and relieve travelers of "taxes." Ba knew he had to watch those operations carefully lest some of his own patriots succumb to temptations to line their own pockets.

"Good," Ba exclaimed. "Patriot Phe, fetch two bicycles for the reconnaissance B unit tomorrow. Patriot Nam, issue instructions to the unit this afternoon to begin reconnoitering the Phu Cuong barracks this week. Our latest intelligence from COSVN indicates that the government garrison is receiving new recruits this month. That will reduce their operational readiness for at least eight weeks while they begin their training. We have never attacked a government unit in garrison, so no one will be expecting anything like that."

Ba felt comfortable snapping out instructions to his staff. It had been awkward at first, but he had rapidly acquired the manner of a seasoned commander. He was not a trained cadreman. He still considered himself a physician first, and hoped that when peace returned to his land he could return to the Pasteur Institute and take up his practice.

For now he maintained his healing skills with the little equipment he had been able to bring with him and the medicines which Phe was able to purchase in the villages. Occasionally he was able to get good French or Japanese drugs, but he was constantly running short. On one occasion Ba had used his last ampule of morphine while setting the leg of a government corporal who had been captured by C-2 unit. Ba wanted to give the boy particularly good care in hopes of convincing him of the rightness of the Movement. Only Mme. Hua's interference prevented him from returning the lad to his village.

The exchange had been heated. Hua had insisted on a private consultation with the D group commander. She accused him of soft headedness and treachery and hinted that he had become too enamored with imperialist ways while he was in Paris. Ba had come close to striking the woman in the fury of the moment, but in the end he relented and gave his consent to the transfer of the prisoner to COSVN. It was not a session that either one of them liked to remember. Ba thought of himself as fair-minded about women, but this one seemed to have none of the graces of her sex.

Ly Nam was the planning specialist. He produced a neat drawing of the Phu Cuong garrison made some six months before, based upon descriptions of the post gleaned from informers and government deserters.

"The sketch may be a little out of date," he apologized. "The reconnaissance B unit will have to reconfirm the details, particularly the locations of the vehicles. As far as we know, there are no new guard posts, and the roads through town are clear. There are police check points north and south of town during the day, but they are withdrawn into the police station at curfew. There is only one machine gun post on the roof of the station, and that can be struck by recoilless rifle from here." He pointed a broken finger nail at a spot on the edge of the sketch.

"We have completed driver training for units A-31 and A-32. Not having operable vehicles, we have had to simulate the instruction in a damaged government tank, but the patriots who will undertake that part of the operation have all read the manual and have been examined by the C unit leader."

Nam reached across the table to a stack of 1:30,000 scale topographic maps. He selected one that had been folded and refolded so many times it almost disintegrated in his hands. Carefully, he laid it out and smoothed it with his palm.

"Here is the garrison. We have selected C unit assembly positions for pre-attack organization within fifteen minutes' march of the post, and B unit reassembly points no more than one hour away afterward. Each reassembly point will be covered with at least one ambush site to discourage pursuit. We plan to use units C-1 and C-3 for the attack. Unit C-2 should set up ambushes and provide porters and guards for the base camp."

The planning session stretched on for three hours. The air in the bunker became thick with the smell of lamp black, bodies, and something else which Ba could never quite identify. At his direction the conferees climbed by ones and twos up through the tunnels to fill their lungs with fresh air, each remaining above ground for only a few minutes. Then they reconvened to go over the details once again.

The sun was falling toward the western tree line when Ba got back to his hut. It had been a good session, he thought, and there would be more after the reconnaissance B unit delivered its report on Saturday or Sunday. Mme. Hua seemed approving of the plan while remaining officially non-committal. There was no requirement to obtain any further approval of the scheme. Ba would have been informed by now if a main force unit were scheduled to operate in the area. But he knew that Hua would seek authorization from COSVN before giving her wholehearted support. That might take as much as a week. Ba resolved to go ahead with the planning — and perhaps even the operation — with or without Hua's countersignature on the official orders. If the operation were unsuccessful Hua's signature might save him from disgrace, but it wouldn't help the brave patriots who would pay the price with their lives.

The twilight offered Ba a precious moment of reflection and escape from his heavy responsibilities. As on a hundred other evenings, he would have liked to have written to his father. The Movement provided a fairly reliable postal service for short notes written on a single sheet of rice paper and folded into a rectangle no more than eight centimeters square. There was a letter box code which covered South Vietnam and insured fairly accurate delivery while providing a modicum of security. Address numbers were changed periodically to complicate the government's intelligence task.

But Ba worried about enemy interception of letters. Only last month a carrier had been run to ground in the province, losing his entire bag of mail. He couldn't permit himself the luxury of direct contact with his family. He had arranged for a relative to provide occasional word, but it wasn't the same thing. He would have liked some news of his friends from days at the Sorbonne who had first interested him in the Movement, too — especially a long haired beauty from Hue. Her name was Hua, too, but she was a far cut from the battle ax he had to contend with now. What was it the American general had said? "War is hell." How wonderful it would be if somehow the two Huas were reversed! Their names both meant "flower," but one was a fresh, sweet blossom, the other a shriveled old weed — and that was just considering their inner spirits. His Hua would be more of a beauty on her worst day than Madam Tran Hua — clearly now damaged goods — could ever have been in the springtime of her life.

In Paris, there had been a little Vietnamese colony of real and would-be poets and ascetics to which Ba had been naturally drawn. The dense cigarette smoke, the familiar music, and the perennial search for "truth" through political debate intrigued him. The process was enormously stimulating, however much it diverted him from his studies. How much had been the dialectic and how much Hua, he couldn't be sure.

At any rate, in time he became a regular auditor, and then a critic, and ultimately a participant in the poetry readings and the heavily charged discussions in the dark, cramped and noisy cafes. The themes, more often than not, related to a dream of a free Vietnam — not just free of colonial masters, but one with a deeper freedom for the common people: freedom from the cartels which controlled the rubber industry, freedom from the Chinese money changers in Saigon who controlled the brutal combat police squads and who forced the countryside to pay homage and taxes to the capital. But most of all, it meant freedom from the Mandarins who, through their interlocking networks of familial, business and political alliances had built a complex system of favors, bribes and quid-pro-quos which had squeezed out practically all other factors in social, business and political life.

Few sons or daughters of wealthy Vietnamese gathered at the coffee houses. Most were, like Ba, young and of modest means, seeking an identity among their own kind. Paris fulfilled their needs for intellectual stimulation, but France was Western and capitalist, and run by a military man turned dictator. That was not to be the path for Vietnam. Ba had become a passable political theorist as well as a physician.

The Diem regime had seemed particularly poisonous: undemocratic, brutal, and given to blatant nepotism, it represented what he thought must be the worst of all forms of non-colonial government. But that opinion proved short lived. In 1960 a group of colonels attempted to overthrow President Diem, but failed. Generals tried again in 1963 and were successful. That seemed to open the way for one coup after another. The countless cabals of generals plotted against each other even before one group came to power. This, Ba thought, must be the worst of all worlds. Each group claims to have the interests of the nation at heart, but in practice they are far more interested in skimming off whatever they can as quickly as they can.

Ba would have liked to have maintained his friendships from the cafes when he returned home, but "home" had become an alien environment — or had he changed? Never before had he been so aware that government informers and secret police were everywhere.

Ba's participation in political discussion had not gone unnoticed in Saigon. It was not long after he had entered his residency at the Pasteur Institute that the police had paid a call on him. It had seemed innocuous enough, but later he sensed that he was being followed. A few relatives and friends mentioned that they, too, had been visited by the police inquiring about his habits. One evening he returned home to find his father with a badly bruised face and his mother in tears, but no explanation of what had happened — only a plea to him to be careful. He became fearful for his life when he was almost run down by a truck on Tu-Do Street. When the invitation came to join others in the countryside working for the freedom of the country, he was psychologically receptive. It was a wrench to leave his family, but he believed that his parents would understand someday. He would return to them when the country was rid of the evils which beset it. His father would toast him again with rice wine. Maybe he would even find Hua again.

# *Three*

## *CENTRAL CORPS HEADQUARTERS, BIEN HOA, SOUTH VIETNAM, 1966*

A year in the United States as a student at the U.S. Army Command and General Staff College and three years of close association with a succession of U.S. "counterparts" had coated Nguyen Van Do with an American veneer that was the envy of his fellow officers. He had long since mastered the stateside idiom, and he took very seriously his reputation as a passable forecaster of NFL football scores. He kept a radio in his office tuned to the GI Armed Forces Network in Saigon ("Good Morning Vietnam!") and regularly leaned on his American friends to get his ballots for the "top ten" on the ''Nam Hit Parade" into the military postal system. Occasionally he had to rely on the black market to maintain his image as a connoisseur of American cigarette brands, but for the most part he could count on a regular supply from his counterparts.

Lieutenant General Vo Van Quoc, the corps commander, was not entirely enthusiastic about Do's apparently unrestrained plunge into the heady waters of Americana. Do was the intelligence officer of the staff, and the commander thought that such a position of trust called for some reserve. Allies or not, the Americans were foreigners and were vulnerable to misunderstanding Vietnamese ways. On more than one occasion confidences disclosed to American officers attached to the headquarters had found their way into the American press. And for some time General Vo had been becoming increasingly suspicious of how much Do was telling his counterparts.

But no one else could handle Americans the way Do could. A succession of visiting U.S. congressmen and senators were visibly turned from semi-hostile skeptics to enthusiastic supporters of the war effort after listening for forty-five minutes to Major Nguyen Van Do describe South Vietnam's plight as the victim of Northern aggression.

"Glad to have you aboard, gentlemen," he would begin. "We in Vietnam share your concern for the spreading menace of communism on a global scale. Eastern Europe, the Middle East, Asia, and even the Caribbean and Latin America have all been targeted by this dreadful malignancy. But we are small, while you are powerful. We are poor while you are wealthy. We must fight in our own back yards, while you have been able, through your farsighted foreign policy, to hold the threat at arm's length. Nevertheless, never doubt that an indomitable free South Vietnam stands shoulder to shoulder with you — here in this country or anywhere in the world. If not in body, certainly in spirit. Yours is a sacred, historic trust. We are honored to be at your side, and everlastingly grateful to have you at ours in our time of peril...."

In fifteen minutes the visitors' eyes would grow misty. In half an hour they would be interjecting, "Hear! Hear!" When he finished, his audience would be on its feet in enthusiastic applause and promises "never to let you down." General Vo could not afford to replace Major Nguyen Van Do.

Do was no fool. As staff G-2 he had access to the best information on the enemy. And the signs didn't look good. Fortunately, the Americans appeared serious about meeting the threat with adequate force. Already there were two U.S. divisions in the corps zone, and an armored cavalry regiment was arriving soon. The advance party of the regiment was already in country, near Long Binh, preparing for the debarkation of the main body.

Maybe — just maybe — the Americans could halt the Northern aggression.

But in Do's view, Northern aggression was not the only problem. Certainly another was the widespread malaise in South Vietnam. The North Vietnamese were unwelcome exploiters of the now chronic instability in the land. Diem, the despot, had been deposed, but he had been replaced by a succession of selfish, corrupt men who seemed intent only upon improving their own positions. Do hoped that the Americans would give the Southerners a chance to sort themselves out. There were serious political and economic problems facing the country, and too many of them were being ignored in the name of meeting the insurgent and Northern challenges.

He turned down the radio to answer the intercom on the window ledge. "Yes, sir, Major Nguyen Van Do here."

"Major Do," the chief of staff's voice crackled and scratched over the ancient device, a relic of the French years. "This afternoon a Major J. Paulding McCandless from the American Tenth Armored Cavalry Regiment will visit the headquarters."

Do took a sudden suck of air into his lungs. "Major Paul McCandless! I know him well, sir. He and I were classmates at Fort Leavenworth years ago. I would be happy to escort him, General."

"Good," replied the unreal voice over the intercom. "Give him the usual briefing on enemy forces in the corps zone. And try to find out how his unit is coming along in getting settled. See if you can get a list of the principal staff officers and commanders of the regiment. We have heard that the executive officer is in temporary command and may be a little crazy. Find out if that is true."

"Yes, sir."

"And, Major ..."

"Yes, sir."

"Watch yourself with this Major McCandless. Just because he is an old friend and classmate doesn't mean he understands things the way we do." The intercom scratch turned into a growl, and the growl into a high pitched whine. Do missed the last few words of the Chief's warning, but he knew what he was going to say anyway.

"Yes, sir."

"That is all, Major."

The little red light went out, and the box went dead. Do turned the radio back up to hear the announcer tell about the new Chevy Bel Aire road tests in Detroit. The sports news would be next.

"Hot Dog! he exclaimed aloud, slapping his hand on the badly scratched desk. "Super Hot Dog!"

Sergeant Vu Minh, Do's chief intelligence NCO, looked up from his work in the next room. He had heard American expressions before, but this seemed a little overdone. He wasn't sure what it meant, but it must indicate a favorable development, judging by the major's animation.

"Sergeant Vu," Do called through the doorway, "an important American officer will visit us today. I want to make a particularly good impression. Have tea and sweets ready. Get my copy of the American staff college year book out, and have it on the table. Find out what time he will arrive, and I'll meet him at the main entrance." The sergeant indicated understanding and hurried out.

"Hot Dog!" Do smiled again, "Super Hot Dog!"

It was three thirty when Paul's jeep squeaked to a halt in front of the Vietnamese corps headquarters. The well-cropped lawns and the bougainvillaea bushes suggested permanence and stability — not at all what he had expected. Then he realized that this was an old French headquarters. The "stability" was deceiving.

Paul climbed out of the vehicle and crunched across the gravel driveway toward the figure emerging from the archway. The sun's glare on the stucco walls made it difficult to make out the man's features.

Have I seen this fellow before? Good God! He looks familiar; what's his name?

Salutes.

"Major Paulding McCandless, welcome to my country. Don't you remember me? We were in the same study group at Leavenworth. I'm Nguyen Van Do." Now it was Paul's turn to gush.

"Do! Son-of-a-gun! What a surprise. Of course I recognize you. You were the smartest man in the class. I'll never forget the time you put the Chinese Republican troops into the Korean war and stopped the commies cold. That was a great solution! I'm not sure you got full credit for that. You sure made the political-military guys wince. What a great thing to find you here. Wait 'till Cicely hears this! I can't wait to write her. How's Thuy? And your little boy? Imagine running into you here like this!"

The conversation was a torrent of questions and partial answers on both sides as the two friends made their way through the dingy corridors to Do's office. The warmth they felt was evident in their gestures; they frequently patted each other on the shoulder and made small references to family incidents that strengthened the sense of intimacy. The bond of respect that been forged at the staff college was alive and well.

"Well, where do we stand, Do?" Paul asked after the sergeant had served tea. What are we up against?"

Do's smile fell from his face. Now it was time to talk business. He pushed the vase of dusty plastic flowers on the table aside and reached behind him for his map board. There were several maps with various categories of information posted on them around the walls of the room, but this was the map Do used to brief General Vo. It had the latest information.

He shifted the board around so that Paul could look at it in normal orientation with north at the top. Paul noticed that it had been printed by the U.S. Army Map Service, but he couldn't make out the date.

"Here we are," Do began. "The Song Saigon flows down this way, and the Dong Nai here. They run together here near the capital and flow on down to the Rung Sat, a foul smelling swamp, covered with mangrove, before meeting the South China Sea. Do you know the Rung Sat?" Paul was glad he could nod "yes."

"War Zone 'D' is here," Do continued, indicating a large area about the size of Paul's hand with his fingers extended on the right hand side of the map — a green featureless blob. "War Zone 'C' is here." Again, a green area devoid of detail.

Do went on, pointing out places that Paul had read about in his area studies back at Fort Meade. Some of them were becoming popular in the weeklies and larger newspapers in the States. The "Iron Triangle" and the "Long Nguyen Secret Zone" were familiar to most readers of *Time* and *Newsweek* now. They would grow in the consciousness of the American people in the months and years to come.

"The VC and *Bo Dai* are here in strength," Nguyen went on. "Saigon, of course, is the target."

"*Bo Dai?*" Paul interrupted.

"North Vietnamese," Do replied. "The growing intensity of the war, particularly the U.S. intervention, has discouraged local VC recruitment, so the proportion of Northerners in the corps zone has increased. We now carry two VC main force divisions in our corps order of battle files. Counting their support units, they have a strength of about 20,000. And I should mention that that represents an increase of about five thousand since last January.

"In addition, most provinces have their own local force battalions made up of local people — men and women — 'patriots' they call themselves. They're full-time guerrillas. Not very many of them are well equipped, but they're plenty tough. Being local people, they move rather easily throughout their areas of operations. Sometimes they help the main force units, acting as guides. They are communist dominated, but the 'National Liberation Front' keeps a few true patriots on its rolls to maintain the myth of popular solidarity. Quite a few of the local force people have been taken in by this and see themselves as freedom fighters. They don't understand the threat that the Northerners pose to the country."

"But Ky himself is a Northerner," Paul protested, referring to the premier in Saigon.

"Yes," Do admitted, "but he's committed to the independence of the South, just as we all are."

Paul wasn't sure precisely what his friend was trying to communicate. Do seemed to be suggesting that the local force guerrillas might have different objectives in the war from the Northerners. Paul had assumed that the enemy was all of one stripe — Red. The North-South nuance was far from clear, but he listened as Do went ahead with his briefing.

"Look upon the *Bo Dai* as the real threat, Paul. They're organized into regular regiments and divisions, and they represent the power of Hanoi — they're hard rock commies. The local VC are clearly communist dominated and supplied, but their make-up is quite different. A number of VC units are left-overs from the old religious and local economic groups that former President Diem chopped up when he was consolidating his power. Some of them are real patriots — genuine people, working in their own way for the kind of independence and freedom they think South Vietnam ought to have. They are badly misguided politically, of course, but their sincerity makes them a hard bunch to beat.

"Our *Chieu Hoi* program brings in a few line crossers from the local village guerrilla groups, but the provincial boys are tough and well disciplined," Do continued, using the government term ("open arms") for the amnesty appeal.

"What's the difference between the local villagers and the provincials?" Paul interjected.

"The provincials are better led and better organized - - and they work at it full time. The village guerrillas are nominally organized into platoons — small companies at best — but for the most part they're farmers and shopkeepers and seldom operate outside their own village areas. Strictly part-time soldiers. But look out for them; the little kid asking for chewing gum with one hand may have a live grenade ready to flip into the back of your jeep with the other."

Paul wasn't sure about his friend's assessment of the North Vietnamese as the greatest threat. The greatest threat would seem to be the closest enemy unit with any real combat capability. If there was a full-time guerrilla outfit loose in Binh Duong Province where his regiment would be operating, he wanted to know all about it.

"Tell me a little more about the provincials," he asked, pushing his slightly chipped tea cup toward the middle of the table.

"Well," Do went on, "you ought to understand a little bit about how they look at their organization. To begin with, they don't use the same maps we do. Even the provincial boundaries are different. The boundaries on our maps — which you Americans have so generously provided — are drawn according to official government districting. The VC use the old system which goes back even before the French days. Everything they do is tied to the old ways, before the country was colonized. They make quite a point of that, and you can see the appeal it has. Even I see some sense in it – it completely removes any connotation of foreign rule.

"I think it even disturbs the Northerners a little. This lower part of the peninsula wasn't their normal run, so to speak, and this kind of independence-minded map drawing in the South doesn't exactly fit in with their plans. They're hell-bent on dominating the whole country from Hanoi. A lot of Southerners, government and VC, take exception to that. Maybe Hue would make a good capital for a unified country — but Hanoi? I don't think so."

"Well, go on about the provincials," Paul prompted.

"Yes, the provincials," Do repeated, almost reluctantly, it seemed to Paul. "They are organized into battalions — 'D groups,' they call them. An 'A unit' is a squad, a 'B unit' a platoon — usually made up of three A units — and a 'C unit' is a company. It is very much like any triangular military organization, except that there usually isn't much in the way of organic support. The main force VC regiments and *Bo Dai* have regular rear area support groups, but the local forces depend pretty much upon families and friends to take care of them. If they need something fixed, like an ox cart or a bicycle, and they can't do it themselves, they just run it into town with one of the local boys and get it fixed at the blacksmith shop.

"They use their own money, you know. I don't know any merchant who has guts enough to refuse to do a job for VC currency. The worst case I ever saw was one time in Bien Hoa when a gas station attendant refused to sell gasoline for VC currency. He called the police instead.

"One of the VC was caught, but a couple of others got away. It wasn't a week before the attendant's body was found floating down the *Song Dong Nai* with VC currency stuffed down his throat. You won't see the money in regular circulation, but it's a brave man who refuses to accept it for services rendered.

"You should understand that these fellows don't just control the ground they walk on. Their influence goes way beyond that. For instance, they deliver their mail throughout South Vietnam. We intercept a lot of it, sure; and sometimes it has some pretty good intelligence value. But I wouldn't be surprised if they were reading more of the mail in the government system than we are of their stuff. The big joke is that VC mail is more dependable, and only occasionally subject to government censorship. And, of course, it doesn't require a stamp. That's hard to beat!

"Then they've got all their infrastructure — little organizations which seem to make a place for everybody. There's the 'Old Farmers Association' and the 'Young Artists Association,' and the 'Young Pioneers Group,' and on and on. There isn't a soul who can't identify with one part of the organization or another. They are geniuses at that."

"Okay," Paul interrupted again, "lets get back to the provincial military. How does it operate?"

"Well," Do replied a little defensively, "just what would you like to know?"

"Well," Paul echoed, trying to formulate a specific question, "tell me about the battalion that operates here in Bien Hoa Province. Who commands it? Is it any good?"

Do got up from his chair and crossed the room to close the door. Paul guessed he was just taking normal precaution before discussing a somewhat more sensitive matter. After all, the group he was asking about was the local outfit, and it would not be beyond the realm of possibility that some friend or relative of a member of the unit could somehow have access to the headquarters.

Do sat back down, drawing a Parliament from its box on the table. He methodically tapped the cigarette on a Zippo that Paul noticed had some kind of inscription on it under the crossed flags of the United States and South Vietnam. Then Do leaned forward and carefully set the lighter down beside the box. He took a moment to align the two with the edge of the table.

"You are asking about the Phu Loi Battalion, Paul," he began quietly. Phu Loi is the VC name for most of the neighboring Binh Duong Province. So far as we know, there's no independent unit here in Bien Hoa, so occasionally the Phu Loi battalion seems to feel free to flex its muscles over here. We don't know a great deal about the unit, but in all candor I will have to admit that it is probably one of the best provincial units they have.

"The commander goes by the name of Van Ba. I doubt that that is his real name. Usually COSVN — that's the Central Office, South Vietnam, the main VC headquarters — assigns cover names to their people.

"We've had a lot of trouble with the Phu Loi Battalion. Some time ago there was a vicious ambush of one of our infantry regiments up near Ben Suc — about here." He pointed with his ring finger while the first two squeezed his cigarette. "We must have lost forty or fifty men. I can't be sure, but I believe it was the Phu Loi Group. We got no prisoners."

"Where are they based?" asked Paul.

"We can't be sure. Their security is very tight."

"Don't you have any idea?"

"Oh, we pick up stray signals from here and there, but nothing we can put our finger on."

"How about a penetration?" Paul persisted. "Can't you get one of your local boys to join up and find out where the bases are?"

"We tried that. As a matter of fact, we tried it three times. The first soldier was so nervous that he blew it right away and came back having received a bad scolding from one of the VC officers and having promised to quit the Army. And sure enough, he did. He deserted within a week and is still AWOL as far as I know."

"What about the others?"

"I don't know. We never heard from either of them again. It could be that they went over to the enemy. Or they could be 'six feet under,' as you say." Do spread his hands in a helpless gesture.

"Oh, come on, Do," Paul protested. "You've been operating against a provincial outfit for — how many years? And you don't know any more about them than that? Where could they maintain a base? What would be the most likely places? How about the Iron Triangle? Have you looked there?" Paul was becoming impatient.

"Of course, Do replied, "we have regular aircraft patrol over the area at least four times a week."

"Four times a week! By air?" Paul had difficulty maintaining his composure as his friend's guest. "Surely you would have to go in on the ground to find anything. There's triple-canopy jungle over there according to the map."

"Oh, sure," Do shrugged off the implied criticism of his reconnaissance methods, "but we have to be much more careful now that the *Bo Dai* have moved into the corps zone in such strength. That's the real enemy now. Imagine what a bind we could be caught up in if we spent all our time out in the jungle chasing a bunch of provincials or locals — guys who know this area the way you and I know the terrain around Fort Leavenworth. Zappo! The *Bo Dai* would hit our garrison with a couple of regiments: artillery, tanks, the works!"

Paul was so startled he flinched. "Do the North Vietnamese have tanks and artillery?"

"Well, we haven't seen any so far, but they come well equipped. I wouldn't be surprised at anything."

"Okay," Paul conceded. "I guess you have your problems. Maybe things will improve as we begin to build up here." Paul would recall months later that he suffered his first fleeting doubt at that moment; but he went on: "The cavalry regiment I'm attached to should be ready to go in short order once it arrives."

Do smiled. His friend had obviously overstepped himself and now felt sorry for it. Perhaps he could press his advantage. "Say, Paul, how is it going with your advance party? I understand your camp is a real show place."

"Oh, sure. We're doing it just like in the movies."

"Movies of the American Civil War?" Do needled him.

"Yeah, I guess so," Paul replied. "Got to keep up appearances for the sake of morale."

"Sure," Do said soothingly, "but isn't that commander of yours a little funny? I mean, I don't remember anything like that back at Leavenworth. What's all the show for?"

"He's not crazy, if that's what you mean," Paul replied defensively. Besides, whatever their friendship, it wasn't any of Do's business how the exec ran the camp.

Do sensed the turn-off and stretched his round face into a grin. "Paul, it is just super seeing you again. If one has to go to war, one should never do it without good friends at his side. Here you are! Just super! I can't thank you enough for coming over."

Paul would have liked to have returned to the matter of the enemy provincial forces. He had seen only skimpy reference to them in the U.S. intelligence reports. Clearly the Americans had been dependent upon the Vietnamese Army for much of their information up to this point, and the Vietnamese either didn't have much or simply weren't talking. The more he thought about the matter the more questions popped into his mind. Just how did the provincials operate? Where did they get their equipment and ammo? How did they manage to maintain such tight security? Paul knew his order of battle "O.B." books were packed with plenty of information on the main force units — their organization, equipment, tactics, unit histories — practically everything you would want to know to deal with them in the jungle. Why is the intelligence so skimpy on the provincials? What sort of an outfit is this Phu Loi Battalion? And — what's his name? Van Ba? Who is he and where did he come from?

Paul sat wordlessly in his jeep with his mind running over the whole conversation again. He was sure that Do's welcome had been genuine. It just seemed to turn a little awkward when Do thanked him for coming — implying that the visit had lasted long enough and that it was time to get on to more important things. The driver respected the major's silence and devoted his attention to picking his way around the pot holes on the route back to the camp. It started to rain again.

Do reported to Brigadier General Don Trong, the corps chief of staff, on the afternoon's conversation. The essentials were that the American cavalry regiment would probably be ready for operations shortly after its arrival. Yes, the acting commander probably was a little crazy. Major McCandless had made no attempt to defend him. It had not been possible to obtain a roster of regimental officers, but that could probably be done soon enough, considering the excellent contact Do now felt he had with Major McCandless. The general asked a few other questions and then, amid a swirl of pipe smoke, swiveled his chair around to face the stacks of reports on his credenza. Do saluted the general's backside and walked out.

# *FOUR*

Van Ba was worried. Three more men from the C-2 unit had come down with malarial symptoms in spite of all precautions. It angered him that the patriots were so superstitious about quinine. Some consumed an entire month's supply as soon as they received it, thinking that if a little was good, a lot would be better. Two of the men he had treated himself. The third was so ill he had to be turned over to the family for care. He probably suffered from malnutrition, too, and would die anyway. Ba issued strict orders to his staff for supervision of all antimalarial dosages.

He was depressed by this latest development, and it took some coaxing by his planner, Ly Nam, to get him to look at a composite sketch put together by the reconnaissance B unit. It was large, perhaps drawn on two or three sheets of butcher's paper and glued together. Even for Ba, who had seen many such sketches, it was surprising in its detail. Without the meticulous labels and with a little more shading in the trees, it might have passed for an overhead photograph. It had an artistic magnetism about it, and Ba clearly felt the tug. He said nothing aloud, but the word "incredible" kept running through his mind.

Here were the streets which led to the garrison. Here were the walls, the wire, the machine gun positions with each sand bag drawn to scale. He could make out each type of vehicle in the park without looking at the labels. The M-41 tanks were lined up in two uneven rows. Those temporarily deadlined for mechanical difficulties were shown on the opposite side of a long shed. Each shed stall housing a vehicle was carefully labeled with the type of vehicle, its unit marker, and whether it had been driven in frontward or backed in. The fuel dump and the office of the motor officer appeared as separate rectangles, off to the sides. Even small details, like oil drums, spare parts and coils of extra tracks for the tanks were shown to scale. Each item had been assigned a code number to facilitate reporting of last minute changes of the locations of items and vehicles up to the moment of the attack. Ba had hoped to have photographs, but this was much easier to read and probably just as accurate.

On a second sheet the artists depicted elevations of the garrison from the four points of the compass. Attached sheets of rice paper contained neatly printed details of garrison routine observed over a period of days. Mess hours, guard changes, garbage disposal and supply runs were all there. The garrison complement was given in round numbers, together with a list of the names and positions of many of the officers and non-commissioned officers.

Ba turned to his planning official. "Patriot Nam, please give my compliments to the reconnaissance B unit leader. This is a superb piece of work. I trust we'll be informed of changes of any critical items of equipment occurring before the operation."

"You'll be informed of all changes, Patriot Ba. I can assure you of that. I have one other report to make, Patriot Ba. This one is quite inconvenient."

"So?" Ba prompted him.

"COSVN reports that there is to be a B-52 heavy bombardment strike in our area sometime this evening. Probably six aircraft, each loaded with one hundred and five 500 pound high explosive bombs. There are reports of a new monster weapon called 'daisy cutter,' but it doesn't seem likely that any will be used in this attack. The new bomb is probably much larger than those to be used tonight."

"How close will it be? Do we have the map coordinates?"

"No, Patriot Ba. COSVN doesn't have that information. But our radio discipline has been good, so it's unlikely that we have been pinpointed. Of course if we remain in the area we'll have to go well below ground when we get the signal. Very soon we should receive confirmation that the aircraft have taken off from Guam. Our Russian comrades will keep us informed of the bombers' progress as they pass the lines of trawlers. We can expect, as usual, that they'll loop around the northern end of Luzon where they'll be refueled by tankers from Okinawa. The final notice will come when they begin their target run just off the coast. We can probably expect about fifteen minutes final warning."

Ba didn't wish to share with his planning officer the fact that he had his own special source for protective information. While it had not proved of much value for offensive operational purposes, it had been of considerable importance in saving the D group from blundering into government traps. The connection was based upon a family tie, so he went to extraordinary lengths to protect it. He accepted the COSVN warning as if he had not heard it before.

Ba was not quite sure how all the information from COSVN was gathered. He knew that Russian trawlers and "fishing fleets" tracked American air and naval activity and reported much of it to Hanoi, which in turn passed pertinent elements to COSVN. But usually, by the time he received official notification from COSVN, he had already heard it from his special source. Unfortunately, his prior notice tended to make him a little less grateful to his higher headquarters than his political officer thought he ought to be. In return, he wondered why COSVN had to send him a woman like Tran Hua to "help" him with the war. He wondered aloud, on occasion, if all political advisors were like her.

"We should interpret the hour of the attack favorably," Ba told his assembled staff. "An evening strike means that there'll probably be no follow-up on the ground. We should be alert ahead of time for any unusual enemy light aircraft activity. Many times their senior officers like to go up in helicopters or observation planes to watch the strike. That should help us pinpoint the area to be hit. Make absolutely sure that we have nothing fragile above ground. If any of our telephone lines are broken I would rather do without communications than risk disclosing any of our positions by radio transmission. Casualty reporting will be by messenger after dark if the lines are interrupted.

"We'll remain in our positions and follow standard pre-strike procedures: nylon lines strung through all tunnel air vents to guide rescue work. All patriots will have digging tools at their sides at all times. Everyone will sing as long as the strike lasts. Six aircraft means that there'll probably be two waves of about one minute each, usually thirty seconds apart. Report back to me when all C units are prepared."

"Comrade Ba." It was Tran Hua.

"Yes, Comrade Hua."

"You have ample warning of this strike. Why don't you order an evacuation of the area? COSVN will be furious if you take many casualties after you have ignored its advice."

"I'm not ignoring anyone's advice, Comrade Hua. COSVN doesn't know exactly where the strike will be." He was trying to be patient.

"You could move the D group a long way before the attack," Hua persisted.

"Look, Comrade Hua. I am the elected commander of the D group, and I am trying to do the best thing for it. If we were to move a little way we could be caught in the middle of the strike area with no prepared protection. If we attempted an emergency march in broad daylight we might be detected by either American or government reconnaissance units which would bring down artillery and tactical air strikes upon us. The fact that the enemy has chosen to attack the area with B-52 bombers indicates that they suspect we, or some other patriotic group is here. They are bound to be looking for any sort of movement on our part. I suggest you go back and read your Marx and leave the tactical decisions to me. We are going to be all right if we follow standard procedures to the letter."

Hua looked around at the other staff officials, but none of them moved. Each face was as impassive as though it were carved in stone. Van Ba has a grip on them, she thought, and it is not a healthy one. None of them exhibits the revolutionary zeal necessary to bring the American imperialists and their government running dogs to heel. She had already commented to COSVN on the political unreliability of the Phu Loi D Group. So far, fortune had run with it, but without a proper political awareness among its leaders it was bound to fail. The Peoples' War is much more than tactics and battles. It's a combination of the awakened soul of the masses screaming for revenge against their oppressors. Van Ba and his clique of staff specialists have no comprehension of the larger dimension of the war. Someday they'll stumble in their blindness and be replaced by leaders with real revolutionary spirit. Hua yearned for the day of correction to come soon. Seated at her field table she jotted down the essence of her argument to dispatch to COSVN if the D group suffered heavy casualties.

The final warning came from COSVN at 1743 hours. It was repeated by telephone to each C unit by 1747. A runner carried the message to the outpost line which had experienced a short circuit in its telephone net during the last heavy rainfall. Just after 1800 the first bombs began to fall. In a dozen bunkers young men and women grasped each others arms and began to sing.

The blasts grew in intensity, and dust began to puff from the ceilings. The singing and explosions intensified. There was a tremendous crash in the tunnel of C-1 bunker as tons of earth and timber collapsed toward the main chamber. The ground heaved and the roar was so intense that neither singing nor screaming could be heard. Two quick witted youngsters struggled to roll a table on its side in front of the entrance way to block the choking dust. When they realized that they were successful, they turned and grinned at each other. And they grinned at their comrades through the suspended dust and the dingy light of the single lantern in the room. Everyone had a wet cloth over his face. With some coughing and spitting, the singing began again.

The bombs moved on. Van Ba ordered a telephone check with the C units. C-1 and -3 reported in. The line to C-2 was broken. C-1 had two known minor injuries, but had no contact with one of its B units. At worst they might have had a cave-in. There was not enough time to investigate before the second wave was due to strike.

Ba looked at his watch. One minute, twenty-six seconds, twenty-seven, twenty-eight, twenty-nine.... Again the bombs began to fall, but this time they were much further away. Everyone was smiling.

"Sing!" ordered Ba. The staff burst forth in a rousing song about a rice farmer who had such an abundant crop that he had to call in the entire village to share it with him. Even Hua joined in. When the raid was over she took the message she had composed for COSVN and tore it to shreds.

An A unit had taken a very close hit. Three young men and a girl were dead. Two others had broken limbs, and they were all dazed and deaf from the concussion. Ba and his medical assistants were up until four the next morning caring for the injured. The dead were transported in slings during the night to their villages and turned over to their families. Again Hua objected to what she saw as a serious breach of security.

"Comrade Ba, I must protest this flagrant admission of casualties. Agents in the villages are bound to note the return of the patriots' bodies. The government dogs will track us down! At least they will put two and two together and determine how much damage the raid did. They will probably even be able to pinpoint the base. We will have to move now. I insist upon it!"

Ba knew she was right, but he was just too exhausted to care. He rationalized that it would take a day or two for the news to get to government military intelligence and for them to figure out what it meant. He was willing to take the risk. Perhaps he could accelerate his operational planning for the Phu Cuong strike and grab the initiative again. Without replying, Ba walked away, leaving Hua standing in morning twilight. He collapsed in his hammock. Whatever was to be next in the war would have to wait. Hua wished she had not torn up her message to COSVN quite so quickly.

# FIVE

The orderly scraped his boots on an empty sandbag outside the major's tent as he looked about for something solid the knock on. He tried the short pole supporting the entrance flap, but couldn't be sure that it was loud enough to be heard inside. He waited for a flight of helicopters to flop-flop-flop their way overhead and disappear beyond the tree line before he tried again.

He cleared his throat and rather self-consciously called out, "Major McCandless, sir. It's Private Thompson."

"Come in, Thompson," a disembodied voice came from within.

Private John Thompson, age 19, had not expected to be called inside. He had figured he could deliver his message and scoot back to the security of the orderly room without having to come face to face with the detachment commander. His perception of military custom encompassed a rigid chain of command between himself and the detachment commander with a number of noncommissioned officers, like Sergeant Garowski, and officers in between. For all he knew, Major McCandless took orders directly from the Pentagon — or maybe even the president. Major McCandless was a very important man, and Thompson felt his heart beginning to pound as he pushed the flap aside and stood up inside. He was conscious that the flap had caught on the muzzle of his rifle on his right shoulder as he saluted with a perspiring right hand.

"Private Thompson, orderly of the day, 145th MI Detachment, reporting sir!"

"Yes, good morning, Thompson. How are you?" The major had pushed himself away from the field desk and was leaning back on a metal folding chair. Thompson recognized the chair as one he had packed in a "Conex" container for air shipment back at Fort Meade. He knew that inch-high letters on the back asserted "DETACHMENT COMMANDER" in bold white-on-O.D. It had made him feel important to pack that chair. Now here it was being used by Major McCandless himself. Thompson felt for the first time that perhaps he was part of the action. The Army was in Vietnam, and he, John Thompson from Texarkana, was part of it. Some of the things he had done — like packing that chair — were already being accepted by important people as an ingredient of the total effort. He struggled to pull his rifle loose from the tent flap without the major noticing.

"I'm fine, Major McCandless, sir." He was doing pretty well. The flap fell away from his weapon. Then he blurted out, "And how are you, sir?" The sound of his own voice speaking to the detachment commander like one friend to another stunned him. He yearned to turn and run. Instead he swallowed hard and wiped his sweaty hand on the damp trouser leg of his fatigues. He had no idea of what to expect from the major in response.

Relief came over him in a flood when the major replied, "Thanks, Thompson, I'm very well. What's on your mind?"

Thank God I haven't forgotten what I came for, Thompson thought. "I had a call from Sergeant Major Abrams, sir. He said that the executive officer wanted to see you right away. I told Sergeant Garowski, and he said to come tell you myself."

"Thank you, Thompson," the major replied. "Please tell the sergeant major I'll be right over. I assume the exec is at the regimental C.P.?"

Panic returned to the orderly. It had not occurred to him that the major might not know where the exec was. That was a high level command matter that might well involve great affairs of military strategy for all he knew. He couldn't think of anything to say.

The major had no difficulty reading the crisis on the soldier's face. He took him off the hook. "Okay, Thompson. Thanks a lot. I'll find him."

Again, a flood of relief. The orderly saluted and turned to go. Again his rifle caught on the tent flap. He unslung the weapon with trembling hands and pulled it loose. Dammit, he thought to himself. The major chuckled inwardly and reached for his pistol belt and steel pot. Thompson would make a fine soldier some day — perhaps sooner that either of them might realize.

Paulding McCandless picked his way through the encampment, jumping over puddles and muddy areas between the tents. He noticed that each tent had at least a four-foot wall of sandbags around it now, and work was progressing on small bunkers every fifty yards or so. There had been a little shooting on the periphery of the camp each night, but he was never satisfied that it was anything more than the behavior of a few nervous American kids sitting on the edge of a humid jungle, thousands of miles from home, listening to the sounds of what they imagined were a murderous band of cutthroats in black pajamas sneaking up on them in the dark. But he couldn't discount the likelihood that the Vietcong would want to reconnoiter the camp at night to discover its security patterns and to test the acuity of the guards. There was no way that the layout could be screened from outside observation in the daytime. The only hope for security was in shifting the perimeter posts and ambush sites after dark.

One night Paul had been awakened by the explosion of a claymore mine sometime after three a.m. It had been followed by a furious tattoo of small arms' fire and the burst of illuminating flares overhead moments later. But inspection of the area after sunup revealed no clue as to how it had started. Paul recognized that any kind of small animal could have tripped the mine, and none of the soldiers he questioned could positively report having been shot at. Once again, he had to ascribe the primary cause of the incident to green troops in a hostile wilderness.

The command post for the advance party was marked with a bright yellow sign — the old horse cavalry color. Emblazoned in the center was the charging mounted lancer of the regiment, and behind fluttered a red and white guidon that would have been at home in any John Wayne movie of the old West. Paul stopped to glance at a makeshift bulletin board that had been erected in rear of the sign. A magnificent cartoon caught his eye from among the official papers posted around it. A grizzled horse cavalry trooper squinted out from under a campaign hat skewered by an arrow. The legend read:

> Yea, though I walk through the valley of the
> shadow of death I will fear no evil, for I am
> the meanest son-of-a-bitch in the valley!

Paul chuckled to himself as he approached the command tent and made a point to remember to tell Cicely about it when he wrote her that night.

Colonel Dreier was on the telephone, apparently talking to someone at higher headquarters. He motioned Paul into the shelter to a folding chair. The party at the other end of the line must have had some rank, Paul guessed, because the conversation was remarkably civilized compared to the usual quality of the exec's communications.

"Look, Paul," Dreier began as he hung up, "that was the Field Force G-3. He says the regimental commander is flying in tomorrow from Hawaii. Colonel Gates left the main body on shipboard at Honolulu to fly on over here for a look-see before the troops arrive. He wants us to meet him at Tan-Son-Nhut and to give him a look around. He particularly wants to see Xuan Loc and the terrain around there. Isn't that where you said the 273rd VC Regiment hangs out?"

"The 274th," Paul corrected him.

"Okay, the 274th. The one that's supposed to be such a hot-shot outfit."

"Yes, sir. It has a pretty good record. Of course it has only had to contend with the 10th ARVN Division, a pretty soft organization by all accounts. I don't think the 10th has ventured out of its compound at Xuan Loc in almost four months. The commander is a political appointee from Saigon. You know the expression here where 'Number One' means the best? Well, 'Number 10' means the worst. That outfit may just be living up to its name." He was about to remark that he hoped people would not get the same impression about the 10th Armored Cavalry Regiment, but he thought better of it.

"Okay. Meet me here at 0630 sharp tomorrow," the exec went on. "We'll have two choppers to take us to Tan-Son-Nhut to pick up Colonel Gates and whoever he might have with him. We'll give them a few minutes to take a leak when they get off the plane, then count on flying direct to Xuan Loc. I will contact the U.S. advisor at the 10th ARVN Division that we're coming. We may make a few loops around the camp here on the way just to show him the area and how we have it organized. You give him an update on the intelligence picture while we're going. Okay?"

"Okay, sir. What about the other staff officers?"

"You let me worry about them. You just be here at 0630 ready to go. Any other questions?"

"No, sir. Got it." Paul saluted and walked out. The heat and humidity of the day were closing in rapidly.

I need a haircut, he thought to himself as he retraced his path back through the encampment. The exec had instituted "shipboard" rules on saluting in the camp, which meant that the men were expected to salute the officers only once when they first saw them in the morning. Paul thought it was an eminently sensible procedure, considering the circumstances, and found himself less concerned with military courtesy on the way back to his own detachment.

He was a little uneasy about the interest the exec had attributed to Colonel Gates regarding the 274th VC Regiment. The 274th was a main force outfit with a good record — no doubt about it — but Paul was a little afraid that he may have overemphasized the unit's importance in some of his briefings. Paul had a great deal more information on the main force units in his "O.B." (order of battle) files because the ARVN supplied much more. He suspected that the South Vietnamese Government might want the Americans to know more about them so that they would look upon the war as a conventional meeting of armies in the field and not as a backyard brawl between relatives. The more the war could be depicted in regular military terms the more the U.S. Government would be inclined to commit its own troops. American units in their full glory of firepower, mobility, and communications could be pretty terrible to behold. But what good could they be in a family squabble? Even city policemen hate to get involved in domestic spats.

Paul worried that perhaps he had not talked enough about the local forces: the village guerrillas and the provincials. He realized that he had not done so because he had had precious little to tell. And Lord knows, Do hadn't been much help the other day. He hoped that he had been mistaken about Do.

How about this Phu Loi Battalion, for instance? Paul thought to himself as he inexpertly jumped a maze of muddy tire tracks, slopping mud over one boot and up his trouser leg. Suppose we were to meet up with them first? I guess we will just have to go to work on the problem as we begin to get the hang of things around here.

The day was routine: more jungle boots in the supply tent, more planking for the floors of the tents, one man sent to the dispensary for stitches in his hand where he had ripped the skin with a saw. Infection in wounds was rapid in this climate, and even small cuts had to be taken seriously.

The departure for Tan-Son-Nhut Airbase was delayed for forty-five minutes by a drenching downpour. The helicopters rose into the air with steam boiling off the ground as soon as the sun came out. Paul and the others were soaked through by the rain, but the rush of wind through the open doors of the aircraft rapidly dried them out.

The countryside was beautiful from a thousand feet up. The air was cool and refreshing, and the reflected sunlight winked at them from hundreds of ponds and buffalo wallows across the landscape. The fields were as green as a child's crayon work, and the red tile roofs of the houses stood out in picture book contrast. How could such a beautiful land be so ugly and dangerous on the ground?

Paul picked out the rivers Do had shown him on the map: the serpentine Dong-Nai, the narrow Roc-Ti-Tin, and the broad, meandering Song Saigon. Not far away lay the "rough neighborhoods:" the Iron Triangle, where the French Group Mobile had been destroyed fifteen years before, and the almost impenetrable Ho Bo Woods where great amounts of enemy weapons were suspected of being stored. Beyond, to the northeast lay the brooding War Zone D, from centuries past the traditional home of outlaws, from yesteryear of the Viet Minh, and now of the Viet Cong. A realization of the relentless succession of tragedies in this poor land overcame Paul for a moment and made him blow his nose and wipe his face.

The regimental commander was waiting for them in the air conditioned office of the flight operations officer when they arrived. He had had time to switch from his travel-rumpled khakis into starched jungle fatigues and looked like a classic picture of the heroic leader. Salutes, handshakes and official smiles all around.

Within minutes the helicopters were airborne again, retracing their route back to the east. Dreier and Paul spent their time pointing out significant features on the ground and correlating them with the map for their commander's benefit. They began by shouting over the racket of the engine and rotor blades, but were soon simply pointing and gesturing. The exec pointed out the ARVN's armored cavalry compound at Phu Cuong with its tanks and other vehicles lined up in neat rows. Colonel Gates could see the saffron flag with thin red stripes and nodded understanding.

After the scheduled loop around the camp of the regimental advance party, the aircraft swung due east along Highway 1 toward Xuan Loc. Paul felt a chill as he recalled Bernard Fall's book bearing the nickname for the northern extension of this road, "Street Without Joy."

"What's going on down there?" Colonel Gates shouted, pointing to a back-up of traffic on the westbound lane. Dreier shrugged and looked to Paul for a reply.

"It looks like a VC tax collection point," Paul shouted back. "See how they have pulled trees across the highway as a barricade."

Colonel Gates was shocked at the almost casual reply. "You mean there are VC down there, right under our feet?" He had to strain his voice to get the question out.

The exec turned and thumped the pilot's helmet to get his attention. He gestured downward to point out the barricade.

The pilot handed Colonel Gates a helmet with built-in earphones and microphone plugged into his intercom. When the colonel had it adjusted, the pilot's voice came on with an electronic crackle, "Sir, there is nothing we can do, other than report it to the ARVN 10th Division. Our choppers have only door guns, and we might hit a lot of innocent people if we tried to use them. Besides, they may have automatic weapons in that tree line covering their operation on the highway."

"What about artillery?" the colonel asked.

"No, sir. Again, we would kill a lot of civilians."

"Well, that's a hell of a note!" the colonel argued.

"The enemy is right there looking at us, and you say we can't do anything about it? I can't believe it. Call Xuan Loc and ask them if they can't send out a patrol to scarf these people up."

On the ground below a half-dozen patriots of the Long Kahn D Group glanced up at the circling helicopters and went ahead with their business; checking identity papers; assessing "taxes" according to the size and weight of each vehicle, its cargo and the number of passengers; and signing receipts for the money received. Government soldiers and civilians were ordered to dismount and to attend political lectures delivered by cadremen in the woods nearby. One soldier who attempted to jump from a bus and run was shot before he could get away. His body lay half in the rain ditch on the side of the road.

"What does ARVN say? the regimental commander demanded.

"They 'Roger' for the message, sir," the pilot replied, "but they don't think they can do anything about it. They said they tried once before, but they lost almost an entire platoon in an ambush down the road."

Colonel Gates was beside himself with anger and frustration, but he couldn't think of anything else to say. Paul watched him take a deep breath and clench and unclench his fists. Paul understood the crisis his commander was going through. It really was one hell of a stinking little war. Finally, the colonel ordered the pilot to proceed on the Xuan Loc.

A small fleet of jeeps was waiting on the ground at the makeshift helicopter port on the town's soccer field. Clouds of orange dust mushroomed out around the aircraft as they settled in on their skids. The American advisor to the 10th Division stood beside a Vietnamese colonel. Officers of lesser rank and a number of drivers stood behind them in little groups. Salutes were followed by a blur of introductions, smiles and handshakes.

Paul was pleasantly surprised to find Do among the receiving party. He climbed into another jeep with a Vietnamese major who smiled broadly, apparently to compensate for an inability to communicate in English.

Paul tried his high school French to find out what was on the itinerary, but the major's French was not much better than his own. Paul understood something about a French rubber factory and a hospital. Whatever was lacking in language was made up by the major's incessant grin and animated gestures.

It was clear enough as they approached the road heading out of town that the major wanted Paul to draw and load his pistol. *"Beaucoups VC! Beaucoups VC!"* he warned.

Paul could see only a pathetic group of rag-picking street children a half block away, but he did as he was told, feeling a little self-conscious as he chambered a cartridge in his weapon. He tried rather weakly to avoid making it appear that he was brandishing a pistol because of the presence of the children. They stared at the column with unblinking eyes as the officers rode by. Paul smiled and waved, but they stood as motionless as gravestones, dirty and unsmiling.

*"Beaucoups VC,"* the major repeated.

Paul tried to take the children lightly. VC or no VC, he thought to himself, I hope I am not supposed to pick up that little bunch of ragamuffins in my O.B. files. And how in blazes would one do that anyway? Lord knows, the manual wouldn't be much help.

But it didn't seem very funny. The unblinking eyes and the poker faces seemed to match the major's warning. Dear God, Paul's thoughts ran on, don't tell me we're here to chase kids with tanks and B-52s! He tried to think about something else.

The small convoy stopped momentarily in front of a row of 55-gallon drums in the road marking the final police check point, and then proceeded on out into the rubber plantation. The canopy of overhead foliage provided a pleasant coolness from the sun, but the geometric alignment of the trunks created an odd illusion as the vehicles passed by. As they rode on in silence Paul thought he detected movement between the tree rows several times, but he couldn't be sure. A plantation worker stood on the side of the road, as expressionless as the children. The major's phrase, *"Beaucoups VC,"* ran repetitively through his mind.

The convoy took a sharp turn to the left and followed a well-worn pair of tire tracks, straight as an arrow through the rubber stand. Paul noticed the rust and disrepair as they crossed the narrow gauge rail line that in more peaceful times had run between Xuan Loc and the markets in Saigon. It had obviously long since been abandoned. The rough road came to an abrupt halt at the wall of a large smelly building with shafts of steam emitting from under the eves. This apparently was the rubber processing plant. A French supervisor was on hand to greet the party, but not many workers were in evidence. No explanations were given for why so few employees were on hand or how operations managed to continue in the middle of a war zone. In twenty minutes they were back in their jeeps and headed back up the trail in the direction from which they had come. Paul had heard how a small French company had continued to operate in Vietnam, minding the business of the great rubber cartels. But it was one thing to hear about it and another to see what was about to burst upon him.

Back on the highway, the convoy had continued driving for ten or fifteen minutes to the east and then turned off into a well tended compound of lawns, palms, tennis courts and stately villas. Silent figures in conical sun hats were bent over their work in the flowering strips beside the buildings, while two bikini-clad European girls batted a ball between them on a court. The luminescent swimming pool had both high and low diving boards awaiting customers. Paul turned to his escort for an explanation, but received only a broad grin and commentary, *"bon, bon,"* for a reply.

No doubt about it, Paul thought, this is pretty *"bon"* any way you look at it. The distant rumble of artillery made the contrast with the Vietnam that he was coming to know all the more poignant.

Beyond the residential area the convoy passed a grass airstrip carved through the trees. Two or three small planes were parked to one side in the shade. Paul noticed that one of them had a red cross painted on a white band encircling the fuselage. Not until later at the plantation hospital did he hear the story from Do that the French maintained the fiction of operating a sport "flying club" from the airstrip on Sunday afternoons.

"Actually," Do went on, "the French are obliged to care for wounded VC at the hospital — no questions asked. Higher ranking cadremen and North Vietnamese soldiers are flown out on the weekends."

"Why doesn't the government stop it?" Colonel Gates asked.

"The government cannot interfere with anything the French do here," Do explained, "for fear of forcing them to leave. At least they keep the economy going and provide jobs, whatever else they do for the enemy."

Paul noticed that Colonel Gates was clenching and unclenching his fists again the way he had done in the helicopter over the VC tax collection point. They were all learning that this was a different kind of war.

The visit to the hospital was aborted at the gate. It turned out to be "inconvenient," and great apologies were forthcoming from a minor functionary for not having had "more time to prepare for a call by distinguished Americans." Paul and Do exchanged understanding glances. No further explanation was needed or offered.

That's all the colonel would need right now, Paul thought, wondering just what the colonel might have done if he suddenly came face to face with VC and NVA patients in a small ward. It started to rain again as they turned back toward Xuan Loc.

Welcome to Vietnam, Colonel, Paul thought as he saw his commander's odd expression when he turned for one last look at the hospital.

# *SIX*

The intercom buzzed again. Sergeant Vu Van Minh jumped immediately to reply. He had spilled his tea getting to it the first time, and still had suffered the wrath of the chief of staff for being too slow to reply. The wire wasn't long enough to permit him to move the box to his own desk, so he had pushed Major Nguyen Van Do's coffee table up under the window to serve as a temporary surface for his papers and had dragged his chair in from the next room to be immediately accessible for a call. His predecessor on the job had been a little too slow in answering summonses around the headquarters and had been demoted and reassigned to an infantry battalion. Minh had heard that the man had disappeared under mysterious circumstances some time later. No one knew whether he had deserted — or whether the government security services had gotten to him. He would have been of some intelligence value to the enemy, which could have made him a target of interest to both sides. In any event, Minh was determined to avoid a similar fate. His voice came out a little louder than he had intended:

"Sergeant Vu Van Minh answering for Major Nguyen Van Do, sir."

"Major Nguyen hasn't returned yet, Sergeant?"

"No, sir. He went by helicopter to Xuan Loc this morning to meet the new commander of the American Tenth Armored Cavalry Regiment. I believe he left a note for you in your office."

"Oh? Well, maybe I have it here somewhere. When'll he be back?"

"He planned to stay overnight, sir."

"Overnight? I didn't authorize that."

"No, sir. I can contact the 10th Division headquarters and have them fly him back right now."

"Yes, do that Vu, and let me know when he'll return."

Minh didn't understand the chief's concern for the major's absence, but he hastened to draft a TWX to the headquarters at Xuan Loc:

> SECRET. PRIORITY: OPERATIONAL
> IMMEDIATE. MAJOR NGUYEN VAN
> DO, G-2 CENTRAL CORPS, TO RETURN
> BIEN HOA IMMEDIATELY. TENTH
> DIVISION WILL PROVIDE AIR
> TRANSPORTATION. BY ORDER OF
> CHIEF OF STAFF.

Within ten minutes he had it authenticated by General Don's haughty aide and delivered to the code clerk for encryption and transmission. He hurried back to his chair by the intercom box in case the chief called again.

At three p.m. a messenger delivered a reply from Xuan Loc:

> SECRET. PRIORITY: OPERATIONAL
> IMMEDIATE. SEVERE BAD WEATHER

FORECAST PROHIBITS DEPARTURE OF MAJOR NGUYEN VAN DO NOW. WILL ADVISE WHEN DEPARTURE POSSIBLE. COMMANDER

Colonel Tuy Van Quinh, the chief's aide, frowned without looking up when Minh showed the message to him. It seemed to be a point with the aide never to look directly at any of the personnel of the headquarters, but to address them only indirectly. The sergeant shifted nervously while awaiting the reemergence of the aide from the chief's office. He could hear voices behind the door, but he couldn't quite make them out. Tuy reappeared, closing the door behind him.

"The chief of staff wants you to inform him as soon as Major Nguyen returns," the aide began, striding back to his desk. "I told the chief that Major Nguyen's assistant, Captain Pham, is sick. That's correct, isn't it?"

The sergeant noticed that the aide's eyes never departed from his desk. "Yes, sir," Minh replied, a bit belatedly.

"And, Sergeant Vu," this time Tuy's eyes were directed to the cigarette he was pinching into a six-inch holder, "is there anything in your current intelligence that would indicate any danger of enemy activity tonight?"

"I don't know, sir. I'm sure Major Nguyen would have informed you — and certainly he would not have left if he had any reason to expect trouble."

"All right." Tuy had his cigarette lit and puffed two almost perfect rings. "Go on back to your office."

"Yes, sir." Minh saluted and departed. He had been left in charge of the intelligence office before, but never without one of the officers being within easy calling distance, and only once had he had to deliver news of enemy action directly to General Don, the chief of staff, himself. Fortunately, it had not been particularly startling, and the chief had absorbed it along with a few puffs of his overly sweet smelling pipe mixture. The aide said that the chief didn't like bad news, and had admonished the sergeant to try harder to reach one of the G-2 officers next time before "barging into the front office with inconsequential details."

Minh busied himself assembling the monthly statistics of enemy action in the corps zone. He noted that all of the figures were slightly higher than the previous month. Attacks by fire on outposts were up 5%. Kidnappings were up 17%. Mine incidents were up 12%. None of the figures were likely to be viewed with particular alarm by the chief of staff. The Americans liked statistics, and Minh had heard the chief comment on the beneficial effect which the growing threat seemed to have on the Americans' commitment to the war effort. These figures would give Major Nguyen additional ammunition for his briefings of American congressmen. Perhaps they would even speed up the buildup of American units in the corps zone.

But Minh felt uneasy about the reports. In previous years enemy activity always seemed to fall off during the rainy season. Now it was on the increase. The June figures had been higher than those in May; now the July figures were above those of June. He wondered whether there was not some relationship between the growing American strength and the increasing enemy activity. Certainly the Americans could multiply their power more rapidly than the enemy, but the figures were not reassuring.

Minh finished his calculations and began to type up the summary in tabular form. The thought crossed his mind for an instant of entering a comment about the higher figures in the "remarks" section of the form, but he rapidly disabused himself of the idea. Major Nguyen could do that if he wanted to, but it would have been a transgression of military protocol — perhaps even of the threshold of politics — for the sergeant to do so. Better just to do his job and let the officers do the interpretation.

An orderly arrived with the evening mail distribution. The soggy envelopes confirmed the weather report of rain for the area. The sun was still shining in Bien Hoa, but Minh knew that it wouldn't be long before a good monsoon storm doused the headquarters. He spoke sharply to the orderly about covering the mail better in the rain.

Normally, Minh would have laid the envelopes on the major's desk, but with both officers gone he felt he had better check through them for anything possibly requiring immediate attention.

Minh cataloged the items in his mind: more statistics, a map of enemy unit locations, some aerial photographs — nothing that can't wait. Just a minute — the photos were taken this morning, but there's no interpreter's report with them. Better send them over to Tech Read-Out for a quick check. I'll be blamed if there's anything significant on the film and it hasn't been gone over by a photo-interpreter — or as Major Nguyen, with all his American slang, would say, a "PI."

It was a couple of hours before the field phone rang. It was the chief PI sergeant — "Nothing of military significance noted. Some old bunkers show up, but we've seen them before."

"Are you sure?" Minh asked, not particularly expecting a different answer.

"Of course. We'll return the film later on," the reply came.

"What is the area of coverage?" Minh inquired as an afterthought.

"It's central Binh Duong Province, around Phu Cuong. We have lots of coverage of the area. It seems Major Nguyen called for the pictures last week, but the Air Force just got around to flying the mission this morning. Pretty routine stuff."

"Okay," Minh replied, conscious that he was beginning to mimic the major's Americanized language. "Send them on back this afternoon and I'll show them to the G-2 tomorrow."

The rain began to fall as he hung up. It started lightly, but was soon pelting the headquarters building with larger drops half frozen into hailstones. Thunder and wind picked up. Minh locked the windows as the lightning began to illuminate the sky. It's a real one, he thought to himself.

By evening Minh had the intelligence wrap-up reports from two of the divisions. The other was probably delayed by a short circuit some place in the line. No cause for alarm. An orderly returned the photos.

He opened the photos while he ate his rice and fish at the makeshift desk. There must have been a dozen or so – just like hundreds of others he had seen in his ten months on this job. His family had lived in Binh Duong until the government made them move to Saigon as part of the "security resettlement" program. He had been to Phu Cuong many times as a boy, and it was interesting to see the town from the air. Things hadn't changed much. The Vietnamese Army had taken over the old French garrison in the center of town. Minh could recall when the post was actually on the edge of town, but houses had gradually grown up all around it.

He could make out the rows of vehicles in the compound, the walls and barbed wire around it, even the people in the streets. The police check points on the roads showed up clearly. He glanced at the other prints of the surrounding countryside. Certainly the PIs were right; except for the old bunkers there seemed to be "nothing of military significance."

Minh repeated the phrase he had heard over the phone — nothing of military significance: no soldiers or vehicles outside the garrison, no new trenches. A vague question began to form in his mind, why did the man say, "nothing of military significance?" Why didn't he say "nothing of intelligence significance," as he usually did? Is there any difference between the two? He wiped a corner of a print where he had spilled a few drops of *nuoc mam* sauce.

There was something odd about the photos of the surrounding farms. He had lived there for years and knew that the farms didn't normally look quite like this — allowing that they were taken from the air. What is it? Of course! There is no one in the fields. The fields are empty! This is the height of the rice-growing season and no one is tending the crops. The photos were taken this morning. A hundred possible explanations ran through his mind.

Maybe it's market day in Phu Cuong. No, there's no unusual traffic on the roads and the frames covering the town show no crowds in the market place.

Maybe there are village meetings. No, no crowds in the hamlets.

Maybe the security people declared temporary restricted access to the area. Minh couldn't remember any recent mention of the Phu Cuong district in the restricted area orders.

Where are the people? And why aren't they in the fields in the morning hours?

Minh finished his supper and rang down to the G-3 operations center. His opposite number, Sergeant Huong Van Teo, answered the phone. The man was new and couldn't yet be considered fully versed in his job, but Minh decided to go ahead and talk to him anyway. Teo had to learn his business sometime.

"Minh here. What do we have going on in Binh Duong, around Phu Cuong now? Any search-and-destroy operations going? Anything that would keep the farmers out of the fields?"

The ops sergeant wasn't sure; he would check. Minh nestled the phone to his ear with his shoulder while he looked over the photos. Sure enough, the fields are empty. Phu Cuong is an island of activity in dead surroundings. Even the livestock are gone.

Teo was back on the line. "Look, there isn't anyone here right now who can answer your question. The G-3 officers are all out to supper. Why don't you call back in about an hour."

"Just look at the main map board, Teo." Minh tried to be patient. "What friendly units are posted around Phu Cuong?"

"I'm looking, Minh. There is the Fifth Armored Cavalry Regiment (minus) and an engineer company in the garrison."

"How about out in the fields around the town?"

"I don't know what they may have out there. They don't tell us every time they're going out to take a crap."

"Okay." Again the American idiom. "You don't know of anything that would account for the fields being empty this morning?"

"Empty of what?"

Minh resolved to call back when the operations officer returned. "Never mind," he said. "I'll call back."

What to do? The possibility of enemy presence in the area is strong. That doesn't necessarily mean that they're there in strength, Minh knew. Maybe just combat scouts. Shall I tell the chief's aide? I really don't have anything else to back it up. That haughty ass will probably dismiss anything I say as wild supposition. Why are both of his my officers gone now? And why, come to think of it, did Major Nguyen request this particular photo coverage anyway? Did he suspect something?

Wait a minute. It was the Fifth Division that didn't call in its daily intelligence wrap-up. Maybe they know something but can't get through the storm. I'll call down to the ops center again.

"Do you have communications with the Fifth Division?" he asked.

"I don't know," Teo answered, "I'll check."

This could be a cracked recording, Minh thought. Minutes passed.

"Hello? Minh? Teo here. We lost contact in the storm. We have men at work on the line now. What do you need?"

Minh ignored the question. "Do you have radio or teletype contact?"

"Well, it's spotty. We'll be back in touch when the storm blows over. What's up?"

"I don't know, but let me know as soon as you have contact."

"All right, but we're pretty busy here with reports. You'd better check back after a while."

"Okay." Minh was becoming agitated. He knew he had to notify the chief of staff. Phu Cuong had to be alerted to possible trouble that night. The blinking lightning, the crash of thunder, and the hammering rain on the roof drove home the realization of the technical problems involved in getting a warning to the garrison if the chief understood his concern.

General Don was at dinner, and according to Colonel Tuy "couldn't be disturbed." The imperious aide seemed a little less imperious than usual when Minh showed him the photographs, but he tended to favor one of the other explanations which the sergeant had discarded in his own mind.

"Get in touch with Major Nguyen Van Do at the Tenth Division headquarters and get his opinion, Sergeant." That was the most positive response Minh could get from the officer. Certainly it would have been improper for him to suggest more action once he had stated his suspicions to the chief's aide-de-camp. Minh sat down in the dingy office and called the headquarters switchboard. All lines to the Tenth Division were busy.

# SEVEN

The C unit had been on the march for three days. Since the path lay through the jungle the patriots marched during the daylight hours and rested at night. As the route entered farming area, they reversed the schedule — crossing open country under cover of darkness. A units scouted ahead, relying partially upon contacts with local guerrilla teams for guidance and security during passage through their villages. The afternoon rains had been a mixed blessing. It inhibited enemy observation from the air, but it soaked the equipment and made the electrical gear unreliable — particularly the telephones and the torpedoes.

The C unit had a radio, but the D group commander had forbidden its use. Patriot Bay, whose assignment it was to carry the device, obeyed orders but secretly wondered why he was required to take it along without ever using it. Once, he had considered admitting his doubts about his assignment at one of the monthly confession sessions. Each patriot was expected to cleanse his spirit by admitting to his comrades any failure or weakness of his revolutionary ardor. But Bay knew the radio was considered an important item and was afraid that he might be reassigned to a position of lesser trust if he appeared to question orders. He had a childlike devotion about him and wanted to please the cadremen. He didn't understand everything, but he had a deep faith in the righteousness of the Movement. He had become a good radio operator, and harbored a secret wish to have an opportunity to demonstrate his skill in the field. He believed he could transmit and receive Morse code faster and more accurately than anyone else in the D group. He wanted terribly to prove it.

The C group relied completely on messengers to maintain contact with the parent D group while it was on the march. As soon as a halt would be called wire teams would begin stringing lines if the distance could be covered before it was time to move again. Patriot Le Van Sau, the C unit leader, drove the teams mercilessly to lay and recover wire while the main body of the unit rested. Only the greatest devotion to the cause sustained the teams, who often had to go for days without sleep while the unit was on the march. American and government radio direction finding units were said to be constantly searching the airwaves for unidentified radio transmissions; the C unit couldn't risk being located during movement, far from the protection of its base areas. Radio was the communications medium of last resort.

The rain grew in intensity. The government weather service had correctly predicted the onset of a major monsoon storm, and several of the patriots made wry jokes about how useful government services were to the Liberation Movement. They likened the announcements to a condemned man fashioning his own gibbet. Each one carried his own weapon plus two mortar rounds or a recoilless rifle round. Men and women from the reserve C unit and from the local guerrilla organizations helped with the crew-served weapons and water. Like all of his soldiers, Sau wore a cloth roll full of unpolished rice in a sling over his shoulder. The grain was bloated and sodden, but it would sustain them until they returned to their base area.

Sau was proud of his C unit. Patriot Ba had hinted to him privately on more than one occasion that his was the best in the D group. Sau respected the confidence, recognizing the discord which open competition could breed among the units. But it was hard to be completely content solely with making a contribution to the success of the Phu Loi D Group. Perhaps someday he could aspire to lead the D group himself.

Sau came from humble peasant stock, but years of perceived harassment by one set of tyrants after another in Saigon had driven him to rebellion. The Movement seemed to offer the best prospect for riddance of graft-ridden administrations and of foreign influence. Unlike some of his colleagues, Sau favored national unification, and he saw no problems with the increasing Northern participation in the struggle. "Uncle" Ho Chi Minh represented the best interests of the Vietnamese people, as far as Sau was concerned, and he was quite prepared to follow the orders of his appointed representatives — in COSVN, in Hanoi, or wherever they served. Besides, promotions usually seemed to go to those who were most enthusiastic about unification.

He watched his weary soldiers plod onward through the storm. Flashes of lightning would reflect off their large conical straw hats and drenched clothing, the rain and darkness melding them into a long serpent-like instrument of the Liberation. There was no talking, only the random slosh and crackle of an army on the move: purposeful, dedicated and lethal.

By one a.m. the C unit was closing into its pre-attack positions. After ten minutes' rest the guides and porters bade the soldiers farewell and withdrew. The soldiers laboriously reassembled into their attack team groupings as they had practiced a dozen times before. Sau dispatched the wire teams to tie into Ba's command post. By two, Sau received confirmation that the entire D group was ready for the final approach march toward Phu Cuong. He awaited the order. Minutes crept by.

The rain was driving down in torrents, springing and bending the slim trees and brush almost to the ground. Sau feared that the water had short-circuited the telephone line, and he cranked the alarm generator again. The line was in working order. Ly Nam, the group planning officer, was at the other end.

"Have patience, Sau," he counseled. "The group commander must be positive that security has not been broken."

"Is there reason to believe that we have been discovered? We have seen no one except our authorized guides and porters for the last three days."

"No, but we have a report that enemy reconnaissance aircraft flew over the area this morning, and the scouts report that the local farmers stayed in their homes all day. They must have sensed something."

"What does Patriot Ba plan to do?"

"I'll call you as soon as we have a decision. In the meantime make sure your patriots remain hidden."

Sau dropped the handset back on its cradle and covered it with the plastic bag. Every move he made seemed to issue the same swishing sound of soaked clothing against soaked foliage. His B unit leaders looked at him questioningly, but he said nothing. They squatted and waited while the storm blew water down upon them, and they worried about their equipment.

At two forty-five Sau checked the line again. Nam advised him to insure the readiness of his soldiers.

Three seventeen. The telephone alarm gave a muffled growl and sparked with the wetness.

"Ly Van Sau here."

"Patriot Sau, the group leader has issued the attack order. Move your C unit forward at once."

"We are on our way!" Sau breathed heavily into the handset. The B unit leaders did not need his order to scramble to their feet and break out of the thicket to rejoin their teams. The lightning caught the dispersing men like a flash camera, seeming to freeze them in awkward postures of flight. Then the darkness closed in and the storm went on. Minutes later the woods came alive with soldiers; mortar shells arched upward toward the black clouds, and recoilless rifles exploded into life. The noise of the storm had been only an overture to the thunderous crash of the attack. Under the umbrella of fire the first two groups of yelling, running, stumbling, scrambling men converged on the disintegrating front gate of the barracks.

# *EIGHT*

"Five tanks! I can't believe it." Colonel Gates was beside himself with incredulousness. "Are you sure about that? A rinky-dink bunch of guerrillas broke into an armored cavalry regimental compound and stole five tanks? You've got to be kidding!"

"No, sir," Paul replied. "Central Corps Headquarters reported the attack and the losses this morning. Besides that, they lost quite a number of men and other vehicles damaged or destroyed. They aren't sure just how bad it is yet. Major Nguyen Van Do left this morning before first light to get back to Bien Hoa."

"Do they know who the bastards were?" Colonel Gates was looking under his cot for his other boot. Paul thought how the colonel would learn to sleep with his boots loosened around his ankles when contact with the enemy was likely.

"No, sir. There were no prisoners. And it wasn't a 'rinky-dink' job. The garrison was apparently taken by complete surprise during the storm, and the results were pretty disastrous."

"Think it was a main force outfit or North Vietnamese, Major?"

"I asked Major Do that before he left; he didn't have much of an answer. But unless he knows something we don't know, I would think it would have had to be main force. It was a professional job."

Colonel Gates had found his boot.

"You had better shake that out, sir," Paul suggested. "Sometimes bugs get in there during the night."

The colonel looked up at Paul to see if he was serious. Seeing that he was, he banged the boots on the floor and peered inside. A little mud fell off. "Tell our pilots we will get on back to camp as soon as they can crank up the birds. I'll give our apologies to our hosts. If we've got a main force unit on the loose in our neck of the woods I don't want to be away from the advance party."

Paul saluted and went out into the hall. There he met his smiling escort of the previous day. The major's admonition *"beaucoups VC"* took on a new meaning this morning. In the last twenty-four hours, Paul realized, he had witnessed a team of VC tax collectors in action and visited an airstrip where the enemy practically ran a scheduled air service to North Vietnam, both with impunity, as though there was no Allied opposition at all. He had also seen a hospital where the enemy treated their sick and wounded, immune from government interference. Now, to top it off, he had just received word of a complete donnybrook at the Phu Cuong garrison where, to add insult to injury, the enemy had broken in and driven off with a whole platoon of tanks. Blazes! Paul thought. Just what the hell is going on here?

But he said *"Bonjour"* to his affable escort. He couldn't think of the French word for pilot so he waved his hands like a flying bird and rolled a series of "r's" through his throat. Fortunately, the Vietnamese was perceptive enough to guess his meaning and proudly led him down the hall to a small mess room where the pilots were making subdued jokes to each other about lousy Vietnamese coffee. They likened it to the foul smelling fish sauce — *nuoc mam* — a staple of the native diet.

Colonel Gates and his staff choppered back to the advance party camp without much talk. Only Colonel Dreier attempted to compete with the clatter of the aircraft in flight, less to convey a coherent thought than to vent steam about what they had seen and heard. Even the regimental commander did not seem disturbed by the pedestrian quality of the exec's language. It was as if his deputy were giving voice to the thoughts of the entire group.

A half dozen officers met the helicopters as they flattened out on their skids. Sergeant Garowski had the engine idling in Paul's jeep in the rear of the group. With a cryptic word of thanks to the pilots, Colonel Gates disappeared into the waiting group of staff officers. Paul saluted his vanishing regimental commander and turned and strode over to his vehicle. The sergeant saluted and gunned the engine. The machine jolted out onto the rough trail with dust billowing up around the wheels.

"Bad news, Major," Garowski said.

"About Phu Cuong? Yeah, we heard," Paul replied. "Any details of the losses — besides a whole goddamed platoon of tanks?"

"Yes, sir, we just received the operational report from Central Corps. I'll show it to you. Of course they claim to have inflicted heavy casualties on the enemy, but that's a crock."

"How do your know?"

"No prisoners, no documents, not even a rifle left behind as a souvenir."

"That bad, huh?"

"Yes, sir. That bad."

Paul spent the day piecing together the scraps of information coming in from both American and Vietnamese sources. Protocol dissuaded him from requesting permission to personally visit the battered garrison. Whatever the incompetence of some ARVN commanders, there simply could not be a flock of American "experts" arriving to critique the action every time a Vietnamese Government unit took it on the nose. "Hell, they've got to do it themselves sometime," was the conventional wisdom. Besides, as

Paul knew, many of the American units arriving in country were pretty green themselves, and it made sense for both the Americans and ARVN to tend to their own business first when somebody blew one.

But intelligence was the major's business; and the first order of business was to find out the identity of the enemy unit or units that had been involved. The reports were vague and contradictory. One estimate of the enemy's strength put the figure at over five thousand. That could include a couple of main force regiments, maybe the better part of a division. That would put the action well up into the big leagues.

What exactly was the evidence? Paul ticked it off in his mind:

One: Total surprise — apparently resulting in complete success, unless the enemy had intended to capture the entire garrison. That wouldn't have made sense, considering the counter-action which combined ARVN and U.S. units could have mounted the next day. Allied forces could have surrounded and recaptured the post in daylight. The enemy could hardly afford to lose its entire assault force. That would represent a one-for-one exchange from his point of view — at best. Nope — the Allies could win that kind of war.

Two: No main force units were known to be within striking distance of the town. However, the surgical precision of the attack would indicate the involvement of a first class organization, well drilled and well led. The total lack of any enemy dead or wounded left in town the next morning was a mark of superb training and discipline. A messy battlefield was the earmark of a sloppy, dispirited outfit.

Three: The enemy force moved with a high degree of security through the province before and after the attack. Air reconnaissance records indicated that a photo mission was scheduled over the area the morning just before the attack. Yet there was no indication of any hostile activity or that anything was amiss.

Paul had received a routine copy of the Vietnamese PI report: "Nothing of military significance noted," the translation read.

Four: Weapons employed included machine guns, 82 mm mortars, and 75 mm recoilless rifles. These are known to be in main force units. Unconfirmed agent reports also have them in the hands of provincials. Inconclusive.

Five: There was no known enemy wireless communication in the area before, during, or after the action. This would indicate that the attack force was not as large as had been reported — probably not larger than a battalion, or a D group, as the VC would call it. A larger organization would have needed mobile communications for coordination. A battalion, or a couple of companies — C units — could have managed it with messengers and perhaps some field wire. Conclusive? Hardly, but a good working hypothesis.

Paul looked down at his paper after he had committed his thoughts to writing. He was tentatively attributing the action to a provincial local force battalion: the Phu Loi D Group, Van Ba commanding.

What did he have in the O.B. files on the Phu Loi Battalion? Precious little. Paul's notes from his conversation with Do were the substance: operational area — Binh Duong Province; previous action — ambush of ARVN regiment at Ben Suc, 40 - 50 friendly casualties, enemy losses unknown; base areas — unknown; code names and letter box numbers — unknown; sources of supply — unknown ... unknown ... unknown ... unknown! Hardly a satisfactory report.

The exec shrugged his shoulders. Colonel Gates read the conclusions with interest and returned the paper to Paul.

"Phu Loi Battalion, eh? Well, send your report to the Field Force chief of staff. General DeWitt may be able to make something of it. There is nothing we can do until the regiment arrives."

Paul tossed the paper on Sergeant Garowski's field desk with just a bit of pride. It meant something, he thought, to have one's analysis sent to higher headquarters. And for all his attempts to be clinical about his business, he was not immune to a little ego trip.

"Colonel Gates wants us to send the report to Field Force Headquarters."

"Yes, sir. I made a carbon copy and put their name on it," Garowski replied confidently.

"O.K., Nostradamus. So you foresee the future. Send it out."

"I already did."

"You already did? What the hell for? You didn't know what we were going to do with it. Someday, Sergeant, you're going to blow it. You've led a charmed life so far. What would you have done if Colonel Gates had found holes in my argument?"

"There aren't any holes, sir. You're dead right."

"You're surer than I am."

"Yes, sir. That's why I sent it out."

The cocky sergeant seemed to have an answer for everything. Paul would have to slow him down.

"I'm going over to Central Corps to see Major Nguyen Van Do. He should have some ideas about this by now. You tend to your knitting, Sergeant, and don't go off dispatching any more reports to higher headquarters without approval. Next thing you know, you'll have your rear end in a sling — or mine, which is worse."

The sergeant would have loved to have followed up on the ambiguity of whose rear end was worse, but he contented himself with a chuckle. "No, sir," he said. "I'll have your driver out of the sack in a minute. He ducked his head to clear the low entrance to the tent. "There's coffee on the burner, Major," he called back from outside.

The Lord doesn't make enough Garowskis for the world, Paul thought as he shook the gummy cream substitute jar over his hot brew. I hope he makes it through this tour all right. And I wonder if there's sugar here some place.

Paul's second visit to the ARVN Central Corps was not much more satisfactory than the first. Do seemed pleased enough to see him, but he was obviously troubled. Paul couldn't tell whether it was the bad show at Phu Cuong on his mind — possibly with some sense of responsibility for having been away from his post at a critical time. Paul made a point to remind him that the aerial photos showed nothing of military significance in the neighborhood the very morning before the attack. Do had ordered the reconnaissance mission himself as part of a program of routine coverage of sensitive areas. How could he feel that he had let anyone down? It certainly wasn't his fault that the storm had prevented him from flying back to Bien Hoa when ordered by the chief of staff. He had taken off as soon as a chopper could fly the next morning.

"Cheer up, Do. We haven't lost the war; just a few lousy tanks. How the VC managed to drive off with them beats the hell out of me, but I'll say this: we'll be gunning for them now. If they want to run a mechanized war, they'll be as road-bound as we are. Don't forget, we have a lot of experience in mechanized warfare — a hell of a lot more than they have. They may have achieved some sort of propaganda victory, but if those vehicles ever stick their noses out of the bush, we'll clean their goddam clocks."

Paul could see that he was not having much effect on his friend, so he let it go at that. "Who do you think was involved on the enemy side, Do? Do you buy my case for the Phu Loi Battalion?

"You may be right, Paul. We have no direct evidence."

"Do you have a final count of friendly losses," Paul asked.

"Yes, it's right here," Do replied, handing him a report sheet in Vietnamese. Before Paul could ask the question, Do went on to explain the columns on men, equipment, and installation facilities. Paul whistled at the figures.

"Turn the paper over. Those are the reports of enemy losses."

"These are greater than the friendly losses!" Paul protested.

"Of course. We can't have them winning the war in the field and on paper, too," Do replied with a wry smile. "You Americans love your statistics, so we're learning to play your game. If you'll do some quick arithmetic, you'll find that the enemy losses are exactly 150 per cent of friendly losses. How would you like some tea?"

A couple of days later the recollection of the conversation with Do offset the excitement that a phone call might have engendered. Paul's report and analysis of the Phu Cuong battle — if it had been a "battle" at all — had been read with great interest, and General DeWitt's office was inquiring whether Paul could be released to join the Field Force staff. The request was extremely flattering on the face of it. It sounded as though someone thought he had a head on his shoulders. On the other hand, it could be just another typical headquarters play to fatten its ranks at the expense of the troop units. Paul couldn't be sure.

But on the positive side, there was an implication of an opportunity to influence some sizable operations in the war, and no less of an implication of an opportunity for promotion. Colonel Gates recognized the implications as clearly as Paul did, and posed no objections to the major's transfer. In fact, he encouraged Paul to take the job.

"We'll manage without you, one way or another," the colonel said. "Never forget that Arlington Cemetery is full of officers who were considered 'indispensable' at one time or another. Maybe you can even help the staff remember that we are real live people out here in the muddy tire tracks and not just machines that can be moved around on a map like checkers."

"Yes, sir." It seemed an inadequate answer, but it was all Paul could think of to say. He mused to himself how often he had thought about opportunities like this coming up during his career. It could be the "big break" which he had heard his West Point classmates talk about so many times, but the anticipation was dulled no little bit by what he had seen of the war in just two short months. Things certainly were going to improve. The regiment would arrive and get cranked up for action, and then we would see the feathers fly. "Charlie" and the *Bo Dai* were riding high right now, but certainly they were riding for a fall.

President Johnson had called for the troops to "nail the coonskin to the wall." Hottcha! That was the way to talk. Paul resolved on the spot to make Van Ba and the Phu Loi Battalion his first order of business — no matter whether Do knew where they came from or who they were. They would be the first to lose their skins if J. Paulding McCandless had anything to say about it.

He was feeling much better when he gathered his men in the evening and told them about his reassignment. He threw in a little of the flavor of Colonel Gates' remarks about the adventure they were all upon. It was good for everyone's morale. So was the talk about fricasseeing the Phu Loi gooks. The beer for Paul's departure party after dark was cooled with ice in Sergeant Garowski's "bath tub." No doubt about it, things were going to improve! The prevailing spirit in the U.S. Army was typified by the slogan, "Gung Ho!" Why should Paul feel any differently?

# NINE

The Field Force headquarters was situated along the principal highway between Bien Hoa and Saigon. Temporary structures of light materials and corrugated metal roofs offered elementary shelter from the elements, but an impressive lawn, plantings, and a couple of flag poles afforded the complex a passable sense of permanence and dignity. The circular drive and flower beds added a note of normalcy and stability in a land which, as Paul noted, cried out for just such influence.

Paul was ambivalent about the appearance of the headquarters. He could understand, but never fully agree with those who deplored the baggage and comforts that the Army brought with it. Air conditioning, portable swimming pools and PX shelves lined with hair spray seemed a bit much, but certainly they were the accouterments of peace rather than war. And the country desperately needed peace — or at least the appearance and structure of peace — if it was ever going to deal with its internal problems. He tended to agree with the American press as it drummed at the theme that this was not a conventional war in which austerity, single minded purpose, and total focus upon destruction of enemy forces in the field would pay off in victory. There were plenty of ribald jokes about combat units "winning the hearts and minds of the people" by grabbing the enemy by the genitals, but there also seemed to be something to be said for contributing visibly to the sense of presence and permanence of Allied strength. Of course Paul would have found the argument more convincing if it weren't for the splendid permanent buildings in Bien Hoa, which had once housed the French headquarters and now accommodated the officers of the ARVN Corps staff. Again Paul found himself struggling to believe that the war effort was on the right track and that it would shortly see better days.

The warm welcome by Brigadier General DeWitt, the chief of staff of the Field Force, gave him no reason to expect the cool, almost hostile, greeting he received shortly thereafter from the man who would be his immediate boss. Any fantasy of meteoric rise to altitudes of influence was quickly drenched by the chilling tone of Colonel Greenwood Dillings, the G-2 (intelligence chief) when they were alone.

"Look, Major whatever-your-name-is, I didn't ask for you to be assigned here. It was the chief of staff's idea — not mine. I'm not sure what I'm supposed to do with you. I don't guess you know much about the corps zone, do you?"

"I'm learning, sir."

"Well, I goddam well hope so. You're going to have to learn a hell of a lot in a short period of time. So keep your ears open. That will be your desk over there. Sergeant Schwartz will introduce you around the staff. Keep out of the way until you know what you're doing. We're busy around here. Any questions?" The colonel's voice seemed louder than necessary.

Questions? Hell yes, I've got questions! Paul wanted to shout back at him. What kind of a chip do you have on your shoulder, you skinny old coot?

The colonel looked like a B-grade movie version of Sherlock Holmes, but without any of the softening attributes of civilization. His scrawny fingers were stained with nicotine, and he hunched his skeletal frame as he talked. Paul guessed that his personal plumbing must have been out of order for some time because he apparently had long since given up any attempt to subdue the noises of excessive gas in his digestive tract. His eyes shone like glass motorcycle reflectors in their cavernous sockets, and bore in on Paul like those of a malevolent beast.

"Just a couple of things, sir," Paul responded quietly. "What's my job?"

"Hell! I don't know. I didn't invite you here. We'll just call you a 'special projects officer.' What else?"

"Where do I sleep, sir?"

"Sergeant Schwartz will take care of that. Anything else?"

"No, sir."

It wasn't a very auspicious beginning. Paul spent the day following Schwartz around the headquarters, meeting the other staff officers and finding where the essential facilities were: the mess hall, the war room, the communications center, the latrine. The latter was a four- holer harboring oil drum halves under a rough bench. The drums would be sprayed with oil each morning and ignited. Enormous black clouds would announce the disposal of each day's waste.

Some of the officers just chuckled when Paul was introduced as the "special projects officer." It obviously meant nothing to anyone. Paul ended his day flat on a cot, staring at the cracked ceiling of an old French barracks, wondering what had happened to him. He had heard about the ruined careers of promising officers who had become stuck in big headquarters or rear-echelon jobs with nothing of importance to do. Good God, he thought, could it happen to me? He was too upset to write to Cicely that night. What was there to tell her anyway?

Events the next morning did little to cheer him up. He leaned against the back wall during a long staff conference while a series of briefers read off reams of statistics having to do with supply levels, troop strengths, construction projects, ammunition consumption — everything Paul could imagine that could have anything to do with the management of a military enterprise on a huge scale. The discussions were couched in the grossest terms: thousands of tons of supply, hundreds of man-days of effort, or thousands of cubic yards of earth moved. It all seemed a little unreal and remote from the business of finding and killing Viet Cong.

The operational briefings were a little more to the point. A snappy looking major in starched jungle fatigues whacked a map in quick staccato fashion with a collapsible pointer while he rattled off the targets of the day's search and destroy missions. He may have had notes, but he didn't use them. Paul thought the officer must have gotten up pretty early to check the orders of a score of different American and Australian battalions and to commit them all to memory. No less impressive was Colonel Dillings' recital of enemy activity of the night before. Rather than pointing to the map, the G-2 described the actions and indicated their locations by giving the six-digit map coordinates the way one might indicate street addresses in his home town. Wow! Paul thought to himself, there is no doubt about the old buzzard knowing his way around.

But Paul had a hard time finding much else to admire about his chief. The man seemed to take some pleasure in being rude to the staff, and it was no less disconcerting to overhear him arguing with the chief of staff about "fancy, hot-shot West Pointers with less than three months in the combat zone who don't know their ass from a hole in the ground."

Maybe Sherman was right, Paul tried to rationalize, "war is hell."

There was little, it seemed, that he could do at the moment but knuckle down and try to make a useful contribution where he could. Patience was not his strong suit, but if he hung on, something might change. Perhaps he might even find a graceful way to get back to the cavalry regiment. Maybe he could get people to look upon his assignment to the headquarters as a "loan" until the full regiment arrived. All sorts of improbable schemes ran through his head.

And there was another thing. It wasn't surprising that a number of the officers on the staff should come from troop units within the Field Force, but it seemed odd that he was the only one to have joined the staff after it had arrived in the theater who hadn't come from one division — the One Hundredth — the "Big Hundred," they called it. Paul had heard rumors about a crazy commanding general, but he had discounted the talk, particularly as people called the exec of his own regiment the same thing. But the presence of so many officers from the "Big Hundred" on the staff was peculiar. Sergeant Schwartz had hinted that at least some of them had been fired from their jobs and "kicked upstairs" to the Field Force staff. Paul wondered how many crazy people there were in responsible positions in the Army. Certainly, the events of the day weren't reassuring. The old joke about there being more horses' asses in the Army than there were horses kept coming back to him.

"Special projects" turned out to be anything Colonel Dillings didn't consider important enough to handle himself. On the G-2's instructions, each evening Schwartz would drop an eight-to-ten-inch stack of new translations of captured documents on Paul's desk. There would be everything from personal letters to hospital sick lists scarfed up in quantity by troop units in their searches of enemy bunkers and tunnels. Paul would sift through them, noting down anything that struck him as having any possible significance. In the beginning it was largely guess work — and he probably made a lot of bad guesses. But after a while some papers began to stand out in the mass as of some intelligence value. He usually finished his work shortly after midnight. Six hours later he would make sure that Colonel Dillings had the essentials in time for the morning briefing for Lieutenant General William Paulding, the Field Force commander. By 0800 each day Paul would find himself at work compiling target folders on suspected enemy base areas for B-52 raids. The details were tedious, but he thought it was educational, and before long the G-2 began to use some of his work as the basis for requesting actual bombing strikes. Dillings invariably described Paul's work as sloppy and inaccurate, but the major noticed he seemed to become more dependent upon it as the days went by. It wasn't too long before the colonel was having Paul stand in for him on some conferences, but never without a stern lecture, with his long, knotted index finger pointed at the major's face and a warning not to "fuck it up."

Afterward Dillings would grill the major on what had happened in a conference and who might have wanted to know what. "Damn you," he would conclude, "if I find out that you gave General Paulding bum dope, I'll have your ass! Understand?"

"Yes, sir" was not the only reply that might occur to Paul, but it was the only one that ever passed his lips.

More often than not, the captured papers included stacks of personal history records of members of the myriads of enemy military and political organizations. Each one might be four or five typewritten pages long. Here was one on Tran Do Hao, age seventeen, laborer, joined the Movement in 1965. Parents were poor farmers. Brothers and sisters were in various menial jobs in the countryside. Tran took part in a raid on the Na Tuc police post in May 1966, earning a letter of good performance. Now Tran was assigned to the C unit at Letter Box Number 100753.

Here was another on Duan Ho Minh, student, age 28. Duan had fought with the Cao Dai sect against the Diem regime in the fifties. His mother, a sister and baby brother had been shot by government soldiers. He, himself, had been wounded twice, once by accident when he was arming grenade fuses, and once during a skirmish with a government combat police patrol. His revolutionary zeal was considered "adequate," but he was less than fully battle ready because he was partially blind in one eye and he no longer had his full strength in his left arm. He was still assigned to the unit at Letter Box Number 104792.

Then there was a list of names of people who had been treated at the "Group 14" medical aid station on November 14, 1965.

Another document was an accounting of rice stores at "Position 6." Still another must have been translated from a torn piece of paper. It indicated that Messenger Tao (remainder of name missing) was to (or maybe had already) pick up two jars of (probably medicine — part of the word missing) at kilometer marker 37 as usual.

Paul passed the papers on to the O.B. section. At his request a young lieutenant kept track of the names, letter box numbers and battles and skirmishes mentioned in the documents. Paul couldn't be sure that the information would prove useful (Colonel Dillings characterized it as "bullshit") but neither could he completely dismiss his fantasy that somehow it might one day turn out to be a key ingredient to cracking an enemy code or some other such dramatic development. Paul consoled himself that no one seemed to have developed any special insight into the enemy's communications or operations, so he pressed ahead with the project, however unremunerative it seemed.

Paul was jolted back to consciousness of his earlier concern with the Phu Loi Battalion when the air liaison officer stood up one morning at the staff briefing and announced that a fighter bomber had knocked out an enemy tank in northern Binh Doung province. Got'cha! Paul thought, That's the first of the batch from Phu Cuong. One down and four to go.

But the details didn't match. The Air Force insisted that the tank was not of US design. Pictures taken after the strike revealed a shape much more closely resembling a Soviet PT-76 amphibious vehicle with its large box-like hull.

"Goddamit, Major," Dillings shouted at Paul, "you've been reading all that captured crap. Why haven't you figured out that the enemy had tanks? Don't tell me that in all that stuff there hasn't been any mention of it."

"No, sir, not a word that I could find."

"Well, now that we have found out from the Air Force about it," the colonel went on sarcastically, "the least you can do is to find out what kind of a goddam tank it was."

"Yes, sir. I'll send up an aerial observer."

The colonel's further commentary on the major's performance was nothing that Paul wanted to remember afterwards. The comments wouldn't improve, he realized two hours later, when the observer's voice came sputtering over the radio saying that he had searched all over the place, but that he could find no evidence of the tank. Paul resolved to go himself.

It took another couple of hours to get another plane – the first one having had to return to its base for some reason or other that was never quite made clear. It was almost 5 p.m. by the time Paul could find the spot where the Air Force claimed to have destroyed the vehicle. Paul ordered the pilot to circle the area while he snapped pictures with a Leica.

The Air Force report seemed basically correct. There was the huge black hole where the bomb had struck. To one side lay what appeared to be the hull of a tank, and beyond that the turret. The only odd thing seemed to be the absence of any track marks in the area. And how come Paul had not run across any mention of a tank in any of the letters he had read? He could only guess that either this was an aberration or that some of the documents were in a code that was so carefully crafted that they seemed to pertain to something else. He had to have a closer look at the objects, so he ordered the pilot to circle lower.

While they descended below 1,500 feet Paul realized that it could well be a trap. The "tank" could be a decoy designed to lure curious observers down within range of hidden machine guns. The plane leveled off at 1,000 feet while Paul studied the surroundings through binoculars. They jiggled and jumped with the vibrations of the aircraft. There were a couple of suspicious looking bushes nearby that might have concealed almost anything. He peered at the "tank" again, trying to steady the glasses.

Goddamit, he grumbled to himself, I just can't make out whether it's a tank or not. The shape seems right, but the size is too small.

It occurred to him again that this was the territory of none other than the friggin' Phu Loi Battalion. They couldn't possibly have a Russian tank! Yet, the wreckage on the ground looked damnably like one. Paul could imagine how word of this was already being flashed back to Washington by the wonderful "Boys in Blue." What the hell did they know about tanks, anyway? They would have loved to have had the enemy loaded to the gills with all sorts of fancy equipment so that they would have something useful to do — rather than flying around over a jungle watching their bombs disappear down through the canopy before exploding, never knowing whether there was a target down there or not. Paul had a healthy respect for the Air Force, but he didn't believe that they were above applying a little bureaucratic leverage when it might suit their purposes.

He had to see what it was. Damn the Phu Loi Battalion; damn the Air Force; and "damn the torpedoes — full speed ahead!" he thought as he ordered the pilot to make a fast dive over the enigmatic rubble below him.

The pilot was no fool, but he was reasonably confident of his own ability to make a difficult target, even down on the deck. "OK, Major, it's your funeral," he called back over the intercom, putting the plane into a steep sliding dive. Paul lost his horizon for a second or two until he realized that the plane was hurtling along at 250 miles per hour with its starboard wing sticking down between the trees. The maneuver brought his stomach up into his mouth. He craned his neck to look up and backward through the top window of the aircraft for just an instant, the instant it took for him to realize that the Air Force had bombed the hell out of a huge shipping crate and knocked a stone cistern, which was just about the size of a light tank turret, askew.

In the same instant Paul realized that he had been suckered into the very trap he had told himself must be there. How stupid could he be? Not more than a hundred yards away a bush fell aside revealing the ugly double barrels of a ZPU antiaircraft machine gun. Two men in black pajamas were spinning the cranks to bring the weapon around onto the aircraft. Other figures in floppy clothes appeared nearby, raising rifles and submachine guns to join in the fun.

"Gun it, Mister!" Paul shouted at the pilot. "We're in a hornet's nest! Go! Go!" Instinctively he tried to push the aircraft forward with his hands and feet.

The little plane strained to get away under full throttle. Bullets bit holes through the wing as it came out of the trees and leveled in response to the pilot's violent jab at the pedals. It took both of his hands on the stick to bring the nose up into the sky and hold it there while the machine raced the hail of shot rising from the ground. A large piece of the tail tore loose and fell earthward, to become a prize of war for the Movement. Paul craned his head again to see if the rest of the tail was going to hold. The damage was serious, but apparently not fatal.

The pilot climbed back to 1,500 feet and leveled off. "Well, Major," he asked quietly, "seen everything you want to see?"

"Hell no!" Paul was furious with himself. "I want to see those bastards clobbered. Get me the artillery fire direction net on the radio. We'll give 'em a dose of their own medicine."

"No, sir, I'm afraid not," the pilot responded laconically. "We haven't got anything that can reach that far. They probably know that and that's why they rigged their little trick up where they did. I understand we've got some pretty big stuff coming into country now, but its all going up north where the main fighting is. Sorry 'bout that."

"Goddam! Goddam!" was all Paul could think of to say for a while. Then he realized that he must sound like Snoopy cursing the Red Baron. Curse you, Van Ba! he thought with a private laugh. You haven't see the last of me yet!

# TEN

Things were going much better than anyone expected. The D group had performed magnificently, and all the patriots knew it. They had assaulted an ARVN armored cavalry regiment in its barracks, destroyed between a third and half of its equipment, and actually driven off with five of the vehicles. When the D group pulled out they left the devastated garrison with the red, yellow and blue banner of the Liberation flying from the flag pole and a totally demoralized town. It had not been practical to take prisoners because they faced a difficult four or five day march over circuitous routes back to their primary base area. Van Ba had issued orders to let many of the government soldiers flee, not so much as a humanitarian act as a psychological one. He knew the shattering effect which the attack would have on the morale of both friendly and enemy sympathizers in the countryside, and he wanted to capitalize on it. He could think of nothing more effective than the flooding of every hamlet in the area with dozens of frightened soldiers who had either fled the scene in disgrace, having thrown their weapons away, or been magnanimously dismissed by a victorious opponent. It would take weeks for the government to pull the garrison back together, and when it had, it would not have a military unit worth mentioning. Instead, the post would be little more than a camp full of scared kids in tattered uniforms, which they would probably want to shed at the first opportunity.

The cost had been somewhat heavier than Ba had hoped, but then the success had also been proportionately larger. Some of the torpedoes, which were supposed to breach the exterior barricades, failed to operate, and precious time was lost in getting into the main compound. The plan had envisioned the garrison pinned down by mortar fire until the leading B units were over or through the walls. But the delay resulted in the mortar crews running out of ammunition before the final assault was ready, and a number of brave patriots fell victim to the fire of some of the more quick thinking government soldiers. At one point there was a murderous fire fight going on, and Ba feared that he might actually have to call off the attack. He could never match the government either in firepower or numbers of men.

The torpedoes were old Chinese models and the weather had been too much for some of them. Ba had heard that the main force units were receiving an improved Russian design, but he knew that it would be a long time before the Phu Loi D Group received them — particularly, as he suspected, with Comrade Hua reporting back to COSVN on how "unreliable" he was.

The "tank" decoy had been conceived as a ploy to throw government and American pursuers off the track. It was hoped that the crate superimposed with a cistern section would resemble one of the stolen vehicles closely enough to divert Allied reconnaissance. The decoy could be moved around at night wherever they wanted it to confuse the enemy. Ba had not counted on the Americans attempting to bomb the structure, but it was reassuring that they had discovered it and took it to be a worthwhile target. Once the bait had been taken, it was simple enough to set up a flak trap to exploit it. Within twenty-four hours two light aircraft had flown over the decoy, and the patriots of C-2 reported that they may have shot one down. Very probably the aircraft was too badly damaged to make it back to its base. The C-2 unit leader had proudly presented Ba with a section of the tail of the plane, inscribed with the names of the gun section members. "Tail feathers" he called it.

Ba ordered the flak trap to be evacuated right away. The disclosure of the ruse, even though the aircraft might not have made it home, meant that stern retribution was sure to follow. While there was no known enemy artillery within range of the site, the American Air Force would probably be back in strength. This time they would bomb the entire area, maybe even with B-52s. The Americans were fabulously wealthy, and they believed in heavy bombardment of targets at the slightest provocation. Ba sighed at the thought of the disproportionate means available to the two sides. His little D group had almost had to cancel an attack because it ran out of mortar ammunition before the enemy post had been overrun. That never happened to the Americans. They had huge piles of munitions all over the country, and had to shoot it up to make room for more. The thought triggered an idea in Ba's mind.

"Patriot Ly Nam!"

The planning officer looked up. "Yes, Patriot Ba?"

"What are you doing?"

"We're discussing what we might be able to do with the tanks we captured. One ran out of petrol, as you know, and had to be abandoned. Of course we removed the machine guns, and we're modifying them for our own use. Unfortunately, we couldn't remove the main gun, but we took most of the ammunition and can use the explosive to make mines. Another tank slid off the trail near Binh Ho, but we still have three in serviceable condition. They're hidden near our regular supply points. We're trying to come up with ideas for their use, assuming COSVN lets us keep them."

"I don't think that's very likely." It was Comrade Hua. "The Liberation will one day mount a great offensive, using the invincible power of the Peoples' main force units in the vanguard.

All of the people of the country will rise as one man to strike the stunning blow against the aggressors! That will be the time for the tanks to roar into the Palace Square in Saigon under the triumphant banners of the masses! Until then, it would be folly to waste such precious assets in cheap side show actions with local guerrillas."

"Comrade Hua," Ba interrupted, "you are entitled to any views you may wish to harbor, but I think it's unlikely that many here would agree that the attack on Phu Cuong was 'a cheap side show action with local guerrillas.' The patriots achieved a magnificent victory, working closely, as you say, with local guerrilla teams. I don't think that denigrates the accomplishment at all. Quite the contrary, I think it shows how well we operate with our brothers and sisters in the countryside. And I think we owe a special note of gratitude to Patriot Ly Nam, here, for his superb planning. Following his recommendations we reached the selected site of battle, won our victory, and returned safely to base. Not long after our return, one of our gallant anti-aircraft A teams probably shot down an enemy reconnaissance plane obviously trying to find us to extract revenge for our attack. I think you would do well to hold your tongue about our planning. You're free to write your complaints to COSVN as you choose, but they're not warmly received here."

"Yes, Comrade Hua," Ly added, "and you might note that no main force or *Bo Dai* unit has ever attacked a government regiment in its garrison and scattered its soldiers to the winds the way the Phu Loi D Group has done. I'm sure Patriot Ba would agree that we will turn over the tanks if we're requested, but in the meantime, we will use the small arms and ammunition in them as we see fit and develop plans for the employment of the vehicles as opportunities present themselves."

Hua was speechless. This attempt at public humiliation of a political officer of the Liberation was tantamount to treason. She turned with a frightful scowl on her simple face and stamped out of the shelter. If there had been a door, she would've slammed it. Ba sighed and turned again to his planning officer.

"I commend your initiative in looking for opportunities to employ the tanks, Patriot Ly, but unfortunately there is considerable truth in what Mme. Hua says. We mustn't lose sight of the larger struggle. I'm sure she'll urge COSVN to take the tanks, and we shouldn't be surprised if they have needs for them. Our drivers aren't very skilled, and we really don't know how to care for the vehicles. Besides, our operations are confined for the most part to this province, and sooner or later the enemy will spot one of them. I understand the Americans have devices which can detect warm objects in the darkness. It would be very difficult for us to employ the tanks effectively under the circumstances.

"We've won both military and psychological victories in their capture. We don't want to become so intoxicated with our success that we lose our sense of perspective."

Ly was disappointed, but he knew his commander was right. He wished that the political officer didn't have to be right, too. "Yes, Patriot Ba," he replied.

"Now, Nam," Ba went on, using his aide's given name, "I want you to consider the enormous stores of ammunition that the enemy has at his disposal. One of the larger depots is being constructed close by here, at Long Binh. That's not in our official operating area, but there's no other local force unit capable of attacking it. We haven't heard recently what's being stocked there; and I believe it's time we took a fresh look. If the enemy's security measures are not too tight we ought to be able to find out what they have. With that information we may wish to consider some type of operation against it, or to destroy it. Artillery ammunition can always be fashioned into mines or torpedoes, and certainly we can make fuses for torpedoes at least as reliable as the Chinese models."

"I understand, Patriot Ba. I hope you will reconsider the possibility of using the tanks if we find a lot of light tank ammunition."

"I haven't closed my mind to anything," Ba replied, "but I think that would be an unlikely development. The depot is primarily an American ammunition stockpile, and, as far as I know, the Americans have only medium tanks. I wouldn't expect them to have 75 mm ammunition for our vehicles."

"Very well, Patriot Ba," Ly conceded, "we'll begin preliminary reconnaissance work right away. We should understand the size of the problem within a week, if that's soon enough."

"That's fine, Nam," Ba replied. "I have no particular schedule in mind."

Ly Nam poured himself into his work. Much as he might have liked to, he couldn't avoid briefing Hua. An operation against an American installation outside Phu Loi Province would have to be checked out with COSVN sooner or later, so he felt that he might as well bring her into it before the planning went very far. Hua took no particular issue with the concept; but, true to form, she reserved judgment pending further development of the details as the situation clarified.

But the situation was slow to clarify. The reconnaissance B unit leader enlisted the assistance of a number of young school girls to make the initial approach in the area of the target. He provided them with bottled Cokes and imitation orange drinks to peddle to soldiers they met, but he deliberately left vague the object of his interest.

The girls were enthusiastic about their mission. They were curious about these tall men with long noses, and either black or white skin, who had moved into their village area, and they found it very easy to sell the dozen or so bottles of soft drinks that they carried in their baskets suspended from shoulder yokes. The B unit leader had to repeat to the girls several times that he was more interested in developing a sketch of the area than he was in making a profit from the sales. They had some trouble taking him very seriously at first, but after a while, and a few mild scoldings, they came to understand that they had to pace off distances between buildings and fences and other features accurately in order to receive a fresh supply of drinks.

An awkward moment arose one morning when one of the girls lost count of her paces between a guard shack and a radio antenna base. She turned and began to retrace her steps. Corporal Ronnie Farring of St. Paul, Minnesota, called to her from the guard shack. "Hey, Momma-san! What are you doing?"

The girl was terrified. She barely saved her shoulder yoke from slipping off her small frame. A bottle of Coke fell out of one of the baskets and pitched to the ground, bursting its cap and spraying the warm, sticky fluid over her ankles with an exuberant hiss. She stopped in her tracks and showed every sign of having a nervous breakdown on the spot.

Farring strode over to her, half expecting the girl to offer him a bottle. His doubts about her were increased as she just stood there trembling. "Have you got an ID card, Momma-San?" he asked.

She muttered something unintelligible and tears began to well up in her eyes. Farring was not sure what to do about her. She was probably perfectly innocent — at least he wanted to think so. But her actions had been peculiar. Farring had heard how the VC would sometimes construct a complete plan of a camp through the use of just such innocent appearing infiltrators. He was greatly relieved when another of the girls ran over with an American quarter coin, indicating that that was what the girl had been looking for, and that the other had just found it. Farring waved them both off in the direction of the highway. They seemed glad to go. Ronnie Farring did not bother to report the incident. He didn't want the paperwork, and besides, if the brass was seriously worried about enemy infiltrators disguised as school girls, they would make sure that civilians were kept out of the base area by erecting more fences, posting more guards, or something. Anyway, he had sent them packing.

The reconnaissance B unit leader was disturbed by the girls' report. It could mean that the Americans had become suspicious of the girls and would sense the imminence of an attack on the base complex. He reported the matter to Ly Nam.

"We'll have to proceed very carefully," Ba told his staff. "The base area is so large, and the presence of villagers around it so common that I don't believe that there is great cause for alarm.

However, in view of this, we had better scale down our plans for no more than a hit-and-run raid. Nam, as useful as a quantity of American ammunition may be to us, I think you should proceed on the basis of a limited concept of infiltration by a few sappers to destroy as much of the ammunition as possible and to escape as quickly as they can."

"Very good, Patriot Ba."

But it was not "very good" in Hua's view. She saw great danger in the venture and argued strongly for suspension or postponement of the operation. "This is insane!" she exclaimed. "One of our scouts is detained by an American soldier, asked for identification, and only manages to escape by the quick wits of a comrade. And you want to proceed with planning for the operation as though nothing had happened! If all of our patriots had that little concern for security, the entire Movement would have collapsed long ago. COSVN would never approve.

"You must remember, this is not a routine operation against the government lackeys of the imperialists. This is an attack on an American base camp outside our area of responsibility, and may have far-reaching consequences. You may be an educated physician, Comrade Ba, but you don't know much about political matters. What you do here can affect the entire outcome of the struggle.

"You think only of your small tactical problems and of the marginal advantage of stealing a few artillery shells. Let me inform you that if that were all we ever accomplished we would deserve to lose. The struggle is not the simple sum of all the petty victories achieved on that scale. We need much bigger victories, victories on a huge scale — and not just on the battlefield. They must be won in the hearts and minds of all peace loving peoples of the earth. We must win the psychological and political battles in Saigon, and in Paris, and, yes, in Washington D.C. Any battle fought by the Phu Loi D Group, if it does not contribute to the much greater battle, is a waste of time and a criminal waste of the lives of our valiant patriots."

"Comrade Hua," Ba answered slowly, picking his words with care. "I believe I have told you on previous occasions that you are free to convey your views on any subject to COSVN. And of course we appreciate your candor with us here. If COSVN agrees with you in this case, we'll have no alternative but to abide by the decision. However, in the meanwhile, I believe that we should go ahead with our planning on the assumption that there is much to be gained from such an operation — both militarily and politically, if you like. It's true that risks are involved, but I believe we must assess the risks objectively and deal with them in perspective."

He turned to his planning officer. "Patriot Ly Nam, proceed as I have indicated. I want to hold another full discussion of the plans next Wednesday. Let me know by then particularly how sappers might be able to get to the ammunition dump and what equipment they'll need.

"Now, please excuse me, Patriots. I have other things to do."

Ba returned to the shelter that had been his home since his election to lead the D group. The dugout was Spartan in its furnishings, but even at that he felt that he had accumulated more baggage than he needed — the wooden wardrobe, for instance, with two unused suits hanging inside. Every day while the group was in the base area he would hang the suits in a pool of sunshine for an hour or two until the sky would darken for a downpour. Even with that precaution, the mildew seemed to be spreading. He consoled himself with assurances that when the war was over, and he would return to the Pasteur Institute, his father would rejoice with him and buy him a new suit of modern cut, for him to resume his practice.

It was a breach of security to sun the clothes, and he took great pains to ensure that only a single narrow shaft of light penetrating the forest canopy reached the suits on their hangers. The spotlight was always so small that he would have to move the clothing every twenty minutes or so. But he knew that it was a losing battle with the fungus anyway.

He sat down at his field desk to draft a message to his special source. The paper had to be very small to be easily concealed, and the text had to appear innocuous in case it were intercepted. With great care he selected words from the pages of a translated edition of Hemingway's *For Whom the Bell Tolls*. On the face of it the note appeared to be a shopping list which any village shopkeeper might carry with him to a market town. Decoded, it read:

> URGENTLY NEED PLAN OF US ARMY BASE
> AT LONG BINH STOP INFORMATION ON
> AMMUNITION DUMP SECURITY MEASURES
> AND TROOP UNIT DISPOSITIONS CRITICAL
> STOP INDICATE YOUR ABILITY TO MEET
> REQUIREMENTS BY OCTOBER FIRST STOP
> BA

In another part of the camp Hua was completing a different kind of message, this one to be addressed to COSVN and marked "ESPECIALLY URGENT AND SENSITIVE." Hua began with a brief resume of her previous messages, summarizing her misgivings about the political reliability and zeal of the Phu Loi D Group leadership. And it wasn't just the commander who disturbed her; it was the whole D group staff and at least a half-dozen of the C and B unit leaders. They all seemed to be under Ba's spell — more interested in tactical efficiency than in correct ideological orientation.

Hua pointed out that while this fundamental weakness might bring numerous short-term victories, it was bound to lead to the downfall of the organization in the long run. The Phu Loi D Group was in serious danger of slipping out of control. Most of its leaders may support the unification of the country, but it was not apparent that all of these saw it coming about under Northern leadership. It would be a grave mistake, she argued, to allow this organization to become accustomed to developing its own philosophy. It could become more of a threat to the Revolution than its servant.

Hua cautioned her readers not to be so entranced with the group's successes that they could not see its dangerous tendencies. If the problem wasn't rectified very soon, the bad seed could grow into a stout tree, floating revisionist seed pods on the winds. The poison would spread. The bourgeois attitudes of the Ba clique would settle among the masses, and all would be lost. Her conclusions:

(1) Ba must be reeducated, preferably in North Vietnam. If that is not possible, it should be at a long distance from Phu Loi.

(2) The request for permission to attack the American ammunition dump at Long Binh must be disapproved.

(3) All offensive operations of the organization should be suspended until the leader undergoes reeducation.

Hua would have liked to have recommended Ba's relief from command, but she knew that that was not possible. Part of the new socialist democracy rested upon the exercise of the popular will of the soldiers. She could not expect COSVN to openly violate its own rules except in extraordinary circumstances. "Reeducation" was the most convenient solution.

# ELEVEN

The Phu Cuong debacle weighed heavily on the entire staff. Since his return from his visit to the battered garrison General Vo had closeted himself with the chief of staff. No one had seen either of them for two days, except the chief's aide, who took food into the commander's office. Sergeant Minh overheard a couple of orderlies joking that the two generals must have gone on an opium drunk together.

Even with some fudging of the casualty figures reported by the garrison and gross inflation of those claimed as having been inflicted upon the enemy, Saigon was bound to react. Do guessed that the post commander would be fired, perhaps the Fifth Division commander as well. There were bound to be official inquiries into the incident, and no one would come through the ordeal "smelling like a rose," as the Americans would say. He suspected that if a shadow were to fall over the corps commander no one on the staff would be safe — least of all himself. As the principal intelligence officer, he was supposed to know what the enemy was up to, and he would make a perfect scapegoat. He hoped General Vo's relation by marriage to the prime minister would insulate him and the staff from a witch hunt orchestrated from Saigon.

He need not have been quite so concerned. Even as the ARVN headquarters was trying to cover up its vulnerabilities, the Americans were charging ahead with proposals for new operations all around the country. There was always the hope that the Americans would be so preoccupied with getting on to the next operation that they would have little time to worry very much about how the last one went. War was an intense business as far as the Americans were concerned, and they seemed always to want to get right along with things at a snappy tempo. As long as they didn't pay too much attention to the Phu Cuong blunder, which could affect their aid deliveries, Saigon might be able to let many things pass with a few wrist slaps to lower ranking officers.

But there was a price to pay for American inattention to foul-ups. In their hurry to move along, they would occasionally come up with awkward suggestions, such as the initiation of a joint US-ARVN field operation on a Friday or Saturday. The suggestion would always have to be treated as though it were perfectly sensible at first. Excuses might be found later for postponing the action to a more convenient time. Do understood the strange American penchant for wanting to do things right away. He tried on several occasions to explain it to the chief, General Don, but cultural hang-ups often have to be felt rather than discussed.

"You have to consider," he would argue, "that the Americans are like automobile mechanics. When they find something 'wrong' they want to 'fix' it. That's the way they go about fighting a war. They think they are over here because our country is in danger of falling to communist inspired subversion. They see themselves helping to 'fix' a 'problem.' With their high technology and their preoccupation for getting to the heart of the matter and 'fixing' it, they think the war will be over in a year or two. Just as we might wish that they could be more understanding of the real situation, we need to be somewhat more understanding of their culture. Don't forget, they haven't fought a long war since their own revolution, almost two hundred years ago, and they don't remember much what that was like.

"At times, when I was at their staff college, I would hear their British and Canadian colleagues remind them of the parties and balls their revolutionary leaders would hold in the late 1770's on their ancestral estates, and of the extended vacations which some of their commanders would take. It was apparently all there in their own historical literature, but they don't read much history. They were always amazed when they thought about it. The real trouble the Americans have is with their own words 'peace' and 'war.' They think the terms are very different — like an electric light switch that has only two, mutually exclusive positions: 'off' and 'on.' They don't understand that 'peace' can be the simple absence of hostilities for the time being, or that 'war' is just a word which may apply only to the most intense periods of struggle.

"As a rule, Americans don't make good classical strategists. They tend to think of strategy as limited to the dramatic sweeps of armies and navies around the globe. They don't understand the many dimensions of the art. They have never really understood Clauzewitz, with his dictum that war is a continuation of politics by other means. And as far as I can tell, they have never even heard of Sun Tzu.

"On the other hand, with experience in two world wars they have a good grasp of the spatial dimension. They are steeped in Mahan, Mckinder and the Italian airpower enthusiast, Duhet. They understand the need for bases and supply lines. They like to quote Napoleon's remark that 'an army marches on its stomach.' Just look at the colossal bases they are building here, at Cam Ranh Bay, and around Saigon. Their investment in either one of those areas would be enough to run the *Bo Dai* for a year. One of their most popular leaders in their Civil War used to say that victory goes to the one who can get to the critical spot 'firstest with the mostest.' Well, they like to go in fast — with a lot.

"But don't expect them to grasp the ideological or cultural dimensions of strategy. Peoples' wars are a mystery to them. They have no idea of what war by attrition is. They want and expect quick, sharp decisions, like the Battle of Cannae, where Hannibal gobbled up a Roman army. They think Napoleon's victory at Austerlitz is the model of all combat. War is something to be fought and won, preferably in the blue environments: in the air, or at sea; but if needs be, on the ground, as long as it is decisive and clean. Just as long as the loser can be expected to show up at the peace ceremony and turn in his sword like a gentleman. Their model for an unsuccessful, but correct military leader is Lee at Appomattox Court House, not Mao-Tse-Tung on the Long March. 'Losers' are not supposed to come back and fight another day. They are supposed to quit, like the Germans and Japanese in 1945 — after which they turn to the business of business, which is where they are more comfortable, anyway.

"Of course, this cultural characteristic manifests itself in American politics, too. Just as President Eisenhower wrote about in his *Crusade in Europe*, Americans tend to think about their political issues in terms of 'right' and 'wrong.' We must be careful that they don't become impatient with lack of quick success in their military expedition here, and jump to a conclusion that it is not in their best interest to pursue it. It would be very easy for one of their ambitious politicians to seize upon the war as a 'wrong' effort and to rise to power on the shoulders of a disillusioned populace. The culture makes them mercurial by our standards, and potentially quick to give up if things don't go their way. We saw it to some extent in Korea, and we could see it again here."

It was tempting for Do to point out how quickly the Americans had tired of President Diem and had encouraged the clique that overthrew him. After that, they had criticized one Vietnamese leader after another, leading to one coup after another, and less and less stability in the country. The major had no faith in any of the men who had climbed to power in Saigon. He thought they were a self-serving lot who were exploiting the situation, but any comment in that direction would have been impolite — perhaps even risky, and might not usefully illustrate his point about the Americans, anyway.

In time the Phu Cuong furor would subside. The Saigon press would be permitted to report only that a battle had been fought there. It was to be emphasized that the enemy had been beaten off, and the official estimates of enemy losses were to be printed in bold type. The government losses, characterized as "moderate" were withheld for "security" reasons. Not until two weeks later would the changes of command of the garrison and of the Fifth Division be announced, and then only as routine matters. Saigon would be satisfied with the heads of only the commanders most immediately involved. The inquiry would not touch the corps headquarters.

Sergeant Minh had rehearsed his story about the aerial photographs and about his attempts to alert somebody about the indications he had had of enemy presence near the town the day before the attack. When he reported his concern to Major Do upon his return the next morning from Xuan Loc, the major evidenced keen interest in it. He had immediately called the chief of staff as he had been bidden, but the aide, Colonel Tuy, had put him off. Whatever it was that the chief had in mind the previous day had been overtaken by the attack. The major had a talk with General Don later on, taking the photos with him, but that was all Minh knew about it. Curiously, when he returned to his office Do didn't even want to keep the photos. He instructed the sergeant to dispose of them in the routine way, along with the negatives.

It was a disappointment to the sergeant to have the matter evaporate so rapidly. He thought he had done a creditable job, first in guessing the significance of the photos, and second in attempting to call attention to the possibility of an attack. He had been frustrated by the balky communications system and by the lukewarm interest of the chief's aide. Also, the inexperience of the operations sergeant had worked against him. Minh would have liked to have confided his thoughts to the major, but he could sense that it was a cold issue. No one was interested. Once it had become clear that the headquarters would not figure in the inquiry, the matter was dead. The photos, together with their negatives, were to be burned.

Minh sat at his small desk fingering the stiff photo prints. What a waste, he thought, to destroy them. At least they would be good for reference, in case anyone ever wanted to know what changes there had been in the area. The PI section wasn't interested. They had said they had plenty of coverage of the area. But he couldn't bring himself to stuff the plates into his burn bag. Instead, he dropped them into a lower drawer, rationalizing that he "would take care of it tomorrow." He gathered up the half-full burn bag and carried it out the rear of the building.

In the courtyard stood a blackened sheet metal incinerator where the waste classified papers were routinely destroyed each afternoon. A good fire was already going in the pit while a corporal from the logistics office shoveled in bundles of papers.

"How are you, Minh?" the corporal asked.

"Thanks Duan, well enough," he replied. "What's new?" He unstrapped the bag.

"Well, we're pretty busy right now. I don't know what happened in that scrap over at Phu Cuong, but it seems that we've just about got to rebuild the whole regiment — tanks, APCs, the works."

"Yeah, they really had a fight. According to Major Do the VC took a lot of casualties, too. But that's just crap. Don't you believe it."

"Well, it must have been pretty bad to judge by our requisitions for replacement hardware. God knows when we'll be able to re-equip them." Minh knew that the reference to a divinity was no indication of the corporal's faith. He doubted whether Duan smelled a joss stick more than once a year — and then only by accident.

"Hey, Minh," the corporal went on, "did you hear that Garowski's back?"

"Who?" Minh countered, with only half interest as he began dumping his papers into the fire.

"You know, the American sergeant, Garowski. He was a PI instructor down in Saigon a couple of years ago. And one of the world's greatest scroungers. If we could scrape up stuff the way he does, we could re-equip the whole Phu Cuong garrison by next week. He was in to see me last week, trying to swap concertina barbed wire for plywood. I suspect he stole the wire, because he seemed awfully anxious to get rid of it. The son-of-a-bitch must be the King of the Junk Yards."

"Oh, yeah," Minh perked up. "I remember him. He's a fine fellow. I suppose he taught me what little I know about PI." The thought of his own ability to interpret aerial photographs stung him again. He was still upset over the total blank he had drawn from the officers when he had accurately called an enemy attack. It wasn't like Major Do to ignore his work. The major had spent a lot of time in America and had picked up enough American democratic ways to make him courteous to enlisted men.

The fire was roaring. The men had to step back to avoid the heat. Minh picked up an iron hoe and began stirring the papers; sometimes incompletely burned papers could be sucked up the smoke stack and blown out the top if the operator wasn't careful.

"I'll be damned," Minh exclaimed. "Where is Garowski assigned now?"

"He's right near here. He's in an MI outfit with the advance party of that new American cavalry regiment moving in near Long Binh."

"No kidding? I'll have to look him up."

"Well, if you're going to, you'll have to be pretty quick about it," the corporal replied. "He says they're going to move out to Xuan Loc pretty soon."

"All right. Maybe I can get over there this weekend. I'm off duty Saturday afternoon. Did he tell you how you can get in touch with him?"

"Don't worry about that, Minh. He's coming back tomorrow to pick up the plywood. I'll tell him you're here."

"All right, that will be great. I wonder how his Vietnamese is now. He used to say it was just like Polish, only backward. I never could figure out what he meant by that. It'll be good to see him, anyway. Much more time in this country, and we'll have to give him citizenship."

Back at his desk, Sergeant Minh found himself smiling inwardly in anticipation of seeing an old friend. Then he thought of the photographs in his desk drawer and how interested Garowski might be to see them. He could burn them afterward. The major had said nothing about showing them to others, and if no one else appreciated his ability to interpret aerial photos, maybe his former tutor would.

# *TWELVE*

Paul sifted through the documents again. They were mostly uninformative personal letters addressed to various letter box numbers that he could associate only with a few villages. But of those with return addresses, almost half of them indicated a single number, 100753. More interesting still, of all the letters bearing that number and with addresses he could interpret, all were destined for recipients living in Binh Duong or Bien Hoa Province. Paul liked to joke that he never was much of a mathematician during his cadet days at West Point, but since switching over to military intelligence, he had to learn to put two and two together. A pattern gradually seeped into his consciousness. Could it be that these were letters from members of a provincial organization to their families? Could it be that 100753 was his *bete noire* — the Phu Loi Battalion? Of course! Van Ba commanding!

Paul was exultant. Maybe he hadn't found the Rosetta Stone or climbed Mt. Everest. Maybe there wouldn't be a sharp new turn in the course of the war, but what fun it was to find something new to think about. He wondered if, with a thousand little mini-victories like that in the middle of the night, battles could be won, and Good could triumph over Evil. Any sense of proportion about his discovery was drowned in his elation over the event. Only when he looked around the dingy room for someone to share his joy with did he realize that it was almost 0200.

The duty sergeant had gone out for coffee. Only two clerks sat by the bank of hot lines connecting the headquarters with its subordinate units. Besides the "Big Hundred" there were trunk lines to the other division, to Paul's former unit, the 10th Cavalry, to the Special Forces headquarters, and to the Australian Brigade. The silence of the "TOC," as the tactical operations center was commonly known, was broken by the dull rattle of the Aussie line where a bored telephone operator decided to make his hourly line check a few minutes early.

Paul realized that the clerks would have little comprehension of any reference to as esoteric a matter as letter box numbers, but he could not contain his exuberance. The clerks listened politely as he jubilantly gave them an exaggerated version of the importance of his find.

"Yes, sir," Paul found himself saying. "The keys to our success in this war may lie right here in our laps among these captured documents. All we have to do is to study them and figure out what they mean."

Paul realized how hollow the boast must have sounded the minute he said it. The clerks exchanged questioning glances when the major appeared to have finished. One managed a sympathetic "Yes, sir" in reply. The other just hunched his shoulders and turned back to this chore of recording the hasty notes of the previous day's phone calls in the permanent log.

Paul would've liked to have said something more convincing, but he couldn't quite frame it in his mind. He decided to save his Big News for a more appreciative audience in the morning. Maybe it wasn't the equivalent of cracking the Japanese code in the Pacific in World War II, but certainly the Field Force commander would grasp its significance, and another feather would be added to Paul's professional hat. The unresponsiveness of the clerks had taken some of the wind out of his sails, but he walked out of the TOC into the cloudless night with a sense of self-justification and accomplishment, nonetheless. He continued to nurture his satisfaction as he stripped for bed in the tiny trailer which had become his home.

For all its Spartan atmosphere, the trailer was a bit of a status symbol. General DeWitt had insisted that the "key officers" be quartered closer to the operations center. Paul's inclusion among those designated for the flimsy trailer accommodations was a point of considerable importance and pride to him. Besides, there was one very practical advantage. The trailer had a built-in john which was connected to a water tank, and Paul henceforth could discharge at least one daily function without resort to the public privy.

Sharing the trailer with Paul was Roger Hutton, an artillery major who might have passed for a textbook model of the ideal general staff officer in any army: quiet, dedicated, diligent, self-effacing. The fellow was friendly enough, but Paul never quite felt at ease with him. He was just too damn modest. He seldom initiated a conversation beyond a cheerful enough "Hi." And he never said a word about himself. He seemed absorbed in his work in the operations section, and monumentally disinterested in anything remotely related to the enhancement of his career. It was not until some time later that Paul learned that Hutton couldn't expect to have much of a career in the service. Like many others, he had been relieved "for cause" from his previous assignment as operations officer of an artillery battalion in the 100th Division.

The incident precipitating the relief was a serious one, but Paul couldn't understand the consequences. One of the batteries in the battalion had mistakenly fired a few rounds into an area occupied by American troops, resulting in a number of casualties. The division commander, apparently given to somewhat volatile reactions, had immediately demanded the relief of both the battalion and battery commanders and the battalion operations officer. As it happened, Hutton wasn't even present at the time of the accident, but as the principal training officer of the organization he had derivative responsibility. Paul thought the relief was harsh, but that was the way matters seemed to go in the Big 100. Hutton's career was a casualty of the war. He would serve the rest of his tour in Vietnam and then probably resign his commission.

Breakfast the next morning was a ritual which had to be endured as Paul contemplated the poignancy of the moment when he would break his news to Colonel Dillings. Maybe the old buzzard would show him a little more respect after this. All sorts of blatantly silly, self-inflating fantasies bubbled up in his mind as he choked down a plate of too-thick pancakes and sulfurous molasses. He tried to guess which elements of the meal had been reconstituted from dried ingredients.

Colonel Dillings wasn't in the TOC when Paul returned. Instead there was a curt note scrawled by Sergeant Schwartz on the back of an official message form. It indicated that the chief of staff wanted to see him as soon as he came in. Paul was irritated that some other matter had apparently come up which, if of any importance, would tend to diffuse the glory of his discovery. Instead of being the focal point of the morning briefing, it might become just another point of interest on a list of several. At worst it could become lost in the background noise of tiresome matters that the staff managers and logisticians were always bringing up and which seemed to absorb too much of the commander's attention. Damn it, anyway. He called the chief's office and was told to come right over. In five minutes he was standing at attention in front of the general's desk with his right hand stiffly and briefly touching his eyebrow. General DeWitt returned the salute and motioned him to a chair.

"Major, we may be in trouble," DeWitt began. Paul noted the use of the plural. That could mean anything. Either the matter didn't directly concern him — or it did, and the general was being polite. Colonel Dillings sat in a chair to Paul's left, but said nothing. Paul sensed that the colonel had been discussing something of importance with the chief before his arrival. This was not the way Paul wanted the day to begin. He waited for the general to continue.

"MACV wants to know why we refused an urgent request by the 100th Division for B-52 support."

"When was that, sir?" Paul countered.

"The day before yesterday."

Paul's mind raced through a jumble of snap-shot images of what he had been doing for the last forty-eight hours. He glanced at Dillings for any sign which might give him a clue as to what the general was talking about. The black beady eyes astride the hawk-like beak serving the colonel as a nose were aimed straight at him. Paul sensed that the "problem" was indeed his concern, and that there was about to be laid before him a question which could carry the most serious implications.

Thus far unstated, but certainly hanging in the air before him, was the possibility of there having occurred some serious encounter with the enemy of which he was unaware. A flash in his mind brought a picture of an embattled element of the "Big Hundred," sorely pressed by overwhelming enemy strength, calling for assistance from higher headquarters. Paul had handled dozens of messages from the units in the past two days concerning planned, on-going or past "Arc Light" strikes, as the B-52 raids were called.

Good God, he thought in the instant. Did I overlook something? Did I skim too quickly over a key paragraph in a critical message? Did one of my men fail to get a message to me? Every question suggested some sort of goof on his part, or on the part of a member of his team in the TOC — which amounted to the same thing in the unwritten code governing military responsibilities.

All his visions of grandeur through penetrating analysis of the enemy letter box system were drowned in terrifying images of American soldiers falling before the sweep of a massive Viet Cong attack. Here is the valiant unit commander standing like Custer at Little Big Horn as the vicious foe crushes his unsupported troops.

Frantic calls, converted at the "Big Hundred" command post to an emergency message to Major J. Paulding McCandless, targeting officer (in addition to other duties) at the Central Field Force headquarters, bring no response. Men die, a battle is lost because Major McCandless is overworked, too tired, too confused to check every goddam square inch of his ill-defined responsibilities every minute of every day.

"I'll have to check the message register, sir. I don't believe we ever received any such request from the 100th Division." That was all he could think of to say. It was obvious that both the chief of staff and the G-2 were skeptical of his reply.

"MACV is sending General Barnes up here by helicopter this morning to begin the investigation," the chief went on. "He will arrive at about 0945 hours. You would be well advised, Major, to have your records ready for his inspection at that time. When he is finished here you will go with him up to 'Big Hundred Forward' where you should be prepared to explain your actions to the division commander. I am sure you realize the gravity of the division commander's complaint."

Good Lord, Paul thought, they're sending the inspector general to investigate an allegation of misbehavior on my part in the face of the enemy. The words "court martial" never crossed the chief's lips, but they didn't have to to bring Paul's entire world down upon him like a five ton truck load of iron pipe.

Back in the TOC Paul searched frantically through the log of messages for the past week for all requests from the 100th Division for "Arc Light" support. Five had been received. One had been canceled by the Air Force because of bad weather, one had been flown with six aircraft. What the devil had happened to the other three?

Paul sent Sergeant Schwartz over to the communications bunker to check the tapes used for the encoding and transmission of messages. Then he placed calls to the intelligence section at the 100th Division command post and to the "Arc Light" operations center in Saigon. The temperamental voice communications links imposed their usual maddening delays, static, and unintelligible garbles of important words. The best he could get in the next hour were promises from each end to make checks of the message records. He consoled himself that at least he had found no evidence that he had received and ignored any request for support. He summarized his findings for General Barnes upon his arrival. In another hour, Paul had confirmed from the Field Force communications center and from "Arc Light" Operations that two more of the requests had been denied by Saigon because of more urgent needs for the bombers further north. One request remained unexplained.

General Barnes was cool and businesslike in his verification of Paul's reports. When he was satisfied that he had seen everything the major had to offer, he stopped into the chief's office to provide him with an interim report. It couldn't be conclusive, but Paul was relieved that the general gave no impression of conducting a witch hunt. The major's shaky hopes for vindication began to beat more steadily.

He climbed into the helicopter behind the I.G.. Not until they were airborne did he remember that he had pulled together what might prove to be important information concerning the Phu Loi Battalion. It was quite apparent now that, for better or worse, it would have to keep. He hoped that the delay would make no difference, but he couldn't be sure. One could never tell when some small piece of information would be just what someone else was looking for. His thoughts leapfrogged ahead to the impending confrontation with the irate commander of one of the Army's most famous combat divisions.

A nauseous feeling of dread, took hold of him. Could it happen now, today, that he would be suddenly transformed from his self image as a promising young staff officer into another casualty around the headquarters, like Roger Hutton? So many former officers of the division seemed to lead zombie-like existences, waiting for their time to expire until they could slip quietly home and out of the Army. Was it a professional frontal lobotomy, or simple castration? He pulled out his handkerchief and wiped his face and the palms of his hands.

The "Big Hundred" was the quintessential American killing machine. Its exploits were legendary in two world wars. It had formed the nucleus of the build-up of forces in Europe in the 1950s to face down Stalin's juggernaut at the outset of the Cold War. Now it was here in Vietnam to lead the way to a similar military solution to the Southeast Asian problem. And it was led by the high priest of attrition warfare, a man who understood the power of the press and of tangible "measures of effectiveness" upon the uninitiated to the amorphous business of war.

The count of cold enemy bodies produced by the enormous firepower of the division would generate statistics back in the Pentagon that like-minded "whiz-kids" from Harvard Business School would cite as evidence of progress in the conflict. The trick, according to this school, was to "kill Cong" faster than they could breed or march down the Ho Chi Minh trail. This struck Paul as a lot like the German naval strategy of the great wars: sink Allied ships faster than they could be launched. Supposedly, England would starve to death and the Allied armies collapse. He often wondered whether anyone noticed how unsuccessful the Germans had been with it, or whether there was a coherent lesson to be drawn.

The chopper settled in on the "Big Hundred Forward" landing pad. Mechanically Paul followed the general out of the aircraft and into a waiting jeep.

Greetings were exchanged between the general and an officer escort from the division staff, but Paul could understand nothing over the clattering helicopter blades. Alert M.P. "shotgun riders" brandished machine guns in the rear of each vehicle.

The division C.P. had been set up in an abandoned French plantation villa. The thick stucco walls were covered with heavy growth, and the interior reminded Paul of a New York City slum dwelling. The graffiti was missing, but the chipped plaster, the broken steps and the debris strewn across the floors had all the hallmarks of modern America at its worst.

One wing of the building had been swept clean, and maps and charts covered the walls. Various calibers of electrical cables snaked through the rooms, and the incessant scream of generators and chatter of radio monitors established a high ambient noise level. Men seemed to be working in random groups around folding tables and packing boxes throughout this section of the building. Others lay stretched out on cots under mosquito netting. Some of the broken louvered shutters had been closed in an attempt to reduce the glare of the midday sun. The escort officer led the visitors through the center hall to the dining room. They had arrived just in time for lunch.

Paul had eaten in general officers' field messes before, but he was surprised at the comforts which the "Big Hundred" provided its leaders and official guests. The extended table was set with white cloths and napkins and adorned with fresh flowers, plucked from the underbrush outside. Each place was set with silver plated utensils and stem glassware for wine. Descriptions of Napoleon's field mess in the late Eighteenth Century popped into Paul's mind as he stepped forward in response to the escort officer's introduction to the division commander.

Paul took a deep breath, saluted, and shook the outstretched hand. In a second it was over. He had met the man who might bring charges against him for dereliction of duty in combat. There was no trace of recognition on the general's face; instead, he seemed to be playing the genial host, smiling and inquiring about the visitors' flight. Paul wondered when the mask would fall and he would turn to the business of the trip.

The mess steward's call to the officers to be seated precluded further speculation on Paul's part. Besides General Barnes and himself there were two newspaper reporters, a congressman and a young relative of the congressman who was introduced as his "staff assistant." An assistant division commander, the principal members of the division staff and a brigade commander composed the rest of the company. Paul was glad to see a good friend, Lieutenant Colonel Frank Roberts, the division intelligence officer, in the group. He hoped he would be seated next to him at the table, and was sorely disappointed when he found his place card on the opposite wing of the "U" shaped arrangement. He badly needed a few moments of confidential discussion with Frank before he faced the general's complaint.

The conversation around the table broke into unrelated exchanges on multiple topics. Paul sat opposite the congressman's "staff assistant" who hardly opened his head. The peace symbol hanging around the youth's neck, suspended from a string of beads, indicated that they probably wouldn't have had much in common to talk about anyway. Besides, Paul was preoccupied with his thoughts, and would have had to strain to make himself interesting to a civilian who obviously hadn't the slightest idea of what was going on. He answered questions from the division staff officers seated around him, but otherwise endured the meal as part of the price for the responsibilities he carried. Why don't they get this over with? he kept asking himself. It's almost like a play. I'm sitting here as a guest, but everyone knows I'm about to be skewered. It is positively grotesque.

At length the dishes were cleared and the division commander turned to Barnes with a remarkably casual inquiry about the nature of his visit to the division. The question obviously took the I.G. by surprise.

"General," the visitor replied, "we are here in connection with an investigation of which I am sure you are aware. Perhaps we can go into it in private at your convenience this afternoon."

"Nonsense," the division commander countered. Paul guessed that the general was playing to the presence of the reporters and the congressman.

"We have no secrets here. Now, if you are looking into the matter of the refusal of higher headquarters to provide the combat troops with support when they needed it the other day, let's lay it out on the table."

Paul saw the reporters dig into their pockets for note pads. Hot stuff. An investigation! Paul cringed at the thought of what must be taking form on those pads. My God, he imagined, I'm going to be hanged in every AP and UP subscribing newspaper in the United States tomorrow morning.

The I.G. quickly summarized the facts as he knew them, mercifully, without any references to Paul by name. The division commander interrupted when Barnes mentioned the as-yet-unexplained fifth message calling for B-52 bombardment.

"That must have been it, General. Here we are, trying to fight a war, surrounded by ever-increasing numbers of infiltrators from North Vietnam, and those fat cats back at Field Force don't even bother to read their mail.

"I'll tell you right now, I won't stand for it. This division has the highest enemy body count of any unit in the country. We have run more aggressive search-and-destroy operations, taken more prisoners, won more medals and sustained fewer casualties than any other division in the war. Now, lets make it crystal clear: we can't fight the whole war all by ourselves. We need air and artillery support, and above all we need the B-52's. I'll guarantee you, General, give us those bombers and we'll clear out this whole wretched jungle. You tell them that back in Saigon."

The reporters were scribbling away on their note pads.

"And you boys tell them that back in the States," he continued, with what must have been intended as a jovial slap on the back of one of the reporters.

"You tell them that the 'Big Hundred' is over here carrying the brunt of this war, just as it has in every war in this century. Gentlemen, you are here at the forward command post of the greatest fighting machine the world has ever known. When you get home you can tell your friends and families that you have seen the cutting edge of American power in the Far East. Never forget it. Your children, and your children's children, will want to hear about it."

Paul was aghast at the color and hyperbole of the division commander's speech. He glanced at the others to see what impression it was having on them. The congressman was smiling and mumbling "hear, hear" after every few lines. The staff officers sat impassive. They must have heard it before. Only the congressman's "staff assistant" seemed to disapprove. He stared at the crumbs on the table in front of him and fumbled with his coffee spoon.

General Barnes brought the discussion back on track with assurances that MACV Headquarters was well acquainted with the accomplishments of the 100th Division and was dedicated to making sure that all of the combat units received all the support they required. Then he zeroed in on the specific complaint of the division commander.

"Can you provide for us, General, a record of your request for 'Arc Light' support the day before yesterday, which was not acknowledged by the Field Force staff?"

"Of course, we can," the commander replied. Then turning to his intelligence officer: "Frank, get the record of that special request we put in on the Ho Bo Woods."

"Which one was that, sir?" Roberts asked.

"You know, the one the G-3 suggested on the high ground, on the north side of the area where the First of the Forty-Second got that small arms fire the other day."

"No, sir," Roberts replied. "I talked to him later about that and we agreed that our information didn't justify a request for B-52's. There couldn't have been much more in there than a few local guerrillas — if there was anyone at all. We never put in the request."

Paul could have hugged him. His spirits soared. Frank Roberts, my dear boy, he thought to himself, you are solid gold! He wished he could have reached over and shaken his hand right there.

"OK," the division commander said, "mystery solved. I'm glad to hear that Field Force isn't taking our requests lightly. We only put in requests when we really need them. I hope you will keep that in mind back there in Saigon."

The anticlimax of the episode left Paul exhausted. He showed only polite interest that evening when Sergeant Schwartz showed him the correct record of 100th Division "Arc Light" requests. There had been only four after all. If he had not been so drained he might have taken a vindictive pleasure in the dressing down the Field Force commander administered to the 100th Division Commander for having gone over his head with a bogus complaint to MACV Headquarters. Paul was slightly embarrassed to find himself standing in front of the Field Force commander as the senior general chastised the junior over a secure phone, describing his behavior as "one hell of a way to run a railroad." Paul's sense of relief smothered any recollection that evening of letter box numbers, the matter which he had anticipated would be his big concern of the day.

It was almost midnight by the time he flopped down upon his bunk. He thumped his boots on the foot rail of the iron cot and stretched and folded his arms behind his head. The cot was barely as long as he was tall, so he had either to rest his feet on the rail or to stick them underneath and let them hang out over the end. The dirt on his boots obliged him to keep his feet on top of the rail. He stared at the juncture of the trailer wall and the ceiling and let his thoughts wander back over the day. He had come through the crisis professionally unscathed, but he felt no elation over that, only fatigue. He half expected to doze off fully dressed as he often did, but the sleep that he would have welcomed didn't come. Too much had happened and too many thoughts kept sweeping through his mind.

Cicely's letters had become somewhat less frequent, and each seemed a little shorter and more generalized than the one before. He wondered if they were drifting apart. When she had written at any length it was either about some family business or to assume a slightly whining tone about how long he had been away. She seemed capable of coping with her day-to-day responsibilities, but she also seemed ready to associate small problems with "stupid Army policies" and to question whether he wanted to stay in the service when he returned home.

"Haven't you done enough?" she would ask. "What else do they want from us?" She would compare the sacrifices which she and the children were having to make with the more normal lives the neighbors seemed to enjoy. She clearly felt that she was being left out of life, and she hated the patronizing tones that her friends assumed when they inquired about how she was getting along.

"No one understands what you are fighting for over there," she wrote, "and I'm sick of trying to explain it." Sometimes she would enclose a clipping from the editorial page of *The Washington Post* or some report of an incident somewhere in Vietnam that would suggest that the war effort was either immoral or futile (or both). Paul had tried to rebut some of the articles, but after a while he just let them go. Their bias and unfairness bugged him, but often they concerned something of which he had no first-hand knowledge, anyway, and couldn't directly contradict. His instincts inclined him to reject most of the stories out of hand. He saw the war as a legitimate effort by the United States, to aid an ally in repelling an invasion by a ruthless communist aggressor, which would probably not be satisfied with overrunning the southern part of the country. Paul could not help but believe that Hanoi would eventually turn upon its non-communist neighbors and seek to enslave the entire population of the Indo-Chinese peninsula.

It bothered Paul more that Cicely would read these things and send them to him than what they had to say. He had been short with her in some of his replies, and he hated the thin wall of disagreement which seemed to be growing up between them. He would have liked to have written her a long letter spelling all of his thoughts, but he didn't have it in him. He would go another night without writing.

# *THIRTEEN*

Garowski seemed to recall Minh from among the sea of faces he had had as PI pupils in Saigon. Even if he didn't, he was glad to pick up another contact on the ARVN side for trading purposes. The conversation hadn't proceeded very far before he was asking about the availability of paint, photographic developer and carbon tetrachloride. Minh guessed that these were just random items on his current "want list" and not necessarily interrelated. Duan hadn't overbilled the American as the "world's greatest scrounger."

Somewhat delicately at first, Minh brought up the subject of the Phu Cuong photos. Garowski's Vietnamese was rusty, and Minh found he had to speak slowly and to stick with generic terms for the most part.

"What would you think of it, Sergeant Garowski, if we had aerial photos of the area around Phu Cuong, but we couldn't find any people in the fields?" he asked.

"Not much," Garowski answered, "they could have been taken on a market day. There are any number of reasons — wait a minute," he caught himself. "Phu Cuong, that's where you had the big scrap the other day, isn't it? And lost a whole platoon of tanks? Yes, I heard about it. That sort of thing gets around."

Minh was not pleased that the American seemed disposed to rub in the defeat of the ARVN garrison. He almost wished he hadn't brought it up. He did his best to defend his countrymen by quoting as many of the official enemy casualty figures as he could recall. Those he couldn't remember he made up. His mind raced. Why not? Someone else invented the official figures, anyway. What difference does it make who composes them? They have no relevance to fact; the important thing is that people — particularly foreigners — should have respect for the Vietnamese Army. Minh wasn't about to let Garowski get away with snide comments injurious to his sense of national pride. Garowski may know a lot about technical matters, but I don't have to concede any sort of superiority to a foreigner — particularly an American.

Garowski understood the signals well enough to wish that he could have rephrased his remark. He shifted the focus.

"Look, Minh, if you have coverage of the Phu Cuong area before the attack showing the fields deserted, it's not unlikely that the villagers knew that the enemy was in the neighborhood and decided to get out of sight. You know that as well as I do."

"Yes, I do," Minh replied. He felt better hearing the American support his own assessment. "Now, what would you say if I told you that I couldn't interest any of the officers on our staff in the photos?"

Garowski checked himself as he almost replied that the officers were stupid. It was OK to talk about the stupidity of officers in general, he supposed, but Minh was talking about Vietnamese officers. Garowski understood the local culture well enough to know that treachery was not as loathsome a trait as stupidity. One was elective, the other a mark of inferiority. He picked up the obvious lead.

"Could it be, Minh, that the officers simply didn't want to know about the photos?" He paused, thinking about it, then went on. "But if that were so, why would anyone have ordered them taken in the first place? What do you make of it yourself?"

Minh avoided the trap. He wasn't going to be the first to suggest that one of his officers may have ordered the pictures for some other, possibly criminal, purpose. If anyone was going to raise that question, it had to be an American, not Minh. It was risky enough for him to entertain the thought of passing the photos on to the Americans rather than destroying them as he had been instructed. Garowski sensed the ARVN sergeant's dilemma.

"You think that one of your superiors may be a VC agent. Am I right? You think he may have ordered the reconnaissance for enemy use, rather than government use. You think that something prevented him from getting the pictures to the enemy at the last minute. Is that it? Then, after the attack, no one wanted to see them. You're even guessing that a number of officers on the staff may be disloyal, right? Maybe they were in collusion. Maybe that's why no one seemed interested after the fact.

"Am I close?"

Minh didn't reply. The American had stated his vague uneasiness in stark terms. Much too stark for Minh's liking. He was confused about his experience and didn't really know what he wanted to do. Above all, he wanted to keep his job, and he began to feel very sorry that he had said anything at all about it. He should've burned the photos, as Major Nuguyen Van Do had told him to do.

Garowski pressed him. "Look, Minh, maybe you'd better let me see the photos myself. We have some new equipment we can put on them which may help us to tell what the real story is. Maybe there's another explanation that would clear up the whole thing. Where are they?"

Minh tried to think of some reason for refusing the question, but his mind couldn't work fast enough. His thought process seemed almost numbed by the enormity of Garowski's guesses about the officers on the corps staff. He fumbled for a moment and then reached into his drawer and picked up the packet.

"Let me have them back by tomorrow. I've got to burn them in front of a witness," Minh said.

The security procedures for the headquarters were clear enough. They had been drafted by an American counterintelligence specialist, but in practice were lax enough to be of no particular inconvenience to anyone. Rarely did Minh worry about having a witness present for the destruction of classified documents. But this was different. He wanted to make sure that he had someone there to swear that he had, indeed, followed the major's instructions to send the photographs up in smoke. The risk of retribution from an irate staff chief over any hint of personal disloyalty by a sergeant was too great a burden to carry, particularly if somehow the chief himself was to fall under suspicion of a more serious kind of disloyalty. Under the present regime, official suspicion of espionage was tantamount to a death sentence. And whatever his part, Minh could see no good coming out of it for him. While he might win some points by fingering disloyal elements in high places, no one would want him around the staff after that. Who could trust him? How could anyone be sure that he wasn't pursuing another self-appointed counterspy investigation. Disloyalty to a superior may not officially carry a death sentence, but it was not an accusation which many NCOs had survived in this war. If a tribunal could not find a capital offense, administrative reassignment of the defendant to an infantry regiment often accomplished the same purpose.

Garowski grasped the problem. He had served long enough in this part of the world to be sensitive to the fundamentals. His respect for the sergeant soared as he received the packet in his hands and stuffed it into his bag. Minh was clearly an exceptional man.

They aren't all "slopes," Garowski thought. This man is risking his job — maybe even his life. I wish they had more like him. I wish we had more like him.

He shook the Vietnamese' hand and gave him a pat on the shoulder, half in reassurance, half in admiration for what he was doing. Then he left. Minh stepped out behind the headquarters building, inhaling deeply. He hoped he would be able to concentrate on his regular duties until he got the photographs back in his hands.

Minh could not have known about the small ambush party staked out on Highway 3 waiting for the first American or Vietnamese government vehicle to come along. He might have given Garowski a general warning about small enemy reconnaissance patrols and terrorist squads in the neighborhood, but he had been preoccupied with the ramifications of letting the Phu Cuong photographs out of his hands. He didn't think to say anything about the redesignation that morning of Route 3 from "green" to "amber." The American Field Force headquarters would be routinely notified in the afternoon dispatch, and someone in the TOC would call the units. The Tenth Armored Cavalry Regiment would duly note it on the S-2 situation map and caution everyone traveling on the ground to avoid the highway.

The claymore detonated with a deafening crash. People along the highway turned to see an almost impenetrable cloud of dirty white smoke blocking the road. It was much too thick for anyone to see the four small black-clad figures dashing out onto the highway to where the American jeep had been passing just seconds before. The figures paid little attention to the wreckage of the machine; they didn't even bother to check whether any of the occupants of the vehicle had survived the explosion. They seized the weapons and ammunition, and would have taken the radio and power pack, but they were too badly damaged to make it worthwhile.

One of the looters noticed a canvass dispatch case wedged under a scorched strip of padding that had once served as the rear seat. He pulled it free and looped the strap over his shoulder. The smoke cleared just enough for the still numbed witnesses to relate to police half an hour later that perhaps a half-dozen V.C. had taken part.

A search of the woods on both sides of the road revealed four shallow fox holes that the assassins may have dug the night before, and a pair of twisted wires leading from one of the holes to the stump of a tree where the mine had been attached. It also revealed a half-completed letter on a small sheet of note paper. One of the assailants had apparently begun to write a message to his family just as the target vehicle had arrived and had dropped it in the press of the moment.

The police notified the ARVN district headquarters, and a young American lieutenant, fresh on the job from the Infantry School at Fort Benning, immediately called the base hospital for a "dust off" — emergency helicopter. Unable to make anything of the incomplete letter, the police forwarded it to Saigon, where it joined the stream of enemy documents which provided the most authoritative insight into the insurgent movement. Unconcerned clerks would shuffle it from one pile of papers to another, spill tea on it, drop it momentarily on the floor, but eventually — perhaps a week later — it would be translated into English and copies would be forwarded to the Americans. The Vietnamese knew that the Americans placed great faith in these odd bits from the battlefield, particularly when they carried letter box numbers as this one did at the top.

The "dust off" chopper had picked up the three bodies lying among the wreckage within minutes of receiving the call. Medics fed fluids into the veins of the one form that still showed signs of life and urged the pilot to speed up the return flight to the hospital. There was an outside chance that the man might survive.

A doctor and two orderlies met the aircraft at the landing pad. The doctor made a hurried check of each of the three forms strapped to stretchers, confirming what the air crew had reported by radio. Two were "KIA," one "WIA," but immediate life-support care was required. The orderlies lifted the wounded man's stretcher onto a dolly and sped their burden through the swinging doors of the emergency wing.

The interior of the receiving room showed the same dull earth tones as the outside of the structure, but a pool of light in the center set the neat rows of instruments glistening like treasure. In seconds a silent team of figures closed around the dirty form on the litter, cutting the jungle fatigues away, and beginning the long, unsure process of restoration of life. Some fed oxygen and fluids into the unconscious body as others probed the multiple wounds for the shards which had ripped their way through the uniform and into the flesh and bone. An orderly copied the information stamped on the soldier's dog tags, and fastened a label around his wrist. The next four hours were crammed with a series of x-rays, probes, operations and bone-setting applications of plaster for the unresisting body. The surgeons marveled at the scars from previous wounds which encircled the torso and two of the limbs. The object of their attention would have more scars to count if he ever regained consciousness. At length the body became another in the almost motionless row of white forms in a dingy extension of the sausage-like links of Quonset huts that made up the hospital.

A matronly nurse in jungle fatigues received the identifying data and long list of afflictions which would require attention in the months to come. While most of the patient's face might eventually be reconstructed, and he might someday learn to walk again, he had lost one arm at the shoulder and was probably blinded for life.

Late in the afternoon, the hospital administrative officer telephoned the TOC to report the day's casualties. No names were given because no one in the operations center would have known what to do with anything as personal as a soldier's name. Casualties were Arabic numerals, statistics — not people. They were transcribed with grease pencils onto large stiff-backed charts covered with clear acetate for display at morning briefings at headquarters throughout the country, and probably in Hawaii and Washington, D.C., as well. Friendly losses were shown in blue, enemy losses — the "body count" — were shown in red, and were usually some favorable multiple of the friendly losses.

No one was quite sure how the term "body count" got started. The conventional wisdom had it that there had been great emphasis in the early years of the war, before American troops became directly involved, upon insuring accurate reporting of casualties. ARVN reports were notoriously inaccurate, so American advisors with ARVN units in the field were encouraged to conduct precise counts of the actual enemy bodies found lying around after an engagement. They also had been asked to provide their own estimates of losses on each side; but the "body count" was supposed to somehow anchor the estimates to what was verifiable.

No one could be sure of this. It was the sort of thing that grew up in the soldier lore of the war. Only generals served involuntary tours in the country longer than a year, so the institutional memory was short. If, indeed, the double reporting ever existed, it no longer had relevance, but the "body count" lived on for no practical purpose that anyone understood.

The clerk in the TOC taking the hospital's report filled the data in on a mimeographed form.

"What were the enemy losses?" he asked mechanically, poising his pencil over the appropriate space on the form.

"We don't know," the administrative officer replied. Of course he never knew. It was pointless to ask. All he knew were the numbers of burned and broken American kids brought in on trucks and helicopters day after day. He could calculate about how many of them would likely survive and how many would not. He also knew how many were brought in for nervous breakdowns, heart attacks, peptic ulcers and the host of diseases which would strike an army of North American natives in an unfamiliar corner of the Asian continent. The clerk noted simply, "enemy losses unknown."

One evening the TOC duty officer, in a cynical mood, noting a similar entry, chided the clerk, "What the hell do you mean 'enemy losses unknown?' There's bound to have been at least one poor bastard who stubbed his toe in the get-away."

Statistics were important. Some said they were the lifeblood of the war. The more sardonic pointed out that if anyone expected the U.S. Government to send men, money and materiel westward there had to be a counterflow of favorable statistics eastward. It was not just a political matter. It was a manifestation of Newtonian law — for every action there must be an equal and opposite reaction. The bureaucratic engines of war at the upper levels of the Pentagon required a daily ration of statistics, ratios and quantification of the unquantifiable to maintain their momentum. And the Army in the field tuned its reports to the harmonics demanded by the statistics keepers. Sergeant Stanislaw Garowski and his companions, like it or not, donated their broken bodies to the stream of alphanumerics feeding the huge, salivating maw of the statistical god in Washington.

# *FOURTEEN*

Paul basked in the momentary credit he received at the morning briefing for his letter box analysis. General Paulding seized upon it as the kind of insight he was looking for, and directed the G-2 to make sure the information was passed up the line to MACV as quickly as possible. He pointed out, to Paul's delight, that with continued dogged pursuit of inside information of enemy units there was a real chance of running them to the ground. He told Paul, in front of the staff, to stick with it, to identify every member of the unit, and to be alert for changes of the numbers.

"I want to know everything there is to be known about every last enemy unit, in the corps zone. I want to know who — by name — is running the show. Where do they come from? Where do their families live? Who are their friends?

"Paul, I want you to put a couple more of your people on this, if you can. Don't let this outfit slip through your fingers. Find out where their base areas are and feed the information to the G-3. Do you understand what I want?"

Paul cringed at the cracked "yes, sir" that came out of his mouth. He cleared his throat and said it again. It sounded better the second time, but he felt silly for having to repeat himself. Fortunately, no one laughed. Paul was proud of his work, but the public acclaim by the Field Force commander was more than he was prepared to deal with. He was glad when the briefing was over and he had only to acknowledge a congratulatory wink from one of his friends and a handshake from the chief of staff on his way out of the briefing room.

The greatest benefit of the incident seemed to be a warming trend between himself and Colonel Dillings. The old codger began to show some interest in his assistant's views; Paul rejoiced at the change. He wrote home to Cicely that the new climate reminded him of the relationship between a senior professor and an eager young pupil. She might understand that, and maybe it would cheer her up. The crusty G-2 was a fountainhead of knowledge on the doctrine, organization and operations of the enemy. He had read widely on the history and culture of the country, and Paul reveled in the depths of the debates they had as each man probed the reaches of the other's feelings and understanding of the struggle. Paul realized how much he had missed in the last months in not having a knowledgeable respondent with whom to thrust and parry ideas. He felt a new excitement which he could not express to anyone else. He wished that Cicely could grasp the sense of adventure and accomplishment that enveloped him, but her now only occasional letters reflected little interest in what he tried to tell her.

The tempo of activity in the Intelligence Section picked up in the next weeks. Most of the officers attributed it to the initiation of planning for a major offensive. Paul ascribed at least some of it to his new relationship with the G-2. Now they were a team. He was sure of that. The totality of their product was becoming much more than the simple sum of their efforts.

Paul was very much caught up in the bustle and activity bubbling up around the staff. Ever since the initial planning conference at which the commander had personally emphasized the necessity for seizing the initiative, an exciting sense of purpose and urgency seemed to bring the officers closer together. Maybe this was to be the first round of a whole new approach to the war.

The scheme was as grandiose as the code name: Giant City. Thousands of troops would take part. The public affairs spokesman had little difficulty finding analogies among the great maneuvers of World War II to stimulate the pens of the increasing numbers of reporters coming up from Saigon and circling the headquarters. Publication of anything related to the operation was embargoed until "D" Day, but the media was free to tank up on background material, pending the opening gun. It was slightly flattering to any staff officer to be buttonholed by a member of the press and asked for his opinion of the plan, but as the days went by some of the officers began to express doubts about the carnival atmosphere that seemed to be developing. Dillings suggested to the chief of staff that he attempt to cool the climate a bit. General DeWitt said he would see what could be done, but as reporters continued to arrive and even a couple of congressmen showed up, Dillings told Paul that he thought that the pressure from above was probably more than the chief could deal with. There was little that anyone could do, other than to go on about his business as best he could in a goldfish bowl. Dillings had insisted on very tight security for the operation in the beginning, but as time went on it became increasingly likely that a leak would develop.

A key element of the security plan had been to avoid informing the ARVN corps for as long as possible. Political considerations made combined Australian and ARVN participation highly desirable, but everyone had long since assumed that the ARVN headquarters had been penetrated by the Viet Cong. The Aussies, of course, as part of the Field Force, were in on the planning from the start. The challenge had been to cook up a cover story for the Vietnamese ally which would serve both to explain the activity in the headquarters to curious ARVN liaison officials and to encourage them to enhance the readiness of their forces in the area for action on short notice. It fell to Paul to put together as convincing a story as possible and to feed it to his counterpart on the ARVN staff.

"Do," Paul began after his friend had made himself comfortable in the small G-2 wing off the operations building, "we're developing a number of contingency plans for dealing with the increasing threat of the *Bo Dai* in the corps zone. When we have settled on something worth talking about, of course, the Field Force commander will want to discuss it with your boss, General Vo."

"Of course," Do echoed mechanically.

"We have been very concerned," Paul went on, "with the increasing numbers of Northerners taking over the insurgent movement."

"Of course," Do repeated.

"Take that prisoner I told you about the other day. He had been on the Ho Chi Minh Trail for over three months. The doctors diagnosed his problems, besides the bullet hole our patrol put in his leg, as a fine combination of beri-beri, dysentery, malaria, and some sort of jungle rot. He's a mess, but he gave us a great deal of information on the formation of an entire North Vietnamese division right here in the corps zone." Paul was warming to his story.

"Do, we have got to be ready to deal with this new threat on an instant's notice. We are increasing the readiness of all our units for reacting to a sudden attack on a larger scale than ever before; and, of course, we believe that General Vo would be well advised to do the same."

Do listened impassively as Paul went ahead with his approved — and rehearsed — explanation for the increased American planning activity. The story was supposed to give an impression of prudent precautions taken in the face of an increasing threat. Hopefully it sounded sensible enough to mask the offensive plans, but Paul could get no hint of how much of it his friend was swallowing. He would've welcomed a few challenging questions, but Do just sat there, smoking his Parliament and nodding his head.

This was a little disconcerting — Paul had always known Do as a bouncy, ebullient, Americanized character, more interested in jazz than in anything serious. It wasn't that he seemed to have reversed himself. Obviously he still liked American cigarettes; it was just that now he seemed to be so much more Vietnamese. Paul supposed that he just hadn't seen his friend in an official role before.

Paul tried another tack. He pointed out some of the more obvious preparations going on in the American compounds in the zone. He thought perhaps he could add credibility without necessarily compromising the operation. He cited new statistics on ammunition stockpiles as examples of the seriousness with which the Americans considered the situation. That seemed to spark an interest in his friend.

"Will you have to substantially increase the size of your stores here in Long Binh?" Do asked.

"Yes, I suppose so," Paul responded.

"Then you'll probably have to expand the size of the ammunition dump. That'll mean clearing out another large section of the jungle to accommodate the munitions, won't it? Will that be any time soon?"

Paul didn't know. He hadn't really thought about it. He was half pleased that Do had shown an interest in part of his story, and half perplexed that his visitor seemed to lock onto a minor detail rather than on to the principal thesis of increased North Vietnamese presence. For the first time since they'd known each other — maybe three years — Paul had a chilling thought that perhaps he didn't understand Do as well as he had supposed. He shrugged the question off with a superficial joke about being an intelligence officer, not a logistician. His reply seemed to dull the shine in the Vietnamese' eyes. Paul hoped he hadn't given offense.

When Do had gone Paul reported to Dillings and related the conversation. He omitted mention of his personal misgivings, feeling a little embarrassed about having developed an ostensibly close personal relationship with a man whom he might not understand quite as well as he thought. To himself, he had made much of the value of having a close friend on the ARVN side, and it was awkward having to face up to a suspicion that his friend might not be as close and open with him as he had assumed. Such an admission might only have provoked another lecture from the G-2 on security and on not allowing friendships to interfere with business. It was even more awkward for Paul to realize that he, himself, had deliberately invited his friend to visit him so that he could give him a misleading story — and one which was probably as transparent as glass to a sophisticated observer like Do, anyway.

Damn it, he thought. Political historians could write about the incongruity of interests of different nations, but it made Paul feel cheap to have attempted to deceive his friend. Damn it.

* * *

Over the next few days the Vietnamese liaison officers made polite inquiries about the American activity, but at no point was there any hint that the story of defensive preparations was not accepted at face value. The American logistical advisors at the ARVN corps headquarters reported that the idea of similar preparations by the Vietnamese had apparently caught on because they were receiving requests for additional stocks of ammunition and petrol. There was some prospect that the ARVN forces would, indeed, be in at least passable shape to take part in an offensive with their American counterparts. A senior staff officer in Saigon insisted that it was essential from a political point of view that the ARVN "tag along," even if all they did was steal the farmers' chickens.

Paul thought the comment was a little more cutting than was warranted. There was no doubt that ARVN was a mixed bag. The Phu Cuong incident was a case in point at the lower end of the qualitative spectrum. But on other occasions most of the officers recognized that ARVN company and battalion-sized units had shown valor and competence which would've been welcome in any army. Paul believed the conventional wisdom around the headquarters that, given time and sufficient American backing, ARVN could shape up into a tough, battleworthy force. The *sine qua non*, of course, was a more stable, if authoritarian, regime in Saigon. The South Koreans had managed it while fighting for their lives a decade earlier. Why couldn't it happen here?

The planning moved ahead. The stated objective was the destruction of all enemy main force units in the CTZ (corps tactical zone) and the capture or destruction of COSVN Headquarters. Paul had read about great victories and how they had changed history, but somehow here, in the everyday world where people goofed or had diarrhea, or sometimes just didn't give a damn and were just putting in their time until they could get out of there, great victories seemed a little remote. Besides, Paul was a little uneasy that maybe the planners didn't quite understand what they were going after. He was very much afraid that he might have given them the impression that COSVN was some sort of super underground fortress, like Hitler's "Wolf's Lair" in East Prussia. There certainly was no evidence to support that. More likely, it was a totality of dozens of different elements in little base areas spread out through the jungle, over perhaps as much as a hundred square miles. Paul wasn't sure that even he would recognize a COSVN office if he saw one. It might be a farmer's shack; perhaps a tunnel complex. Whatever, it probably looked like everything else in the lousy country: dusty, moldy and shopworn. He hoped that the operation wouldn't be judged unsuccessful if it failed to locate a secret Pentagon out in the bamboo some place.

The "destruction of enemy main force units" was no less problematical. American units had usually avoided going after enemy forces in their base areas because of the risk of casualties to booby traps and ambush and of the probability of enemy escape through exfiltration, anyway. Giant City envisioned Allied forces forming a huge encirclement, perhaps fifty miles wide and seventy-five miles long. At best it could go down in history as another Tannenburg or Stalingrad. At least the public affairs officers thought so.

But there were some awkward aspects which Paul thought the planners tended to overlook. First, the series of tiny bases which was being developed for artillery positioning along both flanks of the operational area was bound to alert the enemy to the likelihood of an offensive. Second, little provision seemed to be written into the plan for dealing with possible enemy responses. The scheme appeared designed for rigid execution of juggernaut tactics, expected to so overwhelm the enemy that there was no necessity for alternative maneuvering. Everything Paul knew about VC doctrine led him to expect rapid dissolution of the enemy units until they could slip out of danger and coagulate again. They would want to return to the offensive on their own terms. It wasn't their way to stand and fight an advancing foe. Third, Paul noticed a propensity among the planners to gear the timing of the operation to the seizure of designated terrain objectives and the crossing of phase lines.

How material are these conventional control measures when the stated purpose of the operation is the destruction of the enemy? Paul wanted to ask. How can you count on the enemy being where you want him to be according to your schedule?

The questions were so basic that Paul shied from raising then in their bald simplicity. After all, it was the generals' business to give direction to the prosecution of the war, and there seemed to be plenty of generals in on the planning for Giant City. Paul wanted to dismiss his misgivings as the inner voice of inexperience, but on more than one occasion he had heard Dillings arguing with the G-3 about many of the same points.

And still another thing bothered him. This was to be a sweep of the region aimed at the enemy main force. This was supposed to be Big War — brigade against regiment. But what about the provincial units? What about the local guerrillas? So what if the Good Guys were able to inflict a major defeat on the Bad Guys' main force? What then? Dillings had often said that it was really the local political structure, built up over the years and firmly rooted in village life, that exerted control over the countryside. The political structure was firmly backed by the local guerrillas and by the provincials. What if the main forces did disappear for a while? What would be gained? Paul could only think of partial answers to his own questions, and he wasn't satisfied with any of them. The G-3 would say that the locals and provincials were ARVN's responsibility. Paul worried that the Phu Loi gang and others, perhaps like it, were out of ARVN's league.

He chuckled as he thought about a suggestion one of his younger officers had raised with him a few days before.

"Major," Captain Daniels had said, "you've become nationally famous as the inventor of names for hunks of real estate around here." And it was true that *Time* magazine had quoted Paul when he referred to the border area between Vietnam and Cambodia as the "Fish Hook." It looked like one on the map. "You should have called it 'The Pits'," the captain argued.

Paul's imagination provided him no insight into that. "How so?" he had countered.

"Look, sir. Whenever one of our units gets into a real scrap with a main force outfit, we clobber them, right?"

"Yes, that's right," Paul admitted.

"Well, as soon as they get clobbered they head for the border to get away, right?"

"Yes, because they know we can't follow them into Cambodia. So what?"

"Well, don't you see? That area is just like the pits at the 'Indy 500.' They can run a beat-up regiment in there, refit it with all new equipment, fresh replacements from their manpower pool, give it a few days' rest — maybe some girls — and have it back out 'on the track' in three weeks' time. If that isn't 'the pits' I'll eat my hat.

"And I'll say one more thing," the young captain had ventured. "If Giant City does manage to catch and chew up some of these main force outfits, I'll bet the leftovers make a run for 'the pits,' and that we have a whole new, re-equipped main force out there to deal with in less than two months.

"We've told MACV a dozen times about how Charlie uses the border area for his supply base. Hell, we've even sent them maps of where the depots are, but for some reason they want to continue to fight this war by the Marquis of Queensbury rules. We can't bomb or shell them; we can't go in and clean them out; we can't even send patrols or agents in on the ground to tap their goddam telephone lines."

The complaint was an old one, and Paul had had no desire to rehash all the worn political arguments, pro and con, about enemy sanctuaries. He had just patted the air and waived the officer off. Some matters were just too big to worry about. Paul had resolved to follow the advice printed on the back of a bookmark Cicely had given him before he left home: "Work hard, do your duty, say your prayers and leave the rest to God." He wondered if she would have given him a slogan like that today.

He winced slightly as he thought of Cicely. He hadn't written to her in almost ten days. She had sent him one short note enclosing a vitriolic piece from *The Washington Post* on the illegality and immorality of the war. He had read a few paragraphs and thrown it away. Trash.

And he was uncomfortable about an exchange of letters he had had with Anne. He hadn't sought it out. It just seemed to happen. He couldn't remember how many years it had been since he had seen her, but when her brother, Hunter, showed up in the company of a group of junketing congressmen, his heart leapt at the recollection of his youthful infatuation. Hunter was now a successful young lawyer on the staff of the Foreign Affairs Committee. In the few minutes the two men had to renew their acquaintance, Hunter had taken Paul's unit address and promised to pass the major's "very best" to his sister when he got back to the States.

Anne had been something special to Paul in his cadet days. Perhaps not his first love, but certainly his most intense. The daughter of an Army general herself, she seemed to float with ease through the unique formality of social life at the Academy. She knew many of Paul's classmates and friends, having grown up with them at innumerable military posts throughout the country and across the Pacific in the 1930s and '40s. Paul wasn't an Army Brat, so he had had to swallow his petty jealousy and irritation as Anne would twirl off across the dance floor in the arms of another cadet, laughing and chatting about past years and other places that Paul couldn't share.

Lord, but she was beautiful! The sudden reminder of the girl whom he had loved like he had never loved anyone else, and who had later rejected him in favor of a senior at some New England university, was like an electric shock; it had rendered him virtually sleepless for weeks afterward.

"Yes," Hunter had assured him, "Anne's well and happy and the mother of four fine young boys." The news was both welcome and unwelcome.

"I'm very glad to hear that," he lied in response. "Tell her that I'm well, too." That was all he could think of to say — that and his APO address. He briefed the congressmen on enemy strength and operations in the Field Force zone as he had dozens of such groups before, but it took an enormous effort to concentrate on their questions and to keep his mind from drifting back to that lovely face which had remained etched in his subconsciousness. Somehow he got through the ordeal and accepted his visitors' appreciation for what one described as "the first comprehensible explanation of what is going on in this war" that he had heard. As he had so often, he flopped down afterward on his bunk with his boots propped on the foot rail and stared at a familiar juncture of the wall and the ceiling. He hadn't realized that he had been given to tears until he found himself gasping for breath, and had to get up to get a drink of water to pull himself back together.

While he hadn't really expected it, his faint hope that later on he might sometime hear directly from Anne had crystallized in a matter of weeks. He recognized the handwriting instantly, but turned the envelope over and over in his hands before opening it so he could see her name on the back and see his own name written in her near-perfect script. He relished the idea that Anne would take a few moments to write his name again; and he had barely been able to breathe until he could retreat into a corner of the TOC and break the seal.

# *FIFTEEN*

Ba squatted on the floor of the hut and listened with the rest. The story Comrade Tran Hua was telling seemed to be as closely interwoven with hyperbole as any of her propaganda yarns, but this time she had photographs. Here, indeed, was a photo of the famous American movie star shaking hands with Vo Van Hoa, First Secretary of the Presidium. Here, in another, she was visiting what Hua described as one of the largest hospitals in Hanoi.

One whole wing of the building had been demolished, allegedly by "the barbarous American criminals in Air Force uniform, directed by the fascist clique in the White House and the Pentagon in Washington." Still another showed the young woman accepting an armload of picked flowers from a group of smiling school children.

Why in the world, Ba thought, would the Americans allow that woman to visit Hanoi at the height of the war? Perhaps the photos are fakes, or may be she has been exiled for her views.

Hua went on with her elaboration on the anti-war movement in the United States. She was impressive. She had quotations from prominent citizens, congressmen and senators. They all seemed to echo what she had been saying about the Americans for months: "The war effort is criminal. The war is no concern of the United States. Only the evil leaders and the industrialists, dependent upon fat Pentagon contracts, support the war."

Ba was fascinated, and yet incredulous. How in the world, he asked himself, can responsible people, even in as strange a place as the United States, speak so disloyally of their own government in time of war? How do they get away with it? Why aren't they thrown in jail?

Either Hua's story was a big lie, or the United States was an even stranger place than he had supposed. He was glad that it wasn't his responsibility to provide for the ideological motivation of the patriots. All he had to do was to provide for their welfare, train and lead them. Their zeal for the Cause wasn't his concern. The political officer pursued the task with sufficient zeal for both of them.

Hua broke her audience up into the customary discussion groups for the second hour, making sure that each group had a leader who showed no symptoms of the malaise which seemed to bring the patriots under Ba's personality cult. Ba was not oblivious of Hua's selectivity, but he posed no objection, preferring to conserve his capital for settlement of differences he considered more important.

Besides, he recognized the fundamental necessity of Hua's function. She was abrasive and dogmatic, but often she made sense in a rough sort of way, and she had no more control over the operations of the D group than he allowed her to have. He was still very much in command and no amount of carping on her part could influence what was actually undertaken or accomplished — unless he permitted it.

Only in partial demonstration of his independent authority did he withdraw from the political agitation meeting. He signaled to his planning officer to follow him. The two men filed out the door and down the narrow trail that led from the meeting hut to the bivouac area where the patriots were permitted to build small structures to fit their own tastes. Most were simple lean-tos, providing rudimentary protection from the rain and a modicum of privacy, a commodity never plentiful in the jungle. Close by each structure was a shallow trench, an emergency refuge in case of surprise attack. Ba had insisted that the trenches be as well camouflaged as the shelters, so they constituted a bit of a hazard to anyone walking through the encampment without carefully watching his step. It had become a standing joke among the members of the D group who would break his leg next in a slit trench trying to find his way to the latrine at night.

Ba led the way past the common area to his own bunker. His was the only structure that had been constructed mostly below the surface of the ground. He shoved the canvas flap in the doorway and paused to tie it back with a piece of twine. The flap was a welcome protection from the rain, but otherwise it made the shelter hot and uncomfortable. There was only one chair in the room, so Ba hunkered down on his haunches and gestured to his companion to do the same. The squatting position was a national pastime in Vietnam as it was almost everywhere in the East. Ba had described it once to a friend in Paris as as comfortable to the oriental as the fetal position is to his occidental cousins

"Patriot Ly Nam," Ba began when they were settled, "this morning we received an assortment of documents which were picked up by one of the combat pickets of the C-3 Unit. My English is better for medical than military matters, but as nearly as I can make out, they're mostly lists of different supplies and materials with names and addresses or telephone numbers associated with each entry. The owner may have been engaged in some sort of barter activity. There're also a number of personal and unit papers that rather clearly identify the owner as a member of the Intelligence Detachment of the Tenth Armored Cavalry Regiment."

"Yes, Patriot Ba," Nam replied, "We have known how that regiment has been forming near Long Binh. Our most recent information indicates that it may soon move to Xuan Loc. That would take it out of our normal area of operations, but of course we could encounter elements of it here in Phu Loi Province or in Bien Hoa at any time."

"The most interesting thing," Ba went on, "is the packet of aerial photographs which look to me like the area around the Phu Cuong. And if I read the date-time group correctly here in the margin of the first photo, they were taken the very morning before our attack. What do you make of that?"

Ba spread the prints out on planks to keep the papers off the ground. The two men squatted beside the boards and studied the prints, matching the overlapping areas where they could.

"There's no doubt about it, Patriot Ba. This is Phu Cuong, and I believe you're right about the timing. I wish we had had these while we were planning the attack. They would have been very useful. The reconnaissance B unit had to take a number of chances to get up-to-date information for us. Here we have the entire layout, together with shots of the areas we used for assembly and withdrawal afterwards. What I don't understand is how a C-3 combat picket would find these on an American."

"That puzzles me, too," Ba admitted. "You see, I know why the photos were taken. I have great confidence in you, Nam, and I know you can keep a secret. I asked a special source to get them for us. However, I didn't think it was safe to tell him why we wanted them, and particularly not when, so of course he didn't know they would be too late. I suppose we would have had them in a few days if we had postponed the operation.

"You know," Ba went on, "I never did consider postponement. But when the others spotted enemy reconnaissance aircraft over the target area the morning before our attack, I had to pretend to reconsider our plans. I couldn't let it be known that I wasn't surprised to see them. That's why I delayed the assault for two hours. We can't let the others know about our special source. I know you understand that."

Nam nodded his head and made an upward gesture with his right hand, indicating agreement.

"But I don't understand," Ba went on, "how these photos came into the hands of the Americans. Unless, somehow, they've found out about the special source. Perhaps they caught him trying to get the packet to us."

Ba shifted on his haunches and looked at the ground in front of him. "And I don't like saying this, Nam, but there is another possibility. It could be that something has caused the special source to hand these photos over to the Americans."

Nam guessed how painful it must be for Ba to mention the second possibility. He suspected that the source was a relative of Ba's, maybe even a close one. Treachery in the Movement was not unknown, but when discovered, both men knew, it had to be punished with the most extreme measures. Assassination or kidnapping and execution was mandatory in virtually every case. There were very few exceptions.

"For the time being," Ba said, "I think I'll have to be circumspect in communication with the source. I don't think I should break contact now. If he is operating under American control — or if he's dead, and they're continuing to correspond with us in hopes of tracking us down — I could give away my suspicions by stopping all communications right now."

Again Nam pointed upward. "I think you're quite right, Patriot Ba. You don't know how much the Americans may know. Even if they know about the source, they may not know about how you transmit messages. Assuming the worst, they could close in on the contact patriots if, indeed, the special source uses them. Where does that leave us?"

"I asked the source to provide an assessment of his ability to secure information on the Long Binh ammunition dump by October first. Here it is the fourth of the month and we've had no reply. I'm not sure just what to make of that," Ba replied.

The two men remained squatting on the hard packed dirt floor in silence. Ba gathered up the photographs and slid them back into their manila envelope. He pushed the envelope to one side and reached into his breast pocket. With his index and second fingers he drew out a neatly folded piece of paper.

"I have, however, received a message from the source which relates to the munitions dump to some degree," he said. "For the most part it confirms our information on the Tenth Armored Cavalry Regiment, but as you know, the advance party of the regiment has been stationed in close proximity to the dump. It also contains a paragraph of particular interest to us. Look at this."

Ba spread the paper out on the planks in front of them. The three paragraphs represented the product of decryption and expansion of the standard symbols. The last paragraph read:

> INTELLIGENCE DETACHMENT COMMANDER
> WITH REGIMENT MAJOR J PAULDING
> MCCANDLESS STOP MAY HAVE SPECIAL
> INTEREST IN PHU LOI D GROUP STOP NOT
> CLEAR WHETHER INTEREST PERSONAL OR
> BASED ON MISSION OF REGIMENT STOP

"Either way," Ba said, "I don't like it. We're a very small unit and we don't need an entire American armored cavalry regiment beating the bushes for us. And even if it's only the personal interest of this Major McCandless I don't think we need some intelligence officer making a hobby out of nailing us.

"And one other thing. Note that the aerial photos were taken from a member of McCandless' organization. The coincidence may be significant. I think perhaps we should make an effort to find out a little more about this man. Ordinarily, I wouldn't think that he would be very important, being just a major in an army as big, and with as many high-ranking officers as the Americans have, but we should keep in mind that the commander of the American headquarters at Long Binh is named General John Paulding.

Suppose the major is some relative of the general. What could that mean? In any event, if he's going to concentrate his attentions on us, we should know who he is and how influential he is."

"That won't be easy," Nam supposed. "We have some access to most of the American camps and should be able to locate him. We have sources among the wash women who can look for his name and rank among the uniforms when they do the laundry. It might not even be too difficult to have him assassinated if that were desirable, but I'm not sure how we would do an assessment of his importance or influence. Why don't we just target him for elimination when we attack the ammunition dump?"

"No," Ba said. "Most of this is just a lot of supposition, and I wouldn't want to risk the lives of our dear patriots on a hunch. I am far more interested in the Long Binh ammunition dump than I am in the headquarters. If we were to split our effort between the two objectives we could find ourselves without enough power to accomplish either one very well. We can always go after the major some other day if he turns out to be of any real importance.

"In the meanwhile, talk to the reconnaissance B unit leader. Explain the situation to him. We'll have to keep this rather quiet because we have no knowledge of it other than what the special source has told us. We have to continue to protect him, until we know more about how the Americans got the photographs."

Ba glanced out of the doorway and caught a glimpse of Comrade Tran Hua making her way up the path towards the dugout. He quickly folded the message and put it back into his pocket. He then reached into the corrugated shipping carton that contained his maps and selected one of the Long Binh area. Spreading it out on the planks, he whispered to his companion, "Tran Hua is coming up the path. Pretend that we have been talking about the operation against the ammunition dump. Flatter her. Ask her questions if you can."

Nam looked at Ba, and a conspiratorial grin broke out over his face.

"Yes, Patriot Ba," he said.

Hua stepped down to the entrance to the bunker, slapping the canvas curtain to announce her arrival. Her demeanor was familiar to the men inside: agitated and righteous. They glanced once more at each other before Ba stood up to answer her call.

"Yes, Comrade Hua, come inside. Patriot Ly Nam and I have been discussing the plans for the Long Binh operation. I know you don't believe it is a good idea. Have you received any instructions from COSVN about it?"

Hua was irritated that Ba had guessed that she had already written to her superiors. But she was even more irritated that she couldn't give an affirmative reply, with the additional news that COSVN considered the entire idea ill advised and that the plans should be canceled. Her face seemed to turn a shade darker, but she ignored the question.

"Comrade Ba," she began. "You know as well as I do the requirements for four hours of political agitation and self- criticism among the patriots each week. Today's was a particularly important session, but you did everything you could to sabotage it. You got up and walked out before we had even begun the discussion groups."

Her anger made her eyes glisten.

"You are the elected leader of the Phu Loi D Group," she pointed out, as she always did when administering Ba a scolding. "The patriots look up to you. They look to you for example. Only if you show enthusiasm can we expect that they will show enthusiasm. Now, I want to know why you left the meeting, and why you took Comrade Ly Nam with you. That shows nothing but contempt for orders issued directly from COSVN. Who do you think you are? I suspect sometimes that you may harbor counterrevolutionary ideas and that you're just exploiting your position for your own advantage."

Ba decided not to interrupt. She seemed to have a reservoir of vitriol that she wanted to hurl at him, and he might as well let her get it out.

"I insist, Comrade Ba," she went on, "that you stand up at the next self-criticism session next Wednesday and confess the error of your ways. Specifically, I insist that you acknowledge the mistake you made in leaving today's political agitation meeting early and in leading another comrade astray.

"And as for you, Comrade Ly," she spoke to the squatting figure on the floor, "you have much to regret, too. I shall also expect that you will tell us about your behavioral deviations. It may have been correct for you to have stepped out of the meeting for a moment or two to find out what Comrade Ba wanted of you, but then you should have returned to your proper place in a discussion group.

"This is not the first time that either of you have shown such contempt for COSVN's directives. Nor is it the first time I have had to point out your shortcomings. You probably need the benefits of these meetings more than anyone else in the D group. I hope I have made myself clear on this subject, and I hope that this is the last time that I will have to talk about it. You both carry heavy responsibilities for the Cause, and you cannot discharge those responsibilities in a careless manner."

"You have made yourself abundantly clear, Mme. Hua," Ba replied. He made no effort to respond to her tirade. "I look forward to hearing what COSVN has to say about the Long Binh operation — if they do reply before we conduct the attack. Please let us know as soon as you hear something."

Hua was beside herself with fury. "Comrade Ba, you don't recognize your failings. I have tried to point them out for you, but you don't listen. What would you think if the patriots didn't obey your orders in battle? How would we win victories? Can't you see that the ideological struggle is just as important as the struggle in the field? How can you be so opaque?"

She didn't wait for Ba to respond. Instead, she slapped the canvas flap again, much harder than before. Then she turned her back and marched down the path, head erect, eyes moist with her sense of mission and self-congratulations for having delivered a stunning blow for the Cause.

The two men looked at each other again and breathed deeply. "With the likes of Mme. Hua on our side," Ba joked, "I don't see that the enemy has a chance in this war. Now, go, Nam. You know what we need."

# *SIXTEEN*

"Are you sure?" Paul asked, hoping the reply would be negative. Captain Peter Farnsworth, his successor as commander of the MI detachment with the Tenth Cavalry, repeated the names of the men involved in the ambush.

"I know you knew them all," he said, half apologetically, "so I thought you would want to know."

"Yes, thanks," Paul replied softly. He paused for a minute. There was a click and an officious voice came on the line.

"Is this circuit being used?"

"Yes, yes, operator, we're working."

The line clicked again.

"Well, Pete, thanks for calling me. You say that Sergeant Garowski's OK?"

"I suppose as 'OK' as you can be taking a claymore mine in the side of the head. Fortunately he had his helmet and his flak jacket on. And I suppose Anderson shielded him to some extent on the left. Anderson was driving. I haven't seen Garowski yet, but I understand they may let visitors in tomorrow."

"OK, thanks, Pete," Paul repeated.

Good Lord, he thought as he hung up. You never know what's going to happen next, Anderson and Jacobs dead, Stan Garowski badly wounded. Again! How much junk can a man take into his body in a lifetime? How can he be anything more than a vegetable after this? A nauseous feeling crept over him as he thought about it.

He sat for a long time with his right hand resting on the receiver. The duty clerk sitting next to him sensed the bad news, and said nothing. Others at the far end of the TOC bustled about their work on the map boards, oblivious of the tragedy that had just come in over the phone.

Paul took a deep breath and let it out slowly through his mouth, puffing out his cheeks like a caricature of the north wind on a 17th Century map. He looked up at the G-2 situation map with the crimson flag-like symbols of enemy units scattered across it. Almost aloud he gave vent to his anger and frustration.

Which one of you bastards did it? Which of you hung a claymore on a tree and lay in wait for Sergeant Stanislaw Garowski and Jacobs and Anderson to come by? Which one of you watched their heads blow off? They were better men than all your goddam bloody asses put together. By God, I'll find out who did it, and where you are, and there won't be enough left of your goddam asses for anyone to know what happened. Tears welled up in his eyes as he struggled to still the quiver in his cheeks and lips. Gritting his teeth helped to hold him together in front of the clerks. He got up and walked out of the TOC.

Minutes later the G-2 duty clerk took another call from the Tenth Cav. Among the enemy-initiated incidents reported was one on Highway 3, involving a probable claymore mine attack on a vehicle belonging to the MI detachment: "Two friendly KIA, one WIA, all medically evacuated. Status and disposition of the casualties should be determined from the 42nd Army Field

Hospital." It was all very routine. The clerk plotted the location of the incident on the situation map. He had to move a symbol for an unconfirmed report of enemy personnel in the area in order to pinpoint the exact spot. Unemotionally, he attributed the attack in his own mind to one of the usual local units. It meant nothing special to him.

Sergeant Schwartz had witnessed the major's emotional state when he left the TOC. He replied to Colonel Dillings inquiry as to Paul's whereabouts with a suggestion that unless the matter were terribly pressing it might be best to leave him alone for a while.

"What's wrong with him?" the colonel's voice challenged over the intercom.

"I'm not sure, sir," the sergeant replied, "But I think he's upset over some casualties in his old outfit. He looked to me as though he needed a good walk, He'll come around."

"OK," Dillings concluded. "When he's ready for it perhaps we can cheer him up a bit with the news that he's been promoted. He's been a lieutenant colonel since yesterday."

"That's great." Schwartz was genuinely pleased. He liked the major — now the lieutenant colonel — and was happy for him. But his pleasure also stemmed from a practical consideration. In the subtleties of staff politics a little more rank on one side or the other could make a difference. G-2 - G-3 relations were sometimes a little like the battle of the sexes. Each side has definite functions to perform, but there's always a lot of overlap and not inconsequential competition.

The sergeant would be happy henceforth to precede his conversations with his counterpart in G-3 with "Colonel McCandless has asked me to do so-and-so," rather than "Major McCandless has asked ...." He welcomed all the leverage he could get. For the moment, however, Schwartz advised delay.

"By tomorrow, I think, sir, he'll be ready to hear about it. And the news will do him good. Let him sleep the other news off."

"OK," the voice on the intercom concluded, "but let's hold the information closely overnight. I'd like to tell him myself — or the Field Force commander may want to do the honors."

"Yes, sir," Schwartz replied, "he'd appreciate that, I'm sure." The intercom clicked off.

Silence surrounded Paulding McCandless as he walked with no particular destination in mind around the barren ground outside the TOC. The stars decorated the sky, Christmas card style, but were little comfort. It would be a while before he was ready to philosophize about a larger order of things. He just felt terribly, terribly tired — much too tired to face the stack of translations of captured documents he would have known would be sitting on his desk if he had thought about it. Sergeant Schwartz would ask Captain Daniels to do a rough screening of the stack just to insure that it could all keep for another eight hours.

Paul walked slowly, and only slightly unsteadily, towards his trailer and the solace a night's sleep could offer.

Schwartz's practical psychology paid off; Paul had control of himself in the morning. It was a little difficult at the briefing to recount to the Field Force commander the incident on Highway 3, among the half-dozen enemy initiated attacks in the last twenty-four hours, but he got through it with nothing more than an instant's hesitation.

At the conclusion of the briefing the commander stood up in front of the staff and announced Paul's promotion. The general's aide-de-camp had a second-hand silver maple leaf for the general to pin over the embroidered dull brown leaf signifying a major's rank on Paul's collar. Later that day, a small squad of peasant women would squat in a circle and embroider black leaves on all of Paul's jungle fatigue jackets. While silver was the proper color for dress uniforms, it was much too visible in the field. The military bureaucracy had sensibly specified a substitution of black for silver insignia and dull brown for gold.

The general gave a nice little talk about the importance of intelligence, particularly in this war, and shook Paul's hand vigorously. Paul was ready to smile, and almost beamed as each member of the staff filed by, adding his congratulations. Colonel Dillings seemed particularly warm, and Paul appreciated the sentiment.

In the afternoon, Paul summoned his driver and told him to bring the jeep around to the front of the headquarters. At two fifteen, Private First Class William Hastings had the vehicle standing on the gravel driveway, with the top down and the engine idling. Corporal Thomas Williams was sitting in the back, riding "shotgun." Paul slipped an ammunition clip into his automatic as he climbed in, telling Hastings to head for the hospital. He held his helmet in his hands momentarily, looking at the freshly painted black leaf on the front.

"Looks pretty good, don't it sir?" Williams ventured.

"It sure does, Corporal," Paul agreed. He got the helmet on his head just in time to return the M.P.'s salute as they accelerated out the gate.

Traffic on the highway seemed particularly heavy for the middle of the afternoon. It slowed to a crawl as the jeep approached a bend in the road. A little oversensitive about unanticipated situations on a public road, Paul withdrew his pistol from his shoulder holster and instructed Williams to chamber a round in his rifle, but to keep the safety on. It was unlikely that anything more dangerous than a traffic accident or a road repair gang at work could be causing the tie-up on this stretch, but Paul's was a conditioned response. He pulled at the slide of his weapon and watched the bullet jerk forward into the receiver. A boxy three-wheeled Lambretta bus, struggling along under too many passengers, blocked his view of the congestion ahead.

He stood up, self-consciously holding his automatic at his shoulder with his right hand and grasping the top of the windshield with his left. The bus passengers stared at him as though he were crazy. Over the top of the creeping column he could see a National Police barricade, where civilian vehicles were being stopped and searched.

He sat back down and ordered the driver to double the column. Glancing into the sideview mirror, Hastings yanked the wheel sharply to the left and mashed the accelerator to floor. Paul unloaded his pistol and returned it to its holster. He returned the salute of a police corporal as Hastings swung around the oil drums blocking the highway. In less than a minute, they were clear of the obstruction and zipping along their way.

Paul chuckled sardonically to himself at the thought of the police checkpoint. He knew that this one, like almost all the rest in the corps zone, was a dawn-to-dusk operation. It was too risky to leave a half-dozen officers alone on a highway at night, so most checkpoints were closed at curfew. Paul knew that the enemy had no difficulty in removing roadblocks, or in circumventing them, if they wanted to use the highway. Often the barricades were booby trapped by the police, but the guerrillas seemed adept at dealing with the problem. Often they would simply blow up the obstructions and drive on.

It was not more than four miles to the hospital. A large maroon and white sign announced its location under a canopy of rubber trees. The drab structures sprawled about the area in a seemingly aimless pattern. Sandbags lined the walls of the huts, and ambulances, with their big red crosses emblazoned on box-like bodies, were coming and going like bees around a hive. Hastings slowed the jeep. "Where do you want to go, Colonel?"

"Pull around the left," Paul replied. "The administrative office is over there."

The driver spun the vehicle in a short arc and backed into a visitor's slot. Paul hopped out, bounded up the timber stairs, and pushed the screen door aside. It slammed after him. A harassed orderly, cradling a phone under his chin, shuffled through a card file to find Sergeant Garowski's form. Trauma Ward 8. Paul was encouraged that the clerk said nothing about intensive care or restrictions on visitors.

He followed stenciled signs through the succession of huts. It took a while for his eyes to become adjusted to the bleak light emitted by a sparse series of bare bulbs hanging from the ridge bars of each structure. He noticed that the signs had been stenciled over a couple of times, changing the ward numbers as the complex expanded.

Trauma Ward 8, Paul realized, was for patients with multiple injuries, including damage to the eyes. But for the name tag on the end of the bed, he would not have known that he had found his man. Most of Garowski's face was concealed behind a mask of bandages. His upper torso was swathed in white, as was his left leg, which was elevated through a mechanical device with lines, pulleys and weights. His right arm lay strapped at his side, with a bandage covering most of the hand. Paul was happy to see the tips of five fingers protruding from the bandage. A bottle of clear fluid was attached by a tube to the arm. A lump under the sheet at the bottom of the bed indicated that his right foot was intact. So far so good.

"Sergeant Garowski," Paul began softly. "Stan? Are you awake?" There was a flicker at the mouth hole and a couple of fingers twitched.

"It's me, Major McCandless. Only now its Lieutenant Colonel McCandless. Can you hear me all right?" Paul noticed that there seemed to be no ear opening on the left side — just a tube. He walked around to the other side of the bed.

"You really got zapped, old man. You look like you spent the night brawling in a beer hall. How do you feel?"

The edge of the bandage at the mouth hole fluttered again. Paul leaned over, hesitant to touch the man. He caught a faint "congratulations." A sudden wave of emotion gripped his face, yanking the corners of his mouth downward and flooding his eyes. He struggled unsuccessfully to answer. Blowing his nose, he took a deep breath and tried again. "Thanks."

Silently, he stood beside the bed for what my have been a long period of time. The extent of the sergeant's major wounds were gruesomely apparent. There was no left arm. The only things that weren't apparent were Garowski's certain agony and the answer to the unspoken question of the sergeant's survival.

A prim young nurse in pressed jungle fatigues came to the bedside, motioning Paul to step aside. Wordlessly, she took the sergeant's pulse and eased a thermometer in through the mouth hole.

His jaw must be OK, Paul thought, if he can speak and take a thermometer.

The nurse removed a bag of fluid from the bed, attaching an empty one in its place. Paul counted four lines coming out of the prostrate figure at different places. The nurse made a notation on a clipboard and moved on, dropping the thermometer into a cup on a tray at the foot of the bed.

Paul knew the hospital and was acquainted with the routine. Wounded V.C. scarfed up in search-and-destroy operations or left behind after an unsuccessful attack on an outpost would be brought to the same facility for treatment until they were strong enough for regular imprisonment. Paul would occasionally come to supervise the interrogation of potentially important captives, particularly when there appeared to be a risk that one might not survive and there might not be a second chance to put forth the right questions. The information gained from prisoner interrogation was second in authenticity only to documentary sources.

"Stan," Paul called.

No answer.

"You take it easy, old man. I'll come back and see you when you're feeling a little better. Get a good rest, d'ya hear?"

The mouth hole flickered. Paul leaned over to catch the words. He could swear he heard, "Don't go."

"Look, Stan, you've got to rest. Charlie really laid one into you, and you're got to give these good-looking nurses time to do their thing. I'll come back tomorrow."

"Don't go."

"Don't go? Look, don't you know there's a war on? I've got work to do." Paul was straining to maintain a light hearted tone, but he sensed that the spooky figure had something special to tell him. He bent closer over the bed.

"ARVN had photos..."

"Yes, I hear you, You mean the ARVN corps? What photos?"

"Phu Cuong."

Paul puzzled for a moment. "You mean something to do with the V.C. raid?"

There was no sound for what must have been fifteen or twenty seconds, then, "V.C. raid," and a soft cough.

"I hear you, Stan," Paul said, eager to reassure him. "The ARVN corps has photographs of Phu Cuong during the raid? Have you seen them? What do they show?"

It was a prolonged interview with many pauses and misinterpretations. At length the sergeant stopped, He seemed to have said everything he could or wanted to. A phalanx of doctors, working its way down the row of maimed men, replaced Paul at the sergeant's bedside. Paul would have liked to have reached out and patted Garowski, but he couldn't think of a safe place to touch him.. He parted with a wooden expression of encouragement and a charge to the doctors to take good care of him. It was doubly depressing to walk back out through the rows of white forms, some in grotesque positions, some obviously in acute pain. Paul's nausea returned.

He paused inside the doorway to blow his nose once more and to clear his throat before heading for the jeep. He didn't look at the driver, but ordered him to return to the Field Force headquarters. The air whipping around the windshield gave him an excuse to pull out his handkerchief and wipe his eyes and glasses.

He looked off across the fields as they sped along and reviewed what Garowski had told him. He had little confidence that he had the whole story, but the essentials seemed to be:

One — ARVN corps had requested aerial photographs of Phu Cuong at the same time the enemy was planning an attack on the town.

Two — after the attack the photos were supposed to be burned. Garowski had them but didn't know what happened to them after he was hit.

Three — Garowski hadn't exactly said so, but obviously he believed that there was an enemy agent, in an important position, in the corps headquarters.

Four — the attack on Phu Cuong was almost certainly carried out by the provincial battalion. Maybe Garowski's ambush was made by the same bunch of cutthroats. Maybe they knew he had the photos, and that was what they were after — if that made any sense after the attack had already been carried out. Maybe Do found out that the photos hadn't been destroyed as he ordered. Maybe there was something important on those photos that Do didn't want revealed.

Paul felt a sinking feeling within him. He found himself fighting off conclusions — conclusions prominently featuring Do. The anti-conclusion fight was as difficult as his struggle to retain control of himself when he first heard the news about Garowski. It seemed that a giant vice was squeezing him, insisting that he recognize an ugly truth. He tried to push the whole thing out of his mind, taking large gulps of air from the wind to control his nausea.

The next week saw the kick off of Giant City. It was a huge operation involving practically all of the Allied forces, including air and naval units. High altitude "Arc Light" strikes thundered ahead of the advancing columns; thousands of vehicles clogged the roads for the length and breadth of the corps tactical zone. "Century" series fighter-bombers shrieked overhead, diving to pound suspected enemy strong points and climbing back to avoid ground fire. Paul watched the first waves of air and ground assault units strike the "Iron Triangle," the ancient stronghold of dissident groups from time immemorial. His tiny observation plane rocked like a child's seesaw in the turbulence set up by the attacking jets. Columns of dense smoke springing up on the periphery of a vast circle marked the progress of the front lines.

The Field Force commander had paid a last minute call on General Vo to apprise him of the plan and to solicit his support and participation. Paul hadn't accompanied the commander, but he could imagine an impassive, very oriental visage listening to the plan, making little comment, asking no questions. Then, after a lengthy lunch and a period of consultations while the American commander was entertained with briefings on other matters, announcing that, yes, ARVN forces would take part. In fact, Paul's story to Do had been interpreted as a warning signal, and the American plan was surprising to the Vietnamese only in its scale. General Vo had already planned to join in the operation. Paul was half glad that he hadn't had to face Do at just that moment or to lie his way through an "explanation" of the "modification" in his earlier version of the American scheme.

But his suspicions of the ARVN staff, and of Do in particular, took the edge off his embarrassment. It was quite clear that relationships would be different after this — more correct, more formal. Everyone assumed that the ARVN headquarters had been penetrated by the Viet Cong. Why should he have assumed that any Vietnamese officer was free from taint just because he happened to be a personal friend? Any number of officers in the headquarters could be up to their ass holes in double dealing. As Paul thought about it, it occurred to him that there might be considerable temptation for any of them to play both sides of the fence as long as the outcome remained in doubt.

It's a hell of a set up, he thought. Paul's gut guess about responsibility for Garowski's ambush was confirmed with receipt of the translation of the unfinished letter found in the slit trench by Highway 3. At the top of the sheet was the now-familiar letter box number, 100753. His heart sank as he thought about the colossal operation under way in the field. Men, money and materiel had been committed on an unprecedented scale, but they were aimed at a different foe, at a different objective. Whatever the outcome of Giant City, Van Ba and his thugs were bound to come through unscathed. No one had designated their strongholds for destruction; no one was even looking for them. Hell, Paul thought, the Phu Loi Battalion could be sticking a bomb up our ass right now and we wouldn't even know it. He would have liked to have shared his thoughts with Colonel Dillings, but the colonel was away, working with the small forward C.P. from which the Field Force commander directed the operation. Instead, he just sat and grumbled to himself.

# *SEVENTEEN*

The dry season had come to Southeast Asia. The rice paddies turned to hard, baked platforms and the grasslands turned to straw. The news releases said it made for much easier going for a mechanized army. Things might break down, or become caked with dust and stall out, but no longer would they sink into a bog of slime, or rust or mold away.

And it was a mechanized army that was chasing Charlie this time. The big enemy main force outfits were depicted on all the operational maps as small red flags, shrinking before the Allied attacks, which were themselves dramatically represented by bold blue arrows, three inches long. Air strikes were depicted by jagged circles, like irregular gear wheels. Paul couldn't help thinking that they ought to be accompanied with "Pow!" or "Whammo!" the way the righteous blows of comic book heroes are shown during the final climatic frames of any episode.

After all, he chuckled to himself, here is "Captain America" bringing democracy and clean living to a backward land. The "bad guys" have to be driven out so that the American dream: suburbia, popcorn and the PTA can take root.

Firepower and mobility were the principal ingredients of the offensive. When contact with the enemy appeared imminent "straight leg" infantry would be airlifted into the vicinity by helicopters to make a fight out of it. If the enemy danced away the "legs" would be loaded back up and moved on to the next most promising "hot" landing zone.

Each time, the procedure was the same. Artillery and rocket-firing helicopters would blast the area selected for a landing. Even if the ground wasn't defended it had to be "prepped" to make sure that there were no mines or other unpleasant surprises awaiting the assault troops. Then the troop-carrying choppers would go in in tight formations, vomiting automatic weapons fire in all directions as a precaution against ambush. The "legs" would scramble out of their airborne war chariots before they were even on the ground and head for the tree lines. It was a rare operation that didn't have a guarded perimeter set up within ten minutes. Additional waves of choppers would bring in more soldiers and more ammunition.

Paul could never understand how the helicopter pilots managed these things. How in the world did they keep from banging into one another? More often than not the initial bombardment would set the dry grasses on fire and the entire area would be enveloped in a pale choking smoke. As the choppers would approach touch down, their big thumping blades would set up thick clouds of ash and half-burned straw to further reduce visibility. Paul wondered at the pilots' apparent lack of concern in what he classified as high pucker factor situations.

From day to day leading elements of the assault force reported uncovering all sorts of things — a little like cleaning out an old attic. Tons of rice were found in concealed caches; many different types of weapons and explosives were unearthed. One unit found a printing press, another a complete hospital, with bed pans in tact. The place must have been evacuated in haste, to judge by the fresh blood trails leading off into the woods. Thousands of pounds of documents turned up here and there in tunnels, shacks and tree huts.

The translators in Saigon would be put on triple shifts to turn the papers into exploitable grist for the intelligence mills. No other source of information could provide the breadth and depth of understanding of the enemy's capabilities, and, on occasion, even of his intentions.

After ten days of the offensive the statistics keepers had to make up new categories of things to keep track of. The enemy seemed determined to withdraw in the face of the onslaught, so there were not many bodies to count. A few V.C. or *Bo Dai* would make a stand here or there, wherever they had been locally surprised or trapped, but the statistics on captured bicycles, ox carts, books, flags, uniforms, paper money, jars of fish sauce and bundles of propaganda leaflets were much more impressive than the numbers of prisoners taken. There was no doubt about it, the offensive would knock COSVN's operating budget badly out of line. But, as Paul noted wryly, COSVN's budget hadn't been identified as an objective of the operation. The main force units, and COSVN itself, were the targets, and so far they were evident only in their jetsam.

The little information that did come filtering through about the enemy's whereabouts was not encouraging. While he may have had to "drop his knitting" and move out in a hurry, it seemed less and less likely that any significant numbers of insurgents were going to be trapped. There were just too many ways that small, well-led units could escape. American and ARVN forces began to make contact with one another in the heart of the jungle without having encountered more than a handful of suspicious characters along the way. One young American officer, who probably talked too much, described it to a reporter as "more like an Easter egg hunt than a military operation."

But that was not to be the whole story. Paul studied the map. The enemy had managed to evade the principal encirclement, but what had he done? He hadn't vanished entirely; rather he'd withdrawn to the border areas and stopped. Radio direction finders indicated that he was deployed along a wide arc just outside the Allied ring, and that he was passing a great many messages back and forth. It made Paul uneasy.

"Get the advance CP on the line. See if Colonel Dillings is there," he snapped to the TOC clerk. The more he thought about it the more agitated he became. Captain Daniels' suggestion about renaming the "Fish Hook" came back to him. The enemy might have had to leave a great deal of equipment behind as he evacuated his bases in South Vietnam, but it was all too apparent that he was falling back into "the pits." If the supply depots in Cambodia were nearly as rich as Paul was sure they were, there was considerable risk that the main force could very shortly be "back on the track" like a racing car, completely refitted.

"Yes, sir," Paul was soon telling his chief, "I think we have the makings for a full-fledged counterattack if Charlie chooses to do it. We don't have all the latest information on friendly dispositions right now, but if any of our fellows are out there wandering around looking for souvenirs, or whatever they like to do in that jungle, I think we should give them a little friendly advice. They could be knee-deep in Cong and alligators in another few days."

"How do you figure a few days?" Dillings challenged.

"Well I don't know, really," Paul admitted. "But I think you can figure some reconnaissance and march time, and some time for pre-attack assembly. It really depends upon where our lead elements are right now. I figure you have better information on that than we do." Then he added, "sir." His relationship with his boss was good, and he wanted to keep it that way.

"I'll look at it, Paul," the colonel said at length. "In the meanwhile, see if you can't get us a little extra aerial reconnaissance over the area at night. If those bastards are going to try and come back and hit us I don't want them marching down Highway 3 as though they owned the goddam place. We may not be able to see much, but if we can keep the area lit up with flares we can slow 'em up by forcing them back into the bush.

"And another thing," he went on, "get in touch with the artillery and get them to lay on some H & I fires. We ought to make it as rough as we can on the little bastards."

Paul wondered if he had ever heard the colonel refer to the enemy in terms that didn't suggest illegitimate birth as a widespread social practice in the countryside. But his call for harassing and interdictive artillery fire made sense. It would be impossible to predict what routes the enemy might follow to mass for a counterattack, but indiscriminate firing into the jungle could serve to complicate his problems, if indeed he was coming that way.

"Yes sir, I'll get right on it." He was glad that the colonel had grasped his concern for the situation. It could be the lull before the storm. Giant City could turn out to be Big War after all. He wondered how much time they really had.

Paul had to rely on Colonel Dillings to get in touch with the G-2s of the forward units in the field since they had been out of direct contact with the main Field Force headquarters from the start of the operation. However, he fired off messages to MACV headquarters and to the ARVN corps and prepared a lengthy assessment of the situation for Dillings to give to the Field Force commander. He stapled a little slip to the top of the first page suggesting that the colonel also pass it on to the divisions and to the Aussies. The Aussie S-2 was a particularly bright young major and Paul would've liked to have heard his views on the situation.

He felt a slight twinge of guilt as he slipped the papers into a manila envelope and handed it to Sergeant Schwartz with instructions to get it on the next dispatch helicopter. Perhaps his packet would provide a little extra insight into the dangers of counterattack just then, but he distrusted his own motives. The written record of the war was being compiled by a small historical detachment with the Field Force, and Paul knew that this assessment would find its way into that record. Whether or not the counterattack ever materialized he would be credited with having passed on a warning. If nothing happened no one would ever think more of it again. If, on the other hand, the enemy did regroup and fall upon one or more of the small dispersed units combing the jungle, Paul's performance would be above reproach. That was known as a "CYA" — cover your ass — warning. He tried to convince himself that he really thought that there was a serious risk of counterattack and that he was not just crying "wolf" to cover his posterior against an unlikely contingency. But, damn it, he wasn't sure — either about what the enemy might be up to or about his own true motives. At least some time soon, he reconciled himself, he would find out about the former.

# *EIGHTEEN*

The special source had come through quite well. The list of American ammunition stored at Long Binh was impressive — both because of its detail and its magnitude. Unfortunately, the "as of" date preceded the launching of Giant City so Ba couldn't be sure that the stockpile hadn't been drawn down for the operation. The Americans had a peculiar way of fighting a war. Instead of establishing specific objectives and exhorting each soldier to do his part to achieve them, the way they did in the Movement, the Americans seemed to turn first to their logisticians and rear-area managers to determine what was possible, considering the state of supply. Like logisticians everywhere, these officials tended to be conservative, and would advise against doing anything that might place an undue strain on the supply system. They never can determine what their soldiers are really capable of, he thought.

The Phu Loi D Group had had little experience against American units, so Ba had no real feel for the performance of American soldiers. He did know that some of the American advisors with ARVN units on occasion had practically taken command of the government troops they were assigned to "advise" and had inspired them to fight like tigers. But one couldn't extrapolate these isolated incidents into any generalization about American troops.

Comrade Hua was full of stories about the cowardice of the Americans, and about how the sons of the rich and the powerful in the United States were able to avoid military service by enrolling in expensive universities and divinity schools — the latter the "purveyors of the opiate of the masses." She insisted that the only ones who ever actually ended up fighting in the jungles of Vietnam were Negroes and poor boys who didn't have enough money or influence to escape the draft. She had pictures which she claimed had been taken in Washington, D.C. of young men and women in front of government buildings waving flags of the Movement and carrying signs saying that they wouldn't serve in the Army. Ba couldn't be sure about the authenticity of these pictures any more than about the others she had, but there seemed to be many of them. If they were real, he wondered how the Americans could have much of an army at all. He was well aware of the importance of insuring that everyone in the Movement was wholeheartedly doing his part — even a little bit more. Any doubt on the part of the patriots that someone else in their group was evading duty would have been very damaging to everyone's morale and couldn't be tolerated to even the slightest extent. He had reluctantly agreed to Hua's insistence on the execution of two young members of the group a few months earlier when it became evident, beyond all doubt, that they had lost their nerve and had attempted to persuade others to defect with them. Traitorous behavior in wartime was universally recognized as a high crime throughout the world. It was very hard to believe all that Hua said about the Americans. Perhaps they really were "paper tigers" as she liked to say.

Still, the Americans were rich and had many guns and tanks and aircraft, and one shouldn't be foolish in confronting them.

Ba was reassured by the Saigon papers that Giant City was aimed at bigger fish than the Phu Loi Group, but he would have liked to have had a better idea of how much ammunition had been distributed to local dumps from the Long Binh complex. He certainly didn't want to mount a high risk attack on a dry hole. The early date of the special source's report was a little discomforting. It did nothing to reassure him that the source had not been doubled against him.

However, if the report was to be trusted, the source had done a creditable job in gathering information on the American intelligence officer, Major J. Paulding McCandless. McCandless had been detached from the armored cavalry regiment to join the American Field Force staff. And he had been promoted. The basic information was followed by an extensive profile on the officer's background. It read as though it had been taken from the officer's personal correspondence, with details of his family and associates in the Army. The data on parents, siblings, wife and children was comprehensive — much more than Ba had expected — or that he could see any particular use for at the moment.

Ba had little interest in personalizing the war, but if the man was interested in the Phu Loi Group, Ba was interested in him. The similarity of names between McCandless and the Field Force commander, General John Paulding, might be only coincidental, but McCandless would bear watching, especially if he turned out to be a relative of the general. There was no telling how influential a man in such a position might be. Ba had heard how the popular American president, Kennedy, had appointed a younger brother to high office and how another brother had gained a seat in the national legislature during his administration. For all the disparaging Western talk of oriental nepotism, Westerners seemed to follow similar patterns when it came down to cases. Maybe McCandless' promotion was an instance of favoritism for the relative of a senior officer. Ba realized that he didn't really know much about the United States Army, but he considered the circumstances suspicious.

It was most important to protect the source, and part of that protection was to insure that few others were aware of his reports. However, he realized that the information on Lt. Colonel McCandless could have value at a higher level of direction than his own, and he felt uneasy about holding it to himself. He carefully copied out the significant points of the report and attached a note saying that he had captured a document with the given information. The original paper, he said, was in such a poor state of repair that it couldn't be saved. He folded the report down to regulation size and sealed it for transmission by courier to the Intelligence and Security Section of COSVN. He would have liked to have burned the original message, but he might have need for some of the details later on.

In her own bunker down the trail, Tran Hua lay on a mat and stared at the logs overhead. Why had she not heard from COSVN? She knew that the Americans had disrupted the normal courier connections with their Giant City operation, but she couldn't believe that the leadership of the Movement had allowed itself to be trapped by the enemy. She had been present during many of the discussions and planning sessions, and she knew how many ways there were for the most important sections of the headquarters to escape. Even if some of the functioning offices were completely surrounded they could seal up their tunnels and continue working for days underground, with multiple telephone lines leading through buried sections of bamboo pipes to relay stations miles away. From there the vital heart beat of political and military guidance would be sped on its way to the scores of units, like the Phu Loi Group, and to the hundreds of associations, clubs and cells that made up the fabric of the Movement throughout the country.

Certainly, Hua thought, the devious behavior of the Phu Loi D Group leader was an important matter meriting immediate attention by the proper authorities. Orders should arrive any hour of any day now, relieving Van Ba of his position. At the very least he would be detached for a special reeducation program where he would be led back to the proper revolutionary path. Or he might be permanently barred from high office, relegated to the ranks again where his wrong-headedness could not mislead so many otherwise faithful patriots. The thought was delightful to her. She imagined the moment when she would step out in front of the group at a meeting and publicly denounce the commander. Armed with a message from the highest authority she would recount Ba's criminal pattern and lackadaisical ways which had led to his downfall. What an occasion it would be! She constructed and reconstructed her opening lines in her mind:

"Comrades, I have important news for every ear, direct from COSVN headquarters! Listen closely to what I have to say, for it will thrust cold steel into your hearts and fire your wrath like the coals of a thousand camp fires! We have a traitorous devil in our midst who conceals his crimes behind a mask of reasonableness. But traitorous crimes cannot be veiled from the vigilance of the Cause!

"Hear me now as I lay before you the bare facts in this terrible case, lest those of you who have been deceived and led astray in past months fail to understand the importance of my words."

What a triumph it would be to stand before the entire group and to strip the facade off the traitor, Ba, so that he was finally exposed to the scrutiny and scorn of everyone whom he had misled for so long. The truth would emerge! The Movement would prevail! Ba and his ilk would be cast at the feet of the very people he had sought to deceive. How sweet the victory would be then. Whether the Phu Loi Group survived or not was not nearly as important as the survival and victory of the Correct Way. Revisionism and "practicality" were the greatest enemies of the Movement and had to be purged as quickly and as ruthlessly as possible.

Hua was pleased with her part in the drama. In years to come she and others like her would be revered for their steadfastness in dangerous times. Poets would immortalize the work of the political workers who provided the real direction to the movement. Hua could see People's theaters reenacting the trials and final triumphs of these few cadremen and women who held the entire revolutionary effort together and kept it as pure in purpose as the great leaders intended. The spirits of Comrades Lenin and Stalin, and the sure guiding hands of Mao Tse Dung and Ho Chi Minh were with them at all times and would not let them fail. Her thoughts were breathtaking in their scope, and she slipped off to sleep with tears in her eyes.

# NINETEEN

Do glanced up at the latest postings in the corps war room. Giant City was arrayed on a new set of maps especially assembled for the purpose. Free World forces, shown in blue, seemed to converge on areas which had the least amount of detail. He could imagine young Vietnamese and Americans picking their way through unexplored wasteland, sweating, bruising and cutting themselves on sharp undergrowth. He also imagined them with unquenchable thirst, draining their canteens of the last few ounces of stale water. Only the knowledge that the way back to civilization was probably no better than the tortuous path ahead, to where they were due to link up with other bands of sweating Vietnamese and Americans, kept them going. The denser the jungle the more wary they would become of the dangers of ambush. All manner of flying and crawling insects would engulf them, intensifying their dread of sudden death or mutilation by machine gun fire at close range. Their curses would be brief and muted. There was seldom much idle talk in the bush. Do recalled how he had hated combat patrol duty worse than anything else when he had been a squad leader in the old French Colonial Army. His heart went out to the poor souls represented by the blue marks on the map. No one who had not had to find his way through the jungle could ever understand what misery it could be.

The scale of the operation confirmed what Do had suspected all along — that Paul had tried to feed him a cock-and-bull story about being ready for a big North Vietnamese attack. It was true that the *Bo Dai* were present in ever greater numbers, but Do began to feel that he just might have a better understanding of American politics than they did themselves. It took no deep analysis to discern the need in Washington for a victory to squash the anti-war voices which were becoming bolder and more strident with the publication of each casualty list. Whether Paul and the other officers at the Field Force headquarters realized it or not, it was almost a certainty that increasingly frantic messages from Washington to MACV in Saigon were calling for more aggressive action. (But, of course, more aggressive action with fewer casualties!)

Like water, Do knew, political orders to the military in America flow downhill. Whatever "advice" or "military professional judgment" might be offered back up the chain, the political view calls the shots. It makes little difference what the real military situation is, the political interpretation is the one that counts because that is the one that pinches the officials where they feel it. That was not at all the Vietnamese way. In Saigon the Army was the government.

As it was, Do guessed, there were probably few differences at the moment between the thinking at MACV and that in Washington. MACV probably would have approved the scope of Giant City whether Washington had been on their backs for more action or not. But there were some things that made him uneasy about the whole business.

First, he was deeply disappointed in the way Paul had treated him. Certainly Paul couldn't have believed all the crap he had tried to feed him before the operation. If he did, then perhaps Do had vastly overestimated the acuity of the American's mind. If Paul knew better — and Do believed he did — then why hadn't he leveled with him? Do could have dutifully passed on to his boss any "official" explanation the Americans wanted to convey. Do had hoped that the common experience at the staff college would have bound the two officers a little more closely than that, and that they would have been able to exchange opinions frankly. It wasn't like Paul to suddenly start mouthing some party line. Unless, that is, something had happened to diminish his trust in the relationship. It was an awkward thought.

Another thing that bothered him was the question of the real depth of the American dedication to the war effort. Giant City was a big undertaking. What would happen if the operation fell upon a vacuum in the middle of War Zone C, and they had nothing to show for it? Could the American leadership survive the political cat-calls and scorn of its critics? Do wondered if the VC leadership had made a similar assessment. It reminded him of the old joke that made the rounds among the students at Fort Leavenworth that all the enemy had to do was to lay low until the Americans got bored with the whole thing and went home. But he knew that it could only be a joke. The VC needed victories as badly as the Americans did to keep their grip on the countryside. Revolutionary zeal didn't spring full blown from a pacified population. While anti-government sentiment ran deep among the people, horror and fear of some insurgent methods and distrust of the real intentions of the Northern leadership gave many cause for concern. Religious groups were particularly fearful. However oppressive the Diem regime might have been, few could be sure that the Popular Front would not be worse, and there was always the possibility that the Front was a sham for a takeover by the North. Northerners were fierce, austere people who worked all the time. Rule by Hanoi could mean the end of many of the flabbier, but more tolerable ways of the South.

Do kept his disappointment over Paul's behavior to himself, but he typed up a short memo for General Don on the implications of the Giant City operation for the future of the war. He pointed out the importance of achieving some measurable results to keep the Americans involved. It was probably obvious enough to the chief, anyway, but Do knew that both Generals Vo and Don looked to him for regular commentary on the American approach to the war. They needed his insights for dealing with their big-nosed American military counterparts.

It always amused Do when he heard Americans characterize Asiatics as "slant-eyed" or "yellow bellied." To Vietnamese, the Americans were "big nosed" or "big footed;" either way, it was unflattering.

That afternoon Colonel Tuy, the chief of staff's aide, looked into Do's office and smiled. He hadn't done so very often, so Do snapped to a position of attention and barked out a stiff, "Good day, sir."

Tuy waved him back into his chair. "Good day, Major, sit down, sit down." Do saw that Tuy had his memo to the chief in his hand. He wondered why the aide would bother to come to his office if he wanted to talk about it. He usually buzzed on the intercom for Do to report to him if he wanted something. Do wasn't particularly fond of the colonel, so the democratic gesture of coming to the intelligence officer's office put him slightly on his guard. Tuy wanted something.

"Can I offer you some tea?" Do asked. He couldn't guess how long the colonel intended to stay.

"No, thank you," the aide replied. "Just tell me what's new in the enemy situation."

Do drew a blank. Tuy had been present at the morning staff briefing, and he had accompanied the chief of staff when he came into the war room just before the noon hour. There had been only a few flimsy agent reports since then. The cooler relationship with Paul McCandless had slowed down the informal chit-chat between the two intelligence officers, much, Do supposed, to the detriment of both sides.

"There isn't much new, sir," he replied. He recited a few of the incidents which had occurred during the night and which he had reported at the morning briefing. One "Rough-Puff" squad, as the Americans called the Regional/Popular Forces they funded, had been attacked about three o'clock in the morning as their guards dozed in their shacks outside An Loc. Two dead, three wounded. Enemy losses: four dead, six others probably wounded. A late agent report mentioned formation of a new *Bo Dai* regiment in Cambodia. Reliability of the report: low.

"Thank you," Tuy interrupted. "That's fine." It was clear that that was not what he had come for.

"By the way," he went on, "this is an interesting report you prepared for the chief on the importance of Giant City to the Americans. Do you really think that this could be a 'make or break' operation for them? Are they really that fragile in their commitment to the war?"

"That might be an overstatement," Do admitted, "but there's no question but that the government in Washington is under considerable pressure to produce some results very soon. They've been pouring troops into this country for over a year now, and to judge by what their newspaper, *The Stars and Stripes*, reports of their political problems at home, they had better achieve a significant victory soon or sentiment will turn against them and the entire effort could collapse. The American Government's grip on the country is a loose one by our standards, anyway, and now it could slip completely."

"That's very interesting," the colonel repeated. "What I can't quite make out from your assessment — and what I'm sure the chief of staff will want to know — is what you feel might be most damaging to the American will. Which do you think would be worse from their point of view, a huge effort like Giant City with not much to show for it in the end, or a major battle with some heavy casualties to report back home? It would seem to me that the enemy might either let them have their little game by simply withdrawing over the border, or they might launch a major counterattack. Which do you believe would have the greater impact?"

"Well" Do began, "that's an odd way to put the question. Certainly the Americans have the firepower to break up most large counterattacks, and certainly they haven't had much luck in trapping any significant sections of COSVN Headquarters. However, as bad as an unsuccessful operation might be, I would guess that the worst thing that could happen to them would be to be hit in the rear in their base camps while most of the major units are in the field. That could be compounded by a major counterattack in the field. That could both pile up the casualty lists and make them look silly for having left their rear exposed."

"But they must have adequate defensive cover for their base camps," the colonel countered.

"Yes," said Do, "but that's not the point. The press is unsympathetic to the war effort, and every American newspaper headline would focus on how the enemy had hit them from the front and behind at the same time. Couple that with a casualty list three times the normal length, and you have a formula for destruction of their entire expedition."

"Are they really that vulnerable? Think what a price the enemy would have to pay to mount that kind of an operation," the aide argued.

"I really don't know how vulnerable they are," Do said, "but you asked me what I thought might do them the most damage from a political point of view. I don't think enemy losses have much currency in Washington. Years ago the Americans made the mistake of starting the business of reporting enemy losses by 'body count.' I can tell you that term has come to have a very negative connotation among many in the United States, and a big 'body count' — even a real one — couldn't offset the depressing effect of reports of a 'one-two punch,' as the Americans call it. It could look as though the enemy had snatched away the initiative and was killing American boys in record numbers. Believe me, I've seen the way some of the big newspapers handle stories like that, and it could be devastating for them."

"That's very interesting," Tuy said again. "I'm sure the chief of staff will want to know about that, too. And, by the way, what's new with your friend Paulding McCandless? I hear he has been promoted and moved to the Field Force staff. Is that right?"

"Yes, sir."

"That's good for you to have a close personal relationship with one of their senior officers. Do you think he'll be very influential in his new position?"

"Well, sir, I don't know if 'influential' is the right term, but he's a bright fellow, and certainly the Americans are putting a big effort into their intelligence gathering capabilities. I wouldn't be surprised to see him gain the ear of more senior officers. He was a top student at the U.S. Army Command and General Staff College.

The colonel's eyes took on a reptilian glisten about them. "Of course," he said, "these points must be quite sensitive right now. I suppose we had better not say anything further about them. I'll pass on your views to the chief, and we can let it go at that." The colonel removed the expended cigarette from its holder and dropped it into an ash tray; then he slipped the holder into the breast pocket of his smartly starched jungle fatigue uniform.

"Thank you very much, Major Nguyen Van Do. You are doing a fine job here. If you keep at it I'll put in a good word for you with the chief of staff, and perhaps we can get you promoted."

"Thank you, sir," Do replied, unenthusiastically. He sensed that the colonel was just showing off. Do was at least three years the aide's senior, and it didn't make him feel any better to be reminded that his own professional future could be influenced by the younger man. He was glad to see Tuy leave.

# TWENTY

It was most unusual to receive another message from the special source so soon after the last one. Ba hoped that it contained later details on the ammunition dump. He set about decrypting the jumble of letters. He could hardly believe his eyes as the first few words became clear:

URGENT FOR COSVN REPRESENTATIVE ALONE..."

COSVN Representative? We have no COSVN representative, he thought — unless he means Tran Hua. She's a COSVN political officer. He proceeded with the body of the message. But it didn't make sense. He checked his key words a second time. The lead address to the "COSVN representative" was clear enough, but then the letters jumbled again. He tried the code from the last message. Still a jumble. The principal text was obviously double encrypted, and he couldn't make anything of it. It was frustrating. As far as he knew, Hua knew nothing about the special source, and he couldn't imagine how the source could have known about her. He crouched over the planks where the paper lay and tried to think of what to do.

The source had never used the word "urgent" before. Perhaps it really was urgent and concerned something of major importance. Ba, wondered what it might be and how the source could have acquired a code for communication with COSVN.

He couldn't have been recruited by one of COSVN's regular agent controllers, he reasoned. If he had been he wouldn't be passing signals back through me. He had to have been contacted by someone here in the Phu Loi Group or by the courier. Only one other in the group is even aware that I have a special source. And Ly Nam has no means of contacting COSVN that I know of. As he thought about it his mind began to clear. It had to be Tran Hua. But how could she have communicated and passed on a code? Of course — the courier! Hua must have induced the courier to take her message along with mine.

Ba was growing agitated. That woman will destroy our most vital source of information. The stupid courier can be blamed for taking an unauthorized message, but the poor fellow knows nothing about the source and couldn't have refused the orders of the political officer, anyway. The best he could have done would have been to report the incident to me, but he's probably never been instructed to do so.

It had never occurred to Ba that Hua could have found out about the source or that she might ever attempt to use the military courier to gain control over him. He remained squatting on the dirt floor of his dugout with his eyes closed and his fists clenched against his ears. The pressure of his gritting teeth reminded him that he had a bad molar that probably would have to come out soon.

A thump on the canvas flap announced the arrival of the planning officer.

"Come in, Nam," Ba said. "I have a puzzle here, perhaps you can help me."

Ba explained the situation. The planner squatted beside him and examined the document.

"It appears authentic," Nam remarked, turning it over. "And you say the key words for the signature date worked for the address line? I can only imagine that at some time Hua sent the source a special code for conveying information of vital importance to COSVN — either that, or she has ordered him to accomplish some specific task, giving him the impression that he's working for a representative of COSVN right here in the D Group."

"But she doesn't represent COSVN here. She's just the political officer. I don't have to take any orders from her," Ba argued.

"That may be so," Nam replied, "but the special source wouldn't know that. If she sent the code with your courier the source would assume you were at least aware of the instructions. You can't blame him."

"All right," Ba agreed, "but I can't tolerate Hua working behind my back in an area as sensitive as this. Go find her and tell her to report to me."

Nam stuck his hand in the air to indicate agreement and rose to leave; then he turned.

"Patriot Ba, I almost forgot what I came for." He smiled a little sheepishly.

"What's that?" Ba asked,

"The reconnaissance B unit has reported that the Americans hauled extensive quantities of ammunition out of the Long Binh complex before the current offensive. We don't know if there's enough left to make a remunerative target if you wish to pursue the plans."

"Do we know the lay-out of the dump?" Ba asked.

"Unfortunately not," the planner replied, "and I think we should go slow until we have better information. The recon people also reported that the Americans have taken certain unusual security precautions to protect the dump while their large units are out in the field. If you agree, I'll instruct them to continue to scout the dump and to prepare charts of the lay-out and estimates of the protective strength. They should be able to do that in about a week; then we can consider whether to proceed before the major units return."

"Good, Nam," Ba complimented him. "I want to be quite careful with this. We can't go in there without a clear idea of what we are getting into. It could be a trap. We don't have much experience in operating against Americans and I wouldn't want our first attack to result in failure. You understand."

"I understand, Patriot Ba," Nam asserted. "We'll do our best." He pushed aside the canvas flap and departed. Ba picked up the message and folded it carefully. He itched to unload a piece of his mind into the ears of the political officer.

It was three quarters of an hour before anyone slapped the door flap again.

"Come in," Ba barked. He kept his back turned to show his disdain for the political officer, but he could see her reflection in a small steel signaling mirror he had wedged in the revetted wall.

Hua remained standing inside the door flap. "You asked to see me, Comrade Ba?" she asked evenly.

"Yes, Comrade Hua," Ba replied. "A very serious matter has arisen, and I believe you may know a good bit about it."

"And what is that, Comrade Ba?" she countered. She seemed unsure of what he had in mind.

Ba turned around and rose to his feet. He looked into her eyes and asked, "Did you give the courier a coded message to deliver to a special addressee?"

So, she thought, he knows. He really does have a secret source of information that he has not told me about. But she replied blandly, "What do you mean, Comrade Ba? You know perfectly well that COSVN requires that all special sources be reported through me in order to insure that they don't work at cross purposes with one another. Do you have such a source that you haven't reported?"

Damn her! Ba raged inwardly, but he tried to maintain close control over the tone of his voice. "Comrade Hua," he began, "there are many things which concern us here in Phu Loi Province which needn't be a burden to you or to COSVN. Did you, or did you not, give an unauthorized message and code to the military courier to be delivered to a special addressee over whom I have responsibility? Answer the question." He glared at her.

She wasn't to be trapped so easily. "The Main Political Directorate of COSVN is the best judge of what is of concern. If you have a special source which you haven't reported you can give me the details, and I'll ensure that they reach the proper authority."

Then a light dawned in her mind, Ba has received an answer to my shot-in-the-dark and he doesn't know what to do about it! She was exultant.

"Comrade Ba," she smiled malevolently, "if you have a message for me, please give it to me and let us be done with this little act." She held out her hand.

Ba was speechless. Suddenly he realized the trap which the woman had set for him — and he had stepped right into it! She was completely unscrupulous. He remained frozen, facing her for what seemed like a week. She kept her hand extended with her palm up, waiting for the paper. Her eyes bore directly into his.

At last he broke contact. He looked down at his breast pocket and slipped two fingers in to retrieve the message. He put it in her hand without looking at her again and waved her back out the doorway.

"Thank you, Comrade Ba," she said triumphantly. "In the future please see that such messages are delivered to me without delay. I note that this one is marked 'urgent.' It should be handled expeditiously." She turned to go.

Ba thought that if he had to look at her once more he might break her neck. He was furious with himself for having been so naive. Of course, he thought, she had no idea whether we had a special source or not. She was just fishing, and I walked into the net! He crouched back down on his haunches and squeezed his fists against his ears again. He could imagine nothing but ill coming from her intervention with the special source. Damn! Damn! Damn!

Within an hour Tran Hua had decoded the message and verified that it was indeed urgent for COSVN. Perhaps this would remind the authorities of the valuable part the political officer with the Phu Loi Group was playing in the great national drama. She stripped the original address and substituted the alphanumerics for the Policy Section at COSVN headquarters. Then she appended a note of explanation of how she had suspected that Van Ba had developed a sensitive source somewhere within the ARVN corps structure. She couldn't be sure that the source was actually in the corps headquarters, but she guessed as much since he obviously had an extensive knowledge of, or access to, information pertaining to American operations and practices, and, more importantly, of their political tenor. Tran was convinced that the political dimension of the war was much more important than the military, so she was delighted that the report focused on that side.

She reencrypted the entirety of her report and rang up the courier section on her field phone. The message would be transmitted by radio, but the group leader would permit no wireless equipment within a kilometer of the base camp. Transmitters were targets for B-52 attacks and he wanted no more of them.

"Courier section? Comrade Tran Hua here. I have an urgent message for immediate dispatch to COSVN headquarters. Send a class A courier to my billet now. There can be no delay. The success of current operations may hang in the balance." She rang off without waiting for a reply. A black clad boy in his early teens leaned his bicycle against a tree outside her bunker and slapped at the log over the entrance to announce his arrival. It had been less than ten minutes since her call.

Tran handed the messenger the encrypted document, folded into a small square less than five centimeters on a side. "What's your name, Comrade," she asked.

"Patriot Len Duc," came the answer.

"Good, Comrade Len Duc. This is a most important and urgent message for COSVN headquarters. Do you understand that?"

"Yes, Comrade Hua, I will take it to the transmitter site right away." The woman's tenor was a little unnerving.

"Yes, right away," she echoed, "but first you will sign here on the dispatch record. Your signature verifies that you understand how vital your mission is to the Movement, and that you will let absolutely nothing interfere with your assignment."

"Yes, Comrade Hua, I understand." The boy was glad to sign his name quickly on the clipboard she offered and to stuff the message in his pocket and depart. It had been as he had expected. None of the couriers could ever seem to get away from Hua without some sort of a lecture on their duties. She always seemed to make one feel guilty about the slightest inattention to duty. She was like a stern conscience to the entire D group. The message weighed like a millstone in the boy's pocket until he delivered it forty minutes later to the transmitter station and received his receipt.

# *TWENTY-ONE*

Late in the afternoon fragments of reports of contacts with enemy units began to filter into the TOC. At first they appeared to be isolated incidents of advance units encountering pockets of enemy resistance. It was four days since Paul had sent his warning to Colonel Dillings. As wary as he had conditioned himself to be as the operation had progressed, Paul sensed nothing ominous in the initial reports. Artillery was firing in support of the engaged units, and air support was being called in. The operations sergeant had a radio tuned in on the fire direction net.

"Shhhhhhh," it went. "Garage Three Alpha (squeal) is Awful Digger Niner One. Over. (squeal) Shhhhhh"

"Shhhhhhh, Alpha, Over. (squeal)"

"Shhhhhhh, This is (squeal) coordinates Shackle Alpha, Lima, Four, Niner, Zero (squeal) Shhhhhh ..."

The sergeant turned the radio down. It growled back at him.

How the hell can they ever fight a war with that kind of reception? Paul thought. Victories must be the products of all those compensating errors.

It was six-twenty when Sergeant Schwartz returned to the TOC from early supper with the news that the cold cuts were nothing to write home about, but that there were plenty of fresh tomatoes and lettuce, "so you can make some super 'Dagwoods' if you want to."

Paul immediately saw the irony of the sergeant's report. It was an open secret that the mess steward had a Vietnamese mistress in town who could get almost anything anyone wanted. The vegetables came from the open market where the choicest produce from the highlands was sold. In transit from Dalat to Nai Hoa the trucks had to pass through virtually undisputed VC territory and to fulfill the demands of the enemy "tax collectors" along the way. More often than not, drivers would find two or three tree limbs pulled out onto the highway to form "toll stations," with a couple of mean looking teenagers with Kalashnikovs standing behind them. The prices of the goods could skyrocket by the time they found their way into the market stalls. Then only the most wealthy Vietnamese and those who were buying for the Americans could do business. Whatever the price, good vegetables always disappeared quickly. Paul wondered how much Schwartz's Dagwood had enriched the enemy's bank account.

By seven-fifteen Paul was back in the TOC. The action seemed to have died down for the time being. The ops sergeant was fussing with the radio.

Roger Hutton showed Paul a message which seemed to indicate that the enemy may have broken contact under the pressure of the artillery fire and air strikes. Both sides were probably pulling in their skirts for the night. Paul rocked back on the hind legs of his chair and propped his boots on the top of the camp desk. It was a slightly precarious act with folding furniture, but he had mastered the skill required to maintain an equilibrium of sorts between desk and chair.

Schwartz dumped an eight inch stack of translations of captured documents and interrogation reports from the previous week on the desk. The height of the pile was daunting. Paul squinted at it, calculating that it could take him four or five hours to sort through a bundle that size. He winced at the thought.

"Am I supposed to read all this stuff tonight, Sergeant?" he asked in feigned pain.

"That's up to you, sir," the sergeant smiled. "I sent copies down to the O.B. section, so you'll have plenty of company. They'll have a team going over them all night. If you'd prefer, you can wait 'til morning and get their report."

Paul groaned. "No, I guess I get paid more than they do to look at this stuff. But let me see their report tomorrow, too. Maybe we'll find Ho Chi Minh's secret love letters in here some place. Wake me up if my head flops back over my neck."

The sergeant laughed and went back to work.

The TOC was quiet. The banks of field phones rattled dutifully each hour on a staggered schedule to prove that the lines into the main command posts of the divisions were still working. Broken lines were not a big problem in dry weather. The enemy probably would have preferred to tap into them than to cut them, anyway.

Paul sifted through the letter box numbers. He congratulated himself that he had learned to read quite a few of them the way Dillings could read map coordinates of places of note. Nothing today from the Phu Loi Battalion, he thought. He wasn't surprised — just a little disappointed.

By 11:30 he had satisfied himself of the essentials of the documents. The great bulk came from the COSVN guard regiment and from minor bureaus of COSVN itself. The rest had apparently been left behind by scattered local force units around the central part of the corps zone. Nothing earthshaking. He scribbled a short, rather dry note to Cicely, more to relieve his conscience that to communicate with her. He wrote "free" in the upper right-hand corner of the envelope where the stamp would normally go and dropped it in the carton that served as a mail box on his way out of the TOC.

Maybe the VC use small stationery so they won't have to write so much, he speculated. There are certain advantages to that.

Paul could never recall afterward whether he had actually fallen asleep or not. Somewhere in the twilight between wakefulness and sleep he felt himself being raised from his bunk and hurled against the opposite wall of his living trailer. The iron bunk crashed down on top of him, and the entire contents of the room, together with a spray of glass from the window, flew from their places to envelop him as the entire structure smashed over on its side. The action was accompanied by a tremendous explosion from somewhere outside. Subsequent explosions set his ears ringing and had him gasping for breath. His left leg pained him, and he could feel a warm dampness oozing from his scalp. Other than that he seemed to be okay.

His first thought was that an enemy rocket had hit the trailer, and he half expected a hundred screaming gooks to come piling in through the smashed window — which now faced straight up. He was surprised at how much light there was in the room once he uncovered himself from the debris. It came from the window, now serving as a sky light, admitting the reflected illumination of pyrotechnics accompanying each explosion. The trailer, mortally wounded, continued to shudder as each blast occurred, but at least, Paul thought, it now lay in a stable — if unnatural — position.

Sudden terror welled up inside him as he realized that he was unarmed. He searched wildly for his pistol and his flak jacket, pulling at piles of twisted clothing, bedding and furniture covering the erstwhile wall — now the floor. He couldn't find the jacket, but he recovered his pistol and ammunition belt from under the foot locker. He checked to make sure the automatic was loaded. It was. He swung the belt around his waist, hooked it up, jammed the weapon into the holster and began to search for his boots. It took another five minutes to find both and to get his feet into the right ones. Calls to his trailermate, Hutton, went unanswered.

He tried the door. It was hopelessly sprung and wouldn't budge. It had to be the window — sky light — whatever. He had an odd sensation of standing in the hold of a freighter at sea while a battle raged overhead. He pulled the footlocker free and pushed it up against the floor. Then he wedged the cot frame between the foot locker and the opposite wall and climbed up the exposed springs like a fireman on a ladder. Poking the remaining glass out of the window with a broom handle, he reached for the sill and pulled himself outside. The exertion winded him for the moment.

The scene around him was pandemonium. In the distance huge balls of fire and clouds of smoke rose over the ammunition dump as stacks of munitions exploded, sending shrieking missiles flying in all directions. Closer by, half clad men were shouting and running every which way. Intense fire seemed to be coming from the west. Paul guessed that some enemy might have penetrated the perimeter of the sprawling installation and seized ground between the headquarters and the ammo dump. No one seemed to be shooting in his direction, so he slid down the roof of the trailer and worked his way around to the rear window to see if Hutton was still in his room. He reached through with the broom and probed among the piles of the man's belongings until he was satisfied that no one was there. His trailermate must have been on duty in the TOC when the attack began. Paul turned and started in that direction. He tried to run; pain jabbed at him. He must have pulled a muscle in his leg. No time for that now. Limp, goddamit, but get over there. Fast!

The TOC was bedlam. Every phone seemed to have a man attached, either shouting into the mouthpiece or trying to scribble down whatever some faint voice might be trying to get across over the cacophony of the room. Paul got a quick report from Hutton, who seemed surprised and genuinely pleased to see him. Then he took the phone from the duty clerk handling the line to the forward CP. He caught the tail end of a report. It laid out in code a three square kilometer target for an immediate "Arc Light" strike. B-52s. The big stuff.

"I don't know if there are any birds in the air right now," he heard himself shouting into the receiver. "What's the target?"

"I gave it to your duty clerk there, Colonel," the voice replied. "We're ass-hole deep in VC, and we may have to evacuate this position. We have artillery and tac air coming in now, but we need 'Arc Light.' There must be a million VC out there. What can you do for us?"

"Okay," Paul replied, "I'll see what we can do. Maybe we can get someone else's birds diverted your way. Oh, and by the way, tell Colonel Dillings we're under some screwy sort of attack here now, too. It looks like Charlie's gotten into the ammo dump, and he's breaking up all the dishes. Can you hear that in the background?"

Paul never heard the answer. A huge explosion shook the building, and something smashed down on the side of his head, knocking him virtually senseless. When his eyes cleared he realized that he was lying on the floor looking up at a circle of faces. His head felt as though it were in a vice. A touch to his hair brought out a bright red mess on his hand.

"Just what the hell was that all about?" was all he could think of to say as he tried to sit up.

"You just lie there for a while, Colonel. You'll be okay. We have a medic coming to look at you. You got a nasty bump, but it doesn't look too bad." It was Sergeant Schwartz.

"Hey," Paul called out. "The forward CP is awash in VC, and they need B-52s. Did you get the message?"

"Yes, sir," the sergeant assured him. "We're trying to get through to Saigon now. If there is anything in the air we'll get it."

Paul looked down at his assailant lying next to him on the floor — a large electric fan, probably left over from the French days.

"My god," he groaned, "I came half way around the world to be attacked by GE's most important product. Do I get the Purple Heart for this?"

"If you do," the sergeant laughed, "you'll have to spend all your time fending off jokes about which was worse, the moment the shit hit the fan, or the fan hit you." He picked up the fan and tried to straighten out the guard wire. "You really messed up a perfectly good fan, Colonel. That's government property, you know."

Paul's head hurt too much to take any jokes at the moment. The explosions continued outside, but less frequently than before.

All the big stuff must have gone up in the blast that shook the fan down on me, he thought. He closed his eyes to shut out the glare of the bare electric light bulb overhead and waited for the medic.

"You'll survive, Colonel," was the medic's encouraging word. "We'll get some x-rays as soon as we get you over to the hospital."

"Look," Paul protested, "there's a war going on all over the corps zone. I just got hit by a flying fan. I don't need x-rays."

Two litter bearers had nudged their way through the onlookers. They squatted down, paying no attention to his protestations of ambulatory capability. With the help of a couple of others, they eased him onto a stretcher and strapped him down. In a couple of minutes he found himself being slid into the back of an ambulance. They wouldn't even permit him to sit up in the vehicle to soothe his rumpled self-respect. He felt like a dolt. He had forecast high probability of enemy counterattack in the field, but had sensed nothing which might have indicated an attack on the Long Binh ammo dump. He wondered what the batting average for intelligence officers had been in earlier wars. And he wondered if they got carried out of their operations centers on stretchers just when the action had begun. It was humiliating.

He woke up some unmeasurable time later to see Captain Daniels smiling down at him. The night had been an exhausting succession of x-rays, poking fingers, lights in his eyes, and needles and thermometers stuck into him from all angles. At length he had been allowed to sleep, but it seemed that there was a conspiracy among the hospital staff to insure that his rest was intermittent at best. Finally, he began to feel that he could deal with the real world. Daniel's smile helped.

"OK, Captain, so I crapped out in the middle of the action. What happened?"

The captain's smile broadened into a grin. "Colonel, we cleaned their goddam clocks! We smashed their attack at Tay Ninh, and we smeared 'em here in the base camp. They wasted a lot of our ammo, but I doubt that more than a handful of the bastards got away in one piece. The perimeter force is out chasing them up north now."

"That's great. Any idea who it was that hit us here?" The captain reached into his pocket and pulled out a small piece of paper. Paul took it and glanced at the neat Vietnamese lettering. He was about to hand it back when he noticed what the captain had wanted him to see. He could hardly believe his eyes. The name JOHN PAULDING MCCANDLESS stood out in block letters.

"What the hell is this? Where'd you get it?"

"It was in the pocket of the one of the guys who broke into the compound last night, sir," the captain replied. "We figure they must have been looking for you."

"What the hell for? And how in blazes would the VC know who I am, anyway?"

"Take it easy, Colonel. The sawbones say you have a concussion and are supposed to rest."

"Rest, hell, I'm OK."

"Not for a couple of days, I don't think, sir."

"Don't give me a lot of crap, Captain. I want to know why a gook would be carrying my name around with him on an attack mission. What does the rest of the paper say?"

"We haven't had a proper translation made yet, sir, but it seems the guy who had it was looking for you. It identifies your sleeping trailer by number — look on the back. There's a sketch."

"Goddam!" Paul exclaimed. "This stinking war is beginning to get pretty personal."

"Yes sir. I don't know why they'd be after you, but they must have gotten to the trailer shortly after you left to go to the TOC. There were at least three of them who apparently snuck through the wire just about the time of the first blast in the ammo dump. We zapped two on the way out. And we probably got the other with artillery afterward, outside the perimeter. We have a detail out there scarfing up bodies now."

"How do you know they got to my trailer?"

Daniels laughed. "Just wait 'til you see it, sir. I'll guarantee that if you had trouble with mice or roaches before, Charlie's cured your problem. It's so full of holes now it looks like a screened porch. On top of that, they threw a grenade in the back window."

"That's not my room."

"It is now, sir," the captain chuckled. "There're no walls left inside."

"Good god, did they burn it out?"

"I guess they gave it a pretty good try. But, no. It didn't burn. Sergeant Schwartz has some of his men over there now trying to sort out your stuff. You didn't have anything valuable there, did you, sir?"

Valuable? No. Just Anne's letters, he thought. He wasn't sure he could remember the address. He wished he'd thought of Cicely's letters first. Damn it all. He closed his eyes.

# TWENTY-TWO

Ba was despondent. The attack on the ammunition dump was a technical success, but the price was all out of proportion to the gains. The Americans were rich and would soon replace the munitions which had been destroyed, but it would be a long time before he might again see the likes of the brave patriots who had gone to martyrdom at Long Binh.

He cursed the inflexibility of his orders. The D group had not been ready for the operation. Long Binh was not even in Phu Loi Province. None of the unit's people came from there, and yet COSVN had insisted that it proceed as though all reconnaissance were complete, all planning done, and the enemy could be taken by surprise. In reality, none of these essential factors pertained. The only aspect of the action that prevented complete disaster was the small size of the actual assault force.

There had been no time to acquire sufficient mortar ammunition, and they had to use home-made torpedoes to blast through the Americans' perimeter wire. Home-made weapons could be all right against government outposts in dry weather, but to have to rely on dubious fuses against American troops was highly risky. There was barely time to infiltrate snipers into Ho Nai to harass the Americans as the sappers moved in to plant their satchel charges on the ammunition piles. Worst of all, COSVN had insisted upon dispatching a special mission squad to capture or eliminate an American intelligence officer, but the squad had been unable to locate their quarry and spent precious minutes running from one structure to another trying to find him. Ba's men had to remain inside the American installation, exposed to murderous fires from two or three sides, in order to support the COSVN squad. He cursed himself for ever mentioning the coincidence of names of the Field Force commander and the staff officer, McCandless.

So far, only fifteen of the assault team members had returned. Considering the violence of the American reaction, including tactical air strikes from Bien Hoa airbase, it was quite possible that most of the others had been killed or captured. Tears gathered in the corners of Ba's eyes as Ly Nam read from a list of those known dead, wounded or missing. Ba crouched on the packed dirt floor of the hut he had used as a temporary headquarters and struck the sides of his head with his fists. It was the greatest tragedy to befall the Phu Loi D Group since he'd been elected to command. How could he ever expect to hold the patriots' confidence again after ordering them into such an ill-conceived operation? He felt physically ill.

He realized, too, that he had committed a grievous error in not having kept his focus on the progress of the attack when the first wounded were brought back. It was a foolish risk to run; he might have missed an opportunity to escape an enemy counterattack — or, more importantly, to exploit successful surprise if there was a chance for accomplishing more than what the plan called for. Ba had long suspected that he might be more of a physician than a combat leader. If that were so, so be it. He was only one man.

He had gone immediately to work on young Tran Do Sin, a boy of barely sixteen when the porters carried him in. The lad had a 175 gram chunk of meat excised from his left arm by an American grenade thrower. Miraculously, the projectile had not exploded as it careened off the bone, leaving the boy looking as though he had been bitten by a wild animal. Ba had reassembled the humerus as best he could, removing the slivers for which he could find no fit. Then he had stitched the remnants of the triceps together where he could identify similar tissues. It would be days before he could get the boy under an X ray machine to find out how bad the damage really was. The wounds of the others had not seemed so serious. The patriots who needed his attention the most had not returned. Those who couldn't make it back on their own had grenades they could use if they didn't want to fall into the enemy's hands alive.

Ba tried to refocus his mind on the immediate problems. He had to reassemble whatever was left of his small assault force and get it back to the base area as quickly as possible. Of the better part of his C-3 unit to begin with, only twenty-three patriots could be accounted for. There was, to be sure, reason to hope — no, even to expect — that others had escaped the terrible American firepower. They could straggle in over the next few days if they were not hunted down by American patrols or the government combat police. Ba couldn't risk the safety of the rest of his force by waiting for them. He instructed Nam to alert the local hamlet guerrillas to be on the lookout for them. The guerrillas could take them into their own homes, nurse those needing care, and get them on their way when it might be safe to do so — or whenever it might become more dangerous to harbor them than to put them out.

The march back to the base was arduous. American defoliation flights had turned vast tracts of the jungle into stands of pale gray scarecrows, especially in the traditional havens for outcasts, outlaws, the Viet Minh, and now the Viet Cong. The march had to be accomplished entirely in darkness to avoid enemy airborne spotters who were as numerous as the mosquitoes that swarmed after the little column.

Unlike the main forces, regional units didn't have the luxury of secure, well equipped base camps waiting for them across the

Cambodian border after a combat operation. If they were detected on the march they were sure to be dogged by artillery, aerial rockets and bombs unless they dispersed and sought individual safety in the forest. And often, even after they made it — if they made it — they could expect B-52s to pummel them, perhaps for days and nights after their return.

They often turned toward alternative rest areas to avoid drawing enemy attention to their real destinations. Regional battalions had no Cambodian sanctuary "pits" to flop down into, with waiting cadres to nurse, feed, pay and refresh them. For them, war could be a continuing, sweltering, unforgiving hell. These were the men and women who used the term "patriot" most often, and who took the greatest pride in it.

When at last the exhausted assault group staggered into the base camp at 4 am three days later, it was surrounded by a cheering crowd of Phu Loi warriors. Men and women, boys and girls anxiously ran down along the length of the column, searching for friends and unburdening the marchers of their weapons and the wounded. Men who couldn't complete the march on foot and couldn't be entrusted to hamlet guerrillas along the way had been slung in hammocks and carried beneath bamboo poles.

The reunion began as an event of greater excitement in the darkness than it would end, as the realization of how heavy the losses had been became apparent. Wives began searching for husbands with bottles of fresh, cool water, only to become increasingly fearful and ultimately seized with shock and despair as they learned that their men were not in the column. The marchers smiled wan smiles of appreciation for the gestures of welcome, but they shied from the torrents of questions from their compatriots. They were vague. They were tired. They didn't know. They suggested that the greeters ask others what had become of husbands, sons and fathers. Surely they would turn up. Certainly many others got away who could not get back to the reassembly points. And there were many who were taken in by the people of the hamlets along the way. They would be nursed back to health and would rejoin their loved ones. They were seasoned soldiers and they would survive. Surely. What else could anyone say?

Ba's depression intensified as he entered the bunker to brief the staff on the outcome of the operation. Inside he hunkered down, tipped back against the revetted wall, and let his legs slide out from under him. It was bad form — Western. He didn't care. He was losing his sense of control over events anyway. Let others believe what they would about him. He would continue to do the best he could as long as his compatriots wanted him.

There were no questions about his behavior or about the efficacy of the effort to begin with. The patriots heard him out, taking notes on his comments, each one focusing on matters of particular concern to his area of responsibility. Duan Suc, the supply officer, resolved silently to lay in a quantity of mortar ammunition and Bangalore torpedoes no matter what COSVN said. He would violate the rules and trade materials with friends in the supply train so that the Phu Loi D Group wouldn't again be caught "out in the rain" when it was directed to perform such an attack. He had a brother in a local hamlet guerrilla C group who could hide the goods. He wouldn't let Van Ba down again. He would do it on his own responsibility. No one else need know about it — not even Ba. Le Phe would be the exception. Someone else would have to know in case anything ever happened to Duan, himself.

Tran Hua listened to Ba's report in silence, taking copious notes on every aspect of the operation — especially Ba's comments on the lack of preparation of the D group. Her fingers danced the pencil along the page with phenomenal speed, slashing the letters with diacritical marks, recording virtually every word that was said. Ba wasn't surprised by the woman's attention to detail. He had occasionally joked that the Movement would have a better record of the war with her behind a pencil than the government would have with all its bureaucrats in Saigon.

Ba held nothing back. He related the deficiencies of the assault group — and his own — as though he were describing an event far away involving some third party. Later he would commit his thoughts to paper, but it was important that the staff hear him now so that the members might begin the process of retraining the cadres and rebuilding the C-3 unit. It would take time.

Some of the things he said he half-realized he would probably regret later. Especially since Hua would have a verbatim record. Damn the woman! But he was too tired to care. COSVN had placed too heavy a load on the shoulders of the D group — and on him.

"We are patriots," he said. "We aren't warriors. We never went to war academies in China or the USSR. We don't have large cannon or rockets. Even the tanks we liberated last year were taken from us for use by the *thoat ly*, the main forces. And we have never tried to attack an American base camp before. We were simply playing out of our league, as they say in the West. We were unprepared from the supply point of view, and from the operational view, too. We had made some rudimentary reconnaissance of the camp, but we had no detailed knowledge of the layout.

"On top of that, we had to provide support to a COSVN special mission squad when we really didn't know what they were after. I'm not sure they did. They had to hunt around for their target, and never did find him. In the meanwhile, our brave men had to maintain the escape route under very heavy enemy fire. If it hadn't been for that COSVN team's delay we might not have taken half the casualties we did.

"As far as the ammunition dump is concerned, we couldn't be sure that there were any stocks left, considering all the truckloads we had watched departing for the Americans' aggression against COSVN up north. Fortunately, as it turned out, there was still plenty for our brave sappers to waste with their ingenious satchel charges."

The mention of the satchel charges brought a moment of smiles to the group — particularly to the somber face of Duan Suc. His teams had been collecting the explosives from unexploded 250 and 500 pound bombs scattered around the province by enemy aircraft. It had been extremely dangerous to attempt to disarm them in the beginning, but a team of technical experts from COSVN had paid a visit some six or eight months previous and shown the patriots how to do it. After that, Suc's men had devised some special tools for disassembling the fuse devices and extracting the principal charge material.

Then they had refashioned the explosives into five kilo chunks which were easy to carry and still sufficient for command detonated mines, and more particularly in this case for placing on the American munitions piles at Long Binh. There was a special justice in using enemy explosives to detonate other explosives intended for use against the patriots. Sweet justice. Smiles

When Ba finished his report he looked around the group to see their reaction. There was silence, but they didn't avoid his eyes. That was good. They weren't ashamed of him. They looked at him as they always did. He was their leader. They were ready to copy down any instructions he might have for them; they were ready to do his bidding again if he asked. A gush of emotion welled up inside him, and he had to look aside and pretend to cough to conceal a sob. He loved these men like his own brothers. How could fate treat them so badly, and why had he to be fate's instrument?

"I'll have some specific instructions for you later on, my comrades." That was odd. He seldom addressed them with the correct "comrade" term. But that is what they were: comrades. Why not say it? Ba was no Bolshevik, but he would say what he wanted and have it mean what he wanted. They would understand. If they thought he was insincere they could expel him from the D group leadership. His fate was in their hands as much as theirs was in his. That was the way it had to be.

The small staff waited for Ba to move. He always rose and exited the meeting cell first, but this time he just continued to sit there, looking at them. Finally, Tran Hua broke the silence.

"Comrade Ba, I'd like to have a word with you in private."

Ba looked at her. She was probably the last person on earth he wanted to have a private session with at this moment; but he knew he couldn't say no. She had plenty of ammunition to fire at him, and he might as well hear her out. She would be circulating among the B and C units, spreading her poisonous ideas anyway — especially about him. Maybe she used his name; she was forever talking about crypto-bourgeoise who didn't really understand the teachings of Ho Chi Minh and the great leaders of the North who were purifying the country of its venal rot. The "rot" seemed to infect a lot of people, Ba thought: the rich land owners, the Catholics, the militarists, the Francophiles, the America lovers, the Nung Chinese, the Diemists, the *Hoa Hao*, the *Cao Dai*, the Buddhists, the Mandarins and the shop keepers. Ba wondered how she could hate so many people at one time. He wondered, too, if she had to write them all down in her books just to keep them straight. Keeping book on enemies of the people, he thought, must be a heavy burden for a conscientious political officer.

The others looked at Ba. He nodded, and they rose to file out. Half defensively, Ba pulled his legs back up underneath him and assumed a correct Vietnamese crouch with his tail off the floor. He was damned if he was going to let her criticize him for sitting like an imperialist. Besides, the squat raised his eyes to her level. If she had more political crap to shovel at him he wasn't going to take it on the low side of the balance.

No sooner had the others gone than Hua started in: "I have warned you many times, Comrade Ba, that your neglectful ways in command of the D group would get you into trouble. Because you have paid so little attention to what I've said you've brought great discredit to the Movement, and now disaster to the D group."

"Wait a minute, Hua," Ba interrupted. "As I recall, it was you who opposed our early planning for the attack on Long Binh. No thanks to you — or to COSVN, for that matter — the part we were planning, the strike against the ammunition dump, was well executed. Where we took the casualties was in that idiotic search for a particular American officer. What was that all about, anyway?"

"That was the whole point of the operation," Hua spat back at him. "Your precious ammunition dump caper was permitted only to provide cover to a highly sensitive effort to capture a prisoner of enormous potential political importance. The valiant COSVN fighters, of which you speak so disparagingly, were to seize an officer we believe to be the nephew or other close relative of the American Field Force commander, right there at Long Binh. Of course, you view matters so narrowly that you can't understand the real dimensions of a blow like that. You are so engrossed in petty details of no more than tactical importance that you miss entirely the concept of the political master stroke.

"But that is not your greatest shortcoming. You don't understand what this struggle is all about. You've learned nothing from all my efforts. If it were in my power I would have you expelled from the Movement. But you're fortunate that COSVN has great patience. Instead of complete expulsion for your wrong-headedness, you are being ordered to leave here no later than next week to go to the reeducation center in a neighboring country for three months to learn how to properly lead a D group in the People's Revolution. You'll learn what is really important — how to inspire the patriots with real revolutionary spirit, not this watered-down 'liberalism' you picked up in Paris.

"Comrade Ba, you don't seem to realize how dangerous your ideas are to the Movement right now in its hour of greatest trial. Your kind of bourgeois thinking seems to infect the entire D group. The soldiers think you want them simply to throw the Americans out, along with the evil men they support in the government. You don't understand that we stand for much more than that. We're part of the great world revolution of workers and peasants. We're fighting for a free and independent Vietnam, but one which is united, North and South; one which will provide leadership to our comrades in Laos, in Cambodia, and in Thailand. We will reinspire our brothers in the Philippines, the Hukbalahaps, to rise again to overthrow the fat capitalists in Manila, together with their American masters, who try to enslave them with their deceptive tricks — their 'Peace Corps' and their so-called 'Asian Development Bank.'

"You'll learn all about these things, Comrade Ba, at the retraining center. The scales will be peeled from your eyes, and you'll come to understand how great the Movement is. You'll meet some brothers from other countries and will learn how dependent they are upon the success of our great revolution for the success of their own liberation movements.

"We're part of a great international march for the freedom of all proletarian men and women everywhere. When we gain victory, they gain victory. Then we will have real freedom under the dictatorship of the Lao Dong Party. We'll have a united and peaceful Vietnam, but we'll not lapse into the fat, easy ways of the bourgeoise. We have an historic mission to fulfill. You'll see, and you'll learn."

Ba was only mildly surprised at the news. Hua had been working for this for months. But it was still disappointing. The session with his faithful D group staff had raised his spirits temporarily. The intensity in their eyes had reassured him that they had not lost their respect for their leader. Hua's words brought him back to reality.

"Let me see the order, Comrade Hua."

Hua fished into the pocket of her blouse and brought forth a neatly folded bit of rice paper. She unfolded it and began scanning the sheet, tracing the focus of her eyes with her finger. "Here it is, Comrade Ba, paragraph six."

"Paragraph six! That must be a general message! What kind of security is that?" he demanded. "How long have you had it? Let me see it."

He snatched the paper from Hua's hand, almost tearing it. Paragraph six listed twenty-seven names of patriots who had been selected for "retraining." He found his own near the end. This was COSVN's way of publicly humiliating those who seemed to be deviating from the correct path — and the numbers seemed to be increasing every week.

Ba suspected that it was not so much that more patriots were "deviating" as it was that the rules were changing. He had heard that the elected leaders of the National Liberation Front (NLF) were finding less and less to do in the administration of the Movement. They were Southerners, and while most were sympathetic to the communists, a number were simply nationalists and had no visible ties to the Lao Dong Party. One or two had been replaced since the original appointments, but Ba had thought nothing of that. It seemed natural enough that changes would occur from time to time under the austere living conditions in the jungle. Now, however, there were rumors that some NLF leaders were finding that many of their decisions were being made for them — and that the decisions were being made in Hanoi, not in the South.

Ba had mused at times that perhaps it had been a mistake to accept command of the Phu Loi D Group. Maybe he should have been a full-time physician, with real medical equipment and medicines. He might have worked deep in one of the War Zones. Perhaps there he would've been able to do more for the future of his country than he ever could hope to accomplish as a D group leader. Maybe.

What seized him now, however, was not his lost career, or even the humiliation of removal from command. It was the publicity given his name in a general message. He didn't care about it so much for himself — it wasn't his real name anyway, but he knew that the enemy knew who he was and would be bound to capture a copy somewhere. The Americans or government intelligence could figure out that the Phu Loi D group was in trouble. Maybe they could exploit his absence to destroy the local guerrilla units and infrastructure in the province. A lot of the locals counted on the D group for protection from government patrols, especially the hated combat police, still operating long after their founder, Diem's younger brother, Nhu, had died.

"Comrade Hua," he said, much louder than he intended, "you must get this order rescinded. It's a gross violation of security. The enemy knows that 'Van Ba' leads the Phu Loi D group. They'll hear about this and know that I'll be away for three months. We can't permit that."

"I'll do no such thing," Hua sneered. "I've repeatedly explained to you why the retraining session is necessary. Once should have been sufficient. You're so full of bourgeois ideas you cannot hear or understand anything I tell you. You must do as you're directed or I'll have you arrested and shot. And don't think I'll shirk my revolutionary responsibility."

Ba suspected that she would be only too pleased to give the orders: "Ready, aim ..."

"Look, you stupid woman," he heard himself saying, "I don't care about your silly retraining or about a three month rest for the D group. It certainly needs it. I don't even very much care if you want to have me permanently removed from leadership. I'm sure you've tried many times to get me fired." The bitter words piled out of his mouth like vomit. "This is a matter of the security of the D group, and maybe all of Phu Loi Province. I won't stand for it. Now get your ass out of here and make sure that a copy of the rescission is clipped to every copy of the general message." He was shouting at her now.

But Hua was ready for this. She had dealt with Southern revisionists before. "Comrade Ba," her voice turned oily. "You will address me as you know you should. For all your Western education you have not learned manners. Nor have you learned anything about security. COSVN messages are handled strictly in accordance with the regulations of the Revolutionary Security Committee. They are not distributed to everyone in the Movement."

"Of course they aren't, you bitch." Ba had lost control. "There have to be enough copies made to insure that every enemy intelligence officer gets at least three. Has there ever been a general message that didn't, sooner or later, fall into enemy hands? Damn it, woman, some issues have been reproduced on the front page of the *Saigon Times!* Now get this order rescinded. I'll go if COSVN wants me to. Have them send me a special message, but they must stop this one."

Special messages, Hua knew, were much more limited in their content and distribution. Because they usually pertained to operational and intelligence matters, they went by radio or telephone and could be decrypted only with the use of special message one-time code pads. Consequently, seldom did more than a very few persons know what they said. Hua thought for a moment before replying.

"No, Comrade Ba, I won't ask for a rescission. COSVN knows the purposes of the different types of messages, and it understands the security risks entailed in broader distribution of important information. It is you who does not understand the situation.

"COSVN uses general messages to spread information which it believes important to the Movement. Great victories, like the one just achieved in Tay Ninh against the American imperialists are announced in general messages. We should have a new one soon giving the details. Perhaps it will even include some mention of the Phu Loi D Group's diversionary attack on Long Binh — in spite of your bungling.

"You objected to the attack because you never understood its purpose. If you had been studying more revolutionary warfare and less bourgeois medicine you would have grasped the principle of deep battle. As early as 1922 our Soviet brothers were developing concepts for military operations which will forever be over your head. They invented the idea of simultaneous strikes at the enemy's front lines and at his vulnerable rear entrails. General Vo Nguyen Giap refined these principles in 1954 and gave us the great victory at Dien Bien Phu. Because of his genius, we no longer have to fight your French friends any more. You don't know these things because you're a simple physician playing at war. You read a little Sun Tzu and you think you can command a unit of the People's Liberation Army.

"Comrade Ba, you are a fraud, and COSVN knows it. That's why it has published a general message — so that all the workers of the Movement will know what happens to your ilk. The Movement can't tolerate back-sliders like you. I just hope that the Revolutionary Retraining Center can get that into your thick head.

"Now, I don't think that there is anything more to be said about this. Go and inform the staff and start your preparations for the trip. If you do not, I will have to inform the staff myself. I have plenty of other work to do to get this group back together politically and psychologically after you wasted it so badly at Long Binh. We'll begin fresh revolutionary doctrine lectures this evening. I haven't much time. Better that you pass the news. Now go."

Ba felt utterly defeated. He knew she was right about the way COSVN looked at things. His was a narrow, technical perspective in their view. They attached more importance to public humiliation of "deviants" that they did to the security of a regional D group. They could always recruit — by force if necessary — more patriots to take the place of those who might fall to enemy fire if the enemy were to exploit the intelligence it gained. What it couldn't tolerate was political deviation of a man in a leadership position in the Movement.

To begin with, Ba was a Southerner. He had believed that the South might develop into a free and independent state after the French left. "Uncle" Ho Chi Minh had seemed to represent the aspirations of the Vietnamese peoples, but Ba had worried about some of his colleagues. They didn't say much, but they showed little warmth.

Now that Ho was gone, the leaders of Lao Dong seemed more interested in strengthening discipline in the Movement than in the institution of liberal principles — the very ideas which Ba and his friends had talked about with such fervor in the coffee houses in Paris. And the Northerners seemed considerably more interested in placing themselves in important positions in the South than they were in helping the poor people who were suffering so terribly as a result of the war.

Ba couldn't be sure that COSVN wouldn't replace him with a Northerner. The Phu Loi D group was not a main force unit. If they fired him they might feel obliged, for appearances sake, to accept a replacement chosen by the patriots of the group. Certainly Hua had reported the close relationships which Ba had with his staff and commanders. If one of them was elected in Ba's place, he might prove even less pliable than Ba himself. Maybe that was why he was to be "retrained." It was probably a last effort to press Ba into the mold of the correct revolutionary leader. Shit!

# *TWENTY-THREE*

Paul could hardly wait for the morning briefing to begin. General Vincent Alexander, Commander United States Military Assistance Command, Vietnam (COMUSMACV), commonly known as "Alex," would be there, and for a change, Paul had some good news to report. If his guess was any good, Binh Duong Province — or "Phu Loi," as the VC called it — was about to settle down. The translation of COSVN's general message was right on top of the stack of documents flown up from the translation center in Saigon the night before. In a week or two the news would work its way up through the echelons of bureaucracy which Alex' intelligence chief had built up on the outskirts of the city, but here it was now, where and when it counted. Paul had called the division G-2s in the middle of the night to make sure they had it. He had also tried to call Do at ARVN Central Corps, but the headquarters was "closed." Goddamit! How can they close a tactical headquarters in the middle of a war — especially Sunday night, just when Charlie was most likely to be on the prowl? Paul left a message with the ARVN G-2 clerk to have Major Nguyen Van Do call him as soon as he came in. No call had come by the time Paul had to leave the TOC for the commander's briefing.

The staff was dribbling in to the briefing room, chatting with one another as Paul stepped up to the map boards to mark the points of reported or suspected enemy activity and movement during the night. Paul had briefed the events so often that he had come to know about what to expect from most of the enemy units in the corps tactical zone, as the eleven provinces around Saigon were commonly called. Each enemy unit was represented by a scarlet rectangle with lines and numbers denoting its size and designation.

Paul had also come to know many of the unit histories, the names — or at least the *noms de guerre* — of many of the commanders. He had a rough idea of the status of supply of each, the morale of the troops, their equipment and weapons, and where many of their families lived. Every night he read intercepted letters to and from wives and sweethearts, and self-criticism forms of members of the units in which they detailed their failings in thought and deed — some in past months, others stretching back for years. Paul often thought that a lot of the stuff in his files would probably be more valuable to the police if the people were ever arrested than it ever could be to American military intelligence, geared as so much of it had to be to the big operations and the attainment of high body counts.

Paul never achieved the facility Dillings had for spouting the map grid coordinates for virtually every enemy regiment and separate battalion in the CTZ. But he learned much more about their strengths and weaknesses as the months went by. He knew, for instance, that the spot on the map which "Charlie" called "Work Site 5" was really the headquarters of the 5th VC Main Force Division — as mean a bunch of bandits as roamed the woods. The division was composed of two regiments, at one time called "Q4" and "Q5," the two very different in character. From time to time they would change their names to throw Allied intelligence officers — like Paul — off their trail. Sometimes such games were successful. A prisoner who might have been told that he belonged to "Group 94" would be simply confused by interrogators who wanted to know about "Q4," even though they may be asking about his very organization. Paul's order of battle people adopted a custom of fixing one identifier for reference purposes and then entering other "also known as," or "AKAs," like a professional criminal's aliases, in a book. Q4, and Q5 received fixed designators 274 and 275.

The 274 VC Main Force Regiment was bad news. Well equipped, spirited, and well led — by men like Le Hong Phong, the commander, and Le Van Hai, his deputy, who had grown up in the very villages and towns in which they operated — the organization was a serious threat to any "Free World" force, however uneven the fire power and strength statistics might be. Paul adopted a practice of putting out a special warning to all of the intelligence sections in the Field Force whenever he was in doubt about where the 274 was located. "Unlocated" usually meant the regiment was on the move, and that the commander had some quarry in mind. As often as not, it could be an American base camp, or an air field, or a solitary unit operating away from its parent headquarters. The 274 looked carefully for its prey, like a wolf stalking the sheep dog's puppy, before it went on the move. When it struck it sprang with lightning speed out of the darkness, hurling two thousand battle hardened veterans on the enemy perimeter. If it broke in, it murdered every soul in sight and made off with hundreds of weapons and thousands of rounds of ammunition.

As far as Paul could tell, the 274 had never broken completely through an American perimeter, but it had come perilously close. American fire power was just too much. Scores of automatic weapons, artillery, helicopter gunships and tactical fighter-bombers with huge anti-personnel bomb loads would join in a hellish crescendo to strike back. And then would come the "spooky" or "dragon" ships — converted cargo aircraft, fitted with Gatling guns aimed out of the left side of the bird. The "dragon" pilots would put the aircraft into wide sweeping arcs, banking the wings to bring the gatlings to bear on the ground the VC had to traverse to reach the American positions. The effects were murderous. The electrically driven Gatlings could be set with each of the three spewing out ammunition at the rate of one hundred rounds a second, sounding more like a scream than the staccato of conventional machine guns. The bullets whipped the ground like thousands of claws searching for human flesh. A stream of flares attached to parachutes kept the killing grounds illuminated so that the gunners could do their work. The cargo hold of the aircraft accommodated tens of thousands of rounds of ammunition. The screams of the guns would be only faintly echoed by the human screams from the ground.

The 275 Regiment, on the other hand, was a hard luck outfit. It couldn't seem to ever get anything straight. Paul had read a portion of its log from a couple of months before when it was ordered out onto Highway 2 to see if it couldn't ambush an enemy convoy. The soldiers lay in ditches on either side of the road all day long, swatting mosquitoes and trying to stay out of sight of passers by. Adult pedestrians would hurry ahead, pretending they detected nothing, but betraying their knowledge with furtive glances up and down the road.

An ambush sight was not a place to be when a military convoy hove into view. Occasionally children would wander into the woods to admire the heroes in their battle positions. The soldiers would smile and wave to them, but angry B unit leaders would lecture the children on security, swear them to secrecy, and shoo them back onto the road with severe warnings.

The villagers were never comfortable when VC units were in the neighborhood, especially the 275. The soldiers were well enough behaved — certainly better than the ARVN — but they were notorious for the malaria they brought. They were as unwelcome for their parasites as they were for their needs for food and for their lightening rod like tendency to draw American fire. The 275 had a reputation as a band of bumblers, and the whole neighborhood would often suffer when they provoked a reaction by either government troops or the Americans.

This day the 275 drew only mosquitoes. At dusk the men climbed back out of their ditches and reassembled in the woods to file back to their rest area. Toward the close of the day a civilian, who was not at all pleased to have the unit in his village, rode his bicycle up to a government outpost a few kilometers up the highway and notified the commander of his suspicions of a strong VC presence. ARVN artillery took up H&I fires in the woods for most of the night. Not more than three VC fighters were injured, but no one got more than a few minutes sleep at a stretch.

The next day the 275 tried its luck again. Realizing that the presence of the regiment had been detected, the commander selected a different section of the highway. Again the soldiers scraped out firing positions just in from the edge of the woods. Again civilians walked or rode by, pretending to notice nothing amiss.

But this was Aussie territory. Having received a tip from the ARVN provincial headquarters, the Australians were out to make an issue of who ruled the roads in Phuoc Tuy Province.

Arm and hand signals alerted the VC regimental commander that a target was in sight. The soldiers pulled their camouflage tightly around them and flicked the bolts of their Kalashnikovs to chamber the first cartridges. The growing roar of the Aussie's engines heightened the tension among the soldiers. They looked at one another between the trees in anticipation and passed encouraging gestures.

The first Aussie vehicle to be seen on the highway was an armored troop carrier with its kangaroo pennant whipping in the air from the radio antenna, driving close behind a civilian tricycle Lambretta taxi. The troops held their fire.

More armored vehicles came into view. This was no soft administrative convoy against which great victories might be scored. This had the makings of yet another disaster for the regiment. The 275 had come to know disaster all too well as the war had developed. Here, quite clearly, it was about to happen again. Three hundred communist hearts began to sink. The column slowed, armored hatches clanged shut. The Lambretta engine farted black smoke and squealed its wheels, straining to accelerate out of the way. The steel battle wagons sank their treads into the macadam as they swung right and left off the highway. Dear God, the front rank of terrified soldiers thought, these monsters are coming right at us!

And many of them were. The tracked behemoths clattered forward, yawned across the ditches and smashed into the young trees. Bushes, dirt, rifles and men were ground into homogeneous messes under hundreds of tons of vehicles. Soldiers with the brims of their hats pinned up on one side rode atop the beasts, pouring out jacketed lead missiles by the thousands every minute. A few of the more quick witted VC — or perhaps those with less taste for battle — sprang from their positions, dropping their weapons to run deeper into the woods unencumbered. But the assault was merciless; most were mown down as they exposed their backsides to the fusillade. Only the density of the trees saved the remnants of the ambush teams from immediate destruction.

For many this made little difference. The Aussies had New Zealand artillerists and American fighter bombers awaiting cue to attack deeper into the woods. Napalm canisters wobbled lazily below the aircraft until striking the trees, turning the 275 planned assembly areas into roasting, asphyxiating hell holes.

Paul had noticed that the regimental report was signed by an officer who's name he had not run across before. It was a fair assumption that Ut Thoi (aka Nguyen Thoi) was no longer in command. Not surprising. If the Australians didn't kill him, he probably did the job himself. The O.B. people would pick up the new commander's name on their role of "probables."

Paul's musings were brought to an abrupt halt when an aide banged his fist on the Field Force briefing room door and swung it open in a wide arc. The gesture nearly trapped a diminutive staff officer behind it. The aide stepped inside and announced the approach of the senior American officer in the country, "Gentlemen, the Commander, U.S. Military Assistance Command, Vietnam."

Boots scuffled, chairs scraped, the principal staff of the Field Force, with sundry visitors and "straphangers," struggled to attention, jostling each other in the process. Within five seconds most were erect in neat rows, eyes riveted straight ahead at the backs of the heads of those in front. As further seconds ticked by without additional stimulus, some allowed their eyes to drift off center a few degrees to focus on the map boards Paul had posted for his briefing.

More boots could be heard approaching from the outside in cadence. Paul stiffened his posture, his eyes on the door, a pointer in his right hand, angled at 45 degrees from the floor, as though he were a cadet again preparing to recite a theorem in plebe mathematics. He never was really comfortable in his briefing job. He was reasonably confident that he knew his stuff, but he had a hunch that a professional actor would do better. He just couldn't seem to smack the pointer against the maps as smartly as others did, or to rattle off the statistics with the same alacrity.

This was quintessential military theater. The walls of the room were lined with the crests of the principal subordinate commands, interspersed with beautifully polished specimens of captured arms. Emblazoned over the maps was the insignia of the Field Force, captured in a dramatic pool of light by a strategically placed spot. The device portrayed a stark white arrow thrust upward into a red field. Roger Hutton had blasphemously described it a symbolic rape of the country by white men. Paul had laughed at the straight-faced way in which he had said it, but he was never able to get the symbolism out of his consciousness after that. Like the others, he wore a subdued version of the insignia on the left shoulder of his fatigues, and he was reminded of the analogy every morning as he dressed.

General Alexander's solid image cast a shadow across the open door for an instant before he stepped in. Paul instinctively stiffened his posture the way he had a thousand times before when an upperclassman stepped in front of him in ranks at the Point. The gesture was contagious among the staff. Not the slightest sound competed with the general's rapid stride up the isle toward the front of the room.

The general was every inch in charge in his immaculate starched jungle fatigues. His huge biceps bulged against the roll of his sleeves above the powerful haired arms tapering down to his wrists. A complex black watch covered a two inch swath of muscle above his left hand. On his right hip he wore a 9mm Browning automatic pistol, with extra ammunition clips straining against the confines of their pouches on his polished black general officer's belt. Seemingly huge black stars in clusters of four stiffened the flat of his collar.

Curious, Paul thought. He carries the same pistol I do. He certainly has a general's .32. He must not like it. Paul liked the Browning because it held eleven rounds in the clip instead of the seven in the regulation Colt .45 automatic. Besides, it looked a lot like the .45, and he thought he could get away with it.

Alexander broke the near silence with a formal, "Good morning gentlemen." A chorus responded, "Good morning, sir," but not an eyelid flickered. Each officer studied the back of the head in front of him. Paul's eyes followed the general's progress toward the front of the room to determine if he might make some gesture to which Paul would be expected to react. Alex glanced briefly at Paul. Their eyes met. Paul could read nothing from the look, so he maintained his posture.

Alex reached the front and spun around to face the staff. The Field Force commander started to make a gesture to introduce some of the senior staff in the front row, but stopped himself. Alex had assumed a familiar pose, his feet spread as though he were standing on a rocking boat deck, his hands on his hips, his jaw thrust defiantly forward. He wasn't really defying anybody. He just looked that way.

"Sit down gentlemen," he ordered. "I want to congratulate you all on the magnificent performance the Field Force staged last week in War Zone C. Under your direction and coordination our forces ripped COSVN to shreds and chased the remnants over the border. You've seen the reports of huge quantities of arms and equipment recovered. The insurgency cannot long survive under that kind of pressure. This is just the beginning of Phase II of our strategic plan. From now on we're going to be running the guerrillas to the ground.

"From now on I'll be interested first and foremost in hearing about your operational plans for carrying the fight to the enemy. Now, I don't want you to lose sight of the details of your business, but I want the main thrust focused on the offensive. Do you understand that?" All heads bobbed "yes." A few scattered "yes, sirs" could be heard here and there.

Good God, Paul thought, he won't be interested in enemy activities in the last few days. He probably won't even want to hear about the attack on the ammo dump or the Field Force headquarters. Particularly, he won't be interested in hearing about how they burned out my trailer or how the fan hit me on the head.

Paul's mind raced — what to do? He had maybe thirty seconds to think while the Field Force commander picked back up where he had dropped his effort at introductions. Paul chose his path just as all eyes turned on him to begin the briefing.

"General Alexander, gentlemen," he began. Dammit! His throat was dry and his words crackled. He cleared his throat and plunged ahead. "In the interests of time, we will dispense with the customary details and go straight to the most important intelligence development we have to report."

Not at all sure that the general had the slightest idea of what he might be talking about, Paul assumed a confident tone. "As you know, the Phu Loi provincial battalion based approximately here..." He smacked the map with his pointer, "has been among the most effective enemy local forces in the corps zone. We believe that it might have been the unit that attacked the Field Force headquarters last week, although we don't have solid evidence yet. The headquarters is located outside the battalion's normal area of operations, but the assault was conducted in a far more professional manner than we might have expected from the other possible candidates.

"We don't believe the battalions of the 275 VC Main Force Regiment are in any shape to conduct such an attack. Two of them are still smarting from the aggressive counter-ambush operation by the Royal Australian Brigade at this location," he smacked the map again in a different spot. "The other battalion is apparently undergoing retraining under new cadre recently sent down from the North in an attempt to rebuild it after it suffered very heavy casualties to 'Arc Light' strikes here." (Smack!)

Maybe I can handle this after all, Paul thought, but let's not get carried away.

"The news today is that we believe that the Phu Loi battalion commander, a particularly aggressive fellow, seems to have been recalled by COSVN to attend a three month retraining session. Besides that, we believe that the unit was very badly damaged as a result of undertaking the attack and that it will be virtually incapable of further offensive action in the absence of the commander."

"Well, what difference does that make?" the general interrupted. "I didn't come all the way up here to hear you tell me about every little scratch guerrilla outfit that sends its commander off to school." The facial expression behind the question was not friendly.

"No, sir," Paul replied, but we believe this is a key unit in the CTZ. It is not a main force unit, nor is it as well equipped, but it's considerably more aggressive and effective than many equivalent units of the main force. You may recall last summer it broke into the barracks at Phu Cuong (smack!) and stole five ARVN tanks. Three are still missing." (Paul's pointer missed the provincial capital by at least six kilometers, but the sound was so snappy that no one seemed to notice.)

"Three tanks?"

"Yes, sir. Your headquarters has the details. The point, sir, is that we have a unique opportunity now to extend the pacification effort in the CTZ. The 275 Regiment is out of commission, and never has been much good anyway, under the new Northern leadership. It's likely to be only marginally effective even when it gets back together. It would have a long way to go to reach the Cambodian border, and as poor as their march discipline has been we would probably detect it.

"Now the key provincial battalion, the Phu Loi group, appears to be laid up, too. With the rest of the 9th Main Force Division off in Cambodia, there is an opportunity to get pacification teams into Binh Duong Province and clear out the VC infrastructure — the guerrilla chiefs, the political cadres, the logistics people — the whole works."

Paul waited a moment for the idea to sink in. The unfriendly face didn't change by a whisker.

"Colonel," came the reply, "I don't think you quite understood the point I was trying to make. I said we wanted to go on the offensive — the military offensive. If we bog our people down in every little village, clearing out part-time guerrillas, we'll never wind up this war. No, I have no intention of diverting resources from the main effort — not that I understand why you, an intelligence officer, are trying to run my operations anyway." He turned to the Field Force commander.

"John, lets get on with the briefing."

The commander waved dismissively to Paul, who stepped down, yielding his pointer to the G-3 briefer. Paul felt his face redden and perspiration begin to trickle down from his forehead. Oh shit!

It was a relief to get out of the room. He drew a deep breath. This little episode was no credit to his career, assuming he was going to have one when it was time to go home. COMUSMACV had not exactly humiliated him, but the point was clear. He wasn't the sort of officer the general would want to hear much from in the future. He didn't feel quite as tall as when he had walked into the room forty-five minutes earlier.

# *TWENTY-FOUR*

Ba's departure was unceremonious. He threw a leg over his bicycle and pushed hard on the pedal. The rear wheel skidded for a moment in the dust, grabbed and yanked him forward. When he had his balance he turned for a moment to wave to the little group he was leaving beside the trail. In another moment they were out of sight. No one accompanied him. Soon he was just another peasant among the thousands, working his way along an unpaved road from one village to another with a couple of small bundles of possessions lashed to the rear fender. He could have been anyone. The only difference between him and most of the others was that he did not have a very good identity card. What he had might get him by the more casual glances of bridge guards and such, but it would be a weak reed under the scrutiny of the combat police. Really good cards could be had from COSVN or from Chinese counterfeiters in Saigon, but COSVN favored higher ranking officials, and the Chinese were greatly overpriced. Locally printed cards had to do. As long as Ba stayed off the main roads he would probably be all right.

As well founded as Ba's protestations regarding the security of the Phu Loi D Group in his absence might have been, they were unconvincing to Tran Hua. She had apparently never even relayed his concerns to COSVN. Not that it would have made much difference, anyway. It was certainly not a sure thing that a message would get anyone's attention right now. COSVN was busy recovering its balance from the American offensive, and the objections of a local force commander to an earlier COSVN decision would hardly be likely to garner much interest, no matter what the issue was. The best he could do was to warn his special source that he would be gone until further notice. The source, providing he hadn't been co-opted by the enemy, should understand that any further communications would come from someone else — not from Ba. It was curious how the source's messages seemed to be getting a little mixed up with COSVN business just before the attack on the ammo dump.

Ba found serviceable accommodations along the way. He had enough government *dong* currency to pay for lodging in villages where the Movement hadn't been able to completely impose its discipline. He was uneasy about using his revolutionary script with people he didn't know, but he pushed it where he could, counting on an immediate departure to avoid possibility of arrest by the police in case his host harbored government loyalties.

By the end of the week he was at the Cambodian border. The government had limited control in the area. On the other side he was met by North Vietnamese officers in khaki uniforms who examined his credentials closely. They provided him some rice and fish while they checked out the COSVN general order. After finger-printing, photographing, and completion of a short background record form, he was permitted to rest in a grass hut "dormitory" with others in similar circumstances. He was glad to be among friends, but he noticed that the guards were no less interested in his deportment, and that of his barracks mates, than they were in surveilling the approaches to the camp site.

The next day he and a number of others were loaded into a truck — bicycles, baggage, and all — and trundled off, deeper into the jungle to a spot where much of the undergrowth had been cleared away. This seemed to be some sort of processing center. Here they were issued uniforms, new sandals, mosquito netting, a rain cape, eating utensils, a book of approved readings, and a copy book, such as a grammar school student might carry. Bicycles, money, and personal effects were impounded. Very shortly the group found itself back on the truck for a brief ride to their destination. The arrival formalities at the retraining center were clearly tailored for their shock effect.

"I am Comrade Tien Fue Diem," the commandant shouted. "You are people who have proven unworthy of the trust placed in you in the service of the Movement. I'm here to help you come to a realization of your errors and to try once more to show you the right path of service. I'll be your commander, your teacher, your counselor, and your examiner. In three months' time I hope to be able to certify each one of you as a reliable comrade in the greatest struggle of all time. The education you'll receive here will be forceful, difficult, and comprehensive. You'll be tested and scrutinized at each step along the way. Those failing to show proper zeal and effort will be dismissed from the program and sent to other work sites for other duties.

"You will have no further communication with your friends or family. The staff of the camp and your fellow students will be your friends and family while you're here. But, as in a family, deviation from regulations will be dealt with harshly — by dismissal in the most serious cases."

Ba shrugged inwardly at the speech. He expected as much. He was just a little curious as to what sort of duties might be pursued at "other work sites." Hard labor? The "duties" of prisoners? He would have liked to have asked, but he thought better of it. Better to find out what went on here than to worry about some place else just now. Obviously, Comrade Tien didn't expect a lot of questions in response to his harangue. No need to draw special attention to himself considering he had just been informed that he had proven unworthy of the trust previously placed in him. A circle of *Bo Dai* armed with Kalashnikovs and opaque facial expressions reinforced his second thoughts.

Ba's group was immediately subjected to an intensive afternoon of physical exercises and obstacle course running in the jungle. Following a rudimentary wash-up and an early meal of rice and sprouts, each member was given writing materials and instructions to begin preparation of a more detailed personal history than any of them had been asked to write before. Particularly, Tien wanted extensive data on parents, other relatives, and friends. Then came the first of the "expressive" sessions in which they learned the party songs and marches. They imitated, as best they could, the choruses of militant workers on scratchy records and memorized approved verses for old folk tunes.

Ba didn't realize for a day or two how large the camp actually was. The retraining center was only one of multiple complexes in the installation. There was a large hospital, troop barracks, mess halls, training areas, weapons ranges, lecture halls, an amphitheater, storage warehouses and heavy equipment repair facilities. And everywhere, thousands of troops. At one point he thought he saw a tank that looked suspiciously like one of those his patriots had liberated at Phu Cuong. He felt a particular pang of irony finding himself cast in the role of a "deviant" of the Movement when not more than a kilometer away there may be as many as three tanks captured from the enemy under his direction.

He didn't have to wonder for long about the "deviations" of his companions. Each morning, after exercises and readings from theoretical writings, the inmates would recite from their personal histories the details of their misdeeds. The writing and reciting continued for four weeks while Tien and his cadremen prodded the men to criticize each other's presentations. Ba learned that he showed "too great a readiness to subscribe to bourgeois concepts and principles," and that he "seemed to attach too much importance to his healing skills and not enough to his responsibility for liberation of the masses." Dog shit! But that was how it went. He tangled half-truths with party jargon to paint similar slogans all over his colleagues' talks. It may have been unfair — so what? Who cared?

Ba was impressed by the apparent detachment of the cadremen from the war effort. He could not tell how much they really knew about what was going on. They seemed careful enough to maintain the security of the installation from overhead reconnaissance, but for the most part, their primary concern seemed to be a lot of high-flying philosophical nonsense rather than the more mundane matter of how the war was going to be won. Victory was a given. In their view, it was practically an historical fact. As they saw it, the Saigon regime was already dead. The Americans were on the verge of collapse. Each day was treated as the eve of final disintegration of whatever was left of the opponents of the armies of Hanoi. Not much was said about the Viet Cong. They played a part, too, but the real punch was the revolutionary ardor of Ho Chi Minh and his lieutenants. They constituted the liberating sword of The Cause. This, as far as Ba was concerned, was dog shit, too, but clearly no one was interested in what he really thought.

A major event in the second month of his retraining was an official visit by an inspection group from the United Nations. A Pole, a Czech, an Indian and a French woman, surrounded by an army of North Vietnamese "protocol" handlers, seemed to take their role no less seriously than did the camp authorities. But clearly the purposes of the two were quite different. Tien said as much when he briefed the retrainees on their duties and behavior while the visitors were present.

The visitors had been told, he said, that the camp was a refugee center. The inmates were to answer questions about their home villages with descriptions of how they had been driven out by government search-and-destroy operations and by American bombing. While most of the guards would keep their weapons out of sight, no one supposed for one moment that there wasn't a risk of being shot if he attempted to leave the camp. It was common knowledge that there was a second ring of guards outside the camp with orders to shoot on sight anyone attempting to climb the fence from either side. And the commandant explained that any unauthorized attempt to speak, or to pass notes to the visitors would be dealt with severely. A few retrainees would be selected to play the role of relief workers where required.

Ba wasn't surprised to find his name on the list of relief worker-actors. The prospect even excited him a little. He had had little experience in treating children, but he was delighted to have a chance to play a pediatrician, even if only for a day, rather than simply squat with the others over rice bowls as the foreigners asked silly questions. He asked for, and was given, a general text on children's diseases to brush up on. The book was old and worn, and a few pages were missing, but he chuckled to himself that it beat the book of approved socialist readings.

On the day of the visit, Ba was led to a different compound on the edge of the camp where scores of children were playing in the dust with sticks and whatever else they might have picked up. Most appeared fairly healthy. Some needed care. A few were badly undernourished or had running sores. Ba's role would be to examine and treat as many as he could until the visitors departed. If questioned, he was to say that he was hard pressed to care for the orphans of the war, and to make a plea for medicines and equipment to carry on his work. He should pick out three or four of the sick or injured and make sure that they were shown to any of the visitors with cameras.

Ba plunged into his work with enthusiasm. The clinic was better equipped than he was used to in Phu Loi. He had a small, generator-powered x-ray machine, sterilization equipment, and a good selection of medicines. Perhaps most important was a small electric fan which made the examining room tolerable. He was assisted by three women who appeared to have some experience in health aid. Other women selected the children for his examination and consoled those most fearful of his intentions.

By the middle of the afternoon he had examined the most serious cases. He withdrew from the room and stepped outside to stretch his frame and to eat the rice and bananas he had saved from the morning meal. The table he had to use for examining the children was too low for sustained work, and his back ached. A quiet moment helped lift his spirits.

Just as he finished his lunch and was glancing about for a spot to relieve himself, he noticed a woman out in the yard. A jolt of possible recognition struck him. The woman was bending over a small boy, dusting off his ragged clothing. She turned. He couldn't be sure. He hesitated to call out. Instead, he swung over the railing and half walked — half ran out to her. It was his Hua!

The woman looked up, but her face froze. She seemed to stagger for a moment, and then to thrust the child from her in apparent haste to turn her back. In seconds she was gone, disappearing around the corner of the nursery. Ba raced after her, but immediately found himself struggling through a crowd of waifs no higher than his waist belt. Two other women were herding their charges from one building to another.

Ba grasped the older woman by the arm. Did she know Nguyen Thanh Hua? No, she didn't. Neither did the other. Of course they didn't. No one knew anyone's real name. And Ba had no idea of what Hua was called in the Movement. He felt he had been struck by a boulder. How could the fates have brought him so close to the most fascinating woman he had ever known, only to have her evaporate into the dusty air? And why had she run, anyway? If she hadn't recognized him she wouldn't have fled so abruptly. Why did she run? The question rang in his head like a bell. He thrust his head into the closest buildings. No one seemed to know what he was talking about. He got the feeling that the women didn't really know each other very well. They had been imported with the children for show. No one reacted to his description of Hua. A few looked at each other in a way which seem to hint at some special understanding, but they responded to his hurried questions with downcast eyes and shaking heads. He turned back toward the clinic. Other patients were waiting.

One of his assistants had already stripped a pussy bandage from the leg of a little girl and was bathing the wound with an alcohol solution. Another child with a badly swollen arm squatted beside the examining table. Ba plunged again into the routine of examining, probing, and listening to small, unfamiliar frames as they coughed, wheezed, cried, or sat stoically through the process. After about an hour a cadreman of the camp staff entered and announced the approach of the UN visiting party. Most of the party crowded into the small clinic. All but the Indian spoke French. Ba parried questions as he went on with his work.

"Yes, the children need better care."

"No, we can't take care of the most serious cases."

"Sorry, we have no statistics regarding the care we provide. We just do the best we can from one day to the next." Ba was terrified that the visitors might tarry too long, and that the camp staff might direct the closure of the clinic and take the children away before he had a chance to look for Hua again.

But they had other points to visit. After accepting the congratulations of the foreigners for his "wonderful healing work," he was delighted to see their backs out the door. He continued to work for another fifteen minutes, but when he could stand it no more, he feigned a headache and bolted for the door, promising to return the next day. He had to find Hua.

Ba looked about for guards. None in sight. He returned to the barracks building he had looked into previously. There were cots and lockers, a couple of tables and chairs. A single bare electric light bulb was suspended from a threadbare wire from the rafters. Otherwise, there was no indication that the building was served by any utilities at all. Some of the blackout curtains over the windows hadn't been pulled back, giving the room an oppressive atmosphere. There wasn't enough light to make out the political slogans posted on the far wall. Ba thought of the inside of a half-opened casket.

Quickly he ran to the next building. The sonorous tones of a woman reading what was probably a list of regulations to an unseen audience emerged from within. Ba eased forward to crack the door. He was aware of someone on his right. A soldier, Kalashnikov at port arms, slid between Ba and the door.

"This is a restricted area. Do you have a pass, Comrade?" the guard asked in a Hanoi dialect.

"Yes, of course," Ba replied. "I am Physician Van Ba taking care of the children of the orphanage." He proffered his identity paper from the retraining center.

"There's no orphanage here, Comrade. This is a military installation."

"Look, soldier. You can see by the paper I'm a physician. My clinic is on the other side of this building. I take care of children."

The man was immovable. "There is no orphanage — no children. This is a military installation. You will come with me." He gave Ba a gentle shove with the butt of his rifle.

Again Ba protested, but his argument seemed only to irritate the guard. The next shove might not be quite so gentle. Ba decided to do as he was told. He followed instructions back to the center of the camp with the soldier close at his heels. He felt like a wayward farm animal being chased back to its pen. A second guard stopped the two of men, demanding to know their business. Ba's escort identified himself, and the two were allowed to pass. It was apparent that he was headed for some sort of confinement facility. Sure enough, very shortly he found himself inside a bamboo cage with a dirt floor to squat on. What happens now?

He had about an hour to wait. During that time he observed several C units of men marching by, most of them singing patriotic and socialist working songs. They looked pretty good to a provincial unit commander like Ba. They all had uniforms with sun helmets and carried Kalashnikovs. Ba hadn't done much in the Phu Loi D Group about teaching his patriots parade drill, but they did like singing, particularly when they felt they had something to sing about. Here the soldiers were singing as they marched. The Phu Loi Group couldn't do that. Usually they had to move at night and to be as quiet as they could. And certainly, there were never enough Kalashnikovs to go around.

Another soldier came to fetch Ba. He didn't seem quite as suspicious of Ba as the first one was. He even turned his back and led the way to the camp commandant's building. When they arrived, he simply ordered Ba to wait outside as he knocked at the door and stepped inside. The chap's demeanor wasn't friendly, but considerably less hostile than the first one's. Maybe the matter could be set aside as a misunderstanding. Ba squatted by the side of the hut, waving off a pair of curious flies.

In due time the soldier was back, gesturing for Ba to come in. Ba stepped in, blinking his eyes to accustom them to the interior shade after the brilliance of the outside sun. He was greatly relieved to feel the occasional pass of an oscillating fan. The camp commandant sat on a simple folding chair beside a collapsible desk. A cardboard file of cards occupied the better part of the desk top. The commandant held a card in his hands and was squinting at it. He motioned for Ba to squat on the floor. The soldier did the same behind him.

"Comrade Van Ba," the commandant began, "you were found to be poking around in the barracks in an off limits area this afternoon. Why were you there?"

Ba had no idea how accusatory the commandant planned to be, so he decided to be open with him. The commandant would probably find out anything he wanted to sooner or later anyway. Better sooner. "I had finished my work for the day, and I thought I had seen someone I knew, so I went there to see if that was so."

"Did you find him?"

"No, Comrade Commandant."

"Are you telling me the truth?"

"Of course, Comrade Commandant."

"I believe you are omitting something."

Ba wasn't quite sure what the man was getting at, but he knew that any one of the women he spoke to could have reported that it was a woman he was looking for. Better get that out on the table. "I was looking for a woman named Nguyen Thanh Hua. I didn't find her."

"What's your relationship with the woman?"

"We were friends at school in Paris. She introduced me to many patriots in the Movement."

"Did you have a romantic attachment?"

"Not especially, Comrade Commandant."

"I still don't believe that I am getting the whole story. What else do you have to say?"

"That is all, Comrade Commandant."

The commandant swung around, and the volume of his voice increased. "Comrade Van Ba, is it not a fact that you departed the clinic while there were still patients waiting to see you? Is it not a fact that you told the nurse that you had a headache and could no longer carry on your duties? Is it not a fact that you corresponded with this woman for a period of time, even after you had changed your identity? Is it not a fact that you were hoping to have some sort of tryst with this woman to the neglect of your retraining program duties?

"Comrade Van Ba, have you forgotten where you are? And why you are here? And that we are at war? Have you lost sight of the fact that we are engaged in the greatest struggle in our people's history?"

The rhetorical questions followed in rapid succession. Ba decided to fold up his defenses and reply as simply as possible. Clearly the commandant was not accustomed to dismissing small matters when there was an opportunity for a speech. Ba supposed that the commandant and the Phu Loi political officer, Tran Hua, must have been cut from the same cloth. He half listened to what was said, answering wherever it seemed appropriate: "Yes, Comrade Commandant," and "No, Comrade Commandant." Suddenly he felt as though he had been jabbed with a branding iron.

His eyes popped, his mouth opened, and he dug his fingers into his knees. He couldn't believe what his ears were telling him.

The commandant had just said that this was a highly important military installation for the support of the fighting forces, and that, with the exception of the retrainees, everyone had a primary mission of providing aid and comfort to troop units freshly back from the battle. The woman Ba had been looking for was most likely a "comfort woman" for the relaxation and gratification of the fighting soldiers. Ba had no right interfering with anything such a woman might be doing or diverting her from her primary duties.

Ba was thunderstruck. He had heard that the Japanese had had such "comfort women" — whores — in the World War, but it never dawned on him that the *Bo Dai* might have the same sort of arrangement. And the suggestion that Hua might be involved in such a revolting practice was incredible. Yet the recollection of her expression of distress and her flight at the sight of him burned through his brain like a tracer bullet. Oh, my god! Oh, my god! he thought. Is there no limit to what the Movement demands?

He could listen to no more. Whatever the commandant had to say after that simply didn't register. His mind went blank. Later, back in his own barracks he had no recollection of how the interview closed or whether he had walked or been carried from the room. He had to roll out of his hammock to wash out his mouth and to change his shirt to rid himself of the taste and odor of vomit.

# *TWENTY-FIVE*

"Okay, Paul, so it wasn't your finest hour," Colonel Dillings was saying. "Alex wasn't interested in your pet Phu Loi Battalion. So what? Maybe you've focused too closely on the local war lately. Alex wants everybody to think big. I can't blame you for getting a little excited about 'Charlie' firebombing your trailer — and especially leaving a note indicating he had his eye on you, but, hell, this is war, and that's what it's all about. We have got to get on with it. Grouse if you want to for a while among us here, but don't let the rest of the staff hear you talking like this."

The admonishment made Paul pause. He had to back off a little bit. Maybe he had been talking a little selfishly. The half dozen officers he was talking to had been meeting together in the evenings for a couple of weeks now. It wasn't a formal thing —

nothing anyone could call real staff coordination. It had started as just a bull session to clear the air at the end of the day. They hadn't wanted to talk very seriously over the mess table because a number of local nationals worked there, serving chow and cleaning up afterwards. At worst, one or two of the Vietnamese crew could be enemy sympathizers.

"*Touché*, Colonel," Paul admitted. "Alex got my goat with his put-down. I shouldn't let that happen. Okay. That's his prerogative. He's the boss. But I still think we should take advantage of a weakness in the enemy's structure when we find one. God knows it is seldom enough when we do. I still think we should designate a brigade to go in after that battalion while its boss is off at school. I'll bet we could nail the Phu Loi coonskin to the wall, the way the President says he wants us to.

"Look," he continued, warming up to his argument, "we creamed 'em when they came through the wire last week after our ammo dump — and me. Our air and artillery thumped them all the way back to the Long Nguyen Secret Zone, or wherever-the-hell they went. If ARVN could have gotten its blessed 'ready regiment' out of the sack and into their combat boots in less than four hours we could've had the bunch for lunch.

"No question about it, those slopes hit our ammo big time, but I mean, we really laid it on them. I hear we're still scarfing up pieces of Cong bodies all across the province. I'm not sure I could give you a real good fix on just where they are at this moment — if I could I'd call for an 'Arc Light' strike — but within a day or so they'll be up on the air again and we'll fix 'em close enough to make a brigade search-and-destroy operation well worth the effort. And then, goddamit, with good air cover, and a couple of battalions of artillery, we'd bag the lot of them. Van Ba wouldn't have anything but a smoking hole to come back to. That's what I call offensive action."

"Well that's okay, Paul," his (ex)trailermate, Roger Hutton, replied. "But I'm not sure we could pull a brigade out of the program just now. We've got so many commitments all over the

CTZ, and so many units standing down from Giant City that we would be hard put to do something like that on short notice. You've seen the press reports of the ammo dump attack. Every congressman in Washington wants to know why we aren't guarding our logistical tails better than we are. Hell, I hear the bastards are going to launch a big investigation over who was minding the store while everyone was off beating the bush on Giant City. You can imagine how the anti-war crowd is salivating over that."

"Sure," Dillings added, "and you can bet your sweet ass we're going to get inquiries from Washington on why we didn't have better intelligence on enemy plans. Never mind that you put out that warning of counterattack. You didn't predict exactly what was going to happen." Rolling his eyes in mocking imitation of a Washington critic he added, "Shame on you."

"Well, maybe that's part of our problem," Paul countered. "We're so busy trying to be everywhere at once that we can't really get anything done anywhere. If I'm not mistaken, it was General Giap, after the Battle of Dien Bien Phu, who said that it was more effective to cut off one finger of the enemy's hand than to scar him up all over. Well, we've been fighting all over the place. Christ, we've got a dozen different uncoordinated headquarters all over this goddam country running their own little wars and the thing just seems to get worse and worse. No one has focused on cutting off an enemy finger in a way that anyone remembers from one day to the next.

"Just in the time I've been here the enemy has run two more regiments down the Ho Chi Minh Trail. Now, I'll grant you those poor bastards are in pretty rough shape after their ordeal, but they're probably just over the border now, in camps that we aren't allowed to touch, being refitted and cranked up for action. It can't be too long before we're going to have a whole new enemy O.B. to deal with. And, I am sorry to say, I can't tell you much about them. We haven't run into NVA units around here before. They're bound to be better armed than this crowd we've been dealing with. How they'll fight, of course, is anybody's guess."

"What do you mean 'NVA'?" Roger asked.

"North Vietnamese Army. '*Bo Dai*' ARVN calls them," Paul replied. "This, for the most part, is the core of the bunch that beat the French in the fifties. We've been getting a steady stream of individuals down here right along, but for the most part they've been going into the VC units as replacements. Now they're beginning to form their own regiments, and even divisions."

"Yeah," Dillings interjected, "and that's probably why Alex doesn't want to get bogged down in the little local wars. He's probably looking forward to some bigger actions against the NVA."

"Okay," Paul conceded, "but that time hasn't arrived yet. And when it does, the NVA is going to be reliant upon the local outfits to steer them around the countryside. Those kids from Hanoi won't know which way is up as far as the terrain is concerned. We may be wandering around in the woods to some extent ourselves, but at least we're learning the territory. If they have to square off against us without local support, we'll clean their goddam clocks. I can't help but feel that we're missing the chance to clean out the local rough necks — like that Phu Loi outfit — before we have to take on their big brothers."

"Paul," Roger joshed him, "you remind me of a guy I was talking to the other day — and I will let him remain nameless for obvious reasons. He was arguing that our big problem was that we didn't have a strategy for fighting this war. 'We kill Cong,' he said, 'but with no end in sight. The whole fuckin' war is open ended.' And, I am sure you will be reassured to hear, he placed most of the blame in Alex' lap. 'If Alex doesn't understand this war any better than he seems to,' he said, 'we'll all have to send our grandchildren over here to wrap it up.'"

"Well what was his solution?" Dillings challenged him.

"His task Number 1, Roger replied, was to get rid of General Alexander. It's not that Alexander isn't a competent troop leader or that he can't put on a good show back in Washington in front of the President or Congress. It's just that Alex is out of his depth for coming up with a strategy for bringing the war to a successful conclusion. My buddy says he wants to form a club, which he suggests we call the 'GROAN' Club. That stands for 'Get Rid of Alexander Now,' and the password, he says, should be 'Uhhhhhhhhhh!' Members would moan the password every time they hear his name."

"Not bad," Paul chuckled, "but I'm sure there is something prosecutable under the Uniform Code of Military Justice about joining combinations against authority."

"Nevertheless," Roger smirked, "I think we have the makings of another chapter right here. We're just too chicken to admit it."

"Okay," Paul responded, "you said Alex gets most of the blame. Who gets the rest?"

"Oh, that gets divided up. We all carry a share, I guess, but you know what the old hands call the Ho Chi Minh Trail? 'The Averell Harriman Memorial Highway.' That world renowned diplomat negotiated away control of practically all of Laos of any strategic interest to Hanoi. Yeah, he did that four years ago. He gave the whole thing to the commie Pathet Lao. Now we're not allowed to touch it. With great strategists like that, who needs an enemy?"

"Look, you guys," Dillings interrupted, "That's not funny. You can grouse all you like and make fun of anyone you want to, but unless you can come up with something actionable on a grand scale that will win this war, you can't claim any more smarts than Harriman or Alexander or anybody else. Harriman's as rich as yellow piss and Alex gets to wear four stars. I'm not joining any club until I see one that's got some answers."

"That's fair enough," Paul responded. "We aren't paid to think at that level, and we owe all our seniors our loyal support. But nature abhors a vacuum. If nobody else is doing any thinking about this, then, goddamit, we should. Who knows more about it than we do? We need to really give it some serious thought. I mean, really think about it. Is this war winnable? Or are all the peaceniks right? Certainly it's going no place now. Take that stupid Giant City operation. If we were in the garage sales business we'd all be millionaires by now. How much could we get for a dozen printing presses? Or for a two-year supply of rice? Or how about a few hundred used field telephones and enough wire to plug into Moscow?"

Captain Jim Daniels had been sitting quietly in the session, respectful of the thoughts being aired by his seniors, but the mention of Giant City triggered his pet peeve. "Colonel," he said, addressing Paul, "we can't overlook the political restrictions on the prosecution of this war. I don't know how smart or how dumb General Alexander may be, but we have to recognize that he has to operate within some pretty strict parameters.

"Look at Giant City. Alex did his best to put a force on the Cambodian border to trap the enemy. But he wasn't allowed to use the open areas in Cambodia proper. He had to squeeze all his 'anvil' force into the northern edge of Tay Ninh Province. No wonder COSVN was able to walk around us. There was just no way to seal the border before the enemy departed. So all we got to show for our effort was printing presses, rice and telephone wire. How can we fight a war like that?"

"That's just the point, Jim," whipped Paul, "we can't. And Alex, or somebody up there, ought to be smart enough to recognize it. Yet here we sit, month-in-month-out — maybe it will come to year-in-year-out — working up new operations just like the last one, adding to our stockpile of moldy rice and telephone wire. At some point someone's got to go to the political leadership and say, 'hey boss, you know that little war we're running over thar in Vietnam? Well, it ain't goin' nowhere. I suggest you either let us wrap it up the way the book says we're supposed to or git us the hell out of there.'

"What are we running? About 300 casualties a week? That doesn't go down very well back home — or over here, for that matter."

Dillings was on him. "Okay, Paul, but you haven't told us whether this war is winnable or not, short of throwing nukes at Hanoi — not that that would do it for sure. If we could use Cambodian border territory, would that win the war? Or would we have to go deeper? How far? All the way to Phnom Penh? Then, what does that get you, besides a black eye in the UN?

"The real question is, if you were General Alexander, or the Chief of Staff, or even the Chairman of the Joint Chiefs, what would you be telling the President? 'We can't do it? Get us out of here?' How long would you last in your job if you did that?

"Or could you do it? What would it take? More troops? Another strategy? Or is it simply not worth the candle? Answer that one."

"Well, sir," Paul replied, "I'm afraid we'll have to let that question hang for a bit. We all have work to do before we call it a day. I know Sergeant Schwartz has a nice pile of captured document translations for me to digest before midnight. Let's sleep on this and talk about it some more when we can get together later in the week."

The routine of war ground on. Most of the evening bull session (cum GROAN club) members were caught up in the myriad of staff actions that flood a modern army in the field. For a week no more than two or three found themselves together at any one time to discuss anything. At the Sunday afternoon staff briefing the personnel officer gave the U.S. casualties for the week: 323, not counting two members of the headquarters staff badly injured when their chopper crashed with a mechanical failure. Dammit, Paul thought, that number's worse than I guessed.

As the staff filed out of the briefing room, Colonel Dillings caught Paul by the arm. "Hang on a minute, General DeWitt wants to talk to you."

"What about, sir? Did somebody tell him I was anti-war or something?"

"No," Dillings replied, "you shouldn't be so sensitive. There are other people besides yourself who are concerned about how the war is going. He wants to talk to both of us. The G-3 will be there, too."

"Okay, do I have time to take a leak before the meeting?"

"Better hold it," Dillings smiled, "it can't last long. The chief has to meet with some congressmen at three. Come on, let's go."

General DeWitt was giving some last minute instructions about the congressional visit to his aide when the two men arrived at his office. The G-3, chief of operations, Colonel Tom Cobbly, was already seated at the small conference table opposite the chief's desk. Roger Hutton sat beside him. Roger winked at Paul as he entered.

The general greeted the intelligence officers and waved them toward two vacant chairs at the table. He stepped to the end, slapping a note book down on the rough surface as he plumped into the chair. Everyone seemed to pull 3 by 5 cards from his pocket for taking notes. 3 by 5 cards were as ubiquitous as telescoping chromium pointers among staff officers in Vietnam.

"Look, gentlemen," the chief began, "we don't have much time before the Field Force commander and I have to meet with some Washington types junketing the country. I realize you may not have the complete picture on what General Paulding is concerned about. Greenwood, I'm going to ask you to go over what you and I talked about this morning after I leave. Let me just tell you this:

"There are smart people at every level of command who are concerned about how the war is going, and they aren't all a bunch of 'bean-and-body' counters. That goes right on up the line, to include the JCS. We shouldn't ever get the idea that nobody cares. I know that some of you have been talking about it on the side, and I understand that. But our job is to figure out how to win this war with what we've got, and under the restrictions set down from above. If we can't do it I am sure our political masters will begin to look for some people who can.

"Now, that doesn't mean that we're limited to just what we have in hand now. Our resource levels may change or the political limitations may be either tightened up or slackened off. Further, our thinking doesn't have to be limited just to the Field Force AO. If we have ideas about the larger scope of the conflict, it is our duty to bring them up. We might get into someone else's knickers, but we can't let bureaucratic walls limit our thinking. Let the chips fall where they may.

"What General Paulding wants is some good, sweeping, hard-headed thinking. In effect, he's challenged us to put up or shut up. We are professional military officers. If we, right here in the combat zone can't come up with some better ideas, who can?

"He wants to hear our very best thinking on what we should be doing. He doesn't want a lot of mucking around about how we got into this mess, or the problems we have made for ourselves. And he doesn't want to hear what blockheads there may or may not be running the Pentagon — or even the White House. He wants a professional military assessment. If this were an academic exercise at Leavenworth, and we were playing the part of a planning staff for the commander-in-chief of an expeditionary force, what would we recommend?"

"Well, General, you have hit one hot button right there," Cobbley interrupted. "We don't have a commander-in-chief here. All we've got is the chief of a friggin' 'military assistance command,' whatever that is these days. Alex may walk around wearing four stars, and everybody makes a big fuss over him, but he doesn't have diddly-squat to say about how the air war is run up in the North, or over in Laos along the Ho Chi Minh Trail, either. And there's another button: I'm not sure it is even legal to bomb the trail. You'll have to forget that I even mentioned it."

"Look, Tom," the general replied, "I know that. But that doesn't change our marching orders. If you think the command structure is a mess, say so. But you and I both understand the problems the Government had in getting the other Free World forces to sign on. The Aussies have put their brigade under our opcon, but most of the others haven't. And our European Allies, God bless 'em, haven't even shown up for this fracas. It's a sure shot that we don't want to put our troops under host nation control; and certainly Saigon doesn't want to be under ours. The present system may be a jury-rig set-up, but at least it's here and functioning.

"Look, I'd like to stay here and discuss this further, but I've got to run. Greenwood will fill you in a little more on what the Field Force commander has in mind. Just one last point: General Paulding is going out on a bit of a limb on this. If the press, or maybe even if higher headquarters, got the impression that he was dissatisfied with the war effort and had commissioned a study that might come up with a finding that we're on the wrong track, there would be hell to pay. The general doesn't want this effort known outside this group until he has all his ducks in order. Therefore, gentlemen, I must swear you all to secrecy. If you need the participation of other officers or NCOs, please ask me first, okay?"

The group responded to the general's charge with silence, but all nodded their understanding of the need for keeping the business close to the chest.

"Greenwood," DeWitt concluded, "why don't you take this over to your shop and go over the details there? You've got better maps, and no one will bother you. Get back in touch with me this evening and fill me in on how you plan to go about it."

"Yes, sir," Dillings replied. "Now, don't let those congressmen lecture you too much. I understand this is not a very friendly group this time."

"You know it," DeWitt chuckled, "I hear one of them told his constituents that he was coming over here to put a stop to our 'baby killing campaign.' I'm not sure just how to handle questions like that."

Paul was glad to get a break for a few minutes in the latrine. He'd found early in his tour that the climate made him thirsty and that liquids ran through him pretty fast. He felt much better when the group reconvened in the intelligence wing, off the TOC.

"Okay," Dillings was saying as Paul entered, "we have a charter. Up to this point we've just been beating our gums at each other, focusing pretty much on all the goofy restrictions we've had to operate under and the limitations they have placed on our effectiveness and our ability to prosecute the war.

"Paul, I suppose you are as responsible as anyone for this. You started the evening bull session group. I've heard a lot of griping from — what did Roger call it? — the GROAN Club? But I'll have to say, there may be a serious thought buried somewhere under all that bull shit you guys have been throwing at each other over the last couple of months. I brought it up with General DeWitt some days ago, and he took it to General Paulding. And what do you know? General P. said he was just about to ask someone to look into exactly the same question. But he laid out some guidance for us. Dillings popped up his right thumb.

"First, he said, was secrecy. The chief made that pretty clear, and I think the reasons are obvious.

"Second." Out of his fist came his index finger. "We want a good, professional assessment: How are we doing? Are we winning the war? How can we tell? And if we are, how much longer will it take?" He punctuated each question with a shake of his bony fingers.

"Third." Here came the middle finger. "If we aren't on a track that's likely to bring the conflict to closure, what do we need to win? And by 'winning' he means forcing the enemy to cease military operations and acknowledge the legitimacy of the South Vietnamese Government.

"And fourth, and finally." The ring finger came out with an especially vigorous shake. "If a new strategy is called for, what should it consist of? Here, I think, he gives us pretty fair license to lay out an architecture for victory. Ideally, we would have some choices to offer — alternatives. Everybody likes alternatives."

Having laid out the commander's charge, Dillings fell silent. Paul was impressed. Assuming the colonel had faithfully reported General Paulding's guidance, the old buzzard had essentially put the Field Force commander's muscle behind his own views of what needed to be explored and laid out formally in black and white. The general's "charter," as Dillings called it, was essentially what the colonel said needed to be done at the last meeting of the "club." Paul decided that Dillings would probably make as good a bureaucratic manipulator as he did a G-2. There were clearly some fox-like smarts behind that beak nose and wizened visage.

Colonel Dillings set off a secure soundproof cubicle in his planning space where cleared officers could work and where small meetings could be held. It made more sense to put it there than in the G-3 Plans Office where such projects were ordinarily assigned because of the special sensitivity of the project. Officially, it was just another "special project" for which Paul would be responsible. Both Dillings and Cobbley had confidence in Paul, but they monitored his work closely. As Dillings assured him, "Sure I trust you, but I'm still going to cut the cards."

Roger Hutton was assigned as Paul's assistant, virtually full time. As the work went forward a number of other officers were brought in for their expertise in logistics, manpower, and tactical air support. Special early morning briefings were prepared for the two generals, Paulding and DeWitt, twice a week, on Tuesdays and Fridays.

Everyone working on the project would troop into the Field Force commander's office at 0-six-thirty, or "0-dark hundred," as Roger called it. Paul would summarize the work done since the last meeting and identify issues that needed to be addressed before the next one. The generals would eat their breakfast while Paul talked. Then they might turn to a few of the others with questions regarding details in their specialty areas. The sessions were usually over by seven, whereupon Paul would hurry back to the TOC to prepare his regular morning intelligence briefing for the commander and full staff. After a couple weeks of this he sensed that he was losing more weight than he wanted. He took to eating double helpings at other meals, but the menus weren't always exciting enough to encourage much of that. War is hell, he reflected.

Within a month Paul had assembled a hefty collection of documents detailing trends in the war and assessing their impact on American objectives. They didn't make encouraging reading. They discussed the ramifications of political restrictions on cross-border operations and calculated the likely development of enemy forces in the South over the next twelve months. Some of the findings were jolting:

Item: American offensive search and destroy operations are far less effective than defensive actions. When the enemy masses his troops to attack a U.S. unit or installation, American tactical air and artillery firepower can be brought to bear with devastating effect. Enemy units involved in attacks on American forces may sustain casualties as high as 50 percent — far above their break point for unit coherence. In most cases after such action the enemy units must be completely withdrawn from the combat zone (to Cambodia or Laos) for a matter of months.

Item: Except when directed by ground forces, offensive bombing in the combat zone has little measurable effect. Similarly, bombing of enemy forces enroute along the Ho Chi Minh Trail may inflict some casualties and possibly delay the arrival of units in the South, but the strategic value of the effort is minimal. The best that can be said for it is that it may provide additional time to bring questionable ARVN forces up to minimum combat standards.

Item: The build-up of enemy forces appears to match the programmed build-up of friendly forces. If it continues after attainment of the authorized theater strength levels for friendly forces, there could arise a risk of a serious tactical defeat in the field in the future.

Adding teeth to this possibility was a bit of controversial intelligence. A captured document revealed that the enemy planned to expand the Ho Chi Minh trail into an interlocking system of two lane roads with hard-packed dirt beds surfaced with crushed stone. At approximately one hundred kilometer intervals there would be villages with soldiers and work battalions for maintenance and protection of the line. As many as 100,000 NVA troops may be assigned to Laos for the purpose. Facilities would include barracks, armories, dispensaries, fuel stations, and farms. U.S. Air Force analysts tended to discount the report as propaganda. They couldn't believe that the enemy would attempt such an ambitious project in the face of heavy bombardment.

Glancing down the summary sheet, General DeWitt muttered, “This stuff is dynamite. I hope there’s been no leak.”

“None that we’ve detected thus far, sir,” Paul answered noncommittally. “I would suppose we would have heard about it from somebody if there had been.”

“Yes, very interesting,” General Paulding agreed with his staff chief. “Now, I see that you think it unlikely that we will be able to bring the war to a successful conclusion in the foreseeable future. That’s a pretty broad statement.”

“That’s correct, sir,” Paul replied, “given the restrictions under which we’re presently operating. The key is our inability to isolate the battlefield. As long as we permit the enemy to continue to dispatch troops and munitions to the South, and as long as Hanoi can continue to receive arms and equipment from abroad, the war can go on — virtually forever. We can’t kill the enemy as fast as they breed, raise, and arm them up North.”

“Yes, I understand that,” the Field Force commander responded, “but certainly the losses will have an effect on enemy decision making.”

“That may be so, sir. But we have no way of knowing what level of pain would make them change their mind. There’s no peace movement in Hanoi as far as we know. On the contrary, every indication we have — and those are covered in the study — is that the ruling Lao Dong Party places first priority on the forceful subjugation of the South. Also, I must point out that this is a military — not a political — assessment. From a military point of view, considering the current trends, the enemy can run the war at a troublesome level as long as he pleases. And the prospect, unless we raise the ante considerably in the next year or two, is that enemy performance will become more effective as more Northern units — NVA — are deployed South.

“Okay,” the general said at length. “So lets see the solution. I assume that it’s here on the last page of the summary.”

“Yes, sir. Maybe I can encapsule it better for you here on the map.” Paul rolled out a large board with a map showing the full

Indo-Chinese Peninsula. About half way up was a prominent complex of blue markings running across the waist of Vietnam and Laos, extending westward into northern Thailand. Similar marks extended along the Cambodian coast between Vietnam and Thailand.

"The strategy envisioned here is radically different from that which we currently pursue," Paul began. "Instead of focusing on enemy forces currently active in the South, we orient on the bulk of enemy strength which is still located in the North. We seek to physically block the entry of additional enemy forces southward, thus isolating the battlefield, and setting the stage for the starvation of the enemy effort in the Republic of Vietnam. At current rates of ammunition consumption, the enemy would likely exhaust his mortar and rocket stocks in four to six months with effective blockage of his supply routes. The longer figure would assume his ability to capture small amounts of ammunition currently in friendly hands.

"The effort would be pursued in three phases. Most important initially would be the denial of the enemy's capability for reinforcing his units in the combat zone. In Phase One we would seek not merely to impose a penalty of attrition on enemy units moving south, but to physically block them. We know that practically all of the tactical factors favor us when the enemy is forced to attack us in prepared positions. This scheme would capitalize on our enormous firepower advantage.

"To block the Ho Chi Minh Trail an integrated line of entrenched Free World divisions would be established along the 17th parallel westward from South Vietnam to the Mekong River on the Thai border. Inside Thailand the Thais would be responsible for their own security, backed up where necessary by U.S. rapid reaction forces. The entire line would be heavy in artillery, with strong armored counterattack forces concentrated in the rear. Tactical air support would be on immediate call. The strength of the position would be enhanced by basing it on the south bank of one of the principal rivers flowing into the Mekong. In the rainy season the rivers are exceedingly difficult to cross. There are several options for doing this described in the study. We estimate that five to seven divisions, plus two armored cavalry regiments, would be adequate to hold the 150 mile line.

"In order to block enemy maritime supply routes through Cambodian ports, U.S. and other Free World naval forces must expand their operations to impose complete control over all coastal traffic. Every vessel steaming within 50 miles of the coast must be halted for inspection. No ships or watercraft can be allowed to enter or depart Cambodian or Vietnamese waters without authorization. Naval and Air Force requirements for enforcing this objective, and command arrangements for integrating other national contributions, should be determined separately by U.S. Naval and Air authorities.

"Phase Two of the campaign would be the systematic suppression of guerrilla forces in the South, carried out under the aegis of air tight isolation of the battle area by air, land, and sea forces. The air-ground campaign would not be limited to Vietnamese territory, but could flow into Cambodia, and possibly into Laos when justified in hot pursuit of enemy forces. We should recognize that it is not we who would be expanding the war, but the enemy who has already done so by essentially annexing neighboring territory for use as a huge logistics base and staging area for offensive action in the South. The enormous advantage which this affords the enemy is outrageous and must be eliminated.

"Phase Three, which would not necessarily have to await the completion of Phase Two, would entail the investigation, discovery and destruction of the enemy infrastructure in the country — the political cadres, the support structure, and the controlling machinery, including labor and social organizations presently under communist domination.

"But I must return to the absolute requirement for the effective completion of Phase One, the isolation of the battle area. The enemy ability to move tens of thousands of troops and thousands of tons of war materiel into the South is the Achilles heel of the entire

Free World war effort. If we don't stop that — physically block it on the ground and at sea — there can be no prospect of victory in this century.

"And this in the clincher: there is no other possible outcome in sight. We must complete the blockade of enemy routes of supply into South Vietnam or cut our commitment short here on the peninsula and withdraw. Our present course is a completely open-ended commitment to hostilities in which we are suffering over 300 casualties a week. The prospects for the future are even grimmer. As the mix of enemy units increases in favor of NVA over home grown VC, the sophistication of his forces will increase and so will friendly casualties. The enemy has adequate numbers of physically fit male youths to replace losses at current levels of combat indefinitely. While eventually his losses may impact unfavorably on his national birthrates, it hardly seems feasible to wait the 15 to 20 years it would take for that to become a factor. Our conclusion is that we have no other choice. We must either alter our strategy or get out."

That said, Paul looked at his small audience: General Paulding, General DeWitt, their principal staff officers. No one said a word. Paul sat down in a silent room.

# TWENTY-SIX

Do could feel his blood chill as he listened to the liaison officer's briefing. Lieutenant Colonel Duong summarized the details of the attack on the U.S. Field Force headquarters and the adjacent ammunition dump. The successive explosions, each detonated by a chance hit by a missile from a neighboring stockpile, had been heard at the ARVN headquarters, beginning in the small hours of the morning and lasting until after sundown the following day, so there were few in the audience who didn't have some knowledge of the event. The magnitude of the loss was staggering to most of the officers in the room, having been raised as noncommissioned officers in the French Army where each bullet was accounted for on multiple copies of ammunition reports. An NCO who couldn't account for each round fired by his squad on the rifle range at the end of the day might lose a stripe, or worse, at a company tribunal.

Do had a little better feeling for American wealth than the others, so it wasn't so much the loss of munitions that bothered him. Instead, it was the apparent attempted kidnapping or assassination of Paul McCandless that disturbed him most. How in the world did the enemy know so much about Paul? And why would they care? Was Paul something else besides an intelligence staff officer that Do didn't know about? Was Paul's recent distant manner somehow related to this incident?

Do's first reaction was to get to the American hospital immediately to visit his friend. He had been badly disappointed in Paul's misleading briefing on Operation Giant City, but that might be explicable. Perhaps he had no choice, having been ordered to say what he did. As soon as the briefing was concluded, Do placed an immediate call to the U.S. Field Force headquarters, asking for Paul. A noncommissioned officer answered saying that Colonel McCandless was in conference at the moment, but he would take a message or ask the colonel to call back. To Do's query regarding Paul's health, the noncom replied that the colonel had been in the hospital for only a couple of days for observation. He did have a rather large shaved section of his scalp and some stitches, but he was alive and well and fully back to work. The NCO also indicated that the colonel was exceedingly busy since his return. While Do got no hint of the nature of Paul's current activity, it was clear that he was running at a faster pace than before.

How could that be? Do wondered. What could be more demanding than an intelligence officer's routine duties in a combat theater — especially considering the scale of the Giant City operation? Clearly Paul was involved in some new big project. What could that be? Why didn't ARVN know about it?

Do hung up with a small relief over Paul's rapid recovery, but the conversation had thrown virtually no light on the puzzling situation now gnawing at Do.

First, although not related to the Americans, there was the matter of the aerial photographs of Phu Cuong. Colonel Tuy had told him that the chief of staff wanted them, but he hadn't specified the purpose or the date by which they should be supplied. As a result, they appeared to have been overtaken by events after the VC attack on the garrison. Was it pure coincidence that they were taken the morning before the attack? And what should he make of the point Sergeant Minh brought up — that there were no farmers in the surrounding fields at the time the photos were taken? Normally that would have been a dead give away that military units were operating in the area. The farmers tried studiously to avoid contact with troops of either side in the field. Government troops would steal livestock, and sometimes rape young girls; the VC would grab able bodied people, male or female, and impress them into labor battalions to carry their equipment. Either way, one didn't want to be around soldiers in the bush. But almost all of the cavalry units of the garrison were in their barracks. The enemy must have been near by for most of the day before the attack.

Second, and compounding the mystery, why had the chief of staff shown no interest in the films when Do showed them to him? Had he known something about them before? Had he known that the enemy was going to strike that night? The thought was incredible to the major. The chief was one of the finest officers he had served with — a far cry from so many of the slippery, elegantly uniformed generals in Saigon who always seemed to be plotting a coup or getting involved in some dirty business on the black market. No, General Don was first rate. Do couldn't imagine him disloyal.

Third, Do asked himself, why had the general's aide questioned him so closely about Paul? Could it be simple coincidence that the Phu Loi Battalion would attempt to kidnap or assassinate his friend shortly after Tuy inquired about Paul's influence in the American headquarters? Do didn't trust the colonel any further than he could throw him, anyway, so he had little difficulty imagining the worst of him. Maybe he was making something on the side by feeding little personal tidbits to the enemy. Hell, maybe he was into it Big Time. Maybe he was the guy warning the enemy of the location and timing of "Arc Light" strikes approved by the chief of staff.

Do had wanted to run a special investigation on Tuy's background before — not that he had reason to suspect him of any specific wrong doing. It simply made sense to know a lot more about someone in such a sensitive position. But the chief had told him to lay off. "There are other cases of higher priority," he had argued. Maybe the general was right, but Do was never comfortable with the order.

Fourth, and finally, on Do's mind was the liaison officer's report of General Alexander's remarks to the Field Force staff, including his put-down of Paul over the Phu Loi Battalion. Do winced at the embarrassment of his friend, but the important thing was to know what the general was thinking about. Could it be that Paul was involved in some big new initiative for General Alexander?

No, that didn't seem to make much sense. Clearly the general wouldn't want to deal with Paul after making something of an example of him as representing the kind of thinking he didn't want to hear. But, unlike most other military groups in the world, Do mused, the Americans don't spend a lot of time plotting dark deeds against their superiors. As far as he could tell, they seemed to really believe in the principle of civilian control and in loyalty to their chiefs. Paul couldn't be working on anything counter to the desires of his commander. Cross that out.

Uh-oh, what was that?

Do had done no more than mentally put the notion of disloyalty aside than he was shaken to a sudden awareness of danger. He was on his feet in an instant. His chair clattered to the floor and lay on its side. Within seconds it seemed that dozens of other chairs in neighboring offices and on the floor above were meeting a similar fate. Then there were sounds of running feet in the hall and shouts from the stairs.

Do had heard an explosion, but not like the blast at the American ammunition dump. It was the sharp crack of the small explosion within the cartridge of a pistol. A single shot came from somewhere within the building. Do seized his own weapon from a peg on the wall and chambered a round before realizing that there were no further shots forthcoming. Perhaps it was an accident. But then, why the running? What were people shouting about? Do hurried into the hall. Sergeant Minh was already there, looking down the corridor toward the chief's office. He answered the major's questioning glance with an equally silent shrug. Minh had been around long enough in the days of the coups to know that when single shots ring out from the offices of high ranking officers, noncommissioned officers do well to stay out of the way.

Do handed his pistol to the sergeant and waved him back into the office. Then he turned and ran down the hall on the heels of more senior officers. It was just as well that others were arriving first. If it was anything other than an accident, it would not be good to have to explain unduly prompt arrival. If it was an accident, and someone was hurt, there were medics on call who could deal with it.

The chief's office was pandemonium. Three officers were bending over an inert body on the floor. A .45 caliber automatic lay less than a meter from an outstretched hand. It could have been dropped either by the figure on the floor or by some assailant. Do glanced at the door and noticed that it had been forced open, suggesting either that someone had burst into the office, perhaps to attack the chief, or that the victim had locked himself in and taken his own life, necessitating that someone else break the door down to investigate the shot. A glance over the shoulder of one of the officers attempting to revive the victim revealed that it was, indeed, the body of the chief of staff on the floor, and that recovery was unlikely. The volume of blood around the head both obscured the wound and discouraged hope. Do gasped in incomprehension and grief.

The corps commander was absent from the headquarters on a visit to units in the field. Colonel Tuy elbowed his way through the crowd to assert that he would take charge of matters until the commander could be reached and returned to the headquarters. Colonel Tran Ngo Phu, the operations chief, would continue to be responsible for operational matters, but he, Tuy, would initiate an immediate investigation. He directed all non-medical officers to leave the office and to return to their work. He asked the signals officer to locate the commander and to advise him to return immediately.

Do, as the officer most closely concerned with security investigations, stepped forward to offer his assistance. To his surprise, Tuy refused his help, explaining that this was obviously a personal tragedy and should be dealt with confidentially by the general's own staff.

Do backed off in the face of the colonel's rebuff, but he found himself muttering inwardly that there was nothing at all obvious about it and that it would be a great mistake not to get to the bottom of the matter as quickly as possible. His consternation may have been apparent to the aide, but if it was, the colonel said nothing about it.

Do walked slowly back to his office and plopped down into his chair where by this time Minh had righted it. Do's admiration for the chief of staff and his sense of loss overpowered his thoughts for a while. But as the minutes passed his mind began to clear.

Damn it, he thought. A few minutes ago I was worried about four points. Now I have five. But with the chief gone, his priorities for undertaking background investigations are gone, too, and I must set my own priorities until I receive further orders.

"Sergeant Minh," he called out, "get me the forms for the initiation of personnel security background investigations. We have a top priority one on our hands right now."

# *TWENTY-SEVEN*

It was a week after Paul briefed the Field Force commander on the strategy study before he got any hint of the impression he had made. Colonel Dillings took the call. "Yes, sir, he's here. I'll send him over immediately." Then to Paul: "That was the chief of staff. General Paulding wants to see you right now. Better get going. Give me a dump when you're through, okay?"

"Yes, sir," Paul replied. "Do you think it's about the briefing?"

"I wouldn't know," Dillings admitted, "but you might want to take some of your notes along, just in case."

"OK, sir," Paul said as he buckled on his pistol belt and stuffed a half dozen 3 by 5 cards into his breast pocket. In another five seconds he had buttoned the pocket flap and snatched his cap from the back of the door. "All set."

"Good luck," Dillings wished him.

"Thanks." With that Paul was out the door and around the sandbag blind. The bags were stacked so as to attenuate the blast of near-miss mortar or rocket rounds. Paul often mused about how one had to be philosophical about the chances of a direct hit on the building. That, he figured, would clear out the principal parts of the intelligence side of the TOC: files, maps, desks and all. I guess the war could get along without us, he supposed. Few combat units ever bemoaned the loss of a higher headquarters, but somehow they always looked up to the intelligence staffs for more information. On balance, I think we play a useful role in the larger scheme of things. I hope so, anyway.

General DeWitt was waiting for him in the hall. "General Paulding says he wants to talk to you about the strategy study you presented last week. I think he's been in touch with General Alexander about it and may want you to brief it to him in Saigon. Are you ready to do that?"

"Yes, sir, I think so. When does he want to go?"

"I'm not sure. We'll see." With that he led the way down the hall to the commander's office.

General Paulding was hanging up his telephone as the two officers entered. "Sit down, gentlemen," he said with a sweep of his hand toward a couple of overstuffed chairs. "Coffee?"

The commander's office was known for the best Java in the country. Some said that the subordinate division commanders liked to visit the headquarters just for the brew. Both DeWitt and McCandless accepted the offer and had their orders served by a young corporal.

The general got right to the point. "Paul, I think the main thrust of your pitch last week was right on target. I'm not sure I would agree in every detail, but the bottom line is fundamentally correct, and we've got to do something about it — one way or another.

"I've spoken to General Alexander in broad terms, and he's agreed to have us come down there to Saigon and make our case. I don't know whether he is likely to sign on to our argument or not, but he's a fair minded man and is prepared to hear us out. He says he wants a few key members of his staff to look at your calculations and arguments, so I want you to be absolutely sure, and confident that you have all your ducks in order. Check your sources again. Check your math. Check again with all the officers who worked on the project with you to make sure that they don't have some later information which might make a difference to the findings. You understand what I want?"

"Yes, sir," Paul responded.

"I've gone through your report," the general continued, "and made a few minor notations of points I'd like highlighted in the final text. Let me know if you have any difficulty with any of them, okay?"

"Okay, sir," Paul repeated. His heart soared.

"Fine, now just one more thing. I know General Alexander wasn't entirely pleased with your suggestion pertaining to that VC provincial battalion — what do you call it, Phu Loi?"

"Yes, sir."

"Well, don't worry about that. He didn't say anything when I told him you would be coming down there with me, so I assume he's forgotten about it. At any rate, we're not going to throw you to the wolves, no matter what reaction we get from COMUSMACV or any of his staff. Just stick close to me and you'll be okay. Okay?

"Yes, sir," Paul beamed. "Do we have a date yet?"

"Not yet," the general replied, looking at his watch. "I've got to run now. The chief of staff will be in touch with you when we can get on General Alexander's calendar. Keep a clean set of fatigues packed."

"Okay, sir." Salutes exchanged, Paul was out the door. Hot dog!

* * *

Three days later Paul found himself sitting opposite the Field Force commander on board the general's helicopter at a noisy but cool 3,000 ft. altitude. A second, heavily armed bird tailed the first one in case of any difficulty.

The general was interested in the security situation regarding the bridges on their path to Saigon. Paul was relating recent incidents and attempts at sabotage against them. "In one case," Paul said, "a VC sapper was apparently so nervous about what he was doing that he attached the detonating wires of some spare explosives to his generator rather than to the charges emplaced on the bridge. When he pushed the plunger he blew himself up. The government guards had no difficulty finding and removing the charges on the bridge."

"That sounds as though the sapper belonged to your 275th Regiment," laughed the general. Paul had to admit that he really didn't know.

General Paulding ordered the pilot to circle the construction site for the new MACV headquarters. It was clear that the building was going to be an extensive one — hardly rivaling the Pentagon, but certainly a challenge to most of the defense ministries in Southeast Asia. Paul wondered how it compared with General Giap's headquarters in Hanoi.

Satisfied that he had seen all he wanted — and had consumed the extra time built into his schedule before he was to meet his boss — General Paulding ordered the crew to continue on to the temporary headquarters and to set down next to the command building. Alex' chief of staff was waiting for the visitors at the chopper pad. The staff chief welcomed them to Headquarters MACV and guided them directly to the commander's suite. A small group of colonels and one- and two-star generals were waiting in an ante room. After greeting Paulding, Alex introduced the others whom he had asked to sit in on the briefing.

Paul followed General Paulding through the line of hand shakers, introducing himself. Paulding presented Paul to Alex to complete the circle. Paul searched Alex' face for some sign of recognition or displeasure as he shook the powerful hand, but found nothing but a formal, unconcerned expression. Either he doesn't recognize me or he's a darned good actor, Paul thought. He stepped back against the wall to await the completion of the generals' small talk.

When everyone was seated, General Paulding opened the proceedings with comments about how important he believed the matter to be, however difficult some of the points might be to accept. He roughly outlined the briefing Paul would give, clearly placing himself at the focal point of any controversy, enormously easing the strain on Paul. Paul realized the general could have hung back, letting him serve as a lightning rod for bolts from either Alex or any of the members of his staff. But the general chose not to do so. This was to be the Field Force commander speaking through a trusted staff officer. Lesser officers would think twice about reacting immediately with a lot of flak. Paulding clearly wanted to make sure that the proposition stood or fell on its merits, and not on the hunches of eager sycophants who might guess that there was leverage to be gained in immediately ridiculing a concept which they guessed would not sit easily with COMUSMACV. Alex seemed to understand, judging by the gravity of his face.

For forty-five minutes Paul waded through his by now well rehearsed presentation. Only at one point did Alex interrupt — when Paul outlined the proposed blockage of the Ho Chi Minh Trail by the deployment of troops across Laos. Alex raised his right index finger to say that almost a year earlier he had proposed virtually the exact same thing to the secretary of defense, but had heard nothing further of it. He had followed it up with a similar recommendation to the Joint Chiefs of Staff, but that message, too, was answered only with a polite "thank you for your thoughts."

Paul was pleased to hear that the notion of trail blockage was not foreign to his audience, but he remained on guard against critics. He need not have been. Paulding's personal identification with the scheme discouraged hostile questioning in this meeting. The only point to be closely probed was Paul's suggestion of

Thailand's responsibility for its own defense. "How can you be sure that they can handle it?" challenged a brigadier in the second row.

Paul was ready: "We can't be sure of any specific enemy response to our initiative, sir, nor do we have good data on the Thais' capabilities, but I would point out the following:

"A. To attack Thailand, the enemy would have to cross approximately one hundred miles of Lao territory, then cross the Mekong River, the largest in the region. When they got there the NVA would be fighting as an overt invader against an indigenous force fighting for its homeland.

"B. In a march on Thailand, the enemy would have to turn an exposed southern flank of one hundred miles in length to our positions in Laos where we would have armored forces with a capability for cutting his supply lines at any point.

"C. Even if the enemy were successful in invading Thailand to some depth, he would not have achieved his goal — that of resupplying the Viet Cong or of infiltrating units into South Vietnam. In order to do this, he would have to make a 90 degree left turn and march southward across both Cambodia and Laos, over 400 miles, over unimproved roads and trails, to reach the Vietnam border. During all of that, of course, the enemy would be subjected to intense aerial bombardment and would be highly vulnerable to ground attack and ambush as well.

"In sum, we think it unlikely that the enemy would attempt an invasion of Thailand unless the Hanoi leadership had strong reason to believe that, together with the indigenous communist movement, they could overthrow the government in Bangkok and establish a sympathetic regime. If they were to accomplish that, it would lend credence to the 'domino theory' that the entire Indochinese Peninsula is in danger. That could change the minds of some of the anti-war skeptics in the United States and stimulate a much larger American effort. In any event, we believe that, with continued U.S. economic and military aid, Thailand can probably maintain its political stability.

"As far as Thai units are concerned, it might be preferable from a military point of view to keep their troops at home rather than sending them here to South Vietnam. However, that is a detail which we believe could be worked out after we had authority to change the strategy. The key thing is to persuade the national leadership that we are not on a winning course with the strategy we are currently pursuing. We believe we have three fundamental choices: we can (1) alter our strategy, (2) withdraw, or (3) face the prospect of prolonged conflict with increasing risks and costs in terms of lives and materiel. Of course, Hanoi could decide to cut its losses and quit. But so, of course could we.

"There are no determining factors impelling the enemy to quit at the current level of warfare. What we have now is an option which we believe could change that. We could, with no significant change in troop requirements, physically block the enemy from his objective. Right now, we are cooperating in a contest designed by the enemy. We don't have to do that. We can rewrite the rules so that he has to play our game. We have enormous power at our disposal right here in country. All we have to do is to apply it according to classic military doctrine. As it is, the enemy has the initiative. When he is tired, he can back off and rest. When he is ready, he can attack — virtually anywhere he wants. The best we can do is search the jungles and destroy what we find. We are not permitted to pursue and destroy him. But worse than that, under current rules, we are not permitted to simply freeze him out and to provide the host government with a secure environment for rebuilding the country."

There were no further questions. Alex sat immobile. All eyes focused upon him. Fifteen seconds passed — thirty. It seemed like a week. At length, General Paulding looked at his watch and rose, saying that he didn't want to take any more of Alex' time. He turned to face his commander. But Alex remained riveted in his chair. Finally he looked up. "OK, John, I think you've made your point. I'll take it from here. As far as the actual deployments of units under this proposal, I think we could work them out here at

MACV headquarters. But I appreciate the work your staff has done. I'll take the ball from here. I'll be returning to Washington next week for some consultations and to testify before Congress. I'll make sure this gets into the right hands.

"You know, of course, that the top people in both the White House and the Pentagon are dead set against what they call a 'widening of the war,' so it won't be easy."

"I understand that, General," Paulding replied, "but as Paul, here, has emphasized, this would not widen the war. On the contrary, the enemy widened it when he took over territory in Laos and Cambodia. We seek to confine the war by blockading free enemy movement. Someone back there must understand that."

"Well, we'll see, John," Alex replied. "Thanks for coming down." That said, he ushered his visitors to the door.

The return trip to Long Binh was uneventful. Paulding's aide opened up a briefcase of dispatches for the general's reading. Paul fell silent as he watched the landscape slip under the aircraft. At the landing pad Paul waited for the general to move and then climbed out of the helicopter. There were no final instructions. Paulding returned Paul's salute with a barely audible, "Nice work, today, Colonel."

* * *

General Alexander departed as scheduled for his semi-annual visit to Washington. But in the following days, rather than the usual stream of memoranda and instructions about his visit, the staff in Saigon received virtually nothing from him but one or two messages pertaining to personal matters. At Long Binh General DeWitt placed a number of routine calls to Saigon on various matters, hoping in the process to get some feed-back on the "Field Force proposal," as Paul's briefing had now come to be known. Somewhat perplexing was news of a message indicating that General Alexander's return would be delayed. Another message followed two days later indicating still a later date for his return.

Some of the general's personal staff began to wonder if there was a problem with his health, but there was no indication of that in the press. The general's testimony before Congress was prominently reported in the *Stars and Stripes*, sandwiched between two articles dealing with street protests in Washington while the general was in the city.

Paul met with his evening discussion group — referred to as the GROAN club only by the most irreverent members — on the eve of the second date given for Alex' return. There was still no explanation for the general's delay. Paul imagined aloud what might have happened. Maybe the secretary of defense or the president was really going to take the proposal to heart and order a shift in the way in which the war was being pursued. Maybe history could be changed. The thought was exciting, and Paul made little effort to conceal his enthusiasm. Hot dog! This war didn't have to be a loser after all!

Back in the TOC the next day Paul checked the message log almost hourly to see if something dramatic had come in. He could barely contain himself. Only Colonel Dillings seemed a little skeptical. "Hold on, son," he said. "If Alex is getting anywhere with anybody there in Washington, he'd be letting us know. No news doesn't always mean good news. It's just no news."

The answer was excruciatingly slow in coming. The first hint that it might soon be revealed came in the form of a call from Alex' chief of staff to General Paulding. "Sir, we have been notified that General Alexander's aircraft will arrive within a few hours at Tan-Son-Nhut. The general has particularly asked that you meet him here at the headquarters at 1700 hours this evening. Can you do that?

"Yes, of course," Paulding replied.

"There's no necessity that you bring any staff officers with you," the staff chief continued. "General Alexander says that he has a matter of the highest importance to discuss with you personally. The time seems particularly critical."

"Okay," Paulding assented. "I'll be there."

Paul was ecstatic when he learned of the call for the Field Force commander. The news had to be positive, considering the time-sensitive meeting at 5 p.m. There must be a major announcement coming out the next day in Washington. Alex must have gotten right to the top and convinced the heavyweights of the necessity for change.

But Dillings was a doubter. "If we're going to change our strategy, would we do it with a grandiose announcement in the fuckin' White House rose garden? Hell no. We don't know which troops we would want to use for your great 'Maginot Line' across Laos. We haven't even spoken to the Vietnamese about it. Don't you think we ought to ask some of them how to go about this? This doesn't sound good to me at all. And why do you suppose they don't want you or anybody else to come down there to Saigon with the Field Force commander? I'll tell you why: because COMUSMACV isn't going to say shit about strategy. He may be calling the boss down there to fire his ass. I'll bet this is the last we see of John Paulding. Want to put ten bucks on it?"

Deeply wounded, Paul sat down. "No, sir, I don't want to bet on anything, but how the devil could they turn down COMUSMACV with a proposal for a major shift of strategy without at least studying it? My God, they ought to have the JCS go over that with a fine tooth comb, and come up with a solid, professional judgment regarding its validity. We worked on that beast for almost two months. They haven't had it more than two weeks — assuming that they've looked at it at all."

"Don't take this personally, Paul," Dillings went on, "but there are a lot of very bright people on the JCS. They might even be brighter than you are when it comes to knowing what politicians want to hear. They may know that the SecDef and the Prez don't give a shit about strategy or professional military judgments. Politicians don't have to. They do what their political antenna tell them is propitious. If they wanted to change the strategy they would have done it last year when Alex says he first suggested it."

Paul could barely swallow his dinner waiting for General Paulding to return. He tried to read the evening's document translations, but he couldn't keep his mind focused. His heart began pumping hard as he heard the general's helicopter return to the chopper pad. Minute by minute he sat by his field phone, waiting for a call from the front office. An hour went by, then two. He put his head down on the desk, cradling it in his arms. Still no call.

Shortly before midnight Sergeant Schwartz shook him by the elbow. "Sir, hadn't you better be getting some shut eye on the horizontal? That'll give you a heck of a crick in your neck."

Paul looked at his watch. "Yeah, Okay. I guess I fell asleep. Oh say, Sergeant, save those translations for me, will you? I was thinking about something else all the time and never did get around to really reading or understanding them."

"Yes, sir," the NCO replied. "Goodnight, sir."

"Goodnight."

It was a relief to give only one briefing in the morning. The earlier routine with one briefing on strategy for Generals Paulding and DeWitt while they ate their breakfast, followed by another one on the day's intelligence reports for the entire staff had been a push. Paul arrived in the briefing room refreshed and reasonably rested the next morning. The big question about the strategy study still had to be answered, but Dilling's skepticism had taken much of the edge off Paul's anticipation of the result.

The Field Force commander entered the room at the appointed time, but instead of taking his seat, he walked up to the front of the room and motioned to Paul to hold up whatever he was about to say. Paul stepped back, collapsing his pointer in the palm of his hand.

"Gentlemen, I have an announcement to make," the general began. The room was silent. "I regret to inform you that today I am to be relieved of command of the Field Force." The sound of dozens of pairs of lungs sucking in air was palpable.

"At the same time," he continued, "I want you all to know that the President has decided to nominate me to the Senate for promotion to four star rank."

"Hear! Hear!" someone cried, and cheers broke out from every corner of the room. No one clapped louder than Paul. Paulding held up his hands in a calming gesture, but the applause went on and on. At last the chief of staff had to stand up and ask the staff to quiet down so the commander could finish his announcement.

"Thank you very much, all of you," the general went on. "I just wanted you to hear the news before it's made public. The nature of my new assignment has not been determined yet, so we'll have to await the official announcement. General DeWitt will be in charge of the headquarters until the new commander is designated. I know that you'll continue to give him the outstanding support you have always given to me. I'm enormously proud of all of you, and thank you for all that you have done during my tenure here. God bless you all."

With that, Paulding began to move toward the door, but was immediately surrounded by senior members of the staff anxious to congratulate him on his promotion. When he could get his right hand free, the general gave one final wave to the entire assembly and was gone. General DeWitt motioned for everyone to resume his seat. As soon as the room was quiet he gestured to Paul to proceed with his briefing.

So inured was the staff to the practice of management of war that the morning's presentations unfolded in sequence as though nothing had changed. Paul hoped that he hadn't missed anything important in postponing his perusal of the previous night's documents. He would have to get right back to them as soon as the conference broke up.

But when he got back to his desk it was not the document stack that caught his eye. It was the prim 4 1/2 by 7 inch envelope used exclusively by general officers for personal correspondence. Paul slid a letter opener under the flap of the fine outer vellum. The note was folded double. Three stars on a charging scarlet banner adorned the top of the page. The message was brief:

"Dear Paul:

I am not at liberty to disclose all the events that led to my relief of command or to my nomination for promotion. However, I want you to know that I particularly appreciated your initiative and assistance in the development and presentation of the proposal for a new strategy for Free World Forces in South Vietnam.
I do not know how this conflict will evolve, but whatever the outcome, you can take great pride in your efforts to improve our approach to the many difficulties we face. With all best wishes for your continued success in your chosen profession.

Sincerely,

Jonathan Paulding,
Lieutenant General
Commanding."

Paul sat for a few minutes, reading and re-reading the letter. Something was drastically wrong. How could General Paulding be promoted to four stars without some announcement of what his job would be? It would be great if he were going to take over from Alex, but that didn't make sense. Why would he be relieved of command before the announcement of his appointment? Could Dillings be right? Was the Pentagon just getting rid of a troublemaker in the field?

* * *

A couple of evenings later Paul met with the "club." There was still no announcement of General Paulding's assignment. The general had already left Long Binh for a few weeks leave in the States. The *Stars and Stripes* reported a crush of news reporters after him at his home in Alexandria, Virginia. The major news networks gave the story top billing. Evening TV programs carried interviews with neighbors and friends, but no one seemed to know what was really going on. The general's name was in the headlines of all the big papers from coast to coast. Speculation was rampant that some big change in war policy was forthcoming.

Congress couldn't miss the media orgy. Talking heads on television hinted that they had inside dope on administration thinking which would surprise everyone. The Senate set its calendar for confirmation hearings within three weeks. Editorials and op-ed articles in the *New York Times* and the *Washington Post* led their readers one way and then the other. A leaked report that the White House didn't really have a job in mind for Paulding was given no credibility.

Paul wanted to believe the main thrust of the pundit's speculation, but Dillings' arguments held him in check. The coincidence of the (ex) Field Force commander tying himself personally to the strategy proposal and his relief from command was overwhelming. "No," Dillings said, "things aren't going to change. Mrs. Paulding's pride and joy, Johnny, is just being kicked up stairs to get rid of him. He sounded off on a topic the big boys don't want to hear, so out he goes. He made a bad smell in church. That's the way it is in the big leagues, and he got messed up at too high a level. My ten dollar bet still stands. We'll never see J. Paulding in a job with any influence in strategic or operational matters for the rest of this war. He's done for. And so is anyone else who tries anything like that again. You're just fuckin' lucky, Paul, that you're no higher ranking than you are. They'd can your ass, too."

"But what about Alex," Paul challenged him. "How come nobody knocks him down? He said that he had made exactly the same proposal a year ago. Well now, here he is, back in Washington pushing it again. Why didn't he get clobbered?"

"He's too big a fish," Dillings retorted. "Besides, he plays the game. I heard about his proposal. It was very different turd. There wasn't a damned thing in it about losing the war if we didn't take his plan. That paper you wrote had great big teeth in it, and Paulding signed on for it. He was saying, 'hey guys, you've got to take this or you'll lose the war.' I mean, that's like ramming it up the president's ass — and a hell of a lot different from a timid suggestion of how to 'improve things.'

"Hell, I'll bet Alex carried that report by two fingers at arm's length, holding his nose all the way. He wasn't about to get tied to that personally. He'll still look good in the fuckin' history books, because he's on somebody's record some place as having favored it. But put his ass on the line for something he knows the Prez views like a bad case of herpes? Not on your life."

"Well, what the hell's the answer, then?" Paul challenged him. "We all put a lot of work into that study because we thought it was right. General Paulding thought it was right. For cryin' out loud, Alex, himself must have agreed with the thesis or he wouldn't have suggested it in the first place. The whole country back home is screaming over this war going nowhere. What does it take to get a change in policy, a goddam coup d'etat?"

"No," Dillings answered. "It takes some guys with guts at the top. And I mean guys in uniforms. It's no fuckin' good for some political type to come out arguing for change. They're always arguing for change when they're on the outside because that's how they get back in. It's got to come from the professional military if its going to have any impact. There has to be someone who has the guts to say: 'Look, boss. This isn't working. If we keep this up we're going to lose. We have to change our strategy or get out.'"

"Okay," Paul responded, "that's just what General Paulding said. How could he have made it any clearer?"

"He couldn't. You can't blame him. Of course, he got fired for his trouble. He has some nice new costume jewelry to pin on his collar, but there are damned few four star jobs that carry the clout of a commander of a corps-size force in combat. I don't know what they're going to do with him, but you can bet your ass nobody is going to give him a bully pulpit anywhere. Hell, he won't even draw any more pay, because the fuckin' congress has capped the pay for all the top guys. They're just giving him four stars to shut him up. They're buying him off."

"But what if he doesn't shut up?" Paul protested.

"If he wasn't going to shut up he would have resigned right off the bat. But what good would that have done? Nobody back home has ever heard of him. Some bastard in the Pentagon would just leak some fake story about an investigation of excess casualties, or something, and that would kill him dead. By the time the thing had been investigated, and he had been exonerated, everybody would have forgotten about it. No, he's better off taking the promotion and shutting up. He can put it in his memoirs later on, for all the good it will do him."

"So, what's the answer?"

"Clearly, the only answer is for the top military types — I mean the JCS, and Alex, and guys like that — all the top flag types that people know — to put their asses on the line. 'Dear SecDef or Prez,' they should say, 'if you don't change the strategy you'll have to find some other birds who will continue this bloody war, because we can't in good conscience be a part of it as you've got it tied up now.'"

"Isn't that disloyal?"

"Disloyal, hell! That's the very height of loyalty. It cuts through the bull shit and tells the top guy he's got a problem. A military guy carries more weight in a case like this because he's got more at risk. Once he's out, he's out. Damned seldom do general officers get called back to duty once they quit. Civilians can come and go like people in a revolving door, but not the military. That's it for them.

"The thing you have to understand about politicians is that they get bull shit from the opposition all the time. So they don't think anything of it. But if the chairman of the JCS walks in and asks to be relieved over a major issue, that's like hitting the politician over the head with a two by four. He may be pretty hard headed, but at least you've got his attention.

"Now, of course, the commander-in-chief can order him to shut up and get on with his work, which he would have to do. But the chemistry would be very different. The best you can hope for is that Prez would say, 'Oh, you mean it's *really* important — that's different. Lets look into it.' But no one has talked like that back in Washington, so the goddam NSC just goes ahead smiling at the fuckin' statistics — which everybody, except the SecDef, knows doesn't mean shit — thinking we're winning the silly war. And Alex, God bless him, salutes and follows orders. Draw your own conclusions." Dillings waved his hand wearily and shook his head to emphasize the futility of it all.

"Okay," popped up Roger Hutton, "but why couldn't the president simply accept the resignations of the JCS and find some other guys to run the show? There must be enough ambitious types down the line — or guys like Alex, who may not like the border restrictions, but may believe that we can pull it off with just a few more troops, or a little more bombing, or some other incremental improvement. They would be willing to take over and continue to run things the way they are. They might even make speeches, like Alex did in Washington, promising 'light at the end of the tunnel.'"

"The president might do that," Dillings replied, "but I doubt it. It would be too hot an issue to simply sweep under the rug. This wouldn't be like firing MacArthur. He was a pompous ass, and everybody knew it. Now, you can make a case that he may have been more right than wrong on some issues, but he made a blatant political play out of it. The JCS was 100 percent behind the President in firing him.

"No, we're talking about a very different situation here, and the White House crowd would know that. They may be dumb, but nobody's calling them stupid. They don't know squat about military matters, but they would catch the drift of an argument backed up with a few quiet, off-the-record resignations. The fuckin' problem lies on the military side. Nobody with four stars has got the guts to go to the mat for what he believes.

"If, years from now, we lose this lousy war, it won't be nearly so much the fault of a bunch of knuckleheaded politicians as that of the top guys in uniform who wouldn't jeopardize their precious careers to make the point clear to their commander-in-chief.

"Hell, I don't blame the president. He gets flak from below all the time. Politicians are used to that. So when Alex, or somebody else comes in with some other Grand Plan for winning the war, he sees it as just more flak, and he discounts 90 percent of what he hears. Then when Alex walks out and goes back to business as usual, the Prez thinks he has been exonerated. The message is clear as a bell: all these admirals and generals are just talking flak. He must wonder why they waste his time with all that strategy crap."

* * *

Within a few days a new assignment was announced for General Paulding. Paul grimaced as he read the order. Full General (nominee) Jonathan Paulding was to fill a new billet: administrator of support of Army forces in Vietnam. What a hell of a note, he thought. Clearly John Paulding, arguably the best operational mind in the theater, was to be kept as distant as possible from the business of fighting the war and the formulation of strategy.

Colonel Dillings was right, he reflected. This is a lousy war. The one guy with the brains and personal guts to turn this mess around has just been stuffed under a stone. We're doomed.

# TWENTY-EIGHT

General Don Trong was buried with full military honors in the Garden of Martyrs, just outside Saigon on the Bien Hoa road. The heroic statue of a wounded soldier on one knee, his head bowed, his helmet in his hands, cast its shadow over the gun carriage bearing the general's flag-covered coffin as the procession of official mourners wound its way through the gates. Do watched the proceedings from a rise in the ground reserved for field grade officers of the staff. The foreign commands were well represented. General DeWitt was there from the U.S. Field Force. A number of other generals and admirals represented USMACV Headquarters. Also present were the Australian brigadier and representatives of the Korean, Thai, and Philippine contingents. Several military attaches from other friendly countries were also in evidence, somewhat more elegant than usual in dress white uniforms and gold and scarlet aiguillettes.

Cannon roared eleven times, the internationally recognized salute for a brigadier general. The band played a selection of Vietnamese and French national and military tunes, culminating in the national anthem. A squad of riflemen fired three volleys over the grave, the traditional signal for recovery of the dead from the battlefield.

Do noticed that Colonel Tuy, the general's aide, accompanied the widow, sticking close to her throughout the ceremony. But he also noticed that she never looked at him or spoke to him. Strange. One might get the impression that she didn't much care for the colonel. How could that be? How could he have worked so closely with General Don for as long as he did if there was some sort of tension with the rest of the family? Do thought that maybe his imagination was getting the best of him. Maybe his suspicions were coloring his judgment. He would just have to wait and see what the investigation reports would have to say when they began to come in.

The first report appeared on Do's desk about ten days later, double wrapped and sealed with wire and wax. It was "eyes only" for Do from Mr. Chung, his investigations chief. On the face of it, it was a routine response: the usual details of an officer's life, his family and friends. Do knew most of it, anyway. He skimmed the biography and looked for the financial section. The bank record revealed the routine deposit of Tuy's pay and routine check payments to a variety of creditors. Nothing very remarkable.

But there was something odd about it. What was it? Each month the account was drawn down, virtually to zero, well before the next pay check arrived. How could that be? To believe this report, the colonel paid all his bills in the first ten days of the month, and then lived on credit until the next deposit came in. Did that make sense? Not a great deal. What other explanation could there be?

The simplest explanation would be that there was another account that the colonel had not reported. Why would he do that? Because he had some deposits or payments that he didn't wish to disclose?

Do picked up the telephone. It would have been unwise to discuss the matter on the phone. He asked the investigations chief to come to his office.

Chung arrived wheezing. He was a fat Nung Chinese with small eyes set close together. His round, wire rimmed glasses fogged up from his perspiration. He reminded Do of the fictional American detective, Charlie Chan. The French had suspected Chung of connections with the underworld in the Cholon section of Saigon. Do didn't know and didn't ask. Whatever his connections, Chung knew how to get things done in his shadowy line of work.

"Look, Chung," Do began, "this financial record indicates a very unusual pattern of debt payments. I would like you to dig a little further — confidentially, of course — and see if the colonel doesn't maintain some other accounts elsewhere. Maybe he uses a fictitious name. Tail him if you have to, but find out how he lives during the latter two or three weeks of each month. Also, find out where he spends his money. If he pays any of his debts with checks on other accounts I need to know about it."

The investigations chief responded, "Yes, Major Do. As it turns out, we do believe that we have located one such account. Realizing the close association between Colonel Tuy and General Don, we looked at the general's accounts and found that he had been making some rather large payments to some individuals whom we couldn't readily identify. The bank was able to direct us to the accounts in other banks where they were maintained. One was a dead end. It had been emptied of all funds over a month ago, although the owner never bothered to close it officially.

"The other account is a live one. Hand writing experts inform us that the signature on the account application form and on the checks in process is probably that of Colonel Tuy. He uses the name of Ho Ban Phu. Sometimes he just signs the checks 'Ho.'"

"How large are the payments from the general's account?" Do asked.

"Twenty-eight hundred *dong* each month," Chung replied.

"That's a lot of money. Where's the general been getting so much?" Van asked.

"That's not clear to us yet, Major. We're continuing the investigation. It could be that it's coming from his family. They're not poor. Or he may have a trust he could draw upon without raising any questions. We'll find out."

"Good, Chung. But we'll need more than that. We'll need to know why the general has been paying the aide so much money, and we'll need to know what he's been getting in return. Do you have any thoughts along those lines?"

"I would hesitate to say anything definitive, Major, but I might note that what we have seen so far follows the classic lines of blackmail. As closely as the two have worked for the last couple of years, the colonel could know something about the general's business which would be extremely embarrassing if it were disclosed. Would you have any idea what that might be?"

Do thought for a minute. His respect for the general made it difficult to imagine his chief being involved in any kind of illegal business. "I suppose it could be related to some problem in his family. Why don't you look into that angle. What do we know about the general's family? My understanding is that they were comfortably off under the French when he was growing up. Could one of them be in trouble? Or, just to hypothesize for a minute, could he have connections in the enemy camp that we don't know about. That could be pretty embarrassing for a man of his prominence."

Do was beginning to sense the odor of blood. "Chung," he said, "this could blossom into considerably more that we guessed in the beginning. I sent the request for investigation to you as a priority matter. Let me reemphasize that. We've got to determine the dimensions of this problem. Put some additional men on the project if you have to, but make sure that they're absolutely reliable.

"Now, one thing more: I think we should know everything that is going on in the front office as long as Colonel Tuy is handling General Don's business. Put some taps on the lines. Get some microphones in the office. See if you can't recruit one or two of the orderlies or secretaries to keep us informed. Can you manage that?"

"Of course," Chung replied. "We may already have a secretary on the books. I'll check that out."

"Good. Don't hesitate to recruit whomever you have to."

"All right, Major. Now I think I should move along so as not to take up too much of your time, or people might begin to wonder about that. I'll slip out the back way in case anyone is watching." With that, the investigations chief was gone.

* * *

Three days later Do received a telephone call from the general's widow in Saigon. "I know you worked closely with my husband, Major Nguyen Van Do. I wonder if I could ask you to help me with a problem?" she asked.

"Indeed, Madame Don," Do responded,. "it was an honor to work with the general, and it is an honor to be asked to help you in any way that I can. I am at your disposal. Would you like for me to call upon you at some time?"

"That would be very nice, Major," she replied. "Would it be too much trouble for you to come by our residence tomorrow at 1600 hours? It's a rather personal problem, so I would prefer that we not be seen in public."

"As you wish, Madame," Do said. "1600 hours at your residence. I know the address. You and General Don were gracious enough to include my wife and me at dinner during the Tet season. We are deeply grateful for your hospitality."

"Yes, Major, but it was our pleasure. Your wife sings beautifully. And it's because my husband held such deep respect for you that I feel I can call upon you for assistance at this very difficult time."

"You are very generous with your praise, Madame," Do answered. Then he repeated, "I am honored."

"Oh, just one more thing," Mme. Don went on, as though as an afterthought. "Please say nothing to others about this call — particularly nothing to my husband's aide-de-camp, Colonel Tuy. I wouldn't want him to feel that I am at all dissatisfied with his assistance. Besides, he is very busy with matters at the headquarters, and I wouldn't want to disturb him."

"Of course, Madame," Do assured her. "It will be just as you wish." To himself he muttered, I think I had her pegged correctly at the funeral. Either she doesn't like Colonel Tuy, or she fears him for some reason — or both. The blackmail possibility seemed to loom larger as he hung up the phone.

The next day Do arrived at the general's home at the appointed hour. The security guard checked his credentials and called into the house to notify the Number 1 boy of Do's arrival. Do climbed the steps of the mansion which had been the residence of a French Michelin rubber official at one time. It was only slightly the worse for wear. There was a patched up section of the yellow stucco wall, below the window, that had the tell-tale pattern of automatic weapons' fire. Do remembered that an earlier resident had been gunned down as he sat in the window, reading, during the climb of Diem and his brother to power. Do couldn't quite recall who, or what, the man had been. Probably a libertarian with too many Western ideas. He shrugged off the thought.

Madame Don was most gracious as she welcomed her visitor, offering him tea and inquiring about his family. Do accepted the welcome as genuine, but waited for the "problem" to be described. Clearly, the lady had something very specific in mind.

"I know you're very busy, Major Do, if I may call you that," she ventured after a while, "so I will try to get right to the point of my call. I have heard from a friend that inquiries are being made into some of my husband's personal affairs, and I thought I might speak to you to see if you might have any way of finding out what is going on. These past two weeks have been a tremendous strain, and I would hate to have some scurrilous talk of impropriety arise to stain my husband's reputation — especially now, when he's no longer here to defend himself."

"What sort of talk have you heard, Madame?" Do asked.

"Well, I'm not completely sure," Mme. Don replied, "but it may have something to do with General Don's financial affairs. I understand that some examiners have been asking for copies of his bank statements. Can you imagine how anything like that might happen?"

Sure I can, Do thought. One of Chung's less experienced agents put his footprint down too heavily on the bank. Damn it all! But he replied, "Not at all, Madame. Can you think of any reason why investigators may wish to review his record?"

"Of course not," she said, with just a slight edge of indignation on her words. "My husband was not a corrupt man. He would never have had anything to do with the black market. I'm sure you know that. And I'm also sure that you're aware of my own family's background. We are not rich, but we live comfortably and we do not indulge in shady dealings. I hope you believe me."

"Of course I do, Madame Don. I had great respect for your husband — and still do. I am very sorry to hear that someone might believe otherwise. But you can't think of any other reason why the general's records might be interesting to investigators?"

"No. I am sure that they will find nothing at all."

"Then why do you worry about it, Madame?" Do countered. "If there's nothing irregular, the investigators are bound to discover that rather quickly."

"Yes, but you don't understand," the widow protested, "I'm worried about rumors leaking out, blackening my husband's reputation. Can't we stop it somehow?"

The question stung Do. Of course he could stop it, but this conversation was making him all the more suspicious that the investigation was on the right track. He decided to focus the issue a little more sharply. To her question he replied, "There are many agencies in the government that conduct inquiries, particularly when a tragedy, such as the death of your husband, occurs. Right away they have to make sure that someone has not caused a wrongful death. If there is a killer at large, the authorities have to find that out."

"Yes," Mme. Don conceded, "but I shouldn't think that that would include bank records. They're private documents. They're no one's business but my husband's."

"That may be so, Madame. Have you spoken to Colonel Tuy about the problem?"

"I will be honest with you, Major Do; but you must promise to keep what I say in confidence. Colonel Tuy and I have never been compatible. I ask nothing of him."

"Then why did your husband keep him on his staff, if you don't mind my asking, Mme. Don. Was there something between the two of them which could lead to this great tragedy — or to your 'problem?'"

"Major," she replied, "I think I have said quite enough. If you can't help me I will have to take my problem elsewhere. Please, don't forget your cap on the way out."

At once Do realized that he had overstepped himself. Mme. Don was now an official heroine. And she came from a powerful family. "Of course, Mme. Don," he found himself saying, "we will do everything we can to assist you. Your much admired husband gave his life in the service of the country, and you have every right to expect our full cooperation. I will personally look into the entire matter and let you know as soon as we find out what is behind it all. Please don't concern yourself too much at this point. It's probably just a routine probe stemming from the circumstances of your husband's death. I think I can promise you one thing right now: you should have no worry about the matter leaking into the press — even the American press. They tend to be the most troublesome in matters like this. But I think we can protect your interests in that respect."

Well, Do said to himself as he descended the steps, that ended a little more abruptly than I had hoped, and I would have preferred on a little more cordial note. But I'm sure, now, that we're on to something. And Colonel Tuy is clearly involved. We'll get to the bottom of this — the quicker the better.

Over the next week reports trickled in, and Do began to find substance to underpin his suspicions. The various branches of General Don's family tree included two with missing members. One branch was headed by the manager of a tricycle bus company in Hue; the other by a ceramics factory operator in Saigon. Between the two of them they had three children who had disappeared in recent years — one or two, if not all of them, probably to join one department or another of the "National Liberation Front." Surveillance and interviews with the families by the police in the past had failed to determine any knowledge among those living at home of the whereabouts of the youths. The police maintained voluminous files on the families, but for some reason no one had ever raised the question of a possible connection between General Don and his nephews and nieces. Do wasn't happy about the task, but he felt compelled to pursue his leads.

Chung understood the need for special discretion when probing the roots of prominent families. He had taken a chance in assigning a less experienced agent, Sam Son Duong, to the bank files. That was a blunder, but the feed-back through Mme. Don and the major gave him a chance to cover the matter over. He used another agent, posing as an official of the Government General Inspectorate, to contact the bank officials and persuade them that the investigation was complete and that no irregularities had been found. He could be sure that the news would get back to Mme. Don and allay her fears — at least for the time being.

The matter now was to track down the missing youths. One proved no difficulty at all. Interrogation of acquaintances led almost immediately to a Honda repair shop in Hue, where the lad worked as a mechanic under a false name. Youthful rebellion and avoidance of military duty were apparently his principal motives for disappearing. Chung was content to let the matter rest there — for the time being. There was little to be gained by arresting the boy, and the news would just alert the others.

The second, a sister of 23, was not a great deal more difficult to find. She had apparently taken up living quarters with an American airman, also in Hue, much to the horror of her family. The airman had proposed marriage, but that had simply made matters worse, as far as the family was concerned. At length, her parents severed relations with her. She was working under a false identity as a clerk in the American base exchange, but apparently still met occasionally with her brother in the Honda shop.

The third one, somewhat older, was more of a problem. Born in Saigon, his name was Don Thanh Dzung. He had been a promising student, so much so that he had won a scholarship to school in Paris to study medicine. He had returned to Saigon in 1962 and taken up residency at the Pasteur Institute, but he had seemed preoccupied to a number of his colleagues. They thought, perhaps, that he was considering returning to France to practice, but his abrupt departure, only six months after joining the Institute staff, raised more sinister possibilities. He could have been abducted, or, perhaps even willingly joined the Viet Cong. His family denied ever hearing from him again.

With one exception. Late the following year, his father had heard from Colonel (later to become brigadier general) Don, the young man's uncle, that he might be working in the countryside — possibly with the VC — as a physician. It would have been a considerable embarrassment to the family if the story proved to have substance, so it wasn't pursued at the time. As a minimum, the colonel would have found his career opportunities severely curtailed.

Do fingered the investigation reports, mulling over his options for further probes. He could take the reports directly to General Vo, the corps commander, and let him decide what to do. Undoubtedly the aide, Tuy, knew more about his chief's death than he was telling. Aggressive interrogation might wring the truth out of him.

On the other hand, it might not. The only positive evidence against him was a bank account under a false name. Pretty thin stuff for an accusation of blackmail. And Mme. Don wasn't very forthcoming regarding her reasons for disliking Tuy. No, the case wasn't ready for the corps commander's attention just yet. Perhaps the telephone and office taps would yield something more useful. Better to wait.

# *TWENTY-NINE*

The retraining sessions plowed relentlessly ahead. It seemed to Ba that one day melded into another, but the direction and purpose of the program were gradually becoming more apparent.

Ba would rise with the others before dawn, performing the early group exercises with a shallow gusto. Everyone shouted the cadence, and uttered deep, animal grunts during bayonet drills. By 6:30 it was time to wash up and to fall in line for breakfast.

In the final month, the morning lectures and discussion periods were devoted less to Marxist theory and more to the war and to practical matters of troop leadership in the countryside. Accordingly, Ba found his interest, and that of his colleagues, sharply on the rise. Frequently, experienced C and D group leaders would be brought in from the field to speak to the inmates about specific problems they had had to deal with in their organizations, and the techniques they had used for overwhelming government guard posts and installations. The cadre encouraged questions and debate, and Ba began to feel that the program might not be quite the complete waste of time he had come to believe.

Two or three times a week, at the end of the day, a COSVN representative would arrive to speak about the war from a higher level perspective. Particularly interesting to Ba were the descriptions of the elaborate tactics the headquarters had employed in evading American and government troops during Operation Giant City. Assuming the speakers were giving a candid assessment, there were some small losses, due primarily to mistakes of lower level cadre, but for the most part, COSVN was barely inconvenienced by the offensive.

But it was a talk on the organization and operations of special COSVN strike groups that riveted Ba's attention. These were teams of no more than ten men, specially chosen and trained for conducting precisely targeted strikes against enemy individuals and facilities of direct interest to the high command. The raids were frequently conducted in conjunction with other operations, but not always with the full cognizance of the local commander. The teams would, of course, be known to the forces with which they worked, but information on the exact target and the purpose of the strike mission was frequently withheld for security reasons.

Van Ba broke into a sweat as he listened to a description of an operation against an American headquarters in context of a raid on an ammunition dump nearby. At length he could no longer contain himself.

"Was that at Long Binh just three months ago?" he asked.

"We cannot divulge full details of any of our operations," the speaker replied, "but I can tell you it was a recent operation of high importance to the COSVN intelligence branch. Unfortunately, due to the poor performance of the local force D group to which the team was attached, we didn't achieve all of our objectives."

"You bet you didn't!" Ba heard his own retort. "That was my D group, and your team never did make it clear to us what they were after. We thought they were just coming along as observers. Instead, they had the idea that they could kill or kidnap a particular American officer. They had to search for him, and when it turned out that he wasn't where they expected him to be, my unit had to stay inside the enemy camp, sustaining dozens of casualties, while the hit squad wandered around looking for its target. For all I know, the American may have been right there shooting at my patriots while your team was wondering what to do next.

"While you have mentioned the large stores of ammunition destroyed," Ba went on, "you can take no credit for that. That was accomplished entirely by the Phu Loi sapper B unit — only three members of which survived. And they were all badly wounded."

The speaker banged his fist on the lectern. "I don't know who you are, comrade, but it is clear to me that you don't understand the importance of discipline and obedience in military operations. I do know that your D group suffered very heavy casualties. Clearly that — and the fact that you are now here for retraining — indicates that your leadership skills and political orientation are deficient. I hope you are learning enough here to qualify you to continue to play a role in the Movement."

Ba was losing control. "You blockhead," he shouted, "we had been planning a careful attack on the ammunition dump long before COSVN ordered the larger operation. We were in no condition to take on the whole American camp with the little equipment we had on hand. We could've blown up the dump and been out of there in twenty minutes if it weren't for COSVN's unreasonable demands.

"Had we known COSVN wanted to kidnap a particular officer we could've done that with just a handful of our patriots. We simply couldn't do everything at the same time. The attack on the dump — which was entirely our business — was a technical success, but the losses sustained, because of the crazy attack on the officer, were tremendous. It'll be months before the Phu Loi D Group can again be ready for combat."

The speaker looked to the back of the hall and motioned to two soldiers to come forward. "Take this man out of here and report him to the camp commandant," he ordered. Ba looked at the two with a flashing notion of resistance, but he thought better of it and turned to follow them out. His hands trembled and his eyes filled with tears as he thought of the magnificent patriots he had sent to their deaths because of COSVN's crazy scheme. This can't be an organization worthy of the blood of its children, he thought.

An hour later, Ba stood before Tien Fue Diem, the camp commandant. "Comrade Ba," the officer began, "you've given us more problems than most of our other 'students.' I don't know what you believe gives you that right. I can see why you were selected for retraining, but I can't see that you're worth spending a great deal more time with. You have some notions about behavior that you must have picked up in the West. A few weeks ago you left your post of assignment and probed around in off-limits areas. Today you disrupted instruction by a member of the COSVN staff. You're an embarrassment to us here. Unless you can give me good reason to do otherwise, I intend to recommend to COSVN your dismissal from the retraining program and return to your organization with instructions that you be removed from any position of trust or authority."

Ba said nothing. He was too tired, too disappointed, and too angry.

"Speak up," the commandant ordered. "Is there any reason for me to keep you here?"

Ba looked at him for a moment. "No, I guess there isn't," he replied.

"All right, then, Comrade. That will be it," the commandant said. Shaking his head, he waved Ba out the door.

Within two days Ba had his orders returning him to his unit. He was trucked to the border, given a bicycle, twenty-five revolutionary *dong,* and a role of rice, and sent on his way. If his departure from home had been unceremonious, this one was positively depressing. He tried to make the most of the beauty of the day that seemed at least to welcome him out of the jungle and onto the highway.

The trip back to Phu Loi was only slightly more eventful than his initial trek northward had been. He was delayed for two days in the little village of Son Dang where his host's wife was going into labor. He stayed long enough to deliver a healthy baby boy and to insure that the mother was in no danger. He also examined, cleansed, and gave advice to the parents of a youngster of about six who had injured himself while playing with a grenade primer he had found in a field. The homemade bandages were rancid, and the boy needed minor surgery and antibiotics. Ba had no equipment with him, but he was able to persuade the family to take the boy to a government aid station. Medical care shouldn't be political, he argued, and the parents shouldn't avoid seeking attention, unless, of course, it would make them suspect. Clearly that wasn't the case in this instance.

Eight days after leaving Cambodia, Ba found himself walking his bicycle up the familiar sloping path toward the first guard post of the Phu Loi D Group. Not knowing the current password, he was obliged to squat in the shade while one of the young sentries summoned his B unit leader. Ba rose and smiled when the leader arrived, but received no such reciprocation from the officer. Ba proffered the identification card provided him before he left, but it was an obvious forgery, which did nothing to warm his welcome.

Ba explained the circumstances of his arrival, but found little credibility among his audience of three. The best he could manage was to persuade the leader to send notice to the D group command post that Van Ba had returned. The leader had heard the name, but had only seen him from a distance. As far as he knew, Ba was dead. The visitor's ignorance of the proper challenge and password was suspicious. Ba sensed the delicacy of his position and began to have misgivings.

And well he might. He was, at length, ushered further along the path, to a familiar dugout occasionally used by one of the C units as a troop shelter. There he encountered another leader who recognized and identified him as, indeed, the former D group leader, but he couldn't attest to his status at the present time. The officer's face was familiar to Ba, but he couldn't remember the name. He felt increasingly awkward. He was given fresh rice and water, which was welcome after his trip, but he was obliged to eat it squatting, under the eye of an armed guard.

A couple of hours later a representative of the D group staff arrived, but not one that Ba recognized. He gave his name as Tan So, which meant nothing to Ba. He explained that most of the staff was away, supervising the construction of a new base camp. "I am to advise you that you should remain here until further notice. I'll remain with you to insure that you are comfortable."

"That doesn't make much sense, young man," Ba replied. "I am the duly elected leader of the D group, and I intend to resume my responsibilities immediately."

"I am sorry, Comrade Ba," Tan So replied, "but I have no instructions in that regard. I am sure that everything will be cleared up when the staff returns."

"When will that be?" Ba asked.

"I'm not quite sure, Comrade Ba. Perhaps tomorrow night."

"What do you mean 'perhaps'?" Ba demanded. "Look, Comrade, you get to a telephone and call Patriot Ly Nam at the D group headquarters immediately. Tell him I have returned, and tell him I want a guide to wherever the staff is right now. Do you understand me?"

"Comrade Ba," Tan So spoke soothingly, "I apologize. I may not have made myself clear. There was an election held over a month ago and a new leader was elected."

"Who was elected?" Ba challenged him. "Was it Ly Nam?"

"I'm not at liberty to divulge our new command chain," Tan So replied, "but I can tell you that it was not Ly Nam. As a matter of fact, he may no longer even be a member of the D group."

"How can that be?" Ba jabbed again. "Nam was my planner and second in command. No legitimate election would change that."

"I understand your being upset, Comrade Ba," Tan So said, "but I can't tell you how all the changes came about. I'm sure that it will all be made clear very soon. You must be patient. In the meanwhile, I'll show you to your quarters in the main bunker. I think you'll be comfortable there."

"What do you mean in the main bunker? If I have to sleep here I want to sleep above ground in the open air."

"I'm afraid that won't be possible, Comrade Ba, until the staff returns. We're responsible for your comfort and safety, and that'll be much easier to guarantee under ground than in the jungle."

"What the devil am I, Comrade, a prisoner?" Ba demanded.

"No, of course not," Tan So replied, "but I must insist on this one measure."

"Well, what if I don't want to stay at all? Give me back my bicycle and I won't trouble you further."

"I am afraid that's not possible," the young man replied. "Please follow me to your quarters."

Ba realized he was in a trap — probably one carefully fashioned for him by Mme. Tran Hua who had gotten COSVN to relieve him in the first place. The key question was who was in charge now? Why hadn't the new leader come immediately to meet him and, if not to reestablish his command authority, at least to explain the new situation? How could the entire organization have been transformed in such a short period of time? Ba bit his lip as he followed Tan So down into the tunnel.

Ba's apprehensions were confirmed in the evening as he found that both entrances to the bunker had guard posts just above ground. There was no point in asking what they were there for. He simply nodded to one when he retired for the night.

In the morning, Ba was up before the sun. Already a pail of water and towel had been set out for him near the mouth of the tunnel. It was, he thought, marginally better than his routine in Cambodia. A breakfast of eggs, bananas, bread and rice, served by a smiling woman in a small shack a hundred meters from the tunnel, cheered him slightly. Perhaps this day would turn out better than the previous one.

Tan So joined him in the shack before he finished his meal. "Good morning, Comrade Ba. I hope you slept well."

"About as well as one can in a stuffy hole ten meters under the ground," Ba replied with a touch of a smirk on his face. "When am I going to see the new leader?"

"I still can't be sure of that," Tan So replied. "Please be patient. In the meanwhile, let me invite you to visit the hospital. I'm sure you can make yourself useful there while you are waiting. As always, we're short of trained personnel, and we need all the help we can get."

"I would be very pleased to do so, Patriot Tan So," Ba responded. "How did you know I was a physician?"

"I had heard that you had done some medical work, but not that you were a physician. That'll be very welcome news to our physician-in-charge. He's quite new and doesn't know his way around quite yet."

Ba's spirits soared as he entered the hospital shelter. The head nurse squealed for joy at seeing him, drawing the attention of orderlies and patients alike. A crowd of familiar faces surrounded him as he moved into the central receiving room. It was suddenly as before, with serious work to be done by people with only the best wishes for each other's success. This, Ba thought, is the real heart of the Liberation Movement — not COSVN, not the political lectures in Cambodia, not assassinations of foreign officers — just these good people working and caring for one another. Someday, he strained to believe, it will all be like this.

Phan My, the "physician-in-charge" was not a real physician at all. He turned out to be a bright medical assistant from the Pasteur Institute in Saigon where Ba had begun his work years before. The lad seemed vaguely familiar, and it turned out that they had several mutual acquaintances. That made things easier. Ba washed up, donned a white smock and cap, and went directly to the wards to visit the patients. Phan My and the head nurse trailed after him.

The largest group of patients appeared to be those still recuperating from the attack on the American headquarters at Long Binh. The most serious cases had been dispatched to their families when it became clear that they couldn't be returned to useful duty. Thus, there were few amputees remaining in the hospital. Most of the rest were medical, rather that surgical cases. Malaria and malnourishment were prominent. Ba checked and confirmed most of the regimes prescribed by the "physician-in-charge." A "hmmm" from Ba was enough to make Phan My visibly nervous; Ba's confirmations pleased him enormously.

As Ba entered the last ward he instantly recognized the face of Duan Suc, his former supply officer. "Patriot Suc," he called out, "how good to see you. But what a shame it must be in here."

"Comrade Ba, I, too, am delighted to see you," Suc replied, "but I wish it were under happier circumstances." He patted his head to draw attention to the large bandage encircling the crown. Ba thought Suc looked a little like a potted plant with his straight black hair sticking out at the top.

"What happened to you, Suc?" he asked.

"Ever since the Long Binh operation," the supply officer explained, "government troops have been out searching for us. That's why most of the D group members are away building a new base camp now. Sooner or later this one will be discovered, and we must have more than one alternate to fall back on."

"Yes, I understand that," Ba interrupted, "but what happened to you?"

"Well, I was out requisitioning some materials for the new camp when I got caught in a firefight between some of our lads and a government combat police patrol. I took a bullet over my left ear. I don't really know which side it came from. Either ours or theirs. I hope it was one of theirs — we're too low on ammunition to be wasting it by shooting our own supply officers." The man displayed a wide grin.

Ba laughed with him. "Well, was it worth it, Suc? Did you get what you were after?"

"To tell you the truth, Patriot Ba, I really don't remember. The next thing I knew I was in here all bound up. I thank Patriot Phan for patching me up — perhaps even saving my life."

"Well, that's great," Ba said. "But let's have a look at your head."

The head nurse motioned to an assistant to fetch more pillows to prop the man up. Ba sat on the edge of the cot and began to unwrap the gauze.

"The bullet entered the left rear of his head and exited over the eye," Phan explained. "Another millimeter to the right and he might not have been here now." He opened a file to show Ba the record of his treatment.

"Well, he seems to be doing all right now," Ba said at length. "You should be able to sit up for a while as soon as you feel like it." Then to Phan he suggested, "Why don't you and the nurse finish the round for me. I'd just like to sit and talk with Patriot Suc for a few minutes."

"Of course, Comrade Ba," the young man replied. He was pleased at what he assumed to be a demonstration of confidence in his medical skill by a real physician.

As soon as the others had left, Ba turned back to the patient and asked, "Quick, Suc, what's been happening here? Why hasn't Truc or Ly taken charge in my absence?"

Duan Suc looked furtively over Ba's shoulder and around at the other cots. "Patriot Ba, it is very bad here. Since you left, Comrade Tran Hua has been agitating everywhere to change the leadership. Many of the patriots are afraid that they'll be subordinated to the *Bo Dai* if they don't choose the people she approves. And she doesn't approve very many.

"The new D group leader is Le Van Sau. You know him. He was the C-3 unit leader. He's good, but very ambitious. Mme. Hua's been able to make use of his ambition to influence everything. Since you left she's been in direct contact with COSVN on practically every matter concerning the D group. We don't do anything without her specific approval."

"What happened to Nam?"

"I really don't know. One day he was here, then we were ordered to hold new elections of leaders, the next day he was gone. I don't know where."

"What about the others," Ba persisted. "What about Truc? What about you, yourself? If that bullet came from our side, was it an accident?"

Suc hesitated for a moment. "I can't answer that, Patriot Ba," he admitted. "To tell you the truth, I really don't know. One of the patriots in my own section asked me the same question. I can only tell you this: be careful. Things are very different here now."

"Thanks very much, Suc," Ba replied, patting the man's arm. "I'm glad you're doing so well. I'll look in on you again tomorrow." With that he rose and returned to the reception room.

Tan So was waiting for him there. "Ah, Physician Ba, you have made the rounds of the hospital. Did you run into any patients you knew?"

"Of course I did, Comrade Tan So. You would know that. Just who are my friends, of course, is no business of yours. I treat all patients alike — even enemy ones."

"So I've heard," Tan So replied. "I have some news for you. The D group leader and our political officer are returning to this camp this afternoon and they wish to see you. The leader will receive you in his dugout at 1430 hours. Please arrange your work here at the hospital so that you're not late for the appointment. Comrade Phan will remind you, won't you, Comrade Phan?"

"Of course," Phan said.

It was irritating to Ba to have to make an appointment to visit his own shelter. They're just trying to rub in my fall from grace. Well, let them, what the hell do I care, anyway? I didn't ask to be a D group leader. I much prefer being a physician. This way I can serve the Movement and follow my profession at the same time. That is the best of all worlds.

He almost looked forward to meeting with Hua and her new puppet, Le Van Sau. They must be two of a kind. I'll bet they're both full of the same buffalo crap everyone was so keen about at the retraining center.

Ba asked Phan to join him at the cooking shack for lunch. Phan was flattered, and asked if it was all right for the head nurse to come, too.

"Of course, I'd be delighted to have her with us," Ba replied. He was pleased that they might have a little professional gathering during the meal. They probably would have found themselves within earshot of one another at the shack in any event. The invitations lent an element of style in an otherwise pedestrian situation.

The three picked up bowls and cups. Into each bowl were dumped two balls of rice, some fish and bread. A dark, strong smelling sauce ladled over the mixture gave it moisture and consistency. They had a choice of goat's milk or water to drink. The three squatted in the shade outside the shack with the bowls at their mouths. Ba probed the others about the health of the D group and the availability of medicines between jabs with his chop sticks into the lunch.

The reports were not what he had hoped, but better than he had feared. The greatest deficiencies, as ever, were inadequate equipment for serious trauma cases and for sterilization of surgical instruments. The x-ray machine was unreliable; the generators often shot fuse-blowing power surges into the apparatus. X-ray film and bottled oxygen were controlled items, and Duan's supply people often had to pay sizable bribes to insure adequate supplies.

"Comrade Phan," Ba said, "I can't promise you anything, but I'll do my best to get many of these sorts of problems corrected. "Now, I have about an hour until I must meet with the D group leader. Is there anything in particular you would like for me to look at? If not, I would like to review your records of the cases treated following the attack on the American ammunition dump — I assume you still have them."

"I'm afraid we no longer have the records of those discharged from our care. The only records we've kept are those pertaining to the men still in the hospital," Phan replied.

"Why's that? What did you do with them?"

"Comrade Tran Hua, the political officer, took them, Patriot Ba. She said that COSVN had requested them for a medical study. I know nothing about it beyond that."

"Are you going to get them back?" Ba asked.

"I don't know," came the simple answer.

Ba thought for a minute. If COSVN wanted to do a medical study of the attack, why wouldn't it ask for copies of all of the records? Could the COSVN story just be a smokescreen? Of course! Hua was probably assembling statistics to underpin her case against Ba and his staff. She could add the other cases or not, as they were resolved. Undoubtedly she wanted to focus on the worst cases to strengthen doubts about the quality of the leadership. She is as smart — and as deadly — as a cobra. This sort of report from the field, coming on the tail of the one from Tien Fue Diem at the camp in Cambodia, won't do me much good. He said nothing. Instead he changed the subject. There would be plenty of time to hash out the casualties issue when he saw the D group leader — and Mme. Hua.

The time arrived. Ba walked up the path as he had so many times before. The appearance of his command post as he approached it hadn't changed, but the atmosphere was markedly different. Someone — an interloper — sat at his desk, hung a sun helmet on his peg, gave orders to his D group. Nothing seemed the same.

Once inside, Ba looked at the new leader, and then at his old nemesis, Hua. He liked the moment not at all. He resolved to say nothing until they had explained what they wanted.

Hua tried to break the ice. "Good afternoon, Comrade Ba. Did you have a good trip?"

That didn't merit an answer. Ba looked at the woman, and then back at Le Van Sau. The young man squirmed in his seat. He was clearly uncomfortable facing his former leader in his old command post. For his part, Ba was not about to let the change of authority progress easily.

Irritated by the snub, but determined to maintain her serenity, Hua plunged ahead, "Comrade Ba, as you may have heard, there's been a new election in the D group since your departure. Comrade Le Van Sau was elected to take your place."

Ba said nothing.

"We've also had a new 'physician-in-charge' assigned to the D group, she went on. I understand you've met him. Did you enjoy your talk?"

Ba gave her a more cursory glance than before.

"Look, Comrade Ba," she said furiously. "You have been relieved of all responsibility for this D group. Comrade Le Van Sau is in charge. Do you understand that?" Ba ignored her, keeping his eyes on the new leader.

The young man's uneasiness grew. At last he said, "That's true, Comrade Ba. I'm in command now. COSVN directed the change, and we carried it out. Here's the order." He held the paper at arms length. Ba took it, but set it back on the field desk without looking at it. He never took his eyes off those of the Le Van Sau. The young man wiped his face.

"Comrade Ba, this is not easy for me. You were a highly respected leader of this group until your departure. Then COSVN directed the new elections, and I was bound to respond. Now, perhaps you would like to remain here as an advisor. Also, our 'physician-in-charge,' as you may have noted, is quite inexperienced, and we can use all the help we can get in the medical field. Perhaps you ...."

Hua interrupted with a shrill tone. "Comrade Ba, there is no longer a position for you in this D group. Comrade Le Van Sau is the new leader, and Comrade Phan is the new 'physician-in-charge.' I am in touch with COSVN. I have recommended that you be transferred to some place where your medical skills are needed."

Le Van Sau looked at the woman and blinked his eyes. "You didn't inform me you'd made such a recommendation to COSVN."

"Well, I have, Comrade Le," the woman replied. "There's much that you don't know about Comrade Ba. He's been dishonest in all his dealings here in the D group. I'm sure, for example, that you didn't know that he had an unreported special source of intelligence high in the government army. It was up to me to catch him at that sort of thing. COSVN, of course, was furious. That's one reason he was sent out of the country for retraining. You may not know what kind of traitor we are dealing with here."

Le turned to Ba. "Is that so, Comrade Ba?" Ba nodded.

"See!" Hua interjected. "He admits it! We must get rid of this man as soon as possible."

"Well, let's first hear what he has to say. Please, Comrade Ba, can you clear this up?"

"No, I don't believe I will," Ba responded. "I don't know what happened to the source I had, but my impression is that Mme. Hua either terminated him or somehow took control. It was a source with only very narrow applicability, and would be of no use to COSVN. That's all I'll say about it. Perhaps Mme. Hua will tell you more."

"That's the way he talks," Hua said quietly. "He disobeys standing orders and procedures, he disregards all efforts for self-improvement. We'll be well rid of him."

Le Van Sau was confused. "Look, Comrade Ba. You had better stay with us here until we get to the bottom of this and until we hear from COSVN regarding what they want us to do about the special source. Let me ask you to remain with the hospital staff and to work with them until I find out more."

"You're making a great mistake," the political officer advised him. "Comrade Ba is likely to make trouble as long as he is here."

"Thank you, Comrade Hua," the leader replied. "I'll take that risk. Now, this discussion is terminated."

At least, Ba thought as he stepped back out into the speckled sunshine, there's some hope for that new young leader. I wonder if he'll be any more successful at handling Mme. Hua than I was.

# *THIRTY*

Chung rang up Nguyen Van Do. "Major, I think we have something you ought to hear. When would be a good time to see you?"

"No time is convenient, Chung, but it might as well be now as ever. Come on over."

"I am on my way," came the reply.

A half hour later the investigations chief was sitting in the major's small office with the door closed. Do found himself trying to keep his distance from the rotund, perspiring figure barely fitting into the chair opposite him. He couldn't help feeling that his visitor took up more than his share of space. Do noticed that the man had missed fastening a couple of buttons on his fly. He probably couldn't see them below the bulk of his waistline.

After obligatory small talk, Chung took out a note book with his fat hands and began to relate his story. "Just the day before General Don's death, he made a trip with Colonel Tuy by car to Saigon. The road at the time was considered safe for regular traffic, but they had a two-jeep armed escort, anyway. One in front, the other following.

"The general's driver couldn't hear what the officers were talking about, but it seemed to entail a heated argument. Before they reached town, the general ordered the driver to stop, and Colonel Tuy got out of the car. The colonel walked back to the jeep in the rear and took a soldier's place in the front seat. Then, the general ordered the driver to proceed on to the city.

"The general had several appointments around town during the day, but he didn't seem to have his mind on his business. The driver had to keep reminding him of small things, such as his brief case and his cap whenever he got out of the car. He stayed overnight at the General Officers' Club on Hue Street. The driver didn't see Tuy again until the following morning when the colonel joined the general in the sedan. As far as the driver could tell, the officers didn't speak to each other at all during the return trip.

"Three days later, at the funeral, Tuy took the driver aside for a minute and asked him if he'd seen any of the general's papers. Apparently some were missing. He gave him one hundred *dong* in cash, with strict instructions to turn in the papers if he found them, and not to mention the incident to anyone. He said that the matter was one of great sensitivity and that he, the driver, could get into a great deal of trouble if he told anyone about it. We've interviewed the soldiers who rode in the second jeep, and they confirm most of the story."

"Well, that is an interesting tale, Chung," Do said, "but I don't know where it gets us. Maybe the colonel dropped a cigarette ash from his fancy holder on the general's uniform and ticked the old man off, so he kicked him out of the car."

"I agree," Chung smiled, "except that the driver found this in the back seat of the sedan, with a few other papers, after he dropped the general off at his office in Bien Hoa." He handed Do a sheet of paper, folded in quarters. The major opened the document and read:

TOP SECRET FOR 77495 BIEN HOA STOP
TAKE IMMEDIATE CHARGE OF ALL
COMMUNICATIONS WITH SOUTH SLOPE
STOP FORMER REPORTER AT YOUR
STATION IS TERMINATED STOP

Do took a deep breath and blew it out, rounding his cheeks like balloons. "Well, what do you make of that, Chung? How long have you had it?"

"Answering your second question first, Major, we just got it from the driver yesterday. He had intended to give the papers to the general, but then he heard that the general was shot, and he was in a quandary as to just what to do. He was very worried about giving anything to the colonel in view of the argument between the two men, but he didn't know what else to do. He called the colonel to make an appointment to turn the papers over to him, but we intercepted the call and decided to see what it was all about before we let him go to the office."

"Good work. But what happened when the driver didn't show up at the office?"

"Oh, we just delayed him long enough to make copies of the papers. We had him call the colonel to tell him that he had a flat tire and would be late. The colonel has the original papers now."

"Now, answer my first question," Do prompted him.

"Well," Chung began, wiping his flabby face with an already soaked handkerchief, "I only handle counterintelligence matters, so I don't see everything. For example, I can't tell you what 'south slope' means. Nor do I know the origin of the message. I assume you would recognize it if it were something put out by your spooks. You haven't said anything, so I also assume that it didn't originate here. If it pertained to something being run by Saigon or by the Americans, I expect you could find that out.

"If, on the other hand, we get to the point where we can rule out everything by friendly agencies, then we might venture that either the general or Colonel Tuy — or possibly both — had access to enemy agent communications. That doesn't sound too good if neither you nor I know anything about it.

"We could have this message subjected to cryptanalysis by our own people, but from my experience they're not very sophisticated. Also, I wouldn't recommend having a lot more people in the headquarters have access to the document. If there's an enemy agent here, he could be some place other than the command section. And there could be more than one.

"I know you have a pretty good relationship with that Colonel McCandless at the U.S. Field Force headquarters. I don't like turning the paper over to the Americans, but they are supposed to have a lot of high powered computers and to be more experienced at this sort of thing than we are. I realize that it could be interpreted as an admission of the existence of disloyal officers on our staff, but we may have a serious problem on our hands. The Americans often act as though we were in league with the enemy anyway. Why not see if we can get something out of it? We might even find out something about their cryptologic capabilities. That could be useful for assessing how much they're likely to be reading of our own communications."

"That sounds pretty good, Chung. Leave this with me, and I'll see what we can make of it. In the meanwhile, what can you do to keep the driver quiet? We wouldn't want Tuy to know that we are monitoring him or that we have this message."

"Don't worry about that, Major," Chung replied. "We gave the kid one hundred *dong* to match the colonel's payment, and then we showed him some pictures of 'traffic accident' victims so that he understands what could happen to him if he loses control of his tongue. We have watch on him 24 hours a day — the same as the colonel."

"Okay," Do said. "Thanks very much. I'll get back to you as soon as I can. This time I think you can go out the way you came. We don't want to set any patterns here." Do sighed with relief as the sweaty bulk rose and squeezed out the door, grunting as it went.

Paul was not enthusiastic about taking the call from Do. For all Do's Western mannerisms and bonhomie talk about good times at Leavenworth, Paul couldn't help feeling that the man had another agenda that he wasn't disclosing. Still, to be fair, he hadn't dealt quite straight with Do either. That cock-and-bull cover story for Giant City was an embarrassment, however unavoidable.

"Paul McCandless here. Hello, Do. Good to hear your voice. It's been a long time. I was sorry to hear about General Don. I know you thought a lot of him. How have you been getting along?"

"You want to come over here? What's it all about? Can you tell me on the phone?"

"Okay, I understand. How about 10 tomorrow morning. I should be through the briefing and any staff meeting by then.... It's more urgent than that? Okay, I've got some things going, but if it's real important you can come now. See you in 45 minutes."

An hour later the two officers smiled and grabbed each other's hands as though no rift had ever come between them. Paul poured his visitor black coffee, as he knew he took it. Then he put a level teaspoon of sugar in his own and dusted the top with powdered whitener and stirred the brew with the end of a pencil. Wordlessly, Do unfolded an English translation of the message he had received from Chung and handed it to Paul.

"Well, what's this?" Paul asked as he began to read the lines.

"We may have a problem within our headquarters, Paul," the Vietnamese replied. "The original of this paper was turned in by one of our drivers. It was left in a sedan, and we are initiating an investigation. As I'm sure you can understand, it's a highly sensitive matter, and I thought that you might be able to help us. The first thing I want to make sure, of course, is that it doesn't emanate from one of your offices."

"Well, I can tell you I've never seen it before," Paul responded. "Not that I could necessarily tell you if I had. Do you know when it was transmitted? Or how?"

"No, we don't. I thought that your cryptanalysts might be able to help us out in that regard."

Paul looked at the paper again. "Wait a minute, this mentions communications with 'Xray Tango 852373.' Do the VC use our grid coordinates?"

"No, normally they don't, Paul," Do replied. "I guess that is a little literary license we took with the translation. The actual text said 'south slope.' We have some reason to believe that that is the approximate location on your maps of the area they call 'south slope.' Don't put a lot of faith in it. It's one of a set of names we believe they derived from some older terms used by the Viet Minh back in the French days."

"Okay," Paul said. "Let me check something." He picked up a secure phone and dialed a single digit. "Hello, Sergeant Savi? Colonel McCandless. Tell me something. I have an alphanumeric here that sounds familiar. Ready to copy? Here it is: eight-five-two-three-seven-three-xray-tango. Got it? Right. Now, if my memory serves me right, that's close to the number we were talking about last month. Is that right? Okay, thanks very much."

Paul turned back to his visitor. "Okay, Do, let me make a few educated guesses about what we have here — assuming that it's authentic. I would venture that this could possibly be an enemy back channel message, probably from COSVN and probably to someone in your headquarters. It could possibly be telling him to take charge of all communications to the Phu Loi Battalion — our old friend Van Ba's outfit. Except that Ba is gone. We believe they shipped him out about three months ago for retraining somewhere in the bush — probably Cambodia.

"As you know, Phu Loi has been pretty quiet. After hitting us here and blowing up our ammo dump they went to ground, and we haven't heard much out of them since. I expect we roughed them up pretty badly. If I had had my way we would've run them right down their holes and blown the whole bunch to smithereens. I was glad to hear that some of your chaps kept after them for a while. Do you have any clues as to where they went?"

"No," Do replied. "Unfortunately, we were a little slow getting started and the trail was cold by the time we got out there."

Paul went on, "Their primary radio communications have been pretty quiet, so I assume this is a back channel. We don't see much of this stuff in decoded form. Can you crack this stuff?"

"Rarely," Do admitted. "We got this just as you see it — except for the grid coordinates — from the driver — in Vietnamese, of course. But we need help to get a date, and possibly an indication of the frequencies they're using to transmit this sort of thing."

"I understand, Do. I'll talk to our guys and see what they can do. You must understand, though, that they might not give you back a complete read-out on it. They get pretty ancy about letting other folks know about how much — or how little — they know about frequencies and stuff like that. Even to give you a date would tell you that they're monitoring that channel, and they might not want to let that go.

"This didn't happen to come from General Don's sedan, did it?" Paul queried him.

"Well, as a matter of fact it did. Why do you ask?"

"Look at that last line. 'Former reporter at your station is terminated.' Suppose that were the general, himself."

"I don't know how that could be. He was one of our best. And anyway, he wasn't shot until after the message was found," Do replied.

"Yeah," Paul said, "but they might have known something that was related to his death. Maybe they anticipated it. Hell, maybe they shot him. What does your investigation tell you?"

Do thought for a minute. Then he said quietly, "I'm not sure we had an investigation, Paul. The general's aide took over the whole thing. He said he didn't need any help from us."

"God bless us, Do, it sounds to me as though you need to run a little investigation of that aide. Could he have shot the old man?"

"I don't think so, Paul," Do said. "I was right there within a few minutes, and the aide was nowhere in sight. But I will tell you this. We're running an investigation of him on a close-hold basis. It's pretty clear that he was blackmailing the general. We believe that General Don had a nephew in the Viet Cong and may have been in touch with him. Apparently Colonel Tuy found out about it and demanded money. The general paid for quite some time. Then something happened to bring matters to a head. It may have been too much for the general and he decided to take his own life. Why he wouldn't just shoot the colonel, I don't know. Please keep that under your hat. It's very hard for us in a small country torn by divided loyalties."

"Well, I hope you can get to the bottom of this. We knew that someone in your headquarters ordered aerial photographs of the Phu Cuong barracks shortly before the VC hit it. That was pretty suspicious. Frankly, Do, I'll have to say, it didn't look too good for you. You have charge of that department as far as I know," Paul said evenly. The atmosphere chilled perceptively.

"How did you know about the photographs?" Do asked.

"I'm not sure that I should tell you at this point, Do," Paul replied. "Can you explain how it might have happened?"

"Yes, I think I can, Paul. That's one of the points we're focusing on in this investigation. Of course, there can be no guarantee that our answer will be fully satisfactory to you. I realize we have a lot of explaining to do. You're probably wondering why we were late in getting going after the attack on your headquarters, too. These and some other things are just becoming clearer in light of the general's tragedy. We're hoping we'll be able to clear up everything. If Colonel Tuy has the general's files, there is a chance that we can grab the entire bag and find out just how much damage has been done."

"Wouldn't he have destroyed whatever files he may have gotten?" Paul challenged him. "That would be pretty incriminating stuff."

"That's certainly possible," Do replied, "but greed often has no boundaries. The files would give him a measure of leverage over the family, and that's not a poor family. Also, I might as well tell you, there is a chance that Mme. Don could be under Tuy's control already. She's asked that a major part of the investigation be curtailed. Frankly, I don't know if she is asking that on her own account or whether Tuy put her up to it.

"I think that I have said about all that I can right now, Paul. I hope it is enough to interest you in a cooperative effort for solution of our problem. And, in any event, I must ask you, please, please, don't allow your relationships with Colonel Tuy to shift in any discernible way. He might sense that we're on to him — if, indeed he's working the other side — and he might fly the coop."

"I understand, Do. There are very real bounds on what we can tell each other in this blasted war. Let's just do the best we can and hope that together we can make something work. Maybe sometime after the war we can get together and compare notes — everything on the table."

"Everything on the table," Do echoed. "That would be great."

"Okay," Paul said in a tone intended to conclude the conversation. "Just one more thing. This is obviously a translation of the original. If we translate it back into Vietnamese we're bound to end up with a different document than you started with. That could complicate the analysis. Why don't I send a courier with an armed escort back with you to your headquarters to pick up a copy of the original? Then they could bring it right back for our crypto people to go to work."

"Okay," Do responded. "I guess I should get going right away so your courier can get back before sundown."

No sooner was Do out the door than Paul had his "special security" officer, Major George Lang on the line. Minutes later, Lang was in Paul's office.

"George, I need you to drop whatever you're doing and zero in on this message. I expect to have the original in Vietnamese here in a couple of hours. What can your guys make of the clear text of a top secret, high level enemy message? I want to know everything. Is it authentic? Who wrote it? How was it transmitted? Who, or what, is 77495? And anything else you can find out."

"Well, sir," Lang responded slowly, "we can take a look at it, but it may be a little over our heads. It looks to me like something transmitted by a high grade code system. If you don't mind, I'd like to send it back to DIRNSA for thorough analysis."

"DIRNSA?"

"Director, National Security Agency, back at Ft. Meade. He's my operational boss. I belong to the Army Security Agency, but DIRNSA has all the smarts and gives me my real marching orders."

"Well," Paul cautioned, "I don't want this to become the talk of the town back in Washington. Georgetown dinner parties love spy stories. Can you keep a lid on it?"

"Yes, sir. I can request that it be given a special compartment identifier. That'll keep it under tight wraps — at least until it gets around that there is a new compartment that no one has a clearance for. Then there could be a rush for everyone to get read in. That's when the leaks begin — at the top of course: the White House, the State Department, the civilian side of DOD, anywhere you have people with some sort of political ax to grind and who don't grasp the idea that there might be a risk to flesh and blood in the field very well. You know the old saying, 'the ship of state is the only vessel that leaks from the top.'

"But the compartment could keep the lid on long enough for you to accomplish something specific. A lot depends on what you are thinking of doing with the information. Do you see this as a short or long term requirement?"

"I'll worry about that, George. If you have any technical questions, call Sergeant Savi in O.B.. He knows all about the Bad Guys. You go ahead and send the whole thing in to your DIRNSA. Just make it fast, Okay?"

"Yes, sir," Lang replied. "I'll get this right out. Give me a call when you have the original. I'll come pick it up."

Within two hours Paul had the original, and twenty-one hours after that he had a call from Lang, asking him to come to his shack to look at some "very interesting information." Paul was pretty busy, but he was also aware that security regulations forbid the removal of crypto material from the shack in readable form. The message he had received from Do had now been sucked into the great maw of the American cryptanalysis machine, and, save for a leak or two in Washington, might never see the light of day again. In the language of the trade, it had disappeared "behind the Green Door."

Paul hated that expression. The door wasn't green; it was brown. And he didn't like the shack much either. The sandbags were stacked up over the windows, so only the efforts of two bare 40 Watt bulbs fought back the cavernous gloom. In the center was a table on which Lang laid out special category intelligence according to who was there to read it. Some customers, like Paul, were permitted to see much more than others. From the rear of the building one could hear the hum and clatter of teletype machines and decoding devices. A warrant officer and a half-dozen tight-lipped code specialists moved from one machine to another, ripping off sheaves of paper and filing them in note books and folders. Besides being a key link in the signals intelligence chain, this was the primary communications system for general officers to banter back and forth about critical matters too sensitive to be seen by their staffs, so different matters were handled by different operators. No one below Lang, himself, knew everything that was going on. Even Paul had no access to the generals' correspondence.

"Okay, sir," Lang said after Paul had taken a seat. This message is from a very secure, high level communications net run out of COSVN. Most of the time the base station transmits from an area just southeast of Mimot, in Cambodia. There's a rubber plantation with an airfield and a hospital there."

"Sounds like Xuan Loc," Paul interrupted.

"Yes," the major said. "Many of the plantations were set up by the same French companies, so they tend to look a lot alike. We've been monitoring the principal frequencies they work on, but it's rare that we can read the traffic. Sometimes they use a one-time code pad, so each message is unique. In this case, however, they were using a code which had a daily key. Your clear text gave DIRNSA enough to go on to pretty well break the code for that day.

"Once they're able to narrow the target code down to something less than a quadrillion possible combinations, as we did in this case, you can attack it with high speed computers. Using brute force, DIRNSA said they had it in about eight hours."

Paul found the numbers a little dazzling. "What do you mean, 'brute force'?"

"Just what it says, really. There's nothing very tricky about it. Nowadays, if you've got a large enough memory, you can simply try one possible combination after another against the target. If you can hit it with 20 billion combinations per second, you've got on the outside a little over a half-day's work on your hands.

"Anyway, now that they have the complete key for that day, they're using it for working some other problems. And, what do you know, sir, we're in luck. Take a look at this message that was sent the same day:"

> TOP SECRET FOR TRAN HUA SOUTH SLOPE
> STOP VAN BA DISCHARGED WORK
> SITE 643 TODAY STOP SUBJECT RETURNING
> TO YOUR LOCATION STOP PERFORMANCE
> UNSATISFACTORY STOP SUBJECT MAY
> ATTEMPT DEFECTION STOP KEEP UNDER
> ARMED WATCH UNTIL FURTHER
> INSTRUCTIONS STOP

Paul let out a low whistle. "This is terrific. But, God bless us, it seems that no one likes this blasted war. Poor old Van Ba flunked his finals at retraining camp. Now he's got his tail in a real wringer!

"George, you've got to tell me more about how these commo nets work. Is there any way that we can get into them ourselves — say to send a false message?"

"Well, that's a pretty tall order, Colonel. I suppose if we had the keys we could slip something to the stations we've been able to identify. What do you have in mind?"

"Let's just suppose I could deliver to you a live VC agent who ran one of these stations. And let's suppose he had on him the keys or pads you need. What else would you want?"

"Well, a couple of hefty MPs, for starters, to break his arm if he crossed me up, I guess. Then I'd need an ARVN type who's familiar with the enemy message lingo. And how about a VC clandestine transmitter, while you're at it?"

"Okay," Paul said with unmistakable excitement. "This is just whacky enough for this whacky war. Goddammit, we might be able to pull it off! I'll be back to you in a few days. In the meanwhile, keep it under your hat. If you get anything more on this channel, let me know immediately, okay?"

"Okay," Lang said, wondering if maybe the colonel hadn't gone a little whacky himself.

Within the hour Paul had corralled Colonel Dillings and sketched out the anatomy of a cryptographic operation so fraught with risks that he almost choked on his words as he unveiled it.

"Goddammit, Colonel," he pleaded to his chief, this war is going nowhere. We all know that. But maybe we have a chance to make a difference in a small way that could pay off at some time in the future.

"Right now there's a disillusioned VC battalion commander, with a great war record, who may be on the brink of defecting. He probably doesn't know that COSVN is on to him, or that he's likely to be shot if he tries to jump. Now, here we sit, with a pretty good line on a COSVN agent in the ARVN headquarters, who has just been given the go to take over all communications with the very unit this guy's assigned to. What do you suppose we could make of that?"

"Well, you tell me," Dillings replied skeptically.

"Okay, sir, here's how it looks to me. I hope you don't mind framing an innocent man, as long as he's also a spy and a moral skunk. Tuy's the man. I don't know everything Nguyen Van Do has on him, but I'll take that ten dollar bet of yours that it would be enough to scare the bejesus out of him if we close in and accuse him of espionage, blackmail, and murder."

"Murder?" Dillings' eyes widened. "Who said anything about that?"

"No one has," Paul admitted, "but that wouldn't make a lot of difference. Tuy outsmarted himself by half when he blocked the regular investigation, which probably would have exonerated him. Now he doesn't have that to fall back on. If Do has as good an espionage case as I think he has, it wouldn't take much finagling to make Tuy believe that he would have to face a murder rap, too.

"Hell, Colonel, I'm not talking about court. I'm talking about leveraging the guy to the point of cooperation. We might even sweeten the pot with an offer of cold cash and a one-way ticket to Martinique."

"What do you want him to do?"

"I want him to help us slip false orders to that Phu Loi outfit to turn Van Ba over to us — before they shoot him. That guy could be a treasure trove of intelligence information. Maybe he could give us enough solid dope on Cambodia that we could use to convince someone that we ought to go in there and clean the damned place out. But more importantly, he's been up there at that retraining center getting the hot poop from COSVN on their grand strategy for winning the war. Just because we don't have a strategy doesn't mean they don't. And just because we don't plan to win this war doesn't mean that we don't need to have some idea of how the other guy plans to do it. Hell, Colonel, a lot of men's lives could hang on whether we can get a high level defector — or even a prisoner — like that."

"That's pretty big thinking, Paul," Dillings joshed him. "You don't waste much time with nickels and dimes, do you?"

Paul was quick on the uptake. "No, sir, I don't. I think we've got too many field grade officers — and too many generals — mucking around in nickels and dimes in this war. That's why we're losing. You can't blame it on our troops. They're the best in the world, but they're being led by a bunch of middle managers in Army suits. Damn it, Colonel, let's go for it!"

"Okay," Dillings said, "you've made your point. I think I've heard you on that subject before. Look, let me talk to General DeWitt and Tom Cobbly about this. It's just far enough off the wall that they might go along with it. Of course any flopper would bounce back on me, and I would be only too pleased to note it on your efficiency report."

"That's great," Paul laughed. "I don't expect any of our careers to be worth much after we lose the first war in American history. And while you're talking to those folks, sir, I'll go ahead and call a little preliminary planning meeting of the guys I think we'll need on this — just to size up the problem — okay?"

"Okay," Dillings said begrudgingly, "but don't crank up a lot of stuff we'll have to crank back down. I don't know what the boss will think of this. It's pretty wild."

Within minutes Paul was on the telephone to Nguyen Van Do, setting up a meeting with him and Chung, and one of Do's crypto officers, on the ARVN side, and Roger Hutton from the Field Force G-3 shop, and Major George Lang, the crypto chief.

It was after 8 p.m. before everyone had arrived. The Vietnamese had to wait until they could arrange for a helicopter. Even with the Phu Loi Battalion laid up, it wasn't safe out on the highway at night.

Paul took pains to impress the group with the importance of the strictest secrecy of everything that might be said at the meeting and to rule out the taking of notes or the writing of any kind of memoranda about the discussion afterwards. Everything from then on had to be strictly word of mouth, and spoken only in secure areas on a face-to-face basis. He also asked that anyone who felt that he had to speak to another person outside the group on some aspect of the matter ask the permission of either Major Do or himself first. He and the major would be in close touch with one another as long as the matter was active. Heads bobbed in understanding around the room.

Do wasn't quite sure what Paul was about to propose, but he was pleased that it would be based on a partnership between them. Whatever the bounds of security might be between officers of different nations, he wanted to rekindle his personal and professional bonds with his friend and staff college classmate.

Paul also explained that the operational concept that the group was about to hear was not well developed, nor was it approved on the American side, as yet, but that time was of the essence, and early coordination couldn't wait for protocol. As he began to outline his proposal, the reason became apparent. At any time COSVN could order the Phu Loi Battalion to turn Van Ba over to their control.

Do was the first to speak when Paul finished. "I hope you haven't overestimated the strength of evidence we have against Colonel Tuy. However, I agree with you. We don't need a case that'll stand up in court. We just need enough to make him believe we do. I think that, in addition to charges of espionage and murder, we can add blackmail. That's something we might be very hesitant to make public, because of the implications for General Don's family, but I can tell you we have a pretty good case, with bank records to back it up."

"That's great," Paul said. "Now, as I see it, our first problem is to block COSVN from ordering Ba's return to War Zone C. I take it we can send almost any messages we want, either to COSVN or to the Phu Loi bunch — that is within the bounds of the codes and pads we expect to leverage out of Tuy. Is that right?"

"That's a pretty high reach for us," Lang replied. Maybe the Puzzle Palace back at Meade could do it, but that's a little out of my league."

"We're assuming that we'll have Tuy's cooperation, of course," Paul reassured him.

Do interrupted. "I think we could help you with that. We've picked up a few enemy radios before, and whenever we were able to catch the operator or his code books we could at least confuse their nets for a while."

"For how long?" Paul asked. "24 hours?"

"Well, maybe not that long. But then, we weren't really trying to deceive them for any specific reason. We just wanted to disrupt their channels. We weren't looking for much more than we might have done by jamming them."

"Okay," Paul said, "but this operation isn't one we want to take on with a blunt instrument. We really have to know what we're doing. What are the chances that we could jam COSVN out of the net and then send an imitative message to Phu Loi on an alternate frequency?"

"I don't know," Lang replied. "I would think COSVN would just switch to the other frequency, too."

"I have an idea, Paul, Do interjected. COSVN may figure that we know Van Ba was relieved three months ago, but they probably don't know that we're aware of his problems at the retraining camp or that he's now *chieu hoi* bait."

"*Chieu hoi?*" Lang asked.

"He means defector," Paul explained.

"Yes," Do went on. "If that's the case, why couldn't we have Tuy send a message that General Don's widow wants to meet with Ba, perhaps to turn over some papers of the general's — or perhaps some money."

"But Do," Paul protested, "we don't want to endanger her. She might be captured."

"I'm not talking about using her at all, Paul, just her name. And we may not have to use anyone. All we have to do is delay COSVN from calling for Ba. Once we put COSVN on ice, we ought to be able to send a fake order to Phu Loi to turn Ba over to 'COSVN guards' at such-and-such a place and time. If COSVN bit, Phu Loi would be a relative push over."

"Wouldn't COSVN be able to read our message to Phu Loi?" Paul asked.

"Not if we used a one-time pad," Do said, with what struck Paul as a deliberately inscrutable oriental smile.

"Not bad, Do. Not Bad. Maybe we're getting somewhere now," Paul said enthusiastically. "Now we have the little problem of closing in on Tuy, grabbing all his gear and codes, and convincing him to work for us. How're we going to do that?"

"Leave that to us, Paul," Do said soothingly. Mr. Chung, here, has played that game before. He has a nice picture book of 'traffic accident' victims and you would be surprised how quickly people come around after looking at just a few pictures.

"Did you know that Saigon has one of the highest traffic accident records in the world? And these are not your Washington DC fender-benders. Most are cases of pedestrians being run over by trucks. We have lots of trucks, thanks to your generous aid programs. Of course, our security services have received their share. They may have the highest 'accident' rates in the country. I know you fellows don't get into this very much, so it would probably be best to leave that to Mr. Chung and not ask a lot of questions."

"Okay, Do. I guess that's pretty clear," Paul conceded. "But what if Tuy doesn't have the radio or codes? Suppose he has a go-between who delivers the messages from some transmitter site located somewhere else? As a matter of fact, I would expect this to be the case. General Don, if, indeed, he was involved at all, may have been operating on his own, but once COSVN got into the act I would expect that they would want to establish pretty tight control. They probably look upon Tuy as a sort of loose cannon rolling around on a rocking deck. Also, the fact that the message was typewritten would indicate that there's probably somebody else providing the communications support for this operation — maybe there's a sort of commo central that services more than one agent."

"That's possible, Paul," Do replied. "We'll just have to determine that from Tuy. If he has a messenger, or dead drops, or even if he goes to the transmitter site himself, I think we can handle it. We can explain to him the risks of double crossing us. If greed is his primary motive, as I believe it is, I imagine he'll cooperate. I don't think he wants to be a maimed or dead hero.

"Now, it might be a different story with the radio operator or messengers. Most of these guys are ideologically motivated, and they're quite prepared to risk their lives for their cause. If Tuy tipped off his contacts, I would expect they would wreck the equipment, or burn the codes, or something like that — we could even have a firefight on our hands if we tried to close in on them. But I think Tuy will cooperate when everything is made clear to him. Of course we'll tail him like his shadow if he has to go someplace else. He'll know that."

"Let me say here, Colonel," Lang interjected, "I would be surprised if we found that the commo site was doing much more than supporting Colonel Tuy. That would put them on the air a lot more, which would be very risky for them. As you know, we're looking for that sort of thing all the time, and we just haven't had a lot of traffic. If they come up on the air more than once or twice a day we can usually pin down their location pretty quickly."

"Okay, that sounds good," Paul said. What's next? Oh, yes, how do we scarf up Van Ba, assuming he's delivered where and when we want?"

"That might best fall to us, too, Paul," Do said. "I don't think any of your basketball players with big feet and long noses are likely to pass as representatives of COSVN. The only problem is likely to be the local passwords of the day."

"Couldn't that be prearranged in the message?" Paul asked.

"I guess so," Do replied. "Let's assume so for the time being, anyway.

"Paul, it's almost 10 o'clock. I think we ought to get back to our headquarters and sleep on what's been said here. I will, of course, have to brief General Vo on this, I'm sure you understand that."

"Of course. You may want to wait until I know that it's a go from our end, but that's up to you. I'll call you as soon as we get some word."

"Thanks. I hope its a go," Do said smiling, and he walked out the door.

Paul called Dillings' trailer. There was no answer. Then he called General DeWitt's office. Specialist Ralph Turlington answered.

"Yes, sir," Turlington said. "Colonel Dillings and Colonel Cobbly are still in there with General DeWitt. I took them in their supper a couple of hours ago, but they're still in conference. Do you want to talk to Colonel Dillings?"

"Yes, please, Ralph," Paul replied. "Just ask Colonel Dillings if he can come to the phone for a minute. I just want to bring him up to date on a matter."

"Yes, sir. Please wait a minute."

"Hello, Paul? Dillings. How did it go? Did you get the people you wanted?"

"Yes, sir," Paul answered. "How's it going with you?"

"Well, I've explained the concept. They have a lot of questions, but I think they also understand the opportunities."

"That sounds good," Paul responded.

"Yeah," Dillings said, "but there's another wrinkle that's just come up. I don't think we can do anything about it tonight. Why don't you hit the sack, and we'll talk about it first thing in the morning."

"I wouldn't mind that, Colonel, but I still have a whole stack of new captured documents to get through. I'll be here for a while in case you want to talk about anything before you turn in."

"Well, it looks like we're going to be here for a while, too," Dillings told him. "We have some other things to talk about. There's still a great big goddam war going on out there, so don't wait up for me."

"Okay, Colonel," Paul replied. "I'll see you in the morning. Goodnight."

Goddam war is right, he thought. Cicely, m'lady, you'll have to do without a letter again tonight.

# THIRTY-ONE

"Morning, Paul," Dillings said. "How are the grits?"

"Now, that's a trick question, sir," Paul replied. "You professional Southern types don't believe that we in the North know what grits are. I've been eating them all my life, but my Mom taught me to call them 'hominy grits.' I love 'em."

"Yeah, in a pig's ass. You wouldn't know a cat fish or a black-eyed pea from a whisky soda," Dillings retorted. "Gimme a plate and I'll show you how to eat a breakfast."

"Hey, Sergeant Bonner, got any SOS this morning? I've got to wean my Yankee friend here away from his mother's quiche."

"Yes, sir, coming right up," the mess sergeant answered with a laugh. He repeated the colonel's joke to the cook. They both had a good laugh at Paul's expense.

Dillings pushed the plastic flowers aside and poured a cup of black coffee from the jug on the table. Look Paul, that little wrinkle I was talking about: we're going to have a new Field Force commander this morning."

"Who's it going to be — MacDonald?" Paul asked unenthusiastically, citing the name of the commander of the "Big Hundred" Division, and his tormentor in the false B-52 bomber episode. Paul was well aware that MacDonald was the top contender for promotion in the guessing game around the headquarters. Rodger Hutton, sitting down the table, looked up from his *Stars and Stripes*.

"Look, you guys," Dillings replied, "keep it under your hats for another hour or two. But I think you'll like the choice better than that."

"You mean Wakefield?" Paul's eyes widened, and his mouth stretched into a grin. "Wow! Wouldn't that be something. That guy's a real pro. He may not be the intellectual that Paulding was, but he's a great soldier. Who makes the choice — Alex?"

"I suppose Alex has something to say about it," Dillings commented, "but I think the Chief of Staff carries more weight. Then it's up to the SecDef and the President. It looks to me that they're better at picking Field Force commanders than they are at picking a strategy. Pass me the salt and pepper, will you please?

"The new commander — whoever it is — will be there this morning at the staff briefing. General DeWitt will introduce him, and he may say something himself. Then, right after the briefing he wants you to fill him in on the whole spy business and your proposal. After that he may want to hop over to ARVN Corps to have a talk with General Vo. I don't think we'll get a go-ahead until after that, so hold your water. I know you've got hot pants to get on with it. Do whatever coordination you need to save time if we do get an okay, but don't start something you can't stop."

"I got you, sir," Paul replied.

The choice was Major General Leonard Wakefield, tall, laconic commander of the 20th "Tropic Storm" Division and hands-down favorite for the selection among the members of the Field Force staff. He had a kind of cracker barrel air about him that endeared him to his troops and disarmed congressmen and representatives of the fourth estate alike. Paul was delighted. He had briefed the general several times before at his division headquarters and found him easy to do business with. With respect to the current issue, however, he reminded himself to rein in his enthusiasm lest he blow the briefing and spoil the whole deal. He had seen many an overly enthusiastic briefer throw doubt on his objectivity and undermine his entire pitch.

Wakefield seemed pleased to see Paul, apparently remembering him from his previous briefings. As for the proposal, which had been roughly explained to him by General DeWitt, he showed an open mind. He listened closely to Paul's presentation, tipping back in his chair and sipping white coffee. When Paul finished he rocked forward and set his cup down. "Okay, I think I've got the concept. Now what I would like you to do is to verbally walk me once more through just what you expect to happen when you get approval — if you get it."

"The first thing," Paul said, "would be the arrest and interrogation of Colonel Tuy by Chung's men. They would endeavor to persuade Tuy to serve as a double agent, particularly for the transmission of bogus messages to COSVN and to the Phu Loi Battalion. They would also seek to obtain possession of any clandestine files Tuy may have or know about."

"Now stop there for a minute. How will we know that all this is done. Do we take ARVN's word for it? Wouldn't we want to have one or two of our people in on the action?"

"I must tell you, General, Major Nguyen Van Do and Mr. Chung are disposed to deal very harshly with Colonel Tuy if he refuses to cooperate, or if they believe he is being less than completely candid with them. They appear to have fewer bounds on their interrogation techniques than our CI people have. We haven't been invited to participate in the interrogation, and I recommend that we not ask. I don't want to sound like Pontius Pilate, but I don't think we would want to lend our presence to the business if Tuy is uncooperative and things get ugly."

"Well, I think I'll take a reserve on that. We can return to this point. So what happens then?"

"Then, sir, assuming everything goes as we anticipate, and we either get access to the transmitter and codes, or we are confident Tuy will follow instructions, we'll send a message to COSVN to the effect that Mme. Don wants to see her nephew and to turn over some papers and valuables to him. We don't think it likely that COSVN will necessarily grant the request, but we hope that it will give them pause regarding any action they may be planning to recall him. We would expect that it would take them some time to consider the matter. We're hoping that this may give us at least 24 hours to work the Phu Loi angle."

The general picked up his cup and took a sip. "How can you do that without COSVN knowledge?"

"We hope to get access to Tuy's one-time pad codes, sir. We know they've been used in the past, possibly by General Don. They're time consuming and tedious, but they are almost completely secure. The only real risk we run is that COSVN could have retained copies of all its pads, in which case they might be able to dig the right one out and crack the message. Again, we're hoping that we can move quickly enough to keep a jump ahead of them."

"Colonel," Wakefield interjected, setting his cup down again, "you're beginning to make this sound like a 'B' grade movie thriller. Are you sure we're going about this in a professional manner?"

Paul wanted to answer "yes," but he knew he really didn't know. "General, to tell you the truth, I have never tried anything like this before, nor do I know anyone who has. I'll admit it sounds pretty far-fetched, but I would point out that the risks are not great."

Paul remembered that General Wakefield had long been an enthusiast for wargaming, the principal technique in the Army for smoking out "what if" kinds of questions. He decided to couch his argument that way. "If we try it, and it works, the benefits are hard to gauge, but we believe that they would be considerable." He began to count on his fingers. "First, we get a high level defector, a psychological coup; second, we get insights into both the enemy in the field and enemy high-level planning; and third, we may score a major cryptologic coup. We might even be able to crack most of what COSVN puts out on its clandestine nets — until they get wise to us.

"On the other hand, sir, if we don't try, we miss some great opportunities. That would also be the case if we tried and failed. The difference between not trying and trying and failing would be that if we got access to the radio and codes and made no effort to exploit our position to rescue Van Ba, we might be able to listen in for a longer time. We could use Tuy as a simple double, and it might be some time before COSVN got wise. The Brits were pretty successful in doubling the German agents they caught in World War II. But the psychological value of the defector and his own inherent intelligence value as a live witness could exceed the value of the radio and codes alone. We've talked this over among ourselves, sir, and we recommend that we go for the whole nine yards. The opportunities on the upside considerably outweigh the risks on the down side."

"Who's 'we'?"

"Besides myself, sir, there is Colonel Dillings, Major Roger Hutton, in G-3, and Major Lang, our cryptologic officer. Then on the ARVN Central Corps Staff, there is Major Nguyen Van Do, the G-2, and his crypto officer."

"You said you had some doubts about this Major Do?"

"Yes sir, but I don't believe we are taking any additional risks by working with him on this. And, frankly, sir, I don't think we could do it without him. He brought us the case in the first place."

"How do you know it's not some sort of trap?"

"I guess we don't, sir, but then, I don't see that we're placing any of our people at risk."

"Well, you may be placing my reputation at risk, for all that's worth," the general said without a smile. "If I encourage General Vo to go along with it and it blows up in our faces he won't be very happy with me."

"No, sir. I don't know how that would come out. But I will say this: General Vo took a black eye when the VC attacked Phu Cuong and stole those tanks. If he could come back with the battalion commander who probably pulled off the attack as a *hoi chanh*, and put him on national radio in Saigon, he might find his way back to good graces in the capital. And of course, we would have an intelligence orgy."

"All right. Just one more thing. What makes you so sure that this Van Ba is going to want to defect? Suppose he is horrified at the whole thing and simply clams up?"

"Yes, sir, that's a possibility. But I think he's ready. And when he sees how easily we pulled off his rescue — if, indeed, it goes well — I think he'll be all the more anxious to join us. We've been after this guy for some time now. We know his family, we know his background, and we know a lot about the problems he's been having with his political officer. This Tran Hua is one tough cookie. She's a woman, but mean as sin. In addition to the message traffic and the captured documents I mentioned to you, we've picked up a couple of prisoners and *hoi chanh* that, while not having first-hand knowledge, could pretty well corroborate the story from rumors and talk they had heard."

"Okay, uh, Paul, is it?"

"Yes, sir, John Paulding McCandless. My friends call me 'Paul'."

"Are you related to General Paulding? Aren't you the lucky man the VC were looking for in their raid on the headquarters here last month?"

"Yes, sir — that is, they were apparently looking for me, but I don't know if the general and I are related. We never talked about it. As best we have been able to determine from a prisoner we took, the enemy thought we were, and figured that since the Field Force commander was well protected, I was the next best thing. They probably got my name and address from the wash ladies who do the laundry. They may have seen some of my mail which normally comes with my middle name written out."

"General Paulding is a descendant of John Paulding in the American Revolution," Wakefield said. "His ancestor was the chap who arrested the adjutant general of the British Army, Major Andre, who was negotiating with Benedict Arnold to take over the defenses at West Point. Is that your line?"

"Yes, sir, it is," Paul answered. "I was named for John Paulding."

"Well, that's great. I'll have to tell the general that the VC is way ahead of him in genealogical research.

"Now, to get back to our own war, I think you have an interesting proposal. I'll talk to General Vo about it. If he goes along with it, I'll support you."

"Thank you, sir."

The generals' meeting was scheduled as a working lunch — 12 noon in Bien Hoa. "God, I hope Wakefield doesn't decide to call Alex, or something dumb like that," Paul said to Dillings when they got back to the TOC. "If this gets down to MACV, those guys will tie it up for a week, and probably blow the whole damned thing by wanting to make independent checks of all the details."

"Hard to say how he'll play it," Dillings replied. He eased down in his chair and leaned back, interlacing his skinny fingers behind his head. "Wakefield didn't get to this three star command by keeping his bosses in the dark and pulling a lot of screwy shenanigans. On the other hand, he didn't get there by letting higher headquarters micromanage every goddam thing to death, either. I expect he'll find some way to take care of his boss without stirring up the staff. Generals are paid to play smart games like that. They do it all the time in the Pentagon.

"By the way, Double-O-Seven, let me remind you that there's a war going on here, and you're supposed to be running our intelligence operations. How about letting the generals worry about Mata Hari for a couple of hours and you get your ass into the map room and see what's going on. I understand there's a little firefight under way up there at Phuoc Binh. What do you know about that?"

"Not much, sir. I'm on my way." Paul hurried into the map room. Sergeant Savi was there, posting the latest O.B..

"Good morning, sir. Did you get everything you wanted on the Phu Loi Battalion?"

"Yeah, thanks. What's new?"

"Not a whole lot. There's a little firefight going on up near the special forces camp at Phuoc Binh. The G-3 people are following it. Probably a local force outfit. I know you talked to the S-2 there last week. Didn't he sort of half promise you a prisoner?

"Yeah, but I doubt that we would get much from one of the local thugs."

"It could be something else, sir. The *Bo Dai* are coming down through Laos now in a big way. It could be another package of the 101st NVA Regiment. Those snake-eating green berets like to get out there and tangle with anyone who trods on what they consider their turf. But one of these days they're going to find they've got a tiger by the tail and they'll be screaming for help. I hope we've got someone on standby who could bail them out."

"Good point, Savi. I'll check on it."

Paul crossed to the G-3 operations desk. "Hi Roger. I briefed General Wakefield on our special project. He's having lunch with General Vo today to talk it over. I'm hoping we'll have an answer by one o'clock."

"Sounds good."

"Yeah. How's that firefight going up there by Phuoc Binh?"

"It seems to be quieting down now. No word of casualties on either side yet. On our side we had 5th Special Forces troops and some CIDG irregulars. Haven't heard anything about the other side. What about you?"

"No. But I think we're going to have to watch that area pretty closely. Our O.B. guys are afraid the berets are going to run into NVA troops around there any day now and find they've got more than they can handle. We ought to make sure that we've got some folks ready to go give them a hand, or to help them break off if things get ugly."

"We've got the second battalion of the 17th ready to go at Di An. You think we'll need them?"

"Well, maybe not today, but Hanoi's turning that Ho Chi Minh trail into Route 66. They've got packages of *Bo Dai* marching down there now, practically with bands playing. I know the Air Force is doing its best, but its tough picking out targets under triple canopy jungle. All we've got on the ground is Mr. MacNamara's wonderful 'electronic fence.' My people tell me the enemy collects all the gizmos we drop in there and pulls out the batteries to power their radios. They really like the stuff. And of course it makes for big contracts in the Pentagon. It was a great idea for everybody — except, maybe, for our side to win the war.

"I think we'll have to be a little more alert from now on in that area. I'll tell you what. I'll have Sergeant Savi give your guys all the latest O.B. we have on the area, and maybe you'll want to cook up some plans for getting our guys out in case something big pops. Okay?"

"Sounds good. I'll talk it over with Colonel Cobbley. Thanks, Paul."

Ouch, Paul thought as he walked out the door. Its too goddam easy to get wrapped up in a single project around here. Dillings is right. There is a war going on. Gotta keep your eye on the ball, and there seem to be more balls in the air every day.

Dillings took the call at 1:35 PM. It was DeWitt. "It's a go," he said. "The old man and General Vo are in full accord. General Wakefield is leaving directly from Bien Hoa, flying down to Saigon to brief Alex personally. He wants you to press ahead immediately right along the track Paul outlined.

"Yes, sir," Dillings replied.

"And one more thing, Greenwood. The old man wants to make sure that the operation is off and running before he gets back. He doesn't want to give the MACV staff wiggle room to get into the act and screw things up. You've got to move out smartly."

"I understand, sir. We'll be back to you in an hour or two to verify our status."

"Good, Greenwood. I don't think General Wakefield will be back before 4 p.m. We should have a report for him as soon as he sets down."

"Count on us," Dillings said as he banged the phone back down. Then, turning to Paul, sitting across from him, he exclaimed, "Goddam! That Wakefield is about as smart a son-of-a-bitch as I've run into. I've been wondering how he was going to handle MACV. He's frozen them out. Cold. Paul, you watch that man and you'll learn tricks most generals never even thought of. He's a pro."

Paul smiled. Dillings changed his expression. "Now wipe that silly grin off your face and get on the horn. Make sure Nguyen Van Do and what's-his-name have the word and are moving to execute. Then get over there and see what they come up with. We haven't a moment to lose. Have you got your draft messages ready to go? Better take someone with you. Take Lang. You may need some technical help. I'll mind the store here. Any questions?"

"No, sir," Paul replied. He ran into the next room and immediately rang up Do. An operator came on the line.

"What number did you call, please?"

"Hey, look, operator, I have a flash precedence call to make to Bien Hoa. Can you help me out."

"I am sorry, sir, I'll have to verify any flash precedence call. Who is your supervisor?"

"What the hell are you going to do, write him a letter? I don't care what precedence you put on it, just give me the number."

"I am sorry, sir, but all of the circuits are busy."

"Well then, break in. Override. I don't care. Just give me the goddam number."

"I can't break in without a flash precedence, sir."

"Jesus Christ! I am Lieutenant Colonel Paulding McCandless. My supervisor is Colonel Greenwood Dillings. His supervisor is Brigadier General Ralph DeWitt. Now that we have given the enemy listening in our complete chain of command, perhaps you can put me through!"

"Just a moment, sir. (pause) Your party is on the line, sir."

Do came on. "Paul! I've been trying to get in touch with you. All the circuits were jammed. You would think we were at war or something."

"Yeah, Do. I guess you got the good word."

"Right. Mr. Chung has his assignment. We should be hearing back pretty soon."

"That's great. Look, Do, what if I come over there and join you to coordinate the next step? We don't want to waste any time. I'd like to bring Major Lang along with me, too."

"Sure, that would be fine. I'll have some tea for you. You take milk and sugar, as I recall. If things go well we'll have a party."

"Well, I don't know if we'll have time for a party, but we ought to be able to get things going. I should be there by 2:30."

"That'll be fine, maybe I'll have some news for you."

It was a wonder that Paul wasn't more than an half hour late. The pot holes in the highway, hammered by thousands of two-and-a-half and five ton trucks, were worse than ever. The labor that the province governor might have put into road repairs had long since been sucked up into every manner of job for the high rolling Americans — everything except road maintenance. No longer possible to avoid the holes, Paul's driver, Hastings, had learned how to ease his vehicle in and out of most of them. It was excruciatingly slow, but it was safe and caused no injuries to passengers. The driver was appreciative of Paul's comment, "Good work at the wheel, Bill."

Do did, indeed, have some news. Colonel Tuy had been arrested and was now undergoing interrogation at the Counterintelligence Center. Paul shivered slightly at the thought. He had seen the interrogation rooms and the cells. They didn't have a hospitable ambiance. Would he like some tea? He certainly would.

Paul took out the draft message to COSVN, unclipped a copy, and handed it to Do. "What do you think of this, Do? If you were a COSVN bureaucrat, would it make you delay ordering Van Ba back home? Assuming, of course, that you had intended to do so in the first place. Do looked at the paper. It read:

> TOP SECRET FOR COSVN FROM BIEN HOA 77495 STOP WIDOW OF FORMER REPORTER REQUESTS FACE TO FACE MEETING WITH RELATIVE VAN BA FOR PURPOSE OF DELIVERING PAPERS AND VALUABLES STOP UNABLE TO VERIFY NATURE OF PAPERS BUT BELIEVED TO BE OF CONSIDERABLE INTELLIGENCE VALUE STOP RECOMMEND THAT AUTHORIZATION BE GRANTED FOR MEETING UNDER CONTROLLED CIRCUMSTANCES WITHIN ONE WEEK'S TIME STOP REPORTER WILL COORDINATE DIRECTLY WITH TRAN HUA SOUTH SLOPE STOP

Do scratched a couple of notes in the margin. "This looks fine, Paul. It's just that the VC still use some old idioms that don't appear very often in government documents any more. I want to make sure the translator uses the right terminology." He tabled the message.

"Now, let's see how Mr. Chung is coming along at his end." Do picked up the phone and lapsed into a terse conversation in Vietnamese. Paul guessed that it was not Mr. Chung at the other end.

"He's still in the interrogation room," Do said, setting the receiver back on the hook. "More tea? Major Lang?" Neither of the Americans much wanted it, but both accepted the offer. Within minutes the phone rang again.

"Nguyen Van Do." Again the sing-song language, but this time clearly with greater urgency. Do smiled as he set the receiver down.

"That was Mr. Chung. He wants to come right over. Can you wait for that?"

"We certainly will," Paul replied. "How long will it take?"

"I expect about a half hour. He seemed pretty anxious."

"That sounds mildly positive," Paul surmised. "Let me just call my office and let them know what I'm doing."

"I'll give it a try," Do responded, smiling. "We don't always get through right away." Paul chuckled at the understatement. In due time an operator came on the line with the familiar "DRAGON SLAYER" identifier. Still smarting from his earlier call when he knew he had disclosed too many names, Paul gave Dillings an elliptical report. It was common knowledge that the enemy had access to all but the most tightly encrypted electrical links.

Chung wheezed and sweated his way through the door. It was obvious that he had exerted himself to reach the office quickly. Do translated for his counterintelligence chief. "Here is essentially what he says," Do began, following a few terse questions and exchanges with Chung. "Tuy understands his predicament. He doesn't wish to admit anything, but he is willing to cooperate — 'for the good of the nation,' he says. He says that he thinks he knows where General Don kept his message file, but doesn't wish to disclose it until he has a better understanding with us.

"He also says that there's a courier who picks up messages from a number of dead drops in town. He knows the signals for indicating that there's a message ready for pick-up, but he doesn't know how long it takes the courier to get it. He says he can't be responsible if a message doesn't get picked up."

"What does he have in the way of codes and ciphers?" Paul interrupted. Do looked at Chung and put the question to him. Chung grunted a reply.

"Mr. Chung says Tuy denies having access to anything like that."

"Does Chung believe him?" Again the quick, unintelligible question, but with a more fulsome reply.

"No. Mr. Chung believes that Colonel Tuy will likely have a great deal more to say after he has been interrogated for 12 hours. He says Tuy denied everything at first and had to be persuaded to admit anything. Mr. Chung is sure that there is more to be known, but he didn't want to risk injuring him in view of the time sensitivity of the operation. He's come here now to report that he has gained sufficient cooperation from the prisoner to initiate the operation if we wish to. The longer we wait the more we will learn, but also the greater the chance that Van Ba will be recalled to COSVN."

"I appreciate that," Paul said. "I have clear marching orders to get the ball rolling before General Wakefield returns. He doesn't want MACV to get its tentacles into the operation. I don't know whether we're getting a straight story from Tuy or not, but my tail will be fried if I don't have something ready to report when the general gets back. Unless you think the risks are too great, I say, let's go for it."

Do smiled. "Sounds good to me. Lets give him the first message and see what he does with it. Mr. Chung's men will accompany him to the dead drop."

"I'm not so sure about that, Do," Paul replied. "If Tuy is telling the truth about having contact only through dead drops, how are we going to send a message to the Phu Loi Battalion that COSVN can't read right away? That might blow the whole game."

"I don't believe we have to worry too much about that," Major Lang broke in. "I would bet you dollars to doughnuts that General Don's papers include one-time pads for especially sensitive communications. The great benefit of one-time pads is that only the message drafter and addressee can actually read the text. It cuts out the commo people. They go ahead and encrypt what they are given, but at no point do they have access to clear text.

"These pads are so slow and cumbersome that they don't get used very often for regular traffic. But clearly the general had his own. And, I gather, Tuy knows where they are. I think we should lean on him to produce them."

Do translated for Chung. Chung's eyes opened up and he raised a finger indicating agreement. But Paul didn't like the man's expression. Things didn't look good for Tuy if Lang's argument was fallacious. Paul felt compelled to caution Do against undue brutality in case Tuy really didn't know. Do nodded and repeated the caution to Chung. Chung, too, nodded, but not very reassuringly.

Paul struggled to shrug off his misgivings. "All right, then. Why don't we offer to get Tuy out of the country with a small stipend if we get Ba?"

"I don't think we have to tell Tuy what we're after," Do replied. "He won't even see the messages. They'll be in envelopes. He just has to do as we say — and that includes getting the one-time pads for us. That can't be negotiable. We must get them or the whole deal's off."

"Okay," Paul agreed. "Now, let me show you what we had in mind for the second message." He pulled a second paper from his map case. It read:

> TOP SECRET FOR TRAN HUA SOUTH SLOPE
> STOP SPECIAL COSVN SECURITY GUARDS
> BEING DISPATCHED TO TAKE CUSTODY OF
> VAN BA STOP GUARDS WILL ARRIVE
> BICYCLE XAM CHO 0500 HOURS 4 MAY STOP BA
> MUST BE READY FOR IMMEDIATE
> DEPARTURE STOP PASSWORD DONG NAI
> COUNTERSIGN VICTORY STOP HIGHEST
> SECURITY STOP INFORM NO ONE STOP DO
> NOT ACKNOWLEDGE STOP

Do read the text. "4 May? That's tomorrow."

"Right," Paul agreed. "There's no sense giving COSVN too much time to figure out what's going on. Can you do that?"

Do lapsed into a prolonged discussion with Chung. Paul turned to Lang. "Will you be able to monitor both of the messages, George?"

"Yes, sir, I'm pretty sure," the major answered. "We should pick up the response to the first one, too. Having the clear text of the first one we may be able to shoot that back to DIRNSA and have the keys to the entire day's traffic before we get the response."

Lang lowered his voice. "And, if you don't mind my saying so, Colonel, we might be able to detect any irregularities in the transmissions."

"What do you mean by that?" Paul challenged him.

"Well, clearly there's a risk of some sort of irregularity by the enemy commo people. They may have some sort of indicators they put in a message when they want to signal a warning that they aren't operating freely. But we should also bear in mind that it's not beyond the range of possibility that Major Do or some of his people may be working for the other side. They could slip in indicators, too. Take, for instance, the instructions Do wrote in the margin of the first message. We have no way of telling what he really said. You never want to take anything for granted in this business. DIRNSA will let us know if they spot irregularities. They may not be able to tell us who stuck them in, but maybe we'll be able to figure that out ourselves."

"Excuse me," Do said, conscious that he was breaking into a confidential conversation. "Mr. Chung believes that he can brief three trusted agents whom he expects to select this evening for the mission to Xam Cho. However, he thinks that the timing is a little too close. He points out that we don't yet know how responsive the courier will be to the signal to pick up the first message. Further, he says, we don't even have the proper code for the second one. He suggests that we postpone the rendezvous for 24 hours."

Paul took a deep breath and blew it out. "I suppose he's right. What about setting the rendezvous for tomorrow evening? Couldn't we make it for sundown?" That would save us nine or ten hours."

Do turned back to Chung. Paul watched the counterspy's face while Do framed the question. The chubby, features went from concerned to reflective, and finally decisive. Paul didn't trust the man, but Do's answer was welcome.

"He says 'okay.' We'll amend the message to say 1900 hours. That'll permit just enough light for the agents to make the link up and to get out of town. I think it's good to have the men on bicycles so their exit from town won't be limited to the road, and they can break up if they have to. Of course, they'll have to take an extra bike for Van Ba. The Phu Loi machine may be junk. Mr. Chung says that's not a problem. They have a device that fastens two bikes together when there is only one rider. Chung also says that he'll have them watched until we're sure they're not being followed. Then we'll pick them up. Agreed?"

"Sounds good to me," Paul replied. "But let's go ahead with the first message right away. Things are still going to be tight."

"Right you are, Paul," Do agreed. "We'll have this translated and into the hands of Tuy's interrogators within the hour. Mr. Chung will have agents watching the dead drop until the message is picked up. I'll keep you informed.

"Oh, and just one more thing," Do went on. "The VC normally uses code names for most of the smaller towns. I'll look up what we have on Xam Cho, and if we have something fairly recent I'll plug it into the message. We wouldn't want to use an old term. They might 'smell a rat,' as I think you say. Even the proper name would be better than an old code word. That way they would probably just think that we made a mistake and accept the message anyway. Of course, we could expect a good scolding for violating security. But in any event, we will just have to see how it goes."

Paul rose to go. "Great," he said, "I'm not sure that this is quite the sort of cooperation they were trying to put across to us at Leavenworth, Do, but let's hope for a passing grade, anyway."

"Right on, Paul. We'll give it the old college try. Together, within our work group, we licked bigger problems than this. Give my best to Cicely when you write."

# THIRTY-TWO

Paul was only vaguely aware of the knocking on the door. Having just recently moved into the new trailer, he still had trouble getting his bearings in the morning. He looked at his watch. The luminescent dial indicated 4:17. Yes, it was morning, but hardly his regular hour. Had there really been a knock, or had he imagined it? There it was again, before he could call out. "Coming, coming. Who's there?"

"Sergeant Schwartz, sir. We have a flash message for you."

Paul padded over to the door and opened it, flipping on the light. "Thanks, Sergeant, I'll take it." He held out his hand.

"No, sir. I can't leave it here. It's special category. I'll wait while you read it."

"Okay. Have a seat in the front room, and I'll come right out. Let me get something on." Paul fished around for his fatigue trousers and boots and pulled himself together. He flipped on the light in the hall. "Good morning, Sergeant. Sorry I haven't anything to offer you here. 'Charlie' blew up my coffee maker, along with just about everything else."

"That's fine, sir," Schwartz replied. "I just had a cup before coming over." He fished in an envelope and retrieved a message form stamped, "Flash" and "Special Category — Eyes Only for McCandless."

"Here you are, sir." It was from Do. The text was brief:

> FIRST MESSAGE DISPATCHED. PICKED UP BY COURIER 2015 HOURS 3 MAY. PRISONER DENIES HAVING ACCESS TO ONE TIME PAD CODES. MUST NOW CONSIDER ACTION WITH SECOND MESSAGE IF DOUBLE ENCODING IMPOSSIBLE. SUCCESS OF OPERATION AND SAFETY OF AGENT PERSONNEL AT STAKE. OPTIONS APPEAR TO BE:
> (1) AWAIT COSVN REPLY. IF POSITIVE, ARRANGE CONTACT WITH PHU LOI BN AS PLANNED.
> (2) SEND SECOND MESSAGE TO PHU LOI BN WITHOUT COSVN APPROVAL. MONITOR COSVN TRAFFIC FOR INDICATIONS OF AWARENESS OF OPERATION. THIS OPTION MIGHT BE FEASIBLE IF COSVN RECEIVERS COULD BE JAMMED DURING TRANSMISSION OF MESSAGE TO PHU LOI.
> (3) ABANDON OPERATION.
> DECISION REQUIRED SOONEST. DO

Paul read it twice. "Goddam! Wouldn't you know?" And then to the sergeant, "Has Colonel Dillings seen this?"

"No, sir, it was 'eyes only' for you. I brought it directly here."

"Okay, thanks, Sergeant. Wake up the colonel and let him see it, and then do the same for Major Lang. Tell them I'll be in the TOC working on a reply. I hope you've still got some palatable coffee there."

"Oh, yes, sir," Schwartz smiled. "The 4 am shift usually makes a fresh pot. It should be ready by now."

"Thanks a lot. Don't stumble going down those steps."

"No, sir."

Paul was just reading over the typed draft of his proposed back channel reply to Do when Dillings came in. Paul thought the colonel looked worse than usual. No two strands of his thinning hair seemed to go in the same direction, and he had buttoned his fatigue jacket out of line. It left him with a spare button at the top on the right side and an extra hole at the bottom on the left. Paul turned the paper around and held it out to the bony fingers. It read:

> CONSIDERED HERE HIGHLY UNLIKELY
> COSVN WOULD APPROVE ANY MEETING
> BETWEEN MME DON AND NEPHEW NOT
> UNDER ITS CONTROL. IF NO DOUBLE
> ENCRYPTION OF SECOND MESSAGE
> POSSIBLE WE FAVOR OPTION TWO.
> WE WILL ENDEAVOR TO JAM COSVN
> INTELLIGENCE AND SECURITY RECEIVERS
> DURING TRANSMISSION OF SECOND
> MESSAGE AND CONTINUE TO HARASS ALL
> KNOWN OPERATIONAL NETS UNTIL 1900
> HRS. REQUEST AGREEMENT
> SOONEST. PAUL

"It makes sense to me," Dillings said, returning the paper to Paul. "What does Lang say?"

"I don't know, sir. He hasn't come in yet. We'll see."

"I think you'll have to run it by the front office, too. You heard what Wakefield said about his name being on the line. I don't think he would take it too kindly if you went charging ahead with substantially greater risks and didn't get his okay."

"Right, sir. I just drafted this as a straw man to provoke discussion. I would guess we have until about 11 this morning to decide whether to go ahead or not. But we can't wait until then to complete our planning. I don't know what kinds of birds we need to jam COSVN. Hopefully, Lang can tell us that, and where and how to get them.

"Now, assuming Tuy doesn't relent by then, and lead us to some one-time pads, I recommend that we go ahead without him. He's a crummy scoundrel. I would just as soon see him in a Vietnamese jail for the rest of his life. It's his choice. He thinks he can force us to up the ante by holding out until the last minute. I say 'screw him'."

"Yeah, but don't forget you're raising the risks for Do's people, too."

"Yes, sir, but I didn't make up the options. Do did. If he didn't want to do it, I assume he wouldn't have offered it. He can still say 'no.' If Lang can handle the jamming business, I recommend we charge ahead."

Lang entered the TOC just as Paul was mentioning his name.

"Well, speak of the devil," Dillings said. "I'm going to see if I can get some early chow. Then I'll see DeWitt and Wakefield and show them your proposed reply. Let me have your best copy. You two stay here and work out your jamming operation — assuming that's possible. For God's sake let me know if it's not."

"Okay, sir. We'll work out something."

It was almost noon before George Lang was able to confirm the availability of two special mission aircraft with the right electronic wing pods for blotting out COSVN's receivers. They would take off from Udorn, Thailand, at 1400 hours and be in position to zap their targets at 1430. The second message would be prerecorded and transmitted from a third aircraft at exactly 1448, taking approximately 35 seconds, with no repeat. One jammer aircraft would remain aloft for approximately three hours to jam subsequent COSVN broadcasts. The other would return to base to refuel and stand by to relieve the first. COSVN had to be effectively blotted out until after the planned rendezvous at Xam Cho at 1900. It was chancy, but General Wakefield said he would support the effort as long as General Vo did. And Vo, mindful of his political position, was all for it.

* * *

Mme. Tran Hua received the message just before 4 p.m. She hurried into her shelter to begin the decryption process, and was surprised, and somewhat perplexed, to find that it was already in clear text. It had been decoded at the receiver site. Young Len Duc arrived with it in a sealed envelope, but Hua wondered how many other people might have had an opportunity to read it. There were still many of Van Ba's friends and supporters in the D group, and she could take no chances as long as the former leader was around, whatever his status.

But her consternation turned to delight as she read the text. Ba was to be turned over to COSVN agents. That was wonderful news. Had she not been taught to disdain religious practices, she might have prayed for Ba's removal. But now, here was the news for which she had worked so hard. Now the Phu Loi D Group could be steered along the path established by the leadership of the Lao Dong Party. Victory was sweet, indeed. There wasn't a minute to lose. Guards had to be selected and briefed to accompany Ba to Xam Cho. They might not be able to find food along the way, so they had to prepare rice packets and boiled water to take along.

Hua wasted no time on her way to the commander's dugout. The message said to inform no one, but Hua needed the commander's assent to dispatch an escort with Ba. More importantly, though, the new D group commander had to see and understand the impact of his political officer's influence.

Le Van Sau took no special interest in Mme. Hua's news. He said, quite frankly, that he would just as soon keep Ba with the D group as a physician, but he was prepared to comply with a COSVN order. He didn't raise the issue, but he wondered why the order had been addressed to Hua rather than to him. He made a mental note to look into the matter.

Within an hour Ba had been summoned and introduced to his escorts. Three young patriots, selected from recruits joining the group after Ba's recall, would accompany him to Xam Cho. There they would meet the COSVN agents and relinquish custody of their charge. Each was briefed on the challenge and countersign contained in the message. Mme. Hua spoke briefly to the group, emphasizing the importance of the mission. The guards listened dutifully, raising their arms in the clenched fist salute in response. Hua would have liked a little more spirit in the gesture, but there wasn't time for a complete pep talk. She would return to the matter later.

Ba fell in line second, behind the leader, Ly. The other two followed single file behind. While their weapons were hidden in sacks strapped to the bikes, Ba knew they had them and would use them to prevent his escape. He was resigned to his return trip northward; just where, he couldn't guess.

* * *

Len Duan, the chief radio supervisor in Mimot first noticed the difficulty at about 1445 hours. Heavy enemy jamming occurred on the primary security net frequency, and on both alternate frequencies, and lasted for about ten minutes. The station had no outgoing traffic at the time, but there may have been something coming in that the station missed. Duan quickly drafted an all points bulletin calling for a repeat of any messages intended for COSVN. But no sooner had his transmitter operator powered up his equipment than the jamming reappeared. Duan instructed the lad to try the alternate channels. Same thing. Nothing of the sort had been reported regarding other nets. Very clearly, it was just the intelligence and security net that was under heavy electronic attack. He reported the fact to his immediate superior in the COSVN security section.

Ngo Tan Nu, director of COSVN security operations, checked with the air defense warning section. Yes, there were two U.S. Air Force RF-4C reconnaissance aircraft orbiting in the area. Very likely the enemy was interfering with COSVN security communications in conjunction with some attempt to transmit deceptive traffic to one or more stations in the net. Nu directed Duan to broadcast an alert to all stations using the general command channel.

It took Duan about ten minutes to walk the quarter of a mile to the command net transmitter bunker. It was clear when he arrived, however, that the jamming had been broadened to cover the command frequencies, too. It wasn't continuous, but it interfered enough to require frequent frequency shifting and repetition of messages. Duan realized that it would have greatly overburdened the broader net to load the security traffic on it, too. He would have to activate the back-up facilities on the other side of town. They were slow and cumbersome, but since they were rarely used, the likelihood of enemy interference was substantially less. After alerting his representative there by telephone, he mounted his motorscooter and buzzed out onto the highway. The trip would take about twenty-five minutes.

* * *

At 1745 Len Duc was again summoned to the D group radio station to pick up a message from COSVN for Tran Hua. Double encoded, it bore the symbols of highest priority traffic. A little gun shy from previous encounters with the woman, Duc grabbed the envelope and leapt to his bike, forcing it down the path somewhat faster than he should have. The front tire struck a root and flipped him into the brush. In his fall and his haste to remount, he lost a sandal and spilled half the contents of his dispatch case. It took another five minutes to pull himself together and to straighten the handle bars and seat of the bike.

* * *

At 1800 a battered gray van pulled off the Xam Cho road and into the woods. Three figures in black pajamas and farmers' conical hats climbed out of the back. A fourth, inside the body of the vehicle, rolled four bicycles with side bags out the rear door and into the arms of the first three men. The bikes appeared chipped and worn, but anyone looking closely might have noticed that they were clearly built for high speed, with five gear settings. The men wore gloves and dust cloths over their faces. In a general sense they blended with others in the countryside, but in a number of specific points they did not. One guided a spare bicycle along beside him. They were clearly young men with a mission and in a hurry to be on their way. It would take them forty minutes to reach town. They knew exactly the speed to travel to reach their destination at the appointed time. Peasants who did notice them along the road knew enough about both government and VC special operations to mind their own business.

* * *

Len Duc was perspiring heavily, more from tension than from exertion, when at 1817 he delivered the message to Mme. Hua. She nodded perfunctorily and disappeared into her shelter to decipher it. The message was like a thunderbolt from the blue. Whereas moments before she had been exulting in her final victory over Van Ba, the message hurled her into the blackest of pits of uncertainty, with no knowledge of where the bottom might be. It took no stretch of the imagination to link the COSVN warning to the earlier message ordering the turn over of the former D group leader to 'COSVN agents.' Hua had wondered about the first message, protected as it was by only a single cipher system. Decoded at the radio station, it came to her in clear text. Never had the COSVN security section done that. She had been so entranced by the content of the message that she had totally neglected the form in which it had been transmitted. She crushed the message sheet in her hand and beat her fist on the table. How could she have been so easily deceived?

Her mind raced — just a moment. Perhaps there is yet time to correct the error. She rang up the D group leader's shelter. No answer. She would have to take action on her own authority. She thrust the message, crushed as it was, into her pocket and burst out of the door. The guard center was barely five minutes — five precious minutes — away. She covered the distance in three. Tan So, the guard commander was reading at his desk.

"Comrade Tan So," she virtually shouted. "We have been criminally deceived! Not more than an hour ago we dispatched Van Ba and an escort to Xam Cho, supposedly to meet with a party from COSVN that was to take him back to Tay Ninh."

"Yes, that's right, Comrade Hua. You authorized it yourself."

"That's right, you blockhead, but it was a mistake. The order didn't come from COSVN. For all we know, it may have come from an enemy intelligence agency. Van Ba and our faithful comrades may be headed right now for a rendezvous with government agents. They may all be killed. Worse than that, the traitor, Ba, may be in league with the enemy. You've got to stop them. Now!"

"How do you know that?"

"Never mind how I know. Stop them. Now!"

"I don't know what I can do. What time were they supposed to meet in Xam Cho?"

"1900 hours. That's a half hour from now. Do you have an automobile or truck?"

"Yes, we have a flat bed truck, but I don't know if it's operable. Let me call Chu Ly. He's been working on it." Tan So picked up the field phone.

"Central? Give me Chu Ly."

"Ly? Good. I'm glad I got you. We have an emergency mission of great importance. Is the truck in working order? It is? Excellent! I need it immediately, with a driver and a mechanic if you can get them. Right here, at the guard central. Immediately. There can be no delay!" Tan So replaced the handset and turned to Tran.

"He's coming right now. I'll give you four patriots, three with Kalashnikovs and one with a radio. Are you ready to go? Or would you prefer to have one of my guard supervisors go in your place?"

"Absolutely not. This is my operation. I must lead it to recover the criminal, Van Ba."

"I'm sorry we have no direct telephone connection with Xam Cho. If we did, we might be able to alert the local defense force. There's a village patriots' C unit there. You can make contact through the proprietor of the Long Kanh Refreshment House at the main intersection if you need help. Use the emergency passwords. We have a number of patriots in the D group who come from that area, but it would take too much time to find them. Here's an American carbine and some ammunition. Do you know how to use it?"

"Of course. Thank you."

"All right. Here's the truck now. These four men will accompany you. They're well trained. You can brief them on what you want them to do on the way. Good luck. And good hunting."

Hua climbed into the cab beside the driver while the others scrambled in the back with the mechanic and his tools. The driver expertly pumped the double clutch and the vehicle lurched off toward the highway. Swinging southwest on Route 16, the clattering vehicle kicked up a cloud of dust that drifted out over the swamps separating the highway from the river. Hua urged the driver to speed up. "Drive like the wind, Comrade. Our only hope is to get to Xam Cho before 1900."

* * *

An observer standing by a gray van parked out of sight among the trees on the other side of the road could hardly fail to notice the urgency of the bouncing flat bed, laden with armed youths leaning into the wind. He signaled the driver of the van to start the motor while he climbed into the rear of the vehicle and pulled a black plastic cover off a radio.

* * *

Hua looked at her watch. 1902. Ba and his guards had probably already made contact with the other party. She urged the driver to increase speed. The vehicle swayed dangerously and shook with sickening thuds as the tires crashed into the potholes and slipped in and out of longitudinal ruts. It was all the driver could do to keep the truck on the road on the curves. At one intersection he narrowly missed collision with a Lambretta tricycle bus full of riders on their way home from work. He laid on the scratchy horn and thundered ahead. Still Hua urged him to increase speed.

Minutes later, Hua spotted the first group of guards returning from their rendezvous on the opposite side of the road. She tapped on the rear window of the cab, signaling the soldiers in the back to call to the cyclists to reverse course and follow the truck. The soldiers shouted and waved their Kalashnikovs in the air as the truck thundered by. Hua looked back, peering through the dust. She saw the men stop and turn around. Only then did she begin to feel some optimism for pulling her blunder out of the fire.

Five minutes later the first house appeared. The driver had to slam the brakes to avoid a head-long plunge into the side of an ox cart turning off the road. A civil policeman called out to the driver to stop, but received only a poorly aimed burst of automatic weapons fire in return. He scampered out of sight between a pair of bungalows.

* * *

Forewarned by radio from the gray panel truck, the "COSVN" special operations team wasted no time briefing Van Ba on anything more than the operation of his bicycle. As soon as they had custody of their charge, they turned off the highway and pursued a narrow path out of the village to the southwest. Ba gathered that one of the men had prime responsibility to insure that he would not escape. But who were these men? And why did they head southwest, rather than north? While this direction led through woods, it could only take them ultimately to areas of denser population under government control.

The noise of the flat bed and the gunfire provoked concerned glances by the bikers over their shoulders. It wasn't difficult to imagine how quickly the pursuers might detect that their quarry had turned off the road. At least they couldn't pursue by truck. In a race with dismounted men, the advantage lay with those on high speed bikes.

* * *

Hua felt her hopes slipping as the truck hurtled across the main intersection and approached the other end of town with no one in sight. She ordered the driver to reverse course and to drive back to the Long Kahn Refreshment House. Before the vehicle had even stopped she was out on the running board and leaping to the ground. The commotion had already brought the proprietor and some of his customers out onto the front porch.

Pulling the proprietor out of earshot of his guests, Hua quickly exchanged the emergency password and countersign and explained her critical need to stop the escape of government agents. The arrival of the first guard team provided authenticity to her story and her demands for assistance. After a quick consultation with the cyclists to determine the number and equipment of the enemy group, Hua ordered them to follow the path out of town, the most likely route taken by the enemy team, with Ba in their midst. The other patriots dismounted from the truck and took up security positions around the refreshment house. The lad with the radio walked up and stood beside Hua.

The proprietor motioned to Hua and her radioman to follow him back through his shop. On the way he motioned to three or four others in the room to follow. In the private living quarters in the rear of the building, he introduced Hua to the group and asked her to explain the situation. She was brief.

"I am Comrade Tran Hua of the Phu Loi D Group. We're in hot pursuit of government agents who are attempting to rescue one of our former members, now a traitor. We need immediate assistance in tracking down the enemy. We understand there are three men besides the traitor, all mounted on high speed bicycles. I have three men pursuing them now along the trail to the southwest. What can you do to help?"

The proprietor retrieved a well worn map from beneath a cupboard and flattened it on the table. The entire group hunched over the paper. One of the men, identifying himself as Ho Ngu, looked at the radio and smiled. It was a Soviet model R-105D with a frequency range of 36 to 46.1 megahertz and good for communications up to 6 kilometers. "We'll catch them," he said confidently. In less than a minute he had tuned the device to 38.4 MHZ and began transmitting call signs.

No reply. This time the radio operator assisted him, tightening the connections to the antenna. The rough truck ride had been no more gentle on the equipment than it was on the passengers. However, in another minute they were on the air.

Once Ho Ngu had a response he transmitted his order: "A units one and three: immediate requirement for blockage of all trails west and south of home station. Enemy special operation team, a party of four, mounted on bicycles, attempting to escape. One is former patriot turned traitor. Use all necessary measures to arrest the team. Notify immediately if target sighted."

Then he looked at Hua. "We routinely have one B unit in the woods between here and Hung Loc. As you probably know, enemy patrols from Phu Cuong frequently sweep through that area and threaten us from that direction. We have to be careful."

"I'm very glad to hear that, Comrade Ho Ngu," Hua replied. "Is there anything we can do to prevent an enemy attempt from the barracks at Phu Cuong to rescue their men?"

"I'll see what we can do, Comrade Hua. Perhaps we can set up an ambush. But you must understand that we are not a full time unit like the Phu Loi D Group. We have only a few weapons and rarely more than half our men available at any given time. We are best at very small operations —like catching your traitor." Again Ho Ngu displayed his wide smile. "Now, sit down here, please, and have some refreshment and wait for our patriots to do their work. Do you know my good friend, Van Ba, the commander of the Phu Loi D Group? We worked closely together last summer when his unit was attacking the Phu Cuong garrison."

Hua froze. Her brain almost exploded with the thought, This man is a "good friend" of our traitor! Terror crept over her. How could she keep her quarry secret? She had to steel herself to reply in a manner unlikely to encourage more questions, "Yes, I know him."

Thirty minutes passed. The sun had already disappeared. "It must be quite dark in the woods," Hua said. "What'll your men do now?"

"They're accustomed to working at night," Ho Ngu reassured her. "That's when we do all our offensive operations. The Government tried to station a Popular Force unit here in Xam Cho last year. We burned down their house in the middle of the night." He showed another big smile.

* * *

The group leader raised his hand and ordered the men, including Ba, to dismount. He motioned to everyone to clear the trail and had a quick consultation with his companions. Then, turning to Ba, he ordered him to lie down behind a tree and not to look toward the trail. One man crouched behind another tree about three meters away where he could watch both Ba and the trail. Ba realized the men were setting an ambush for whoever might be in pursuit. It was a mistake.

Ba attempted to rise, but his guard swung his rifle around and warned him to stay down. He tried to whisper.

"Look, if you ambush the men behind us the noise will give away where we are. I know the local patriot unit here. They're bound to have been alerted by now and are probably searching for us. You heard that truck and the shooting in town. We could have an entire C unit looking for us."

The guard motioned to his leader to come hear what Ba had to say.

"How can we believe you?" the young man wanted to know. "For all I know, you're still VC. If we're captured, I can guarantee you that you won't live to see it."

"You can believe what you want," Ba replied, "and I assure you I don't want you to kill me or any of the members of my former unit. But that has nothing to do with what I'm telling you. The ambush is stupid. You may kill a number of your enemy — and me — but they'll also get you, and everyone loses.

"Let the pursuers go by. If there's an ambush it's bound to occur further down the trail where the local patriots lie in wait. Let our pursuers run into that if they must. I'd like to prevent that, too, if I could, but I don't see a way. What I can do is to show you a way out of here. If you can reach your friends by radio, I can show you where you can arrange for a helicopter pick up. How would you like that?"

The team leader was about to respond when one of the others snapped his fingers and pointed to the trail. Seconds ticked by. Nothing. Then rapid steps, and again silence. The pursuers were approaching in short rushes to minimize vulnerability to ambush. Through the trees Ba could make out a man with a Kalashnikov at the ready. He ran ahead a short distance and disappeared into the brush. A second man could be heard some distance behind. The second leapfrogged ahead, and then, himself, disappeared off the trail.

Ba looked to the team leader to see what he would do. The others instinctively did the same. The leader hesitated. A third VC soldier vaulted ahead of the first two on the trail. If there was a moment for maximum impact of ambush, this was it. Ba held his breath. He was just about to cry out when the leader held up his hand in a cautionary gesture. Ba realized immediately that he had won his argument. The leader would allow the enemy to pass.

Ba's guards remained in their positions for another five minutes to make sure that there were no further pursuers. The leader turned to him. "I understand that you're a physician and that you have become disillusioned with the rebellion. Is that true?"

"I don't call it a rebellion. It is a revolution. It will forever change the country."

"Does that mean that you plan to continue to work for Hanoi, and the Chinese and the Russians?"

"I've never worked for Hanoi, or the Chinese, or the Russians. I work for my country, South Vietnam."

"You stupid bastard. You're so full of that communist crap that you really don't know what's happening. You're not a *hoi chanh*, you're a prisoner of war. That makes no difference to me. I wouldn't trust you one way or the other. But I'll admit one thing: you may have been right about the ambush."

"Thank you," Ba said with just the trace of a smile.

"I didn't say you were right," the leader shot back. "That remains to be seen. But now, even while I can't trust you, I want to hear your idea about how we might escape from here. How do you know this area so well?"

Ba was tempted to boast about his group's performance at Phu Cuong, but he felt the better of it. "Oh, I've wandered through here before," he said. "There's an historic pagoda about a kilometer further to the southwest. If we could reach that, your friends would have no difficulty finding us, even at night. The problem would be to make sure that the local patriotic forces do not have many soldiers around it. They occasionally use it for a temporary reporting post and aid station when they're in the field. Today might be such an occasion. If that's so, you can probably still sneak up and take them by surprise."

"All right, you lead the way," the leader replied.

"But I make one stipulation," Ba went on. "You mustn't shoot any patriots in the area unless they resist. Can I have your word on that?"

"I can't promise you anything like that," the leader protested. We must surprise them if we're going to be successful in extricating ourselves — and you — alive. Any of these thugs would shoot us on sight."

"No, they won't," Ba contradicted him. These people have few weapons. The little they have is largely homemade and distributed to A units guarding the trails. Those at the Pagoda may have nothing more than a shot gun and a couple of knives. You must promise me that you'll make every effort to avoid bloodshed if I take you there."

At that moment an explosion occurred down the trail, followed by the sound of rifle and heavy automatic weapons fire. "It sounds as though your friends ran into an ambush," the leader said with a smile. "I guess you were right, after all."

Ba said nothing. He would have wished otherwise.

"All right," the leader continued. "You have my promise, Mr. Physician. We'll find your pagoda, but there's no way we can make it there in this darkness. We can't use the trails, so we'll have to wait for morning. Ky, see if you can raise the base with your radio. We can give them a situation report and alert them to the need for helicopter extraction early tomorrow."

# THIRTY-THREE

Again Paul found himself opening his door to a nocturnal knock by Sergeant Schwartz. "Another special category flash message for you, sir. It seems that your correspondents only work at night, now. You don't suppose there are vampires or werewolves in this country, do you?"

"I am sure there are, Sergeant," Paul responded, "but I don't think they're sending me messages. What time is it?"

"About 2:15, sir. You're both too late and too early for fresh coffee at the TOC tonight. Sorry 'bout that."

"Yeah, I am, too. Hold on. I'll be right out." Coming into the light, Paul took the message and read:

CONTACT ACHIEVED WITH SPECIAL

MISSION TEAM. CURRENT
LOCATION XRAY TANGO 885090.
VAN BA IN CUSTODY. ALL WELL.
ENEMY LOCAL FORCE UNIT
SEARCHING AREA. ALL TRAILS
BELIEVED BLOCKED. TEAM
PLANS TO WALK TO PAGODA AT
XRAY TANGO 880085. REQUEST
HELICOPTER EXTRACTION WITH NO
PREPATORY FIRES AT PAGODA SITE
0715 HRS NEXT. CAN YOU
ARRANGE?

"Hell, yes, we can arrange it. Okay, Sergeant, take this over to Colonel Dillings. Tell him I'm working with G-3 to get the choppers. I'll ask for four gun ships. They clearly don't want us to go in guns blazing, but it could get hairy. It would be good to have two standing by while the other two go in to pick up the troops.

"Is Major Hutton here?"

There was no answer to the sergeant's knock on the major's door.

"He must be over at the TOC," Paul said. "I'll get him there. Thanks a lot."

"All in a night's work, sir. Sorry to have to get you up."

Ten minutes later Paul was in the TOC talking to Hutton about the availability of armed helicopters. "You've got a high priority project there, Paul," Hutton said. "I see no problem getting two, but more than that could be sticky. Why doesn't ARVN put up a couple?"

"Well, I guess they could, Roger, but that would be risky. We need a team of guys that's worked together on high pucker factor operations like this. How about the Special Forces birds? Those guys are fat cats. Let me have theirs. We should be able to return them by 10 a.m. — noon at the latest."

"Yeah, but they may come back full of holes. Colonel Broderick doesn't like our scratching up his birds."

"What does he care? He does it all the time. Those guys don't think they've earned their pay unless they lose metal on a mission."

"I'll take it up with Colonel Cobbley, Paul. I can promise you two for sure. He'll have to okay any more."

"Okay, thanks. Do your best. Tell him the fate of the Republic depends upon it."

"Which republic do you mean?"

"I don't know at this hour of night. But if we don't do it right we may be accused of working for the Democratic Republic of North Vietnam. I want four gun ships and I want them armed, gassed, and ready to go at 0530. Got it?"

"Yes, sir. Four at 0530."

Paul got three gunships. It took a fist bouncing session on the desks between Dillings and Cobbley at 4 o'clock in the morning, and the cancellation of a lower priority special forces operation, but the compromise allocation of aircraft was ready and waiting at 0530.

The birds made impressive implements of war. Each carried two externally mounted, electrically fired, M-60 "flexguns," capable of spewing out 2,400 rounds of ammunition per minute. The weapons sucked up ammunition like water from twelve boxes stored in the cargo compartment of the aircraft. In addition, they mounted door guns on each side and fourteen 2.75 inch rocket launchers outside the cabin. The ten pound rockets could be fired singly, in pairs, or in salvos.

Paul climbed aboard the lead ship and instructed the pilot to move the flight over to the ARVN compound. There he met with Do, Chung, and an ARVN special forces officer, a Captain Kiem, whom he hadn't met before.

"Kiem works for me," Do told him. "The team on the ground bringing in Ba is from his company. They are all what we call *'Luc Long Dac Biet'* — Special Forces, to you."

"Glad to meet you, Captain Kiem," Paul said with a wide smile. "It sounds as though you have a good group on this mission."

"The best, Colonel," the young man replied in perfect English. "If anyone can bring in your man, they can."

"Well, we still have a chancy bit to go," Paul said. "By the way, where did you learn to speak English so well? Here in school?"

"No, sir. We concentrated on French in school. For the most part I picked up my English in the States. I'm a graduate of UCLA and of your infantry school at Fort Benning. 'Benning School for Boys,' they called it."

"Well, you're damned good." Paul opened his map case and laid it out on the hood of Do's jeep. "Now, let's get the pilots together here and you can tell them how you want to go about it. Those are your troops on the ground. I had to lean on our operational people a bit, but I was able to get you three gun ships."

"Thank you, sir," Kiem replied. "We've been requested not to fire any preparation in the area before the pickup, but it will be reassuring to have the firepower available. I propose to take the lead ship myself to pick up the team and your Mr. Van Ba. For that reason, if you have no objection, I will pare the first aircraft weight down by unloading the rockets and the extra M-60 ammunition. If we have sufficient space we'll land. We'll be counting on the ground team to notify us if and when it's safe to touch down. We'll take extra radios to drop in case we have trouble communicating with them on the ground.

"I would also like to have two extra men available in the second aircraft for emergency assistance to the team on the ground. If we have any casualties we may need to put a couple of additional men down to provide help with their protection and evacuation. The third aircraft should orbit and provide armed overwatch of the operation. I would suggest, sir, that you, Major Do, and Mr. Chung, if he wishes to come, ride in that aircraft. By maintaining altitude you should be able to maintain good communications both with us on the ground and with the operational base here. I've been assured that we can call on long range artillery support and close air support if we need it. Does this meet with your approval?"

"What do you think, Do?" Paul asked.

Do was pleased that Paul appeared to defer to him.

"It sounds pretty good to me, Paul. I don't remember having a problem quite like this at Leavenworth, but maybe we should have. My only concern is our problem of continuity of operations with respect to Colonel Tuy and our link with COSVN. I think it would be better to leave Mr. Chung here to keep an eye on his business — just in case you and I run into problems."

"Like what? Getting shot down, you mean?" Paul feigned surprise at the suggestion. "Hell, we're going to be in the highest bird aloft. I don't know about you, Do, but I'm planning on meeting our friend Ba, welcoming him to civilization, and being back at work by noon. But you're right. We shouldn't trouble Mr. Chung. He has important work to do."

"Okay, Do said. "What's our flying time to the pagoda?"

"About twenty-five minutes, sir," Kiem replied. We'll be flying a somewhat circuitous route to avoid tipping our hand to the enemy. We have the route marked on these maps for the pilots.

"Are all of you comfortable with the basic plan and with the route to the objective area?" Kiem asked the pilots. They nodded agreement. "Okay, then. Let me make one more check with our communications center to make sure that nothing new has come in. In the meanwhile, please strip down the lead ship to minimize the weight. When I return we can get on our way."

Twenty minutes later the war birds lifted off in swirling clouds of dust. The lead ship turned southward, following the broad waters of the Song Dong Nai. The sight of the river reminded Paul that there were other VC units in the area, especially the Dong Nai Regiment, larger and perhaps better armed than its Phu Loi cousin, but no better led. If the VC awards battle streamers to combat units, Paul thought, the Phu Loi Battalion should be high on the list of honors. For now, he hoped to bring that to an end with the capture of its former commander and one of the enemy's best leaders.

Before reaching the confluence with the Saigon River the small helicopter formation turned west, passing over the infamous Route 1, the southern extension of the historic "street without joy." Then, over the town of Thu Duc, the group turned northwest, on course for the objective area. The door gunners swung their M-60s out into the air stream and yanked back the bolt levers to chamber the first cartridges. The copilots on the second and third aircraft checked their rocket launcher consoles. If it was to come to a firefight, everything had to be tightly coiled for instantaneous eruption of overwhelming firepower. Hesitation, even if only of a second or two, could make the difference between success and failure. And life or death.

Kiem called back to the following aircraft that he had contact with the special forces team on the ground. He read off the radio frequency, and the copilots cranked their receivers around to tune in on the traffic. The ground unit was momentarily approaching the pagoda. Thus far there was no enemy in sight. Kiem led the flight group slightly off course to give the ground team a little more time to determine whether the spot was clear. The birds went into a wide orbit east of the Pagoda where enemy spotters would have to look up into the rising sun to see them.

A second message, received simultaneously by all aircraft, told of a brief encounter with three or four enemy who had fled southward from the pagoda at the approach of the ground team. Minutes later came word that the team was on the pagoda, but receiving intermittent small arms fire from the tree line to the south. The men were ready for pick up, but called for some suppressant fire on the tree line about a hundred yards away. The ground wind was about 3 knots from the east. A moment later saffron smoke billowed up from a point close to the base of the pagoda, indicating the best spot for pick up.

Kiem directed the second aircraft to fire two bursts of aerial rockets and continuing M-60 machine gun fire into the woods. He was going in for touch-down, if possible.

Paul and Do watched as the second ship delivered its ordnance and Kiem's aircraft approached the pagoda. Kiem seemed just about to touch down when an ugly, thick cloud of black smoke belched from the engine compartment. Paul felt a sudden shortness of breath as the machine appeared to lose power and fall six or eight feet to the ground. Fortunately, it remained upright and figures could be seen running from the wreckage. Paul counted five men. That should be all of them, he thought — and prayed.

Minutes later the ground team leader was on the air again calling for fire on the tree line and immediate pick up. There were two men wounded, he said, one of his own and one injured from the downed helicopter. The pilot of the second ship, having exhausted his rockets, called to the third to cover him while he attempted touch down. "Bring the wounded first," he told the ground leader.

Again a barrage of rockets slammed into the trees while the door gunners sprayed the flanks of the enemy position. The second bird was on the ground and pulling men aboard on one side, while the gunner on the other fired his machine gun red hot. In seconds the aircraft was up and out of the line of fire. The two aircraft circled while the pilot of the freshly loaded one took a head count to determine who was still on the ground. There were ten men aboard, counting the aircraft crew, indicating that five remained below. It was time for the third aircraft to go in.

With all rockets expended, both ships had to improvise to maximize their firepower. Paul and Do took up M-16 rifles and blasted clip after clip of ammunition through the open doors of the aircraft into the dust and smoke outside. God knows who's there, Paul thought. Whoever it may be, I hope he has enough sense to keep his head down until we're out of here. He had to stop firing to help pull one of the Vietnamese aboard. He wondered if it might be Van Ba.

"We're loaded and outta here," the pilot shouted over the intercom. "Hold on, everyone." Smiles broke out everywhere as he gunned the engine and the ship climbed back into the sky. The pilots headed due east, for Bien Hoa. One man, apparently with medical training, tended a wounded companion with a badly lacerated shoulder.

Paul turned to Do. "Which one's Van Ba?" Do repeated the question in Vietnamese. Two of the men shrugged and showed no comprehension of the question. Another gestured over the pilot's shoulder toward the leading aircraft. Paul felt a slight disappointment, but immediately exchanged it for a sense of concern.

"Holy cow, Do, I completely forgot. That bird we left on the ground has a lot of good stuff on it. The VC will be all over it, dismantling the machine guns and everything. How can we get the artillery?"

"I'll call Kiem. Hold on." He pressed the radio switch clipped to his jacket and spoke into the mike. Paul could hear the reply, but without understanding. "It's okay," Do said. "Kiem says he's given the location of the aircraft to the artillery and asked for destructive fires. They're trying to figure out how to do it without damaging the pagoda. That's a no-no. They may have to get someone else to do it. The battalion designated to support Kiem's team is located east of the pagoda, and with the aircraft wreckage so close, the dispersion of the fire could damage the structure. It would be much better to find someone who can hit it from either the north or the south. As you know, lateral dispersion is never as bad as range dispersion. At any rate, the problem is in the hands of the professionals. Let's not worry about it."

The cool tranquillity of the flight plunged everyone aboard into silence. The contrast with the heat, dust, and danger of the few minutes on the ground was overwhelming.

Paul was dying to pin down Van Ba and ask him a thousand questions. Once on the ground, he hurried over to the group just dismounted from the lead ship. Kiem was talking to a skinny, unarmed man in black pajamas.

"Introduce me, will you please, Captain."

"Of course, Colonel. This is the object of our operation, sir, Physician Van Ba." Paul could recognize only his own last name in the captain's address to the Vietcong leader.

There was no handclasp. Paul folded his arms. "I've been reading a lot about you, Doctor," he said. "I feel I have known you for some time." A smile crept across Ba's face as Kiem translated.

"How do you do?" Ba replied stiltedly.

"You speak English? I should have guessed," Paul said, matching his interlocutor's smile.

"Not so good, I am afraid. I too, have heard of you, Colonel."

"I believe you have. I think you may have tried to kill me a few months ago when you attacked our headquarters and blew up our ammunition dump."

"Not I, Colonel. My patriots did attack your ammunition dump, but it was someone else's idea to kidnap you."

"Why would anyone be interested in me? There are lots of lieutenant colonels in the United States Army."

"You have the same family name as the Field Force commander. Is that not so? I think that our high command would have liked to capture a general, but most of them are too well guarded. We had heard that you and your commander had the same ancestry. Some of our leaders have sought to capture the relatives of American leaders. Have you no kinship with your commander?"

"I am afraid you would have been badly disappointed," Paul said. "General Paulding and I may have a common ancestor, but I'm afraid that the link goes back so far that it has no importance to either of us personally."

"That is too bad," Ba replied. "I did not think that it was a good idea, and I lost many patriots in the battle to find you. I could do nothing about it, though.

"But you must tell me, Colonel," he went on. "How had you heard of me?"

"Until you left your battalion, Doctor, you were famous among our intelligence officers. Under your leadership, it caused our forces great concern. I have many questions to ask you about the Phu Loi Battalion."

"I do not believe that you will be very satisfied with my answers, Colonel. Under the Geneva Convention you have only the right to ask me for my name, rank, and serial number. As for that, I am Van Ba, my rank is physician, and I have no serial number."

"I don't think that will do," Paul replied. Van Ba is not your real name, you were a battalion — or 'D group' — leader, and you probably do have a serial number, whether you know it or not. Further, there is no limit to the questions which you may be asked under the Geneva Convention. There is only a limit to the questions which you may be forced to answer, and the treatment to which you may be subjected to obtain those answers.

"And I should add, much depends upon your status as a detainee. Do you want to be considered a prisoner of war or a *hoi chanh?* I expect you will have a choice. Prisoner status would provide you with the nominal protection of the Geneva Convention, but you can't expect that you would have much opportunity to perform anything more than manual labor in a camp. As a *hoi chanh* you would be considered a reformed deviant from acceptable behavior, but you would enjoy some personal rights and opportunities of citizenship. You might even eventually return to your former position in the Pasteur Institute. Would you like that?"

"What makes you think that I was at the Pasteur Institute, Colonel?"

"I understand that there was a young man there a few years ago, a graduate of the Sorbonne, named Don Thanh Dzung. Have you heard of him? Speaking of relatives, he was the nephew of Brigadier General Don of the Army of the Republic of Vietnam. As a matter of fact, he may have been in communication with General Don before the general died. Did you know the general was dead?"

"Yes," Ba replied. "I read it in the newspapers."

"Look, Mr. Van Ba — or Mr. Don Thanh Dzung, whichever you prefer — you will have to make up your mind how you would like to be treated. If you choose *hoi chanh* status, we would expect you to cooperate with us fully. You know much about the insurgency in the countryside that both my government and that of South Vietnam need to hear. And I don't mean just military information. Governments are concerned with all sorts of political, social, and economic matters as well.

"Of course, you may be considered a traitor by your former comrades, and a price might be placed on your head. As I am sure Major Do will tell you, the South Vietnamese Government will do everything in its power to protect you and your relatives.

"On the other hand, if you prefer to become a prisoner, you will probably be tied up immediately and assigned to one of the places designated for prisoners of war. As you may know, we Americans keep no prisoners. We are here at the request of the South Vietnamese Government, and you must expect to be handled within the Vietnamese system. I don't know how much you know about South Vietnamese prisons."

"I know much about government prisons, Colonel, but the choice is not as easy to make as you seem to suggest. If I choose the *Chieu Hoi* Program, I assume I would be handled by the government anyway. Is that not true?"

"Yes, that's so, Doctor. Nevertheless, you must decide. No matter what, you'll be under the jurisdiction of Major Nguyen Van Do, here. Do, let me introduce Doctor Van Ba. Am I not right, Do?"

"Quite right," Do replied. "I have many questions I want to ask you, too, Van Ba. It really makes little difference which status you choose right now. No matter what, your interrogation will begin immediately under the supervision of my counterintelligence chief, Mr. Chung. As a precautionary measure we'll place hand cuffs on you and keep you under armed guard. We'll treat you as a suspicious detainee until you have told us enough to clarify your status."

Do asked Captain Kiem to have his men take charge of Ba and turn him over to Mr. Chung. "We'll let you know later, Paul, how this goes. I can't thank you enough for your leadership and for your cooperation in this entire matter. With the exception of the two men injured in the operation, and the loss of your helicopter, it's been a great success."

"I agree, Do. This has been a significant accomplishment. You and Captain Kiem, and all your men have done splendidly. I am sure General Vo will be hearing from General Wakefield about how pleased he is with the entire operation. I wish we could always work so closely together.

"But, Do, let me caution you regarding Van Ba. As you know, he's no routine detainee or prisoner. Mr. Chung should understand that. Interrogation is fine, but it must be conducted strictly according to international accords, especially in this case. We can't have him hurt under any circumstances."

Some of the joy went out of Do's voice. Paul's caution sounded heavy, like a big brother lecturing a younger sibling. Damn it, he thought. Why does every American always have to be so patronizing, just when we seem to be getting together on something? But he said, "Of course, Paul. We understand."

Actually, General Vo's order to have Ba prepared to appear on national television and radio within the week underscored the point. From his point of view, it wasn't nearly as important what Ba might say or not say, as it was that he appear healthy and coherent. Only the renegade's presence could begin to restore the government's confidence in the corps commander. Ba would be a peacock-sized feather in the general's hat.

As it turned out, Ba was a rather dull interviewee, disinclined to comment in public on the war or on the fortunes of the Phu Loi Battalion. He spoke mostly about his youth and his involvement in political discussion groups in Paris. He did say that he was glad to be back in Saigon and appreciative of the government's lenient attitude toward him as a returnee. Vo beamed with pride over that.

What other commander was able to deliver his principal tormentor's head on a silver tray the way he had?

But Ba drove a hard bargain for his cooperation. He steadfastly refused to provide information of operational value against his former unit. Chung's interrogators leaned pretty hard on him, but he refused to budge. The issue was contentious; so much so that ultimately it had to be resolved in the prime minister's office. No one in the *Chieu Hoi* Program had ever been granted such immunity before. But neither had such a big fish ever offered to cooperate on so many other matters. He was too valuable to lose over some tactical issue.

As soon as Ba's status as a defector was established, Paul arranged, through Do, for a joint session with Ba to seek answers to their highest priority questions. Dillings and Paul, plus a Colonel Daniel Williams from the MACV intelligence staff, would represent the U.S. side; Do and Chung, together with a Lieutenant Colonel Chun Phu Diem from the ARVN Joint Staff, would speak for ARVN interests. Ba asked that henceforth he be addressed by his true identity, Don Thanh Dzung. Further, in honor of his uncle, he suggested that the short title, Dr. Don, be used. It was agreed that Paul and Do would conduct the interrogation, adhering to a prepared list of questions of high priority.

"Dr. Don, I understand that you have elected to use your family name primarily for its identity with General Don," Paul began. You are proud of your uncle, aren't you?"

"Yes I am," Don replied. He was a great patriot, a man who loved his country, South Vietnam."

"How can you say that?" Do challenged him. "The general was in touch directly with you while you were in the service of the enemy, and he was providing you with information of high military value. Sooner or later he would have been caught, and likely died before a firing squad if he hadn't shot himself first."

"You see only half of the man from your perspective," Don countered. "Yes, we were in touch while I was in the field. But you may not know that he gave me credit for saving the life of his infant daughter from pneumonia a few years ago when other physicians had given her up as a hopeless case. I did no more than I would have done for anyone, but he felt deeply indebted to me. I didn't want to take payment from him, as a member of the family, so I simply suggested that perhaps we could stay in touch if ever I were to be forced to leave town because of my somewhat libertarian views. He wasn't a very political man, and he saw little danger in the anti-Diem youth group to which I belonged. He knew I wasn't a communist and that I didn't support the subservience of South Vietnam to Hanoi.

"At the same time, he understood the risks of maintaining contact with me, but he also knew that it would have imposed a much greater risk upon his brother — my father — if I had attempted to communicate directly with him. When I went to the field, my family was placed under continuous surveillance, and occasionally subjected to severe interrogation. General Don served as the link between myself and my father. He did it for love of us both."

"Well, that sounds noble," Paul admitted, "but it doesn't explain how he developed a regular communications channel with you, or why he provided you secret military information."

"That came later. He knew that the Americans were subjecting all of us in the field to heavy B-52 bombardment, and that we were suffering from it. He began to send us a warning when he thought we might be targeted. His motive was to save our lives — my life, in particular. The tragedy is that as time went on it really wasn't necessary. We received ample warning from COSVN over their air defense net. The Russians reported to Hanoi whenever the aircraft left Guam, and then tracked them all the way to Vietnam. Hanoi passed word to COSVN, and they warned all the units in the expected target area."

"Why didn't you tell him to stop? You knew he was placing himself at considerable risk in what he was doing."

"I wanted to, but that might have compromised the COSVN air defense system just to save my uncle. I couldn't tell him that we had another way of getting the information. I simply cautioned him to worry less about me and more about his own safety. I told him I wanted him to survive the war, too."

"That's very interesting, Doctor," Paul said. "But now I would like to turn to the matter of your attack on our headquarters and on our ammunition dump. You said it wasn't your idea. Whose was it?"

"I said it was not my idea to kidnap you," Don replied. "Now that I hear that you have no close relationship with the Field Force commander, I feel exonerated. It was a great mistake. We paid a terrible price."

"You would have paid a higher price if the designated force had gotten out of bed to hunt you down," Do said. "I'm embarrassed that it took them several hours to get out of their barracks."

"Don't judge them too harshly," Don cautioned him. "It was not their fault. My uncle deliberately withheld the order in order to give us time to get away."

"That sounds like high treason to me," Do countered.

"I am sure you could make such a case in a military court, Major Do, but my uncle did not see it that way. He was determined to give me any assistance he could that would help me to survive. I probably would not have been here today if he had ordered the troops out right away. The Americans had inflicted terrible blows upon us. We practically had to crawl our way back to our camp."

"Where was that camp?" Paul interjected.

"I am sorry, Colonel. I cannot answer that question. And I must remind you of our agreement, approved by the prime minister, that I am under no obligation to disclose information of exploitable military value."

"Okay, Doctor," Paul said. "Did the general give you any information regarding our headquarters?"

"No, but I did ask him about your ammunition stocks. We did not know whether it would be worthwhile attacking the ammunition dump, considering how much we had seen taken out to support your attack on COSVN — Giant City, I think you called it."

"Did he give you what you asked for?"

"Yes, and no. He gave us an inventory of the stocks on hand, but it wasn't of any real use. It was dated sometime earlier, and we couldn't tell whether the ammunition was still there or not. We notified COSVN what we were planning, and they were anxious to have us go ahead to take the pressure off them. In addition, they had heard about your name, Paulding, and your promotion, even though you had not been in the war zone very long. To them you appeared to be a promising 'target of opportunity,' as you Americans sometimes say. They sent a special mission team down to capture you while we were in the ammunition dump. They could not find you, so they delayed our withdrawal so that they might have more time to search. It was a great mistake."

"It sounds as though General Don didn't really help you when you were on the offense, but then extended his arm when you were on the run," Paul observed.

"That is exactly right, Colonel."

"What about your attack on the barracks at Phu Cuong last year. That was your operation, wasn't it?"

"Yes, it was, but the general was no help to us there. I asked him if he could get us some aerial photography of the area before the attack. Of course, he did not know when we planned the attack, and it appears that the reconnaissance mission was not flown until the morning of the day we had planned. We never did get the photos from him. And, frankly speaking, I doubt that he ever would have given them to us. He might begin something with the intent of helping us, but then his conscience would get to him and he couldn't finish the task. He became a torn and tortured man."

"Then how did you know that the photos were taken?"

"We saw the aircraft. It wasn't until later that we captured the prints. One of our patriots picked them up from an American soldier caught in an ambush."

The thought of Garowski in great pain made Paul's skin crawl. "Yes," he said with some vehemence, "and that American soldier was one of my dearest friends. I would have happily blown your head off if I could have caught you." His voice was rising. Dillings reached over and touched his arm. Their eyes met, and Dillings shook his head.

"I am sorry for that, Colonel," Don said quietly. "Was he killed?"

"No — no thanks to your 'patriot,'" Paul added. "He may be blind, though."

"I am truly sorry," Don said. "I have tried to save more people through the practice of medicine than I have been responsible for killing in this terrible war. I hope your friend recovers his sight."

"Thank you, Doctor. I guess you are sincere."

"I am."

"Let me get back to your uncle," Paul said evenly. "Major Do, and, I am sure, others had great respect for the man."

"That's right," Do said. "It's hard to believe that he could become wrapped up in something like this."

"I think I am beginning to understand," Paul said. "Not that I condone it. I suspect he saw himself as a man trying to protect the life of a relative to whom he owed a great deal. That's not an easy problem to deal with. I would prefer not to judge him.

"But let me ask you a technical question, Doctor. I assume he had a radio. Where did he get it? Did you give it to him?"

"Yes, I had it sent to him, along with codes and instructions for operation."

"What kind was it? Chinese? Russian? One of ours?"

"Russian, R105-D."

"How could he communicate with you with that," Paul asked. "That would have too short a range."

"I had a relay station — actually two of them. Didn't you ever pick them up?"

"Now it is my turn to refuse to answer, Doctor. Maybe we did, maybe we didn't."

Don shrugged.

"Did you have one-time pads for security?"

"Yes."

"Did you know that another officer was aware of the general's contact with you and that he was blackmailing him?"

"Not directly, but I heard such a rumor. My uncle was under enormous pressure in the final month. I think he felt that he had gotten far more involved with me than he ever intended. Then there was the blackmail, and finally, the pressure of blame for the losses at Phu Cuong. It was too much for him. He sent me a message a few days before he died rather hinting that he did not expect to survive the war. He asked that I look out for Mme. Don — which I plan to do as soon as I am free. If there was any single factor that made me decide to become a *hoi chanh*, it was my promise to my uncle that I would look out for his widow if he were killed.

"But, to be quite candid with you, I never fully believed the story of my uncle's suicide. That sounds too convenient for the government — and maybe for General Vo, too. With all due respect, Major Do, you may wish to clarify the matter some day."

Do's eyes flashed. "I can clarify the matter for you right now, Dr. Don. He either shot himself, as I believe, or he was possibly shot by someone in his office. I know. I was there."

"Did you see him shoot himself?" Don asked.

"No, but I heard the shot, and I was there within a minute or two."

"Did you have an investigation of the matter, Major?"

"No," Do replied.

"Then I do not believe that you have clarified the matter very much," Don concluded. "What you mean is that neither you, nor any member of your organization murdered him, as far as you know. Well, that may or may not be very reassuring. There are many intelligence and security organizations operating in the country, Major Do. Even if we wanted to eliminate your organization from the list of suspects, which I am not sure we should, I think the matter remains open."

Paul noticed that both Colonels Williams from MACV and Diem from the ARVN Joint Staff were taking copious notes. He also noted that Do gritted his teeth, but did not respond. This was thin political ice. Paul realized that the notion of Do's possible involvement in political assassination hadn't crossed his mind before. I guess I'm learning about the Orient, he thought.

"My final question, Doctor," he went on, "concerns your political advisor, Mme. Tran Hua."

"So you know about her, too," Don smiled. "Perhaps your intelligence is better than we have given you credit for."

"Well I don't know about that. Perhaps that is another open question. Explain to me how she had the power to have you relieved."

"First, Colonel," Don responded, "you must understand that the insurgency in the countryside did not begin as a communist organization. I, for example, have never been a communist, yet I became an active participant. Our organization was called *'Phong Trao Dan Toc Tu Quyet Mien Nam Viet Nam,'* 'The Movement for South Vietnam for the South Vietnamese.'

"You must realize that communism is an absolutist concept. It cannot abide competition in any form. The Lao Dong Party uses others, such as myself, as instruments for achieving its objectives, but in the long run, it has to control everything. I was a double threat. Not only was I non-communist, but I had deep reservations about the Northern domination of the war. When I shifted from the political struggle to the military conflict — we called it *'Dau Tranh Vu Trang,'* 'the violence struggle,' — it was a civil war. But now, as you are probably aware, it is rapidly turning into an invasion of the South by the North.

"In order to discredit me, all Tran Hua had to do was to point out to her superiors how badly I fit into the communist scheme of things. I thought I was fighting for a new life for the common man in South Vietnam. I found I was really serving as a stand-in for a communist regime in another country. I had been too ready to accept Hanoi as a friendly partner. I did not understand that the leadership there planned to take over everything. Now you see me as a man who has lost his war. I didn't realize who the enemy was. I thought I was on the winning side. Actually I was on the losing side — or perhaps one of the losing sides."

"Well, that brings me to the final question I had for you today," Paul said. "How do you think the war is going?" By coming in under the *Chieu Hoi* Program, have you now joined the winning side?"

"Not at all," Don said waving his hands. "I have elected to become a *hoi chanh* largely for personal reasons. I have probably left one losing side to join another. The Saigon regime cannot withstand the single-minded drive of Hanoi. The government here doesn't even realize that it is in mortal peril.

"Look outside. There you will see thousands of young men running around town on their motor scooters, listening to their high fidelity recording machines. Read the newspapers. There you will learn about the latest rumors of military coups. This government is going no place. I dislike saying this to your face, Major Do, but you are on a losing side too. You may win a battle or two, but you will lose your war, if not in the field then in the corridors of power here in Saigon."

"How do you view the effort of the United States to assist the government here?" Paul asked him. "That must alter the balance of power to some extent."

"Of course it does," Don replied. "But it will not affect the outcome. You must realize that your high command has chosen to leave the initiative in Hanoi's hands. Have you read your great Western military genius, Clausewitz? I have. And I can tell you that he argued strongly that victory goes to the side which seizes the initiative.

"You have come over here to fight battles in South Vietnam. You don't realize how Hanoi uses other countries, like Laos and Cambodia, to attack you here. When Hanoi's troops are weary, they retire over the border for rest. When they are ready, they come back again. That can go on forever. Hanoi argues that the final battle will not be fought in Vietnam. It will be fought in Washington where those too weary to continue will overcome the diminishing numbers of people who want to continue. Then the forces of the North will subdue the South Vietnamese.

"North Vietnam understands the principle of the isolation of the battlefield much better than your government does. Hanoi fights tactical battles here, not strategic ones. The strategic battle is the isolation of South Vietnam from its allies. Once the United States tires of the conflict and leaves, everyone else will leave, too.

"Your government has no comparable strategy. Unless you can come up with something better than the very limited one that you have, you will lose your war, too."

Paul looked at Dillings. He was grimacing. Dr. Don had struck too close to Paul's heart for him to respond. He looked at Do. "Do you have anything else you would like to ask him today, Do?"

"No," the major replied. He, too, had been scored — doubly so, by the implication of involvement in General Don's death and by the prediction of failure in the war effort. All of the men were quiet as they walked back to their vehicles. The interrogation hadn't turned out as the glowing crown for their achievement as they had expected.

"You know, Do," Paul reflected, "I suddenly feel much older than when I drove in here. I had the idea we were going to hear some sort of congratulations from the doctor about how we had outsmarted our enemy. Instead, what we've heard is a rather sobering analysis of how we've all been losing our wars.

"Certainly Don has lost his — to his political officer. Now he says you will lose yours — to corruption and divided loyalties, I guess. And, for our part, I can't argue with his point that our war makes no strategic sense. We've lost touch with the basics.

"Hanoi denies even being a party to the conflict, but it seems to be the only winner. There's little doubt that the NVA is becoming more active every day, but if we accept what Don says, most of our losses are self-inflicted. I don't know how we're going to write this up."

The men exchanged subdued farewells and promised to remain in touch.

# *EPILOGUE*

Dr. Don was confined to Mr. Chung's compound, but provided with an office and secretary, and reasonably comfortable living quarters. Close overwatching security was established, nominally to protect him from possible retribution by the VC. He dined in the officers' mess with those responsible for his keeping and interrogation, which was no small shock to some of his keepers to begin with, but most of them eventually came around. Occasionally he took his meals at his desk or in his quarters. He was permitted visits from his family and others he identified to Mr. Chung. Considering that the country was at war, his living standard was quite comfortable. Certainly it beat life in the bush. He created his own diversions through exercise or by working in the post dispensary.

Don's principal vocation was his participation in a seemingly unending series of protracted and exhaustive interrogations and his drafting of an autobiography. The interrogators appeared at regular intervals as teams, representing practically every department of the

Vietnamese Government, and many from Washington. His testimony was assigned high security classifications and he was considered "hot copy" by every office with any sort of bureaucratic ax to grind. Not by accident, some of his interviewers who were not particularly pleased with aspects of the story he had to tell, were known to "interpret" selected comments in ways more congenial to their predispositions. More than one "turf" battle in Washington would grow out of such interpretations of Don's comments.

Paul and Do paid occasional visits to clear up various points. Dr. Don determined from his aunt, Mme. Don, that the second bank account into which his uncle had transferred funds was owned by her under an assumed name. General Don had been concerned that Colonel Tuy might find out the full dimensions of the family finances. It was determined that the general's brother, Dr. Don's father, had assisted the general in meeting Colonel Tuy's blackmail demands. It was a warning from the brother that he might be unable to continue to meet the payments that brought the general to the point of suicide.

In retrospect, it is clear that one of the most important revelations in Dr. Don's testimony was the first hint of Viet Cong preparation for the "Tet Offensive" the next year. The doctor reported that COSVN representatives in Cambodia made frequent references to a new training program for fighting in urban areas. The training may have even begun in the Phu Loi Battalion during Don's absence. This early warning assisted intelligence officers in evaluating other indications as they surfaced. By the time the offensive began many commanders had made adjustments in their troop dispositions to deal with the onslaught.

Colonel Tuy delayed admitting to the possession of the general's codes and ciphers in hopes of securing greater concessions from the Vietnamese Government. However, rather than increasing their value, his delay rendered the codes virtually worthless. COSVN soon realized the extent to which the allies had penetrated its intelligence and security communications net and changed the entire system. Tuy's gamble rendered him less, rather than more useful to the government.

In August 1967, Lt. Col. J. Paulding McCandless completed his tour of duty in Vietnam. Lt. Gen. Leonard Wakefield, the Field Force commander, invited General Vo and Major Do of the ARVN Central Corps to attend a small award ceremony in the colonel's honor. Wakefield surprised the company by presenting Legion of Merit medals to both Paul and Nguyen Van Do.

In a final interview with Dr. Don, attended by both Paul and Do, Paul advised the other two that they should remember that they would have a friend in the United States if they ever found that they could no longer live in their native land. The three would remain in touch by mail for a number of years.

In one of his letters to Paul, Do enclosed a clipping from the *Saigon Times*, together with an English translation, reporting on traffic accidents about the country. Municipal Police, it said, were investigating a fatality in Cholon. The name of the victim could not be determined pending forensic examination of the remains. Police sources said the nature of the accident was of such violence that officials could not be sure of the identity of the body. However, there was some speculation that the victim may have been a colonel formerly assigned to the Central Corps staff. Do insisted that he knew nothing more about it.

Paul recognized that the eventful year of separation had been erosive to his marriage. He and Cicely would need a prolonged period of readjustment to heal the doubts which had come over both of them, particularly if he was to continue in military service. In a moment of resolution he wrote an apologetic "final" letter to Anne, and destroyed most of hers. But not all. Only time could settle that matter one way or another.